She wore a mask again.

This one was a deep, rich chocolate satin that matched her gown and complimented her hair and complexion. Grey didn't mind that she chose to conceal herself from him again. He had worn his mask as well.

"I didn't think you'd come," he said as he closed the door to the private suite behind him.

She rose from where she sat on the side of the bed, the snug gown hugging every curve, the tiny sleeves threatening to slip from her exquisite shoulders. "I almost didn't."

That was a little honesty he could do without. Then she added, "I thought you had surely changed your mind, and so I thought to save myself the disappointment."

Changed his mind? He couldn't have stayed away if he'd wanted to. His will simply wasn't that strong.

"You do not know the strength of your charms, madam."

Romances by **Kathryn Smith**

Night after Night
Before I Wake
Let the Night Begin
Taken by the Night
Night of the Huntress
Be Mine Tonight
Still in My Heart
In the Night
In Your Arms Again
For the First Time
Into Temptation
A Game of Scandal
A Seductive Offer
Elusive Passion

When Seducing A DUKE

Kathryn Smith

AVON
An Imprint of HarperCollinsPublishers

This is a work of fiction. Names, characters, places, and incidents are products of the author's imagination or are used fictitiously and are not to be construed as real. Any resemblance to actual events, locales, organizations, or persons, living or dead, is entirely coincidental.

AVON BOOKS
An Imprint of HarperCollins*Publishers*
10 East 53rd Street
New York, New York 10022-5299

ISBN 978-0-06-134029-1
www.avonromance.com

First Avon Books paperback printing: October 2009

Printed in the U.S.A.

10 9 8 7 6 5 4 3 2 1

This book is for all the readers who asked if I was ever going to return to "regular" historical romance. And to Janet, who demanded to be the first to read this book the day I told her the plot. Of course, this book is also for Steve, who treats my characters like real people too. Thanks, Babe.

Chapter 1

London, May 1877

There were few things Greyden Kane, Duke of Ryeton, had been denied in his privileged life. Generally his every whim was indulged with cheerful abandon. Despite such fortune, life was not without its ironies and Grey had often been given things he never once asked for or, for that matter, wanted—such as the six-inch scar that ran down his left cheek. A scar that was hidden for the time being beneath a supple leather mask that obscured most of his face.

And so self-denial became something His Grace sought, but like all things, the taste of it often dulled.

It was that same sense of denial that had driven him to Saint's Row that evening. Like the society it catered to, the club located on that abbreviated lane gave the appearance of propriety and good manners, but beneath that façade—if one sought them out—there were all manners of scandalous and seductive delights to be found. In one section, proper ladies and gentlemen might attend a special ball or spectacle of some kind. In another section, less decorous patrons could indulge in their fantasies without risk of their carnal delights ever being found out.

In short, it was a place where elegance and debauchery often crossed paths, but were never formally introduced.

The large, cream stucco building sprawled like corpulent King George IV, during whose reign it had been built. Back then it had been intended as a theater and had continued as such for fifty years before the owner, one Mr. Threwsbury, lost it and everything else he owned years ago in a card game. That he would risk his livelihood was scandal enough. That he lost the club to a woman . . . well, Threwsbury had to leave England—not just to escape his creditors, but to avoid being a laughingstock as well.

Vienne La Rieux was no ordinary woman. That soon became apparent when she assumed ownership of the Saint's Row theater, and took it from tattered street urchin to diamond of the first water in its first six months. Now it was a high-class club open to any man or woman wealthy enough to afford the price of walking through its doors. Oh, there were balls and parties, and a restaurant open to the public, but balls like this one, where everyone wore a mask and spirits flowed freely . . . those were open by subscription only. The only way a non-subscriber could attend was as the guest of a member.

Archer was there as his guest. Not because Grey needed his brother's support, but because he knew how futile it was to attend such an event without his younger brother tagging along.

And tonight, Grey had a need that would no longer be ignored regardless of his brother's presence. Saint's Row bustled with energy and gaiety and, beneath that, a frisson of sensual promise. It was this promise that Grey chased as the ball ebbed and swelled beneath the balcony where he sat, watching. Waiting.

Archer, younger by a scant ten months, sat with him. The younger Kane hadn't Grey's particular fussiness when it came to women and was ready to dance and subsequently romance with whoever would have him. Arch had the look of a racehorse about to storm the gate.

"Sweet Christ, Arch." Grey couldn't keep the edge from his voice. Being watched over by his brother like a governess hovering over a precocious charge was as maddening as it was humiliating, especially since it was obvious Archer would rather be elsewhere. "If your bollocks are that backed up, go find some lady willing to relieve your discomfort and leave me to my own."

Archer shifted against the padded velvet chair. Like his brother he wore a simple black mask. "My bollocks are just fine, thank you. See anything you like?"

Turning his attention to that brilliant swirl of a crowd beneath him, Grey shrugged. "Not yet."

"I don't understand this impossible criterion of yours. Is not a pair of fine eyes, a pretty smile, and a willing nature enough for you?"

"No," he replied, never lifting his gaze from those damned dancers. "They are not." Grey's needs in a partner weren't quite so disinterested, or so noble. His desires went beyond simple companionship to border on something uncomfortably like obsession.

All he required was thick dark brown hair, cupid's-bow lips, and a lush figure. That was enough for him to pretend that his partner was the woman he really wanted.

Rose. The last time he'd laid eyes on her sweet curves and big brown eyes had been several months earlier when he visited his estate in Kent. Bramsley was close enough that he could visit more often if he so chose, but with just enough miles between it and London that he could always find an excuse to play absent. Why torment himself with the agony any more than necessary?

The full pressure of that torment bore down upon him as he observed the merriment below from the darkness of the box. Silent as a shadow, he drained the last of his champagne and set the empty flute on the table beside him. He was a patient hunter, but the hunger inside him frayed the edges of his nerves to raw, jagged strips.

Still, he would wait.

"Ah, there's a pretty little bird who looks eager to do some nesting." Archer leaned forward in his chair, anticipation clearly etched on his angular face. They shared the same thick wavy hair, though Archer's was almost black while Grey's was more of a reddish sable. Their pale blue eyes were almost identical, though Archer's often held far more merriment. And Grey was very certain that his own cheekbones weren't as high, nor his nose quite so sharp. Still, for all their differences, there was no denying their shared heritage. Kane blood always showed. Their younger brother Trystan and sister Bronte were proof as well.

Following his brother's eager gaze, Grey saw a slender auburn-haired woman of indeterminable age standing on the fringes of the dancers clad in a smoky-green gown. She was obviously looking for companionship given the way she kept passing her gaze lazily over the others in the room.

At one time she would have more than whet Grey's appetite. At one time practically every woman in this club would have served as a way to scratch his itch, but not anymore.

The lady looked up, her eyes glittering behind a violet mask trimmed with downy feathers. Her gaze fell on Archer and a smile curved her full lips. Grey's brother smiled back.

"You'll excuse me, then?" Archer was already on feet.

Grey waved him on his way with an indolent flick of his wrist. As much as he loved his brother and enjoyed his company, he would much rather bide his time alone.

Archer clapped him on the shoulder. "I will see you in the morning, then." It was an accepted fact that Arch never crawled home before dawn, reluctant to leave the supple embrace of his companion. Grey, on the other hand, didn't linger long enough for the fantasy to spoil.

Grey acknowledged the farewell with a slight dip of his head. "I'll have a place set for you."

He didn't take his gaze away from the throng below, but Archer's exit caught the edge of his vision. Once he was alone in the box, Grey let out the breath he'd been holding and slouched in the chair, stretching his legs out before him.

What the hell was he doing? He asked himself this very same question every time he came here. And he never liked the answer.

He was here because he wanted what he couldn't have—what he had promised to never touch. Would never dream of defiling.

Laughter echoed in his ears—loud and unwelcome. It stirred memories of that night long ago when he'd felt cold steel lay open the steaming warmth of his cheek. It reminded him that he was alone while more than a hundred people gathered beneath him, just out of his reach. He didn't like people, and that feeling only intensified when they gathered in groups like vultures hovering over a dying stag.

If he didn't find her soon, he would have to leave. Find relief in more auspicious and unsavory environs.

And then, like the answer to a prayer he'd never uttered, he spied *her*.

Grey leaned forward in the box, fingers curling around the smooth, cool brass rail. There, in the glittering meadow of hothouse flowers, was a wild bloom of a woman who quite literally robbed him of all breath.

Time ground to a halt, as did the beating of his heart.

She wore a low-cut gown the same vibrant burgundy of a rose just past first bloom. The tiny sleeves were trimmed with the same bronze lace that flitted around the rest of the gown, and sat low on her creamy round shoulders. From where he stood—when had he left his chair?—he could see the deep valley of her cleavage, the swells of her beautiful breasts flushed under the chandeliers.

The snug bodice of her gown hugged her across the ribs, nipped in sharply at the waist and then flared over hips and a backside that didn't need the little flouncy bustle to draw his attention.

His gaze lifted, and his heart began to beat once more as he took in the coffee darkness of her hair shimmering with the faintest hint of copper beneath the twinkling light. Her skin was the right shade of ivory, her hair the correct color and thickness, twisted into a high, loose knot. Beneath the bronze lace mask her nose had just the right tilt, and her mouth . . . her mouth was ripe and plump, just begging to be kissed.

Christ in heaven. If he didn't know better he'd swear this woman—this dream—was truly Rose.

But it couldn't be. Rose was a single young woman. She would never come there alone, and no one who knew her would bring such a gently bred young woman to a masked ball meant for seduction. Everyone familiar with Saint's Row knew what happened at these private functions. And there was no way a lady as sheltered and removed from London as Rose Danvers could ever pass through these doors. No, this wasn't Rose, but she was as close a twin as he could ever imagine—ever hope to find.

And he'd be damned if he'd stand there any longer, staring like an idiot, and give some other man a chance to have her.

Pivoting on his heel, he swept from the box, pushing the heavy velvet drapes aside to exit into the corridor beyond. Here, the lighting was almost as dim as in the box itself, with only a few sconces to illuminate the way. But Grey knew the interior of this club and his feet were sure as they carried him swiftly and silently along the thickly carpeted hall. He spared the slightest glance at the couple against the wall, the woman with her skirts bunched around her thighs, the man with his hand beneath. Their sounds of pleasure teased his ears, spurred him onward.

Halfway down the stairs he encountered Madame La Rieux herself. She was perhaps his age or a bit younger. Handsome and fair with shimmering copper hair that appeared as natural as the shrewd blue of her eyes. She was tall and slender, clad in an elegant and simple gown of butter yellow silk that could only have been made by a master such as Mr. Worth.

"*Monsieur le Duc,*" she greeted huskily in her delicate French accent as she curtsied demurely. "May I be of assistance to you?"

Manners and habit dictated that he bow in return, though what he truly wanted was to brush past her to find his delicious wildflower. He opened his mouth to ask her pardon, but then a thought occurred to him. "A private suite, madam. Have you any available?"

She smiled, carmine-tinted lips curving but not parting. "For you, Your Grace? Of course." Long, slender fingers dipped into the bodice of her gown and withdrew a small brass key on a delicate chain.

She offered the key to Grey. "The last chamber on the right at the end of the hall. You will have complete privacy."

The filigree key was warm from her skin and Grey held it tight in his fist. "Thank you. You will add it to my account, of course."

She inclined her head. "Of course. Shall I send a bottle of champagne as well?"

"Yes. Please." He slipped the key into his pocket. "And now if you will excuse me?"

She smiled again, coy but not debauched. "Have a pleasant evening, sir."

Grey nodded and hurried down the stairs. Only once he reached the bottom did he slow his harried pace. It wouldn't do to appear too eager.

He entered the ballroom blinking as his eyes adjusted to the brighter environment. He wasn't used to being out in the open like this. Usually he kept to the shadows, avoiding being seen at almost any cost.

Chandeliers burned overhead, but it was the gaslights camouflaged as antique sconces that gave the most light. Still, the room was bright without being overly so. No lady need worry that her complexion be judged too harshly or scrutinized too closely.

The cavernous room was like an open box of bonbons, decorated in shades of cream, chocolate, and gold. There was just the right amount of decoration as to be elegant rather than gaudy—a feat difficult to achieve these days. The lighting, now that he was accustomed to it, was just bright enough to see clearly, but not enough to abuse the eye, and the music was at the perfect level to titillate the ear, but not so voluminous that it ruined all hopes of conversation.

Not that he was in the mood for talking.

Hardly anyone glanced in his direction as he strode into the room, which was how he preferred it. Masked balls of this sort were known for discretion and anonymity. Of course, there were always those who noticed power and position when they saw it. He ignored them, his gaze scanning the room with one person in mind. And then, he spied her. She was alone, standing on the outskirts of the dancers, looking around the room as though she was waiting for someone.

Her gaze fell upon him, locking with his. The impact shook Grey right down to his toes. For a second, he swore he saw a flash of recognition, but it must have been a trick of the light, because it was gone in a blink.

She stood as still and poised as a gazelle as he approached, and just as likely to bolt if he conducted himself in the wrong way.

Patience, Kane, he told himself. Patience.

He walked up to her, every step measured and unhurried. Her head reached just above his chin, and she tilted it back to look up into his face. Sweet lips parted, revealing the moist pink flesh inside. He wanted to touch her, feel that slick moisture against his finger. He wanted to taste it with his tongue.

He held out his gloved hand. "I would like very much to dance with you, my lady."

There was no hesitation as she slid her silk-clad fingers over his. "I would not dream of denying you, my lord."

A thrill of anticipation raced down Grey's spine as he led her onto the dance floor, the other dancers swallowing them into their ebb and flow.

Denial? No, there would be no more of that tonight.

When he had offered his hand, she took it. There was the slightest tremor to her long, delicate fingers as his own closed around them. He led her onto the dance floor where they joined the other couples doing a more seductive version of the waltz than most ballrooms ever witnessed. It gave him a convenient excuse to hold her just as close. The corseted swell of her ribs rose and fell with her breathing beneath the flesh of his palm. He made her nervous—the rapid rise and fall of her spectacular breasts was proof of that, as was her inability to raise her gaze to his.

A little anticipation was a good thing, but he did not want her afraid of him. He wanted her as eager for him as he was for her.

"Shall we converse?" he asked.

She looked up, giving him a glimpse of dark, sparkling eyes behind her frilly mask. "On what topic, sir?" Her voice sent a delicious shiver down his spine. It was deeper than Rose's, and a little breathy, but close enough that his body reacted with such enthusiasm he thought he might embarrass himself by arching a massive erection right here on the dance floor.

"Whatever suits you," he practically growled. "I will be content to watch your lovely lips move."

Her eyelashes fluttered; clearly she was not used to flattery, or even flirtation. She really was perfect.

"You flatter me. Perhaps I have little conversational skills. I should hate to bore you."

He shook his head. "I find you fascinating."

Her head tilted and a slightly mocking smile curved that gorgeous mouth. "Sir, you barely know me."

Grey pulled her closer. His thigh brushed her hip. It was like bumping up against a hot stove, so great was the shock to his anatomy. "In my heart we are the most intimate of friends."

She opened her mouth—probably to protest—but he robbed her of the words by claiming her lips with his own. In the middle of the ballroom, he let her mouth scorch his, tasted her with his tongue. Hot and wet, his assault ignited a fire in them both. He could feel her body's answering arousal as she pressed her sweet self against him. She brought her tongue to his as she dug her fingers into his shoulder, clutched at the hand he had wrapped around hers. She tasted of champagne and warmth, and her lips were every bit as delectable as he suspected they would be. He wasn't aggressive in his pursuit, but she could have no questions as to his intentions.

Hell, no one within a mile radius could have doubts as to his intentions!

When he finally lifted his head, breaking the kiss, she stared at him, her eyes slightly glazed behind the mask. She licked her lips, and Grey knew with a strange, sensual certainty that she was savoring the taste of him.

"Let us not play games, love," he murmured, his mouth still very close to hers. "The moment I saw you I rushed down here to claim you before any other man could try."

"You did?" She sounded genuinely surprised—and delighted.

Grey bit back a groan and managed a grin instead. He let go of her hand, and reaching inside his coat pocket, withdrew the key Vienne La Rieux had given him. He raised the filigreed metal for her inspection before gently inserting it between her breasts. She gasped as the cool metal touched her skin, went completely still as his fingers settled on the warm swells. Her skin was like silk, smooth and fragile. He wanted to run his tongue over the delicate blue veins barely visible beneath the surface, taste the salt in the valley between.

But here was not the place.

"It's for a private suite," he explained. "Shall I meet you there, or will you break my heart and refuse me?"

In the space of a few agonizing heartbeats, he waited. Then her fingers closed over the ones that lingered upon her breast and a sweet but teasing smile curved her lips. "I could never live with the guilt of knowing I had broken your heart, sir."

"How long do you require?" Christ, he was as hoarse as a boy!

"Ten minutes," she said instead. "Is that agreeable?"

Hell, no. "Five."

There was no denying the shudder that racked her frame, no denying it was anticipation that wrought it. "As you wish."

Somehow Grey managed to release her and let

her walk away. His hungry gaze followed her as she moved across the floor, moving through the crowd as she made her way toward one of the exits along the far wall of the ballroom. Once she stopped and glanced back over her creamy shoulder at him. Perhaps it was his imagination, but he reckoned he could see the desire in her gaze despite the distance.

Five minutes. Not that long. A mere three hundred seconds. Why, he spent longer than that on his appearance in the evening. And it wouldn't do for him to seem too eager, would it? Wouldn't want his lover to know just how badly he had to have her.

Leaving the ballroom and making his way to the back stairs took thirty seconds. Climbing the stairs another twenty. Still, he had told her he'd give her five minutes before he'd even come to the room. He still had to wait.

He skulked in the shadows until he could wait no more. Two minutes early, he moved down the plushly carpeted corridor.

Denial was no longer an option. Tonight was all about indulgence, and he intended to indulge so lavishly and wholeheartedly that neither he nor his mystery lady would be able to walk properly for a week.

He was almost to the door when a hand grabbed his arm. Annoyed, he turned to face the intruder.

And that's when he saw the fist flying toward him.

Chapter 2

Grey ducked and the man attached to the fist fell into the wall, a victim of his own momentum.

"Bastard," the man spat from the floor where he slid. "I'll kill you."

"Not tonight," Grey remarked dryly, straightening his cuffs. "Perhaps when you are sober you could give it another go, however."

His assailant stared at him through bleary eyes. It wasn't the first time Grey had been the victim of a surprise attack, but the last one happened some time ago and his reflexes were not what they ought to be. His heart hammered shamefully in his ribs. The arse had actually surprised him.

"Do I know you, sir?" he asked, wasting time studying the man's familiar features when he should continue on to his lovely lady.

Spittle flew—intended for Grey but landing mostly on the man's own chin and lapels. "You shagged my wife, you filthy bugger!"

Grey's brows rose. A strange amusement filled him. "I'll have you know I bathe regularly, sir." He frowned. "Martingale? Is that you?"

The man huffed, tried to push himself upright and

failed. "You know it is, you . . . you fussbudget."

He would laugh at the absurd insult if he hadn't realized the man had every reason to want to kill him. He had shagged Lady Martingale—many years ago. He'd shagged their daughter as well. Mother and daughter had gotten into a very public row over him at the theater one night. Bad form all around.

Grey offered the man his hand. "Let's get you to a carriage. You should go home."

Martingale slapped his hand away with a snarl. Somehow the man found enough strength in his alcohol-saturated muscles to stand, though he had to cling to the wall to do so. "Go frig yourself."

"Come now," Grey said softly. "Let me assist you." It was the least he could do given all the harm he'd done. Of course Lord Martingale wasn't a saint either. He'd been doing some burlesque dancer while Grey dallied with his womenfolk, but Martingale had been discrete and Grey . . . well, he'd never been known for such virtue.

Martingale shoved him, but it was the drunken earl who stumbled rather than Grey. "Sod off. Those men should have cut more than your face, you piss ant."

"Yes," Grey replied coolly. "But they didn't. And you should have taken better care of your wife."

The two of them stared at each other for a brief second, Grey still and composed, Martingale unsteady and filled with drunken anguish. And then, all the fight seemed to abandon the earl, leaving him deflated and bent. He turned and staggered down the corridor, leaning on the wall for support.

Grey watched him go with some regret. Of course he wouldn't have welcomed further altercation, but perhaps spilling some of his blood would have given Martingale the satisfaction he wanted, granting Grey some atonement at the same time.

Instead, he was left feeling oddly empty. Perhaps he ought to leave. He hardly felt romantic at the moment. Still, it wouldn't be gentlemanly of him to keep her waiting. He should at least apologize.

He turned and moved toward the room where she waited. The door opened just as he raised his fist to knock, and his lady stood there, gasping when she saw him.

Grey frowned when he saw the reticule in her gloved hand. "Were you leaving?"

"I was, yes," came the cool reply with a lift of her round chin. "I do not appreciate being kept waiting, sir."

Grey smiled, all thoughts of his own departure evaporating at the challenge she presented. He stepped over the threshold, forcing her to retreat into the room. "Anxious, my lady?"

The room was made for assignation. The wallpaper was heavy and obviously costly. Huge bouquets of colorful Oriental flowers bloomed against the flat black backdrop. The plaster on the high ceiling was the same golden beige as the trim around the windows and door. Heavy drapes framed the window, designed to keep out all light or intrusion the city offered. The floor was walnut, polished and buffed to a high-gloss shine, and accented with plush rugs in the same colors as the wallpaper. The bed—a massive four-poster monstrosity—was hand-carved mahogany, covered in black bedding—with gold satin sheets turned down for the occupants.

Had waiting here, knowing what was going to happen between them when he arrived, made her nervous? Had she sat on the edge of the bed squeezing her thighs together in a vain attempt to assuage the itch deep inside her?

"I was anxious," she informed him more than a little haughtily. "Waiting has a way of cooling ardor."

He laughed then, as he closed the door, sealing the two of them into the room. Was it just him, or had the temperature gone up several degrees?

"Do you reckon?" He stepped closer. "I've always found that the more I have to wait for something the more I want it."

She stood her ground, but he could sense that she might bolt at any moment. They were so close their torsos were almost touching—hers rising rapidly with every breath. Grey's entire body was tight, tingling. Dark eyes rose to meet his. "Then you must want me very badly, sir."

There was no denying the spark of desire in her gaze. Golden flames seemed to burn in the chocolate depths, drawing him toward their heat as though he was nothing more than a powerless moth. "I do." His voice was rough, but if her shiver was any indication she didn't mind. "I want you very much."

Soft lips parted, but no sound came out. She simply watched him with that molten gaze, driving out all thoughts other than that of possessing her.

He wished she would take her mask off so that he might see all of her face, but she might expect him to do the same, and he couldn't have that. He didn't want her to see the damage done to his face, didn't want to face her questions, spoken or not.

He lifted a hand to curve around the back of her neck, drawing her closer. Her breath was warm and sweet against his face as he lowered his head. She came up on her toes, fingers clutching at the lapels of his coat, as he claimed her mouth with his own. She kissed him with the same hunger he felt in his soul—and when they finally broke apart, he wasn't the only one breathing hard.

"Champagne," Grey rasped, releasing her. Did she even notice that he'd loosened the lacing that held the back of her gown together? A few tugs at the shoulders and he could peel the snug garment off with little difficulty. But he didn't want to rush this. He'd found the perfect fantasy and he meant to savor every inch of her.

He tossed his coat over a nearby chair and unbuttoned his waistcoat as he moved toward the champagne waiting on ice. As he poured a flute for each of them, Grey untied his cravat. There, now he could breathe properly again. Christ, he was a mess!

When he returned to her, a glass of champagne in either hand, she was sitting on the edge of the bed, studying the base of his throat through his open collar. Grey didn't think his neck was all that fascinating or different from any other—not that he had ever compared that particular part of his anatomy to another man's.

He sat next to her on the bed, and she took the champagne he offered, downing a healthy swallow. Ah, his little bird was so sweetly innocent, something he would have found amusing in his younger days, but now . . . it was sweet.

"Sip it," he encouraged. "We have all night."

She glanced at him. "Do we?"

He nodded, dipping his index finger into the cold liquid in his glass. "We do." He didn't want to think that she might have someone to return to before the sun rose. He refused to think of anything but the two of them together in that room. Nothing else mattered.

He brought his finger to her mouth, tracing the curve of her lower lip, brushing the sensitive flesh just inside. She met his gaze boldly, and flicked her tongue against the pad of his finger. The wet heat of her touch sent a wave of lust over him. She was a temptress—an arousing mix of sensual promise and innocent wonder.

If he survived the night he would be sure to thank God for sending her to him, not that he deserved such a gift.

They took turns caressing the features of each other's faces. Never once did he try to remove her mask, nor she his. She seemed to understand his need to remain hidden.

Her fingers brushed against him like the softest of feathers, so delicate and warm. Grey closed his eyes, giving himself up to the exquisite torture of her exploration. Her thumb slid across his lower lip and he flicked it with his tongue as she had done to him. She gasped in delight—surely the loveliest sound he'd ever heard.

Glasses empty, Grey set both flutes on the table once more. This time when he came to her, he took her into his arms and brought her to her feet. The champagne made her relaxed and languid, but not unsteady. She stood, still letting Grey's fingers tug her tiny sleeves gaping at her shoulders. Gently, he pulled them down her arms, and when they refused to go any further, he reached around her and tugged on the laces of her gown again. Slowly, the bodice loosened and finally drooped. The gown's bustle was built in, so when the burgundy silk bagged around her hips, he was able to push it to the floor. He hooked an arm about her waist and lifted her out of the pool of fabric, setting her before him once more.

No false modesty, no confident preening. This beautiful specimen of womanhood stood before him with nothing but honesty as his hungry gaze raked over her. She was still clothed, layers of delicate underthings hiding her flesh, but his mouth was as dry as desert at the sight of her.

Grey's gaze fell to the swells of her breasts, straining against the edge of her pretty pink satin corset. They would fill his hands, pliant and warm beneath his fingers. As she breathed, the blush hued petal of aureole peeked over the tiny rosette trim. He reached out and settled his fingers there.

"Beautiful," he murmured, lowering his head to place gentle kisses on the top of either breast, and then up to her collarbones and neck. "You smell like spring rain," he told her, breathing in the gentle warmth of her skin.

"Do you like rain?" she asked, breathlessly.

"I do." His gaze held hers. Her eyes bright as twin moons as he raised his fingers to her jaw. "It cleanses the world, leaves everything fresh and new in its wake. And it's so clean and pure." He dragged his thumb along her lips, down her chin. "So sweet and wet."

She smiled saucily at him. "Lucky for you England is such damp country."

He grinned. Even her wit was similar to Rose's. "Indeed."

Then he kissed her again, this time with more hunger and passion than he'd shown before.

His fingers—surprisingly unsteady—managed to make short work of the busk front of her corset, as her hands tugged at his shirt, pulling it free of his trousers. Grey released her long enough to pull the garment off and toss it across the room. When he reached for her again, she stopped him by bracing her hands against his waist. Her hands were so soft and warm, he sighed at the feel of them against his skin.

"Wait," she whispered. "I want to touch you."

Grey let his arms fall to his sides. "Then touch me." Damn her for putting that note of pleading in his voice, but he was too far gone to let pride stop him now. She could bring him as low as she wanted so long as she kept touching him like he was something rare and special rather than the all too flawed man he was.

She ran her hands over his flesh, tracing the dips and swells of his torso and chest. Then up to the bones of his shoulders. She seemed to find his form fascinating, a fact that inflated his confidence as well as his cock. Every place she touched quivered at her touch, as though his body had been starved for such contact.

Grey hauled her against him once more. "Now it's my turn to touch you."

He kissed her again, untying the ribbons of her chemise. He pushed the fragile fabric down her arms until it slid free and pooled at her feet. Her arms came around his neck, fingers tangling in his hair as he tore his hands away from her long enough to unfasten his trousers and dispatch them. It wasn't until he swept her into his arms and set her on the bed that he realized she wore nothing but her stockings, and that he wore nothing at all.

Greedily, he raked his gaze over the full length of her. Her legs were long and shapely, the calves slightly muscular. Her hips were full, belly soft. Between her thighs, soft dark hair beckoned for his touch. Her waist was narrow, her breasts full, topped with delectable pink nipples that hardened under his appreciative gaze. Christ, but she was all pink and dusky cream—a delicacy that made his mouth water in anticipation of tasting every inch of her.

Her appraisal of him was every bit as frank and appreciative. Her eyes widened as her gaze fell upon his erection, stroking his self-satisfaction to a new level of smugness. He'd never been one of those men who doubted his size or prowess, but this woman made him feel like a stallion, or a god of some kind.

She reached out and touched him there, curling her fingers around the length. Grey hissed in pleasure. She stroked him, and he thrust against her hand, prick pulsing in delighted response. He let her explore and pleasure him until it became too much, then he covered her hand with his own and gently drew it away.

"Did I do something wrong?" she asked.

He laughed—a rasping sound. "Christ, no. I just don't want to come in your hand."

She flushed the prettiest rose. "Oh."

Grey smiled at her, touching his fingers to her cheek. His heart pinched at the contact, a response that struck fear in his chest.

It was only sex, he told himself. This emotional reaction was because of her similarity to Rose, because she seemed so genuinely taken with him. It was nothing to worry about. Nothing that wouldn't go away once the sun came up.

Bracing himself on his elbow, Grey lowered his head and took one puckered nipple into his mouth. Heat rushed through his blood as she moaned in pleasure, fingers digging encouragingly into his scalp. Her back arched, and when he sucked harder, she cried out, pressing those lush lips against his, parting her thighs for him.

He repeated the process with her other breast, rubbing the length of his arousal against the damp cleft of her body. She was all wet heat and willing flesh. It would be so easy—it was so tempting—to slid into her tightness and lose himself there. But not yet. Not yet.

He slid his hand down her torso, his fingers tracing the faint ridge of her ribs. Down the soft curve of her belly he moved with excruciating stealth, circling her navel and then down, until finally he found the damp and wanting place between her thighs. She didn't have to ask, didn't have to make a sound, for him to know what she wanted. Little moans escaped her mouth regardless, and she lifted her hips in invitation. One of his fingers parted the dewy lips of her sex to slide within, and found with surprising ease, the spot where he knew she ached to be touched. His lover cried out when the tip of his finger stroked and teased the little knot, and Grey acknowledged her pleasure with a gentle nip of his teeth against her nipple. Then he replaced his finger with his thumb, letting his fingers ease down through her wetness.

She gasped when he slid the length of one finger deep inside her. Her hips jerked upward, and he delved deeper, moving his finger, exploring with it until he found the ridge that made her squirm and moan. He became ruthless then, stroking and teasing until she ground herself against his hand, beautifully, beyond caring or shame. And then, as his thumb ruthlessly brought her closer to oblivion, he slid a second finger inside her.

Strong muscles clenched at his hand, urging him on. She was soaked between her thighs and his hand moved easily against her slick flesh. His own body was so tight and tense Grey felt as though he might come apart at any second, and yet he could not bring himself to deny her this pleasure, nor deny himself the pleasure of watching her face as climax claimed her. He raised his head to look at her.

And then she exploded. It was like nothing he'd ever seen before. Her chest and neck were flushed with the same blush that infused her cheeks. Her soft lips were parted, letting her cries ring out without censure. Her entire spine arched like a delicate wave, giving herself over to the sensations igniting every nerve.

She was beautiful.

When Grey came up on his knees over her, he knew the smile he gave her was beyond smug. "Did you like that?"

She blinked at him. "How can you even ask me that question?"

Grey laughed. Hands on either side of her head, he bent down and kissed her once again, nibbling on the sensuous curve of her lower lip. He nudged her thighs apart with his knee and she spread her legs willingly.

Reaching down, he guided himself to the entrance of her sex, where she was so very warm and damp.

And then he pushed forward, slowly parting her flesh as he eased his own inside. His lover dug her fingers into his back, lifting her legs to better adjust the angle of his intrusion. The walls of her sheath eased to accept him. She stiffened just for a moment and he thought . . . but no. She wrapped her legs around him, urging him deeper inside.

"Christ, you're tight," he rasped, shuddering just a little as he finally came to rest fully within her.

She stilled. "Don't you like it?"

Another harsh laugh. "My love, you feel so good I don't know how long I can last."

Then the vixen moved her hips beneath him, eliciting a groan from deep within his chest. "You naughty wench."

She laughed—a throaty chuckle that cut off abruptly when he thrust inside her. That would teach her to tease him, he thought smugly. And oh, dear Christ, she felt like Heaven!

Every slick thrust brought him closer and closer

to the edge. Every time she raised her hips to accept him he lost a little more of his control. Grey didn't care. He was too far gone to care. He withdrew only to bury himself inside her, over and over again as her nails scored his back and his fingers dug into the bed.

They clung to each other, bodies undulating. Grey could hardly think let alone speak. His mind was numb as his body came alive with every sensation and feeling. His heart seemed to swell within his chest as the tension within him grew. He'd had plenty of meaningless encounters in the course of his lifetime, but this wasn't one of him. He'd fallen headlong into infatuation a few times as well, but nothing had ever come close to this.

What was it about this woman? Was there something special about her? Something other than the fact that she reminded him of . . .

"Rose," he whispered.

If she heard him, she didn't let on, thank God. It was inexcusable of him to speak another woman's name during intimacy, even he knew that. But he hardly had time for regret as he could feel her limbs tightening around him, feel the strain in her muscles as she teetered on the edge. He thrust hard and deep, quickening his movements until the hot wet grip of her undid him and they came together, cries of pleasure blending so that he couldn't tell her voice from his own.

It was only by the grace of God that he remembered to withdraw at the last minute and spend on the sheets rather than in her.

They lay together, tangled and sweaty, breath

coming in shallow gasps for what easily could have been an hour or mere minutes. Normally he would have been up and dressed by now, but Grey found himself in no such hurry, and when his lover started to pull away from his embrace, he stopped her. "Don't go yet."

She looked at him, and damn her she must have seen the desperation in his features because she said nothing, only lay back down beside him, allowing him to draw her against his chest.

Grey brushed his lips against the silky skin of her bare shoulder. "I want to see you again."

"I don't think that's a good idea."

He cupped her jaw with his hand, turning her head so that she was forced to meet his gaze. He didn't care if she thought him pathetic or desperate. Nothing else mattered but that she acquiesce. "Please."

"When?" Her voice was a little hoarse, not nearly as low and breathy as it had been all evening. Damnation, she even sounded like Rose.

"One week from tonight," he replied, heart dancing for joy. "I won't be able to get away before then."

"All right," she agreed. "Where?"

"Here. In this very room. I'll make the arrangements."

She nodded. "Here. One week from tonight."

Grey smiled. Her voice had been stronger this time, her tone more enthusiastic. "Thank you."

And then, in case she mistook their conversation for dismissal, he pulled her close and covered her body with his own once more. He kissed her softly, tenderly, patiently waiting for her to fully recover before launching a second seduction. He kissed the edges of her mask, her cheeks and finally her lips until she began to move against him, hips seeking his.

He made love to her a second time, and afterward, when they'd both collapsed limp and replete, Grey allowed himself the luxury of falling asleep in her arms. How long had it been since he'd spent the night with a woman? Too long. He'd forgotten the pleasure of soft flesh pressed to his own, the feel of a lush bottom against his thighs.

As he began to drift off, he realized that he didn't know her name, and had no way to find her should she not return the next week. If she changed her mind she would be lost to him forever. Part of him knew that he could get over the disappointment if she decided to neglect their appointment. And another part . . .

That was the part that had him wrap his arms around her and hold her as tight as he could.

Dawn was still some hours away when Rose Danvers opened her eyes.

Good lord, how could she have allowed herself to sleep? It was late. She had to get going if she was going to catch the first train—if she was going to trick her mother into thinking she'd spent the night in her own bed.

She couldn't waste any more time lying there watching Grey sleep, listening to his gentle snores and soft sighs.

Though, truth be told, she could stay like this

forever. He was so beautiful it broke her heart. The mask he wore hid nothing from her, she who had memorized every line and detail of his face years before. Even that ragged scar couldn't diminish the perfection that was his every feature. His eyes were closed now, but when open they were the clearest, loveliest blue with a hint of spring green. His nose was long and strong, his cheekbones chiseled, and his jaw broad. But it was his mouth she loved most. She loved the way his lips moved when he spoke, curved when he smiled. And most of all she loved the way they felt against hers.

Thank you, God. Thank you for giving me this gift.

She couldn't help but touch him one last time, even if she risked waking him. She lightly brushed a lock of hair from his forehead, feeling the dark, silky strands between her fingers.

Had this night really happened or was it a dream? Had she truly given her virginity to the one man she held above all others? And had she actually heard him whisper her name, or had her heart imagined it?

So many thoughts swirled through her mind and yet she couldn't seem to concentrate on any one. She had done what she set out to do and she would not regret it. If there were to be consequences then she would face him. She didn't expect anything of Grey, but she hoped . . .

She hoped that now she might live without her incessant desire for him defining her every waking moment, every action. Perhaps now she would be free. And yet, she'd agreed to meet him the next week. That wasn't freedom, that was the beginning of an affair. An affair she couldn't afford to continue. It was too risky.

Quietly, she crawled off the bed, her legs shaky, muscles trembling. The tenderness between her thighs told her it was indeed real and not a dream. She dressed as quickly and completely as she could. She would fix her hair and check her appearance in one of the retiring rooms downstairs before rushing out to hail a hack.

At the door she hesitated, glancing back at the man on the bed. It felt wrong to leave while he was asleep, without leaving something of herself behind. She reached down and tore one of the rosettes off the bottom of her gown. There were so many no one would notice that six, let alone one, was missing. She placed the burgundy silk blossom on top of the table near Grey's discarded cravat.

There, at least he would know she thought of him before she went.

And then, she cast one last glance at the man who had changed her forever before gently opening the door and ducking outside. She hurried down the stairs, checked her appearance as she planned, and then ran outside into the predawn street to hail a hack. Lucky for her, there was a steady stream of them traveling the length of Saint's Row. Apparently there was no shortage of early morning departures from the club.

She gave the train station as her direction to the driver and climbed in the back, settling against the cushions.

The coach hadn't even reached the end of the

street when the tears started coursing down her cheeks. What the devil was wrong with her? She'd just had the most amazing night of her life—a soul stirring experience with the man who haunted her dreams and made her feel like no other.

So why, then, did she feel so awful?

Chapter 3

She was gone.

Grey woke to the sound of rain beating against the windowpanes—a gentle tinkling sound that made him want to roll over and wrap himself around the delicious woman in bed beside him. That was how he realized he was alone. He hadn't even heard her leave.

Instead, he gathered the pillow she'd slept on close, and inhaled the lingering scent of her into his lungs. Her smell—fresh like the rain pattering outside—filled him with a longing so intense it damned near unmanned him.

Who was she to fulfill his fantasies so completely? Had she been a dream?

Tossing back the blankets, he sat up and swung his legs over the side of the bed. There was no point dallying if he was alone. He had to get back to Mayfair and prepare for the arrival of his guests. Facing the "real" Rose would be so much easier now.

Completely dressed save for his cravat, Grey reached for the discarded strip of silk and found a single, rich wine-colored rose ensnared in the length. It was from his lady's gown. Smiling, he raised the delicate bloom to his nose, even though he knew it would have no scent. So she hadn't left without thought or feeling. Why that should warm him so was a mystery. It was only sex. Still, that she should leave him a faux rose, when she was indeed his faux Rose . . . well, the irony wasn't lost on him.

It would be a long week until he saw her again. As he wrapped and then tied his cravat around his neck, he thought about how it had felt to be with her—how tight and hot and wet she'd been. Almost shy. He had no trouble believing she was every bit as virginal as Rose would be.

Next time he wouldn't have to be quite so careful, though he would have the patience to explore much, much more of her than he had last night. The mere thought of what they might do to each other was enough to waken his cock. He had to stop thinking about her, else he'd embarrass himself.

Grey left the club through a private members door, where there was less chance of being seen by others on the street or leaving the club. Of course, the hackneys knew about it, which made it all the more agreeable. No one had to feel obliged to make their driver wait all night, coat of arms on display for any and all to see. He gave his direction to the driver, climbed inside, and was soon on his way home.

The interior of the carriage was nowhere as fine as his own, but it was clean and comfortable—all that he required. He'd certainly been in worse. In his younger days, long before the incident that left him scarred and changed his life, he had been quite the rake, enjoying any and everything that was debauched, debased, and decadent. And he hadn't cared who knew of it either.

Amazing how a torn face and vicious beating could change a man's priorities.

The hack delivered him to his front door. Ryeton House was a sprawling throw back to another era—a Palladian design with neoclassical elements added by Robert Adam almost a century earlier. Grey supposed it was his turn to add a little something to the design, as his predecessors had, but he hadn't the heart to make the poor old girl endure any more "dressing up." He liked her just as she was.

The interior of the house was much like the outside—old, but elegant, and owing much of its style to each generation of Kanes who had lived there. Never once had the dukedom passed outside of Grey's direct bloodline, and though he knew his chances of producing a legitimate heir were slim to none given that one had to marry for any offspring to be recognized, he took comfort in knowing that Archer or Trystan would no doubt provide the necessary boy to take over when Grey was long dead.

The smell of breakfast greeted him as he crossed the hall—buttered eggs, sausage, ham, fresh bread . . . Grey's stomach growled in response. He was famished. Instead of heading upstairs to his bedroom, he pivoted on his heel and, after tossing his overcoat, gloves, and hat onto an obliging table, entered the dining room.

Archer, freshly shaven and bathed sat in Grey's usual spot, sipping coffee and reading the *Times*.

"Get your arse out of my chair," Grey barked by way of greeting.

His younger brother bent his newspaper—Grey's newspaper—and peered over the top with an arched brow. "Well, well," he intoned, dry as burnt toast. "Look who finally decided to crawl back to the roost. You look like shite." But despite the insult, Archer rose and moved his plate from the head of the table to a spot on the right.

Grey smiled. He had stayed out longer than Archer. That hadn't happened for a long time, and he was decidedly smug about it. "Thank you."

He sat down at his usual place, flipped a snowy white napkin over his lap, and removed the mask that had been stuck to his face all night. It felt good to free his skin from the snug leather. He would remove the traces of spirit gum left behind, later in the bath.

"You aren't going to bathe before breakfast?"

Grey loaded his plate with a selection of everything. "No." He was too hungry—and not at all in a hurry to wash away the lingering scent of his mystery lover. "Anything of interest in the paper?"

"The usual drivel. Lots of dithering about Russia and Turkey, and the fact that the Princess of Wales is in Greece." Archer snapped the paper shut and set it aside. "I ran into Aiden and Blackbourne last night at Saint's Row. They said they overheard Martingale bragging about taking a swing at you. Since you don't look the worse for wear, should I squelch the rumor soundly?"

"He took a swing at me all right, and then fell flat on his arse." Grey poured a cup of coffee. The whole debacle seemed much more amusing in the light of day. "But don't bother saying anything. Everyone knows he's a lousy drunkard who couldn't hit the broad side of a coach with a cricket bat." It was unlikely that society would believe Grey left the house let alone lost a fight to such a man.

Archer's dark brows hitched. "You're very chatty this morning. Not to mention almost congenial. Shall I assume your evening was satisfactory?"

"Assume whatever you like." He shoveled a large forkful of eggs into his mouth. Sublime.

Archer scowled. "Bugger. I'd tell you."

Grey inclined his head in agreement as he ripped a chunk off a still warm roll. "You're not as discreet as I."

"What rot! Since when?"

Pale, creamy butter melted on the soft bread in Grey's hand. "Since always." He popped the delicious morsel into his mouth. Had food always tasted this good?

His brother snorted in disgust and Grey took pity on him. "My night was lovely, Arch. How was yours?" More than lovely, it had mellowed him to such a state that he wasn't the least bit anxious or agitated about seeing the real Rose. In fact, he'd wager this time he could take her into his arms and give her a welcoming embrace without wondering what it would be like to feel her nipples against his tongue—a thought that had been a genuine low for him given that Rose had been seventeen or eighteen at the time. He'd been eight and twenty and old enough to know better.

Accepting the bone he'd been tossed, Archer

helped himself to a roll as well, only he slathered his with strawberry preserves as well as butter. He grinned. "Enthusiastic," he replied with a touch of bravado in his rich baritone. "You might even call it downright athletic."

Grey picked up a chunk of ham with his fingers and bit off a large bite. "What did you do, bugger the entire Cambridge rowing team?"

A piece of sticky bread narrowly avoided striking him in the eye and hit his cheek instead. "Twat."

As he wiped the jam off his face, Grey laughed—a genuine from-the-belly chortle that felt so good he could hug his insolent younger sibling. It wasn't long before Archer was laughing with him.

"I'd give my right nut for a night as lovely as yours must've been," the younger man commented as he refilled both their cups with rich, black coffee. "What was she like?"

Grey sobered and lifted the cup to his lips. "She was everything I've ever wanted." But as soon as he said the words he knew them to be a lie. "Or as close as I'll ever have."

Archer regarded him carefully, popping a piece of his strawberry-soaked roll into his mouth. "Let me guess—dark hair, fair skin, and an ass you can sink your teeth into?"

He didn't know whether to laugh at the accurate description or cuff him for his impertinence. "Something like that."

His brother nodded, took another bite, chewed and swallowed. "You know, I've never understood why you just don't marry Lady Rose."

And here he'd thought he'd managed to conceal his

obsession with Rose. "Because she's not for me."

"That's just more rot and you know it."

Grey sighed. How often had he had this same conversation within himself? It didn't matter what argument the side of him obsessed with Rose made, the few shreds of decency he had left inside him knew what was right.

"It's not up for discussion."

Archer shook his head, a sneer curving his wide mouth. "Jesus, Grey. If I were lucky enough to find a woman I wanted that badly, I'd do whatever it took to have her."

Another forkful of eggs. "But I can't have her. There are too many reasons why she and I would never work."

"Name one."

"She's enamored of parties and balls and longs to be a social darling."

"So get rid of the mask, get your arse out into public, and join her."

"I'd rather take out my eye with the jam spoon."

Archer shrugged. "Obviously you don't think that much of her, then."

Grey's fork clattered to the plate. "Fuck you." Now he was as foulmouthed as his brother.

The other man was unruffled. "It's a damn shite excuse and you know it."

"How about the fact that I'd never know if marrying me was just a way to say thank you for my saving her family?"

Archer made a face, as though it was obvious. "You could ask her."

Grey slouched back in his chair, regarding his

brother as though ten years rather than months divided them. "Would you want to know the answer if it was you?"

His brother didn't have a quick retort for that. And it was plain as the fading sneer on his face that Grey had made his point. "I suppose not."

His appetite gone, Grey tossed his napkin on the table. "I'm a decade her senior. I was a friend of her father, and I'm sure she looks upon me like a benevolent uncle. Even if she didn't, I promised Charles I wouldn't lay a hand on her." The Earl of Marsden had been one of his dearest friends—practically his only friend. A promise to such a friend should not be easily broken.

Archer jerked back, disbelief coloring his angular features. "Why the hell did you do that?"

Grey shrugged. "He asked it of me."

Shaking his head, Archer exhaled a breath. "You never told me that before."

"I suppose I was ashamed." And hurt, even though he understood his friend only made the request to protect his only child from a man whose sexual conquests had resulted in his being marked for life. Were the situation reversed, Grey might have very well demanded the same promise. And despite being a libertine, he was a man of his word.

Archer stared at him for a long moment, elbow braced on the table, chin resting on his thumb as his index finger stroked his stubbled upper lip. "Devil take it, Grey. Charles Danvers was one cruel bugger."

A bitter smile curved Grey's lips at the insult to his late friend. "Quite."

* * *

"And I think you should wear the blue Worth to your first ball. Perhaps the pink Pingat to the second. How kind of the duke to pay for such beautiful gowns! You must remember to thank him."

Rose acknowledged her mother with a faint smile. The older woman had scarce drawn breath since they'd left Bramsley. While she loved seeing her mother so animated—she'd been practically on a shade in the last two years since Rose's father's death—she really wished for a little peace to gather her thoughts before they arrived at Ryeton House.

"I will thank Gr—the duke, mama. I promise."

Her mother smiled and clasped her hands together in her lap like a child overcome with joy. She peered out the carriage window, her gaze lit with joy. "It's been so long since I've been to London, I've forgotten how much I missed it."

Her mother hadn't been to London since her father died. Rose at least had the advantage of visiting her friend for a few days last year when the family was in town. Not during the Season, of course. This was her first Season in almost three years. Three long years since she'd had a new gown that wasn't black or gray. Three years since she'd danced or put flowers in her hair. So long since she'd dressed up and made herself pretty so a would-be suitor might notice her.

Three years—until last night.

One more thing to add to the list of things to thank Grey for. At this rate she'd spend the next week doing nothing but showing him her appreciation.

Part of her couldn't shake the feeling that last

night had been wrong—she had done something sinful. But she had wanted to do it. Wanted it more than she'd wanted anything—more than she wanted her father not to have lost all their money.

And it was wonderful, more than she could have imagined, but it had been awful too, because as much as Grey might have pretended that it was she who he had made love to, he believed it to be someone else. He would never know the truth, and that tarnished the beauty of their night no matter how few regrets she had about it.

Her mother adjusted the black silk of her skirts. She refused to come so far out of mourning as to wear any kind of color. Fortunately, she was one of those women who looked rather fetching in black, giving a kind of sad elegance to her appearance. Rose fancied not even Queen Victoria herself could find fault in her mother's mourning of her husband. Her black hair was pulled back in a tight chignon that would have looked severe on a less striking woman. Her skin was so fair—more so than Rose, who favored her father in coloring as well as looks. And her eyes were as green as spring grass. So lovely, was her mother. It almost hurt to see her looking so happy. She deserved to be happy.

"And what will you wear to the balls, Mama?"

Her mother shrugged. "I'm sure I have several gowns that will suit."

All black. All simple and plain. Her mother wouldn't want to be noticed, and that fact alone would garner her unwanted attention. Her looks would guarantee gentlemanly stares. Only the black armor she wore would protect her.

Leaning across the short distance between them, she seized her mother's hand, careful not to wake the little gray terrier snoring on the seat beside her. "You will let yourself have some fun, won't you?"

Smiling as only a mother indulging her child could, her mother placed her free hand over Rose's. "Of course." Meaning she would take the brunt of her own happiness from whatever joy Rose managed to find.

Not that Rose should take responsibility for her mother's happiness, of course. That wasn't the expectation and Rose knew it, but that didn't stop her from feeling the heaviness of the burden upon her shoulders.

"Perhaps you could call upon some old friends," she suggested, leaning back against the cushions as the carriage rocked, bouncing lightly over the cobblestones. "Renew old acquaintances."

Her mother looked vaguely surprised by the notion. "Why, yes, I suppose I could." She smiled. "It would be lovely to see some of those ladies again."

The pressure around Rose's chest eased, pressure that she hadn't even noticed until it was gone. "I'm certain they would enjoy seeing you as well, Mama." The ones who had been true friends would anyway. Others might care about Rose's father's loss of fortune and cut her mother, but there would always be those who could overlook that in favor of the Duke of Ryeton's guardianship.

Good lord, the list kept growing.

Rose stretched her back. How much further was it to Ryeton House?

Her mother must have noticed her discomfort. She cast a glance out the window at the passing scenery. "We're almost there."

The next thing Rose knew, they were rolling between the thick stone columns of a gate. The wrought iron swung closed behind them, and they continued up a smooth gravel drive that led to a shady courtyard.

Ryeton House. Her heart gave a tremulous thump against her ribs. They had arrived.

What did she hope would happen when they entered the house? That Grey would come to meet them, realize she was his lover from the night before and fall prostrate at her feet? Maybe he would beg her to marry him as well, giving her no choice but to fully defy her father's wishes and consent to be his wife.

What she would truly like was to face Grey and not feel as though the world was quivering beneath her feet when he looked at her. She would like to know that the degree of emotion she felt for him could be felt for another man as well. She had to hope that was true.

A footman in the Ryeton livery opened the door and released the steps for them, then reached in a gloved hand to help first her mother, then Rose from the carriage. Her mother held Maurice, the terrier, against her chest as she stepped out into the afternoon air.

Rose followed. The air was reasonably fresh compared to the stuffiness of the carriage, but not as sweet as she was used to in Kent. Still, it was London air, and that made it lovely all the same.

While the footmen collected their luggage, Rose and her mother continued up the steps to the house. The door was opened by Westford, the butler, who greeted them both with a polite but genuine smile. "Lady Marsden, Lady Rose. Delightful to see you again."

Inside the house, Rose's heart began to pound a little harder. Would Grey meet them? Or was he away from home? Perhaps he was still at Saint's Row, in the bed where she left him . . .

"Camilla, Rose!"

A tremor raced through her at the sound of his voice. Only he would be so familiar as to call them by their Christian names. Her parents had insisted upon the intimacy, especially after he saved them. It was more than most married couples allowed, but somehow, it seemed right to grant him such liberties.

He came through the hall dressed in dark gray trousers and matching coat. His shirt and cravat were snowy white, stark against the tan of his skin. His dark hair was brushed back from his face, and the mask he'd worn last night was no where to be seen.

He felt comfortable enough with them to show his scar.

It was a jagged white line that ran from just above his left temple all the way down to his jaw. It was about a quarter of an inch wide, but it wasn't the scar itself that was disconcerting, it was how he came to have it.

He walked up to them, greeting her mother first. Rose just stood there, staring stupidly as Grey took her mother's hands and kissed her smooth cheek. She didn't hear what they said to each other; she couldn't think over the rush of blood in her ears.

And then, Grey turned to her, offering an embrace that could only be described as brotherly. "Rose, I'm so glad to see you."

Looking at him, she could tell that he meant it. He was happy to see her. He also had no idea that he had seen her just that morning. He didn't know. Face-to-face with her, holding her in his arms, how in the name of all that was holy could he not recognize her as the woman he had made love to the night before? Did her hair not smell the same? And what of her scent? Did she no longer smell of spring rain? Or had it all been a lie?

How could he not know her? Was it so impersonal for him that he didn't recognize his lovers when he saw them? Mask or no mask, surely he could tell. She recognized him without his mask. She would know him anywhere.

Had she completely misjudged his attraction to her, his feelings for her?

Or perhaps, she thought a little bitterly as she stepped out his embrace, she was simply getting what she deserved for deceiving him in the first place. Perhaps she should be happy that he didn't recognize her. She should be thankful right then and there that despite his obvious desire for her, she'd made no more of an impact upon him than the women he used to take pleasure with and then cast aside.

And she was thankful. Then she wouldn't have to explain why she'd done what she had done. If he didn't know her then he couldn't be upset with her when she failed to show up for the tryst the following week.

And make no mistake, she was not returning to Saint's Row.

Chapter 4

"Lady Hilbert requests the pleasure of our attendance at a tea at her home next week," Rose said, scarcely looking up from the soft pink invitation in one hand as she placed a delicate teacup back into its saucer with the other.

Since it was just the three of them taking tea in the parlor, Grey used the intimacy as an excuse to watch her openly, a faint smile upon his lips. He'd meant it when he told her he was glad to see her. She was like a ray of sunshine after a week of rain. Thanks to his lovely companion of the night before he was able to enjoy the sight of beautiful Rose without the onslaught of unslakable lust and longing that usually hung over his head at their meetings.

Not that his desire for her had lessened. It hadn't. In fact, his mystery lover had only served to deepen the fantasy. He could imagine now that he had actually made love to Rose, could imagine that the supine arms that had wrapped around him so tightly had truly belonged to the gorgeous creature sitting across from him. He wanted her all the more for it, but without the usual desperation.

Could she see it? Was that why she'd barely

glanced at him since her arrival? If he didn't know better he'd say she seemed almost embarrassed to look at him. Was it the scar? It had never bothered her before, or had she become so very refined since they last met?

Absently, Grey's fingers went to the jagged strip of satiny flesh that ripped down the side of his face. The flesh around it was vaguely numb, like a child's nose after an afternoon of snowman building. He followed the scar all the way down to its thickened end, remembering all too clearly how the serrated blade had burned and tore as it forged its bloody path.

"Ruin that pretty face of his," one of his attackers insisted. But this was as far as they got. Were it not for the interference of Rose's father, his dear friend Charles, he might not have gotten away as lucky as he had. The man who cut him had obviously enjoyed his work and intended to apply himself to a job well done.

Camilla, Charles's pretty widow, sat across from him, the perfect lady on a stiff-backed settee. "Do you know Lady Hilbert, Your Grace?"

He favored the older woman with a charming smile. It was an expression he rarely wore these days. "My dear friend, how many times must I remind you to call me Grey? Or at the very least Greyden."

Her answering smile was as endearing as he'd come to expect from her. "A few more, I'm sure, *Greyden.*"

Grey helped himself to a cucumber sandwich and took a large bite. He chewed and swallowed before speaking again: "To answer your question, I've known Lady Hilbert most of my life. She was a good friend to my mother." Then he addressed Rose, "I would view it as a personal favor if you were to accept her invitation."

That made her raise her head. Her gaze locked with his—like a doe in the woods. "I wouldn't dream of refusing."

There was a huskiness to her voice that recalled murmured words of passion, so sweet and real that his prick—impudent thing—stirred at the sound.

But then she went back to her task. The invitation from Lady Hilbert she set to her right. There was a smaller pile to her left, and the larger unopened batch still in front of her. "Those on your left, are those ones you plan to refuse?"

Her smooth cheeks—normally a dusky ivory—flushed as sweetly as her name. "I think it the wisest course."

A perplexed frown tugged at Grey's brows. "Forgive me, but after such a long absence from society I would think you eager to attend any and all functions." Especially given how excited she'd been to return to the rat infested sewer that was the London *ton*.

She looked at him with something like indignation in her gaze. Was that resentment as well? Ridiculous. After all he'd done for her and her mother, why would she have any reason to think ill of him? He'd never been anything but obliging—and certainly would never dream of telling her how to live her life or which parties to go to. Hell, it wasn't as though he ever attended any.

"Because one of these invitations is from Lady Francis. The other from Lady Devane. Were not both of those ladies suspected of having a hand in the attack against you? Or did I misunderstand the discussion you had with my father?"

"Rose!" Camilla was positively scarlet, obviously embarrassed that Rose was indelicate enough to bring up such a subject. Grey was made more regretful than humiliated by the reminder. In fact, he was oddly touched that she would snub two hostesses because of him.

"You should never have heard that conversation," he lamented. "But since you did, I cannot deny the accuracy of it, though I've never seen sufficient evidence to damn either lady. I do not wish you to turn down an invitation on my behalf, but neither would I have you attend a gathering that would make you anything less than comfortable."

Rose looked away, returning to her previous shyness—avoidance. "They only invited me so they could ask about you, I'm sure."

"Rose," her mother chastised. "That is quite ill natured of you."

The young woman shrugged gently rounded shoulders, hugged snugly by her dark blue day gown with crimson piping. "Be that as it may, Mama. It makes the statement no less true. I do not wish to be social with any lady, no matter how grand, who could be considered capable of such vileness."

Grey could kiss the chit senseless for her misguided allegiance. She might be all righteous indignation on his behalf, but he'd deserved what had happened to him that night. In fact, that incident had changed his life forever, and for the better he believed.

There were those who thought he shunned society out of humiliation or fear. People who thought he could not bear to face them with his "pretty" face not so pretty anymore, but that wasn't true. Grey no longer went out in society because he despised the ugly lie of propriety and civility that lurked beneath the surface. He avoided society because it disgusted him.

"You've a great deal of honor and nobility in you, Rose," he said—to the side of her head since she wouldn't look up. "You remind me of your father in that way."

She looked up at that—a glimmer of tears in her big brown eyes. "Thank you."

Charles Danvers had been the best of men, but he'd no head for business or money management, like many of their class. That was what led to his undoing. Years of free spending, on himself, his wife, and his precious daughter led to a slow downfall. Grey had been just as ignorant as anyone else, since Charles never said anything. So when ruination struck, it struck hard.

Poor bloke never recovered from it.

Grey continued to hold Rose's gaze, fairly drowning in the dark depths of her large eyes. How long they stayed as such he had no idea, but when Camilla cleared her throat, he knew it had been too long.

"I've never had a chance to properly thank you for all you've done for us, Your . . . Greyden."

"My dear madam, that is quite unnecessary." It

might sound as though he was merely being polite, but it was true.

"Still," Camilla pressed on. "Your kindness to Rose and me . . . sponsoring Rose for the Season . . . I can never thank you enough."

Grey's gaze flitted to the young woman sitting silent and pink-cheeked at the desk. "Seeing Rose happily married will be thanks enough."

Camilla chuckled with happiness, as any mother would at the thought of her daughter's marriage. Rose, however, went from flushed to chalk-pale in seconds. She looked at Grey as though he'd punched her.

"Not that my wants should be a consideration in your quest for a husband, Rose." It occurred to him that a goodly portion of London society might be present at Rose's wedding. It also occurred to him that she might be embarrassed to have him, a scarred, masked freak there as well.

It also occurred to him, like a well-aimed kick to the head, that the idea of watching Rose marry anyone was something he looked forward to about as much as he would castration.

Possibly less.

He cleared his throat, aware now that there was a strange silence in the room. "You may take your time in your search. I will see to your comfort for as long as necessary."

"Oh!" Camilla gasped, hands pressed to her generous bosom. "You are all kindness, sir!"

Grey managed to flash a tight smile before returning his attention to her daughter, a girl who took up way too much of his thoughts as it was.

"Have you any traits that you require in a husband, Rose? I might know some gentlemen who would please you." None half so much as he would like to please her. None who would kneel down before her and worship her as he did.

Forget his obsession with her; he respected her as well. He'd watched her go from a spoiled girl to a brave young woman who stood beside her father during his ruin. A woman who had helped nurse him after his attack. A woman who'd supported her mother when they both lost the only man they could depend on. So Grey had stepped into that role, because he'd never had anyone love and need him like those women had loved and needed Charles Danvers. Taking over their care had done so much more for him than he would ever be able to do for them.

Rose toyed with an unopened envelope, her fingers tracing the edges. Her gaze fell to the table before her, then up to meet Grey's own. This time at least she didn't look so hesitant, but there was still a trace of defiance in her gaze that puzzled him.

"My requirements in a husband are simple," she informed him smoothly. "All I want is a man who will hold me above everything else, including his horse, his fortune, and his pride."

Hearing that simple yet seemingly impossible declaration was like a blow to Grey's solar plexus. She was going to be so disappointed, the poor thing. How perverted was it of him to secretly rejoice over her wants? She might find a man who could love her more than his horse, perhaps even more than his fortune, but never would she find a man willing to sacrifice his pride—not without that same man coming to hate her for it eventually.

"More than his horse?" he joked. "My dear girl, you ask too much."

He flashed a bright grin to let her know he was only teasing, and it seemed to do much to warm her toward him. He'd never felt this withdrawal from her before. They'd always been such good friends despite the torment it gave him. So, when she returned his smile with a tentative, then full-fledged, one of her own, it was like a gift from heaven.

"Perhaps I could be persuaded to overlook that requirement if the gentleman is handsome enough."

The three of them shared a chuckle, and soon settled back into an easy companionship. Grey snatched another sandwich and watched Camilla make a plate for her daughter.

"You have to eat something, Rosie. I won't have you wasting."

"Wasting?" Her daughter laughed at the notion. "If I want all the gowns Grey bought me to fit properly I shall have to be very careful what I put in my mouth."

Immediately Grey's gaze dropped to that mouth. A sweetly curved upper lip rested tenderly above a full, pouty lower. He could think of at least one thing he'd like to slide between those lips.

Christ, he was such a cad. A despicable cad. It was thinking of women this way that got him in trouble years ago, but it seemed he had yet to learn his lesson. He might not whore around like he used to, but his libertine ways hadn't been completely obliterated.

Rose indulged her mother and took the plate of sandwiches and biscuits she offered. She even went so far as to eat a little of it before setting it aside to return to her invitations.

How many of them were from people who were sincere in their request for her company? Probably less than half. Some would have acted out of a sense of what was expected of them given that Rose was the daughter of an earl—albeit a ruined one—and, thanks to Grey, had a large dowry. Others would simply view her as a way to gain a little titillation by using her as a way to find out gossip about him. Those people would no doubt be sorely disappointed. His lovely Rose was nothing if not loyal. She would not talk about him—not in the way society would relish. In that way she was one of his most steadfast friends. One of the few people who refused to turn against him even when it would have been in her best interest to do just that.

His attack happened before Charles lost everything, so it hadn't been a sense of self-preservation that drove her loyalty either. She was simply not capable of turning her back on someone she cared for.

That realization humbled him more than any serrated blade ever could.

"Thank you," he blurted. Startled glances shot his way. "Both of you."

Camilla, paused in the middle of pouring herself another cup of tea. "Whatever for?"

"For your kindness." A huge lump seemed to have formed in his throat as his gaze locked with Rose's. "I am honored to have your friendship."

Rose's expression softened into something he

couldn't read, but it seized his heart all the same. What the hell was wrong with him? A few hours in her company and he already unmanned himself.

"You shall always have it," she told him quietly. Then, a quick glance to the woman near him. "Isn't that right, Mama?"

Damn it all, in those few seconds he'd forgotten about Camilla. "Of course," she replied with a gentle smile as she laid her hand over one of Grey's. "Always."

Somehow, he managed to smile. Then he made some foolish excuse so that he might leave their company. He felt Rose's questioning gaze upon his back as he left the room, and he had to force himself not to look back. Because if he did, there was no telling what insanity he might get up to.

He had his pride, after all.

"You simply have to try some of this cake."

Rose knew better than to argue with her friend Eve, so she obligingly opened her mouth and allowed her friend to deposit a bite of soft, chocolaty goodness inside. She would have to eat light at supper that night or she really wouldn't fit into any of her gowns.

"Mmm," she agreed as the cake melted on her tongue. "That's divine." They were on the terrace of Eve's family's London townhouse. The Viscountess Rothchild held a tea at this time every year to celebrate the opening of the Season. It was barely two weeks into May, but her lawn and terrace were awash with ladies of all ages in prettily-colored day gowns and lacy parasols twirling under the midday sun.

"I might have to help myself to another slice," her friend allowed with a sigh. Blonde with ivory skin and cornflower blue eyes, Eve had the delicate grace of a spring lily and the determination of an oak in a storm.

Rose eyed her shapely friend in disbelief—and a little envy. "If I ate like you I'd weigh twenty stone."

Eve set the empty plate aside and dabbed the corners of her mouth with a napkin. "It's only because Mama watches everything I put in my mouth when we're alone. She hardly lets me eat a thing."

Looking around the gathering of chatting ladies and gentlemen, Rose easily spotted Lady Rothchild laughing with her mother, who looked like a black orchid amongst a field of bright spring blossoms. "Won't she notice how much you eat today?"

Her friend licked a spot of chocolate off her lip. "She's too busy being hostess. Besides, if she asks I'll say I'm getting it for you."

Rose laughed. "Just like the time you got caught with two of your father's cheroots?"

Eve's patrician nose wrinkled. "Nasty things. And you got into far less trouble than I would have had I told the truth."

That was true, though she didn't voice it aloud. Eve's mother was something of a termagant, always finding fault with her sweet, pretty daughter.

"Then you should go and get another slice of cake before it is all gone."

Eve rose demurely from her chair and made her way to the sweets table where a livery-clad footman waited to serve her.

Rose took advantage of the time alone to look

at all the ladies in their finery. Most had welcomed her warmly when Eve's mother made introductions. Of course no one would be obviously rude and risk Lady Rothchild's censure. And despite the scandal clinging to Rose's past, she was still the daughter of an earl. Her father's title had been in the family for centuries and was one of the oldest in England.

And there were some who were genuinely overwhelming in expressing their pleasure at seeing her. She renewed a few acquaintances and had invitations to call whenever she wished.

So far her reentrance into society was everything she'd hoped it would be. Of course, the true test would be her first ball. She tried not to think about it, but she hoped it would be all she remembered—all that she dreamed of. Her gown was perfect, the height of fashion, and she looked quite fetching in it if she said so herself. If her dance card wasn't full, it didn't matter. So long as she had a few names on it, she would be happy. So very happy.

Even if Grey wasn't there to dance with her. The realization diminished her enthusiasm.

When Eve returned, Rose realized in horror that she had brought two plates, each with an enormous piece of cake on it!

"Eve," she groaned. "You want me to get fat, don't you?"

"Of course not, although knowing you as I do, you would no doubt manage to be pretty even if you did weigh twenty stone." Her friend forced the plate into her hands. "I want you to be happy. Eat it."

A wry smile curved Rose's lips. "Am I to find happiness in a piece of chocolate cake?"

Eve already had a forkful en route to her mouth. "I stake my reputation on it."

"Oh," she replied dryly. "Surely heaven is just a bite away."

"Speaking of heaven," Eve said a few minutes later when Rose thought she might expire from the bliss the dessert inspired, "tell me about your evening at Saint's Row."

"Ssh!" Her paranoid gaze darted around to see if anyone had overheard, but there was no one standing close enough to their whitewashed bench.

"Don't shush me, Rose Danvers. I'm your best friend and you've kept me waiting four whole days! I demand details."

Cheeks flushed, Rose stared at the half-eaten cake on her plate. Eve's timing might leave something to be desired, but at least she'd stopped Rose from eating the entire slice.

"What do you want to know?"

Eve's expression was incredulous. "Everything, of course." Then, as though realizing who she was talking to, she sighed. "Did you find him?"

Rose nodded. "I did." The fire in her cheeks burned hotter, and she looked away. "Oh, Eve!"

Her friend grabbed her wrist, clattering fork against plate. "That arse didn't hurt you did he?"

"No!" Then, lowering her voice, "And he's not an arse." Using such rough language made her feel daring and bold.

The scowl on Eve's face eased. "Then . . . he was good to you?"

Rose nodded, leaning closer. "It was the most amazing experience of my life."

The blonde giggled, bringing her head nearer to Rose's. "Tell me everything."

So Rose did, within reason, looking up every once in awhile to make sure no one could hear.

Afterward, when she was finished, Eve looked at her with a peculiar expression. "It sounds wonderful."

"It was."

Eve's ivory brow tightened. "So, why do you sound so . . . disappointed?"

Rose sighed. "It's going to sound so pathetic, but when I saw Grey the next day he didn't recognize me."

"But I thought you didn't want him to know it was you."

Rose laughed darkly. "I don't. That's the rub of it." She turned to more fully face her friend. "But part of me wanted him to realize it was me, Eve. I wanted him to see me as a woman, not as his responsibility or burden."

"I'm sure he doesn't view you as any such thing."

Shaking her head Rose set the plate of cake aside, her appetite gone for good. "I thought this scheme would make everything better, and it's only made things worse." Worse because her feelings for Grey hadn't lessened as she'd hoped they might, they'd only deepened.

Eve worried her upper lip with her bottom teeth. "Are you going to meet him again?"

Another shake of her head, vehement this time. "No."

"But. Rose, he wants to see you."

"Not me, her." This was said with a bit more

bitterness than Rose was willing to admit. He *might* have whispered her name, but it wasn't *her* he wanted to meet.

Eve chuckled. "But you are her." She squeezed her wrist again. "Rose, don't you see? You're who he wants to see again, whether he knows it was you or not."

Rose hadn't looked at it that way. She wasn't quite convinced her friend was right, but it was enough to make her doubt her own conclusions. She shook her head again. Blast, but she was making herself lightheaded. "I just don't know."

"You'll figure it out," Eve allowed. "You always do. Oh my God."

Rose's head jerked up at the gasped words. Eve was staring just over her shoulder, eyes wide, mouth agape. Of course she turned to see what had her friend so discomposed.

"Oh my God," she repeated dumbly as her gaze fell upon the man who had just arrived. He was tall, with thick wavy hair, velvety dark eyes, and a grin that could charm the habit off a nun. Once, a million and a half years ago, she had thought she would be his wife, but then her father lost everything, and the honorable Kellan Maxwell never proposed. She didn't blame him anymore. After all, no gentleman of standing wanted to marry a penniless young woman whose father's death was awash in scandal. Kellan was a younger son of an earl with a large fortune and family connections. The match never would have been welcome.

"I can't believe my mother invited *him*," Eve remarked hotly. "Rose, I'm so sorry."

"Don't be." She meant it. "It doesn't bother me at all seeing him."

Kellan turned his head. His gaze locked with hers, and Rose watched with pleasure as surprise and genuine joy lit his handsome features. He looked older than he had last time she'd seen him, which of course only made sense. He had to be in his late twenties now, if not already thirty.

He turned and came toward them, a wide smile curving his lips. It was contagious, because Rose found herself smiling in return.

"Lady Rose," he greeted, his voice as warm as his smile. "How delightful to see you again."

Rose extended her hand, which he took in his larger one. "Hello, Mr. Maxwell. I'm very pleased to see you as well."

His gaze flickered to Eve. "Lady Eve."

Her friend's reception was a tad frostier than Rose's. "Mr. Maxwell."

Dear Eve, so protective.

"How is your mother, Lady Rose?" Kellan asked. "Is she in good health?"

"She is, sir. Thank you for asking."

His eyes twinkled. "I shall have to call on the two of you some day."

Rose found herself grinning. "That would be lovely. We're in Mayfair at Ryeton House."

Some of the light left his eyes. "Of course. I trust His Grace has no objection to you and your mother receiving callers?"

"Of course not." Although secretly she hoped Grey did mind. "You are welcome at any time. Mama will be delighted to see you." That was true as well. Her mother always harbored a soft spot for the youngest Maxwell boy. She was more disappointed that he never proposed than Rose was.

Kellan grinned. "Excellent. By the by, will you be attending the Shewsbury ball Friday evening?"

"I shall, yes." It would be her first. "Will you?"

His smile turned flirtatious. "I plan to now."

Rose blushed like a young girl, even though she knew Eve was behind her probably rolling her eyes. She would definitely wear the Worth gown her mother suggested. "Then I suppose I will see you there."

"I hope you will honor me with the first waltz?"

Gracious, he certainly wasted no time! But Rose knew better than to have any expectations where he was concerned. Grey might not want her, but she wasn't ready to set her cap on the first man to show interest in her.

"If you wish to dance with me, I have no desire to disappoint you." Who was the flirt now?

Kellan bowed over her hand, brushing his lips across her gloved knuckles. "I shall count the days until then. Good day, Lady Rose. Lady Eve."

"Good day, Mr. Maxwell."

Pleased with him as well as herself, Rose watched him walk away, but took pains not to let her contentment show. It would only give the gossips something to twitter over, and she knew better than that.

"Promise me you won't fall victim to his charms, Rose," Eve murmured near her ear.

"You needn't worry, Eve," she replied, patting her friend's hand. "I'm not the green girl I once was."

And that was truth as well, because the girl she

once was never would have been so suddenly sure of a man's interest. Nor would she consider using that interest to her own advantage—not in any harmful way, of course. She may no longer be green, but she wasn't an "arse" as Eve so eloquently put it.

But still, if Grey didn't want her, then he wouldn't mind if someone else did. Would he?

Chapter 5

Anticipation kept Grey from eating much at dinner Thursday evening. Only the fact that his cook was so adept at her job made the meal palatable at all. Like a lovesick boy, his stomach churned and twitched as the hands on the clock refused to move fast enough.

It was just past eight o'clock. In another three hours he would see his lovely mystery lady.

She would stoke, and eventually bank the fire within him, and make it possible for him to get through a dinner without wanting to take a bite out of the young woman sitting to his left, close enough to taunt, but too far away to touch. Not that he could touch her even if she was closer—Camilla might frown upon such liberties being taken with her daughter.

No man in his right mind could blame him for entertaining thoughts of setting Rose on top of the dining room table and shagging her senseless. Anyone who saw her in her dinner gown of soft peach and tea-dyed lace would think she looked good enough to eat, especially with the candlelight deepening her cleavage and highlighting the soft swells of her breasts.

They hadn't spoken much in the last few days—not that he was avoiding her. Rather, it seemed the opposite. Had he done something to offend her? For the life of him he couldn't think what that might be. And yet, despite knowing that it was probably for the best that they didn't spend much time together, he couldn't help but feel . . . disappointed.

He hadn't been aware of staring, but when her questioning gaze locked with his, Grey felt as though he'd been smacked upside the head by the open palm of idiocy.

"Is something troubling you, Grey?"

He loved the sound of his name on her tongue, and hated that he loved it. She made him weak and stupid. One sweet glance from her and he was ready to drop to his knees.

It wasn't love. It wasn't even infatuation. It was pure unmitigated lust. He could admit that. Hell, he embraced it. Lust could be managed. Lust could be mastered. And lust would eventually fade once she was out of his care and out of his life. That was the cold, hard, blessed truth of it.

"I was wondering if you were eagerly anticipating Lady Shrewsbury's ball tomorrow evening?" How easily the lie rolled off his tongue as he lifted a bite of poached salmon to his mouth.

She smiled softly, obviously looking forward to it very much. "I am. Thank you."

Camilla shared her daughter's pleasure judging from her coy grin. "Rose has renewed her acquaintance with the honorable Kellan Maxwell. He requested that she save the first waltz of the evening for him."

The fish caught in Grey's throat. He took a drink of wine to force it down. "The same Kellan Maxwell who courted you during your first season?"

Rose's smile faded a little. No doubt she heard the censure in his tone, his disapproval. "The same," she replied with an edge of defensiveness.

The same idiot who abandoned his pursuit of Rose when Charles lost everything and scandal erupted. The little prick who hadn't loved her enough to continue his courtship regardless of her situation.

"Mm," was what he said out loud.

Rose scowled at him. "We had no understanding. We were not engaged, and Mr. Maxwell behaved as any other young man with responsibilities would have."

"You defend him." It was difficult to keep his disappointment from showing. He never thought her to be the kind of woman who would forgive disloyalty when she was so very loyal herself.

She tilted her head. "I appreciate your concern, but I'm no debutante, Grey. If I'm to find a husband this season I shouldn't show prejudice."

Common sense coming out of anyone else. Coming out of her it was shite. "You deserve better."

She smiled a Mona Lisa smile. "We do not always get what we deserve, or even what we desire."

She knew. Christ in a frock coat, *she knew.*

Her smile faded. "If we did, Papa would be here with us, and Mama and I wouldn't be your responsibility."

She didn't know. Damn, what a relief. "The two of you are not a responsibility. You are a joy."

For some reason that only made her look sadder, but Camilla smiled through happy tears. She thanked him profusely, but Grey had a hard time hearing what she was saying—he was too intent on Rose, who had turned her attention to her plate and was pushing food around with little interest.

He could bear this no longer. He didn't know what was wrong with her, or why she seemed so strange with him. And he couldn't stand that he cared.

"Ladies, I'm afraid I must beg your pardon and take leave of you."

Rose glanced up. "So soon?"

He pushed his chair back from the table. "Yes. But I will see you at breakfast in the morning."

She turned back to her dinner.

Grey bid farewell to Camilla and then strode from the room as quickly as he could. If he survived the Season it would be a miracle.

"I think it's lovely that Grey is so protective of you."

Rose might have laughed if her chest didn't feel so tight. Lovely indeed. "Shall we ring for dessert, Mama?"

Rose hadn't much of an appetite for the ginger ice cream Cook had prepared, but she ate it anyway. It was delicious, and she made herself enjoy it. She wasn't going to let this mess with Grey spoil anymore of her dinner. She had engineered this situation—had deceived the most important man in her life since her father—and now she had to face the consequences, all the way to the end.

Obviously Grey couldn't wait to leave her company, but was he running away from her, or toward the woman he was to meet that evening? Would he even show up at Saint's Row, or would she sit there alone and wait?

Were she a strong and decent woman she would keep her earlier resolve and not go, but if there was even the slimmest glimmer of hope that he would come to her, her heart demanded that she be there to receive him.

And truth be told, she was already humming with a different kind of anticipation—the carnal kind. It made her feel dirty and excited at the same time. And it would not be denied.

She had thought giving herself to Grey—indulging in her fantasies—would ease her desire for him, but it hadn't. If anything, it had made things worse. She wanted him more—craved him more—than she had a week ago, despite the fact that nothing would ever come of it.

After dessert, she went to her room to change. Her mother believed that she was spending the evening with Eve at her home. She didn't feel bad about lying. It was far preferable to the truth in this case.

With the help of her maid, Heather—youngest daughter of Miller, the butler at Bramley—she changed into a pretty chocolate-colored gown and redressed her hair. Then, she said good night to her mother and took one of Grey's carriages to Eve's. She managed to avoid taking her maid by giving her the rest of the evening off. Such a ruse never would have worked had she been going anywhere but Eve's. Once the carriage drove away, she walked just down the street and hailed a hack to take her to Saint's Row.

She remembered to put on her mask before walking up to the door. "I'm a guest of the Duke of Ryeton," she told the doorman who received her. He moved aside and let her in without question. He handed her a key as she passed. Rose didn't look at it until she was at the foot of the wide sprawling staircase. The fob attached had a room number on it—the very same room they had shared the week before. Clutching it tightly in her fist, she climbed the stairs to the suite and let herself inside.

Would he come?

She sat on the edge of the bed and took off her gloves.

Would he come?

And then, hopeless fool that she was, she waited.

She wore a mask again.

This one was a deep, rich chocolate satin that matched her gown and complimented her hair and complexion. Grey didn't mind that she chose to conceal herself from him again. He had worn his mask as well, but then he always did the few times he risked being seen in public.

"I didn't think you'd come," he said as he closed the door to the private suite behind him.

She rose from where she sat on the side of the bed, the snug gown hugging every curve, the tiny sleeves threatening to slip from her exquisite shoulders. "I almost didn't."

That was a little honesty he could do without. Then she added, "I assumed you had surely changed your mind, and so I thought to save myself the disappointment."

Changed his mind? He could no more do that than ask night not to fall. There had been no question as to whether or not he would keep his part of their bargain. He couldn't have stayed away if he'd wanted to. His will simply wasn't that strong.

"You do not know the strength of your charms, madam."

"I do not doubt my own attributes, sir, merely their ability to hold the attention of a man such as yourself."

"And what kind of man is that?"

"A man who prefers to make assignations with women whose names he doesn't know."

Grey laughed. He wasn't the least offended by her, in fact he found her honesty as amusing as it was bold. "The same could be said of you, madam."

"I do not think so, Your Grace."

He stilled as he hung his discarded coat on the rack in the corner. He only had to turn his head the barest inch to see her. She stood, hands clasped together in front of her, shoulders back as though waiting for him to do something.

"You know who I am?"

She nodded, hands clasped in front of her. "I do."

Moving away from the coat rack, Grey moved toward her, keeping every step measured, every move careful. "You know the stories about me, then?"

Another nod. "Yes."

"And yet here you are."

"Here I am." She held her arms out slightly at her sides, a gesture of supplication if ever he saw one. "Are you surprised?"

"To be honest, yes, I am."

She smiled then, the lush bloom of her mouth curving invitingly. "Perhaps it is you who underestimate your charms, Your Grace."

"Don't call me that."

"What would you have me call you?"

Darling. Lover. Best fuck ever. "You may call me Greyden."

"All right."

"And what may I call you?" He couldn't really call her "mine." Could he?

"Whatever you wish."

"You have my name but refuse me the same confidence? Why?"

"Because you have a reason for your mask, Greyden. And I a reason for mine. Give me whatever name you wish."

"Rose. I will call you Rose."

Was it his imagination or had she froze, just for a second? Of course she had. He was an ass to make such a suggestion. If she knew who he was, then she no doubt knew who Rose was as well. "As you wish."

Grey held out his hand. "Come here."

She did, slipping into his arms as though she belonged there. "Mine," he whispered roughly against her ear. "That's what I want to call you." It wasn't the first time he'd made such a declaration, but it was the first time he'd ever meant it.

She pushed against his shoulders, angling herself so she could look into his eyes. "Why? You don't even know me."

"I don't know you, but I've been looking forward to tonight ever since I woke up that morning last week and found you gone." He slid his hand up the graceful curve of her spine to cup the back of her head. "And so have you."

He cut off any reply—any denial—she might have tried to make with his own mouth. Her lips yielded so sweetly beneath his, easily parting for his tongue to slip inside and taste the warm wetness of her mouth. She affected him like the most potent wine, making him lightheaded and warm. She made him lose all control, all reason.

It was a feeling he wanted to cling to as long as he possibly could.

They undressed each other slowly, making a sensual game of it. When he carried her to the bed she wore nothing but her stockings—a sight more arousing than any he'd ever seen.

They came together easily, her body slick and ready for him. The humid vise of her sex wrapped around and held him with a tightness that made him grind his teeth in an effort to maintain control. Christ, she felt like heaven. He could stay inside her forever.

But forever wasn't possible, so he settled for most of the night. Sometime just before dawn, they fell side by side on the damp and tangled sheets. He disposed of the last sheath he'd used, and closed his eyes in sated oblivion. His fingers fumbled and finally found hers as they rested against her thigh.

Her hands were so soft.

When the darkness came he fought it, knowing that the night would end when sleep came for him. But Hypnos, god of slumber, would not be denied, and even Grey's will was no match.

He woke the next morning alone. Again. But this time, a soft brown mask lay on the pillow beside him, and beneath that a sheet of Saint's Row stationery upon which was written two words.

Next Thursday.

Chapter 6

It was late Friday afternoon when Grey returned from taking tea with his mother, Archer, and Bronte.

It had been a good visit, he reflected as he left his mount with one of the grooms near the stables. His mother hadn't bothered him about finding a wife. She seemed to have given up on that dream and moved on to Arch. Plus, she had Bronte to concern herself with as well. The youngest Kane sibling was on her third Season and had already turned down four proposals of marriage since her come-out. With a sizable dowry and investments of her own thanks to their brother Trystan, Bronte was in no hurry to "sell" herself as she put it. Grey couldn't blame her. She was only twenty, and wanted a man who saw more than her fortune. He wished her luck, as she might be in for a bit of a wait. Fortunately, any man worth his salt realized that women became more interesting and attractive as they got older, so he had no doubt that Bronte would eventually meet someone who saw her true worth.

Speaking of interesting women . . .

There, on a blanket spread over the lush green of

the back lawn, was Rose. She wore a wide-brimmed straw hat to protect her from the sun, and a coral-colored day gown with very little adornment or trim. Not for the first time, Grey was struck at how much older she was than when she'd come into his care. She wasn't a girl anymore. She was a woman.

Not just a woman, she was obviously a bloody siren, because no matter how much he intended to carry onward to the house and take care of some business before bathing and dressing for dinner, he found himself walking across the freshly cut grass toward her, mesmerized by the ruffling of her skirts as the warm breeze tugged at them.

She was engrossed in reading a magazine, which she held in both hands to keep the wind from picking up the pages. In fact, she was so involved in her reading that she didn't seem to notice his arrival.

"And what is the popular color for gowns this Season?" he asked with a smile when it became necessary to announce himself.

She gave a little start, and when she raised her face to look up at him, her cheeks were pink, her eyes wide. She looked, for lack of a better comparison, like a child caught doing something she oughtn't.

"Oh! Hello, Grey." She glanced away. "Um, blue seems to be very favorable this year."

Arching a brow, he nodded at the periodical in her hand. "Beg pardon. I thought you were reading a ladies' magazine."

"I am," she replied with a coy smile. "But fashion is not one of its main areas of interest."

With an expression like hers—very much like

the Cheshire cat in that book by Lewis Carroll—he doubted it was an article on housekeeping that put such becoming color in her cheeks.

"May I?" he asked, holding out his hand.

Her grip on the magazine tightened, reluctant to give it up. "Only if you promise not to tell Mama you saw me reading it."

Oh, this was trouble. Still, it was none of his business what a grown woman of three and twenty read. He was curious, that was all. "I promise."

She hesitated, then put the pages into his hand.

Placing his finger between the thin sheaves to mark her spot, Grey flipped to the cover. Christ on a pony!

The magazine looked fairly harmless—the sketch on the front showed a demure young lady in a stylish gown and hat, sitting on a park bench. Only upon closer inspection could one notice that the object of her attention—and rapturous smile—was the young man bathing in the lake just on the edge of the page. He was bare-chested—quite possibly bare everywhere, but that key part of anatomy was carefully hidden with a line of text that read, "Ten ways to keep a gentleman at home—and in bed."

He didn't want to see what she was reading. He had heard of this magazine before. *Voluptuous* was a racy publication for women, filled with erotic stories, advice, and articles about sexual relationships, how to conduct oneself to avoid scandal, etc.

He could take her to task for reading it, but what would be the point? No doubt the information in it would serve her wisely someday. He gave the magazine back to her. "I have to confess, I'm a little surprised to find you reading such . . . material."

She shrugged. "I was curious. My parents were so happy in their marriage, so very much the opposite of most of what I've heard. If I'm to make a match as good as theirs, I need to know as much as I can about how to have a satisfying marriage."

Grey almost groaned. The image of Rose "satisfying" herself filled his mind with such clarity it was difficult to remember he'd never actually seen such a delightful sight. His body stiffened at the delectable images his mind conjured, and he had to fold his hands in front of him to hide his growing arousal.

"There's just one thing I don't understand," she remarked, setting the periodical aside for a moment.

"And that is?"

She tucked her skirts around her legs, denying him further glimpses of her ankles. "Would you by chance know what gamahuching is?"

Grey would have thought himself far beyond the age of blushing, but the heat in his cheeks was unmistakable. "Good lord, Rose." His voice was little more than a rasp. "That is hardly something a young woman brings up in casual conversation."

Oh, but he could show her what gamahuching was. He'd be all too happy to crawl between those trim ankles and climb upward until he found the slit in her drawers . . .

Rose shrugged. "I suppose it might be offensive to someone of your age, but women aren't as sheltered as they once were, Grey. If you won't provide a definition, I'm sure Mr. Maxwell will when I see him tonight." And with that threat tossed out between them, the little baggage returned her attention to her naughty reading.

His age? What did she think he was, an ancient? Or was she merely trying to bait him? Tease him? Well, two could play at that game.

And he refused to think of Kellan Maxwell, the bastard, educating her on such matters.

"I believe you've mistaken me if you think I find gamahuching offensive," he replied smoothly, easing himself down onto the blanket beside her. "I have quite the opposite view."

Beneath the high collar of her day gown, Rose's throat worked as she swallowed. "Oh?"

"Yes." He braced one hand flat against the blanket near her hip, leaning closer as though they were co-conspirators. "But I'm afraid the notion might seem distasteful to a lady of your inexperience and sheltered upbringing."

Doe eyes narrowed. "If I am not appalled by the practice of frigging, why would anything else done between two adults in the course of making love offend me?"

Christ, she had the sexual vocabulary of a whore and the naiveté of a virgin. There were so many things that people could do to each other that very well could offend her—hell, some even offended him. As for frigging, that just made him think of his fingers deep inside her wet heat, her own delicate hand around his cock, which of course was rearing its head like an attention-seeking puppy.

He forced a casual shrug. Let her think he wasn't the least bit affected by the conversation. Hopefully she wouldn't look at his crotch. "Gamahuching is the act of giving pleasure to a woman with one's mouth and tongue."

Finally his beautiful innocent seductress blushed. She glanced down at the magazine in her hands, obviously reimagining some of what she had read. "Oh." Then, her gaze came back to his. "Thank you."

Thank God she hadn't asked if it was pleasurable because Grey wasn't sure his control could have withstood that. Still, glutton for punishment that he was, he held her gaze. "Anything else you would like to ask me?"

Rose shifted on the blanket. Embarrassed or aroused? "No, I think that's all I wanted to know."

"Be careful, Rose," he advised as he slowly rose to his feet once more. He had to keep his hands in front of him to disguise the hardness in his trousers. Damn thing didn't show any sign of standing down either. "Such reading may lead to further curiosity, which can lead to rash behavior. I would hate to see you compromise yourself, or give your affections to the wrong man."

She met his gaze evenly, with a strange light in her eyes that unsettled him. "Have you stopped to consider Grey, that I may have done that already?"

And since that remark rendered him so completely speechless, he turned on his heel and walked away.

She was such an idiot.

Standing to the side of Lady Shrewsbury's ballroom, Rose waved her new bamboo-and-silk fan to cool the flush under her skin, cursing herself for behaving as she had earlier with Grey.

It had been stupid to ask him about gamahuching. Stupid to let him see what she was reading. He probably thought her a terrible, loose woman now. Never mind that he was the one who had made her loose in the first place. He didn't know that.

Perhaps he was the stupid one.

Regardless, she didn't think she could continue with this ridiculous masquerade. It hurt too much to see him in her daily life and not be able to touch him, or kiss him. They rarely spent any time alone, and when they did, he treated her like a stranger. How could he do that when just the night before he admitted to wanting her? Surely telling her "other" self that he wanted to call her Rose could mean nothing less.

She was jealous of herself. Jealous of the woman she pretended to be, who could make that proud, beautiful man tremble with a touch. He treated her like something beautiful and desirable within the walls of Saint's Row, but outside, in the daylight, she was nothing more than his responsibility, and though he might want her, he obviously couldn't wait to be rid of her.

If only she'd never snuck off to Saint's Row in the first place. If only she'd never hatched that rotten scheme! If only her mother had caught her and talked some sense into her.

If only Grey hadn't done exactly what she wanted him to—with the exception of revealing his feelings to her. He had revealed them to an extent, but only when he thought she was someone else.

It was time to stop playing games. Bedding him hadn't lessened her feelings, and it certainly hadn't made it easier for her to find a man to marry. And she had to marry. Being a spinster wasn't an option for someone of her class, despite the awful rumors of her father's ruination and death. Rose refused to believe any of it. It had been an accident; her mother said so.

As much as she hated to admit it, Rose's feeling for Grey went beyond physical, beyond the gratefulness she felt that he had taken them in when her own father's family would not. He fascinated her, made her want to protect him—made her want to defy her father even more than she already had and be Grey's forever.

And there was the rub. He had already made it abundantly clear that he would never marry. And even if he broke that vow for her, she would be miserable spending all of her evenings at home, even if those evenings were spent in bed. How long would it take before she began to long for company? How long before she began to resent his reclusive nature and called him a coward to his face?

Care for him as she did, Rose had no illusions about Grey. It was pride that kept him from society. He never used to hate it at all. In fact, she could remember a time when her father commented on Grey being out every night of the week for more than a month.

Grey blamed society for his scars. It was so much easier than blaming himself. She didn't hold that against him, but did he think it was easy for her, being out in public when every one knew that she'd be as penniless as a church mouse without Grey's help? That it was easy knowing that people still speculated about her father and would judge her for it? Yet, here she was, because unlike Grey, she didn't blame society for her situation, and she was determined to make a better one for herself.

And if that meant confronting Grey and telling him how she felt, then she would do that. Better to give him the opportunity to reject her than to continue on pining and wishing he would change. One thing was certain, she would not be keeping their engagement for the following week. This time she meant it.

But that was six days away, and right now she was at her first ball of the Season, and she was wearing a gorgeous Worth gown of cobalt blue that had cost Grey a small fortune. Too bad he wasn't there to appreciate her in it.

A squeal to her right made her turn her head, a smile jumping easily to her lips. She'd know that sound anywhere.

Eve rushed up to her and embraced her with great enthusiasm. The slender blonde was dressed in icy green satin edged with cream lace and delicate rosettes.

"You look beautiful!" her friend gushed, golden curls bobbing around her ears. Her hair style was terribly intricate—only something Eve could wear with ease. Rose kept her own hair more subdued, but still she was very pleased with the twist Heather had woven her thick locks into. Her hair was piled high on her head, smooth and glossy with nothing but a large diamond comb for ornament. She wore her mother's diamonds at her ears as well—the two pieces of jewelry she'd managed to hide. Managed to keep.

"So do you," Rose returned. She glanced around the crowded, warm ballroom. "Is your Mr. Gregory here?"

Eve rolled her fine blue eyes heavenward. "He's not my Mr. Gregory. At least not yet."

It was whispered about in certain circles that Bramford Gregory, a well-known up-and-coming politician, had his eye on Eve for his future bride. Not once had Rose heard it referred to as a poor match despite the difference in station. Everyone knew he was expected to become prime minister one day. And then Lady Eve would be married to the most powerful man in England. In fact, everyone seemed to think the entire affair a done deal. Only Mr. Gregory had yet to propose.

"But is he here?" Rose pressed. In all of her years as Eve's friend, she'd yet to meet this mysterious would-be suitor.

"Yes." Her friend smiled coyly. She gestured over Rose's shoulder with her fan. "He's the tall gentleman with blonde hair standing with Lady Shrewsbury."

Rose turned to look. Her gaze fell upon an older—much older—gentleman who was indeed talking to Lady Shrewsbury. In fact, he seemed to be charming her with remarkable ease. He had a confident but kind smile, and a face that the years had obviously been kind to. She judged him to be in his early forties, fit and full of life.

"He's very handsome."

"Yes," Eve agreed. "He is. I shouldn't mind being his wife at all, if he ever asks me."

It was at that moment that Mr. Gregory looked up and caught them watching him. He smiled and raised his glass of champagne to them.

Eve smiled in return before turning to snatch a similar glass for each of them off the tray of a passing footman. "See? He catches me staring and he barely reacts. Most men would be halfway across the floor already."

Rose took a sip from the flute her friend had given her. "Perhaps he is so confident in his intent to have you that he feels he needn't exert himself."

The blonde made an indelicate sound. "He'd better reconsider exerting himself, otherwise I'm likely to find someone with less confidence."

How Rose wished she had that kind of self-value.

The orchestra began the opening strains of a waltz, and suddenly Kellan was there beside her, dressed in impeccable black and white, his thick hair brushed back from his handsome face, a teasing smile upon his well-formed lips. "I believe this is my dance, Lady Rose?"

She grinned. How could she not when faced with such good humor and good looks? "Indeed it is, Mr. Maxwell."

"Excuse us, Lady Eve," he said with a bow before leading Rose onto the dance floor. As they joined the other dances, she caught her mother's attention from where she sat with other chaperones. One look at her partner, and her mother's face lit up like a Christmas candle. It was all Rose could do not to chuckle at the sight.

"You look lovely tonight, my lady," Kellan said for her ears alone as he took her into his arms—not too close, of course.

His flattery pleased her but did not discompose her as Grey's did. Rose smiled sincerely in response. "Thank you, sir. Might I say that you are in very fine looks as well."

"You always know exactly the right thing to say to woo me, Lady Rose." He grinned as they moved through a turn. "Have a care, else you're likely to break my heart."

"If it is so easily broken, perhaps you should hold it a little more dear," she advised archly.

He winced, but it was apparent that he had taken the remark with the humor she intended. "She mocks me."

"You are mistaken, sir. I am merely thinking of your best interests."

They shared a smile and were silent for a turn.

"I am surprised that Ryeton allowed you to come tonight."

Rose raised a brow. "The duke does not dictate where I can and cannot go." Grey might be her benefactor, but he was not her guardian.

"That is good to hear," Kellan replied, ignoring the edge to her tone. "So he cannot prevent you from taking a drive in Hyde Park with me tomorrow afternoon."

She chuckled. "No, I suppose not. But first, you might want to ask me if I care to take a drive with you."

"Do you?"

She did. Did that make her awful? Just a few

minutes ago she'd been missing Grey and thinking about how much she cared for him, and now here she was flirting with Kellan and fluttering over the prospect of going for a carriage ride.

It wasn't fickleness, she told herself. It was practicality. She was doing what she was supposed to do. Kellan had yet to lay any claim to her feelings or her heart, but she owed him the opportunity to try. She would never get over Grey and find love if she didn't try as well.

And it wouldn't hurt Grey to see another man take interest in her. Perhaps a little jealousy would do him good.

"I would be delighted to accept your invitation."

Her partner didn't bother trying to conceal his pleasure. "Excellent. I shall call for you just before five."

Ahh, the fashionable hour, if her memory served. She hadn't been to Hyde Park since before her father's ruination. She'd always loved it there, and looked forward to seeing it again—and being seen there with the man who had walked away from her before. Would people mock her for allowing him into her life once more? Probably. But for Kellan to approach her again after all this time, it had to mean he regretted his previous behavior. After all, he needed neither her money nor her pedigree, and could get either from any other single lady in London.

The dance ended far too soon, and Kellan escorted her to her mother, but not before making Rose promise to favor him with another later in the evening. She agreed, but if he asked for a third, she would refuse. No sense in giving the gossips more fodder than they deserved.

She danced with several other gentlemen before having to take a break for the ladies' retiring room. She made use of the facilities, washed her hands, and pressed cool, damp clothes to the back of her neck and chest to cool and refresh herself.

"It's ungodly hot, isn't it?" remarked an attractive slightly older woman standing beside her at the mirror.

Rose nodded. "It is. I do hope this isn't a portent for the rest of the Season."

The woman ran a smoothing hand over her neat, honey blonde chignon. "Doubtful. Lady Shrewsbury insists on burning candles rather than using gaslights like the rest of the civilized world. No doubt your next ball will be much more comfortable. I'm Lady Margaret Devane, by the way."

Rose looked at the hand extended toward her like a snake crawling out of the grass. The dowager Marchioness Devane. One of the women suspected of being behind the attack on Grey. Suspected. It had never been proven. Rose thought she would be older, less attractive.

Swallowing, she accepted the handshake. She couldn't afford to be so rude as to cut a woman of her stature. "Lady Rose Danvers."

Lady Devane's green eyes widened. "Charles and Camilla's daughter?"

"Yes," Rose replied with a slight nod.

The older woman clasped her other hand around Rose's as well, destroying any chance she might have had of breaking contact. "I was so sorry to hear of your father's passing."

She sounded so sincere, it made the backs of Rose's eyes burn. "Thank you."

And then, a bit slyly, Rose thought, "You are under the protection of the Duke of Ryeton, are you not?"

Rose stiffened at Lady Devane's use of the term protection. Did her ladyship think Rose so green and stupid that she wouldn't know a euphemism for mistress when she heard one?

"His Grace has been a great friend to my mother and me." Rose pulled her hand free. "I think of him quite as an older brother." Lie, lie, lie! But an effective one.

Lady Devane appeared duly chastised. "Oh, my dear girl! I meant no offense. I simple meant to say that Ryeton had appointed himself knight errant of yourself and your dear mama."

That took some of the sting out, and relaxed Rose's backbone. "No offense taken, Lady Devane."

"I don't suppose he will be joining us this evening?" There was an edge of hopefulness to the older woman's tone that Rose would have to be a simpleton to miss.

"No. He will not."

Lady Devane didn't look surprised, but her disappointment was genuine, unless she was a better actress than Rose wanted to give her credit. "That is too bad. You will tell him that I send my regards?"

She dared ask such a favor, this woman who might very well be responsible for the scar that ran down his face?

But of course she dared. She had been Grey's lover once upon a time. If that didn't give her leave to be so arrogantly intimate, what did?

"Of course," Rose replied with false warmth. "I will see him at home later this evening and I will gladly relay your message. I'm sure he'll be touched by your consideration." She hadn't meant to put an edge to the words, but it slipped out anyway. Lady Devane did not miss it.

"Thank you." She cleared her throat. "Well, enjoy the rest of your evening, Lady Rose. I'm sure we will meet again over the course of the Season."

Rose forced a smile. "No doubt. Good evening, Lady Devane."

When she exited the room, Rose went in search of champagne and Kellan and his request for another dance. She desperately needed something to take her mind off that awful conversation with Grey's former lover, and not just because Lady Devane might be responsible for the attack that could have killed him.

But because the entire encounter was another painful reminder of everything that stood between Rose and Grey ever having a future.

When Camilla and Rose returned home that evening, Grey took one look at Rose and wondered how much she'd had to drink, and why her mother seemed oblivious to the fact that her daughter was half pickled.

Oh, she didn't act drunk, but he could tell she was. She was far too relaxed and happy in his presence. Not to mention that she was smiling this silly little smile that made her absolutely adorable.

Add that adorableness to her already stunning appearance and was it any wonder his heart kicked up a fuss at the sight of her? The dark blue silk gown she wore was embroidered with even darker flowers that seemed to shimmer in the light. The wide neckline left her neck and shoulders bare, giving him a delicious amount of pale flesh to admire.

She was beautiful. There was just no getting around it.

"Did you have a good time, Rose?" he asked, needlessly.

"Oh, yes!" She grinned happily at him. "It was lovely."

Odd, he almost wished he'd been there to experience it himself based on that simple testimonial. How long had it been since he'd missed the stuffy confines of a ball, the poor food of a midnight supper?

Never. The ball wasn't what he'd missed that evening.

"I'm off to bed," Camilla announced with a smile that didn't quite reach her eyes. "I'm not used to city hours yet."

"Good night, Mama," Rose said and hugged her mother. Grey bade her good night as well, and once she had disappeared up the stairs, Rose turned to him, much of her high spirits having seemed to disappear.

"She's missing Papa," she explained quietly, weaving just a little. "She didn't say anything, but I can tell."

Grey couldn't imagine ever loving someone

enough to marry them, let alone how it would feel to lose them. It had to be awful. "You must miss him as well."

"I do." Her gaze was still fastened on the staircase. "But not like she does. He was her life."

"And the two of you were his." That much he could tell her truthfully. No one who knew him would ever argue what Charles Danvers felt for his wife and daughter.

"Yes," Rose replied not without some harshness as she finally turned her gaze to his. "It was his desire to please us, to give us everything we wanted that led to his losing everything. There are times, Grey, when I wish he had loved us a little less."

There was nothing he could say in response that could make that any easier, so he remained silent.

And then she said the damnedest thing. Standing there, in the middle of his foyer at half past three in the morning, with all the servants gone to bed except for the poor maid who would have to remove the evening's finery and tuck her mistresses into bed, Rose looked at him with a gaze that was unnerving despite its slightly unfocused glaze.

"Do you love me, Grey?" she asked softly.

His heart slammed so hard against his ribs he thought something might be broken. He couldn't draw breath.

"Of course," he replied lightly, though it felt as though he was being strangled. "You and your mother mean more to me than you know."

"No," she insisted hotly, a wavering finger in his face. "It's you who do not know. How can you not know?"

He frowned at her. This situation was about to spiral into something better left avoided if he didn't figure out how to diffuse it. "You're right," he said, taking her by the elbow and steering her toward the stairs. "I don't know. Why don't you explain it to me over breakfast, when you're sober." Of course, there was little chance she'd remember to do just that.

She turned on him so quickly he hadn't time to react. Before he knew what she was about, Rose was pressed against him, her arms tight around his neck.

Dear God, he had fantasized so many times about having her touch him like this. And now, all he could think of was getting her safely to bed before she made a commotion and someone saw.

"Rose," he said softly. "Rosie. Let go."

She shook her head. Her eyes were just wet enough that his resolve melted under the sight of them. What he would give so that Rose never cried except for tears of joy.

"I wish I could let go," she told him, speech slightly slurred.

And then she kissed him. And oh, dear God, it was sweet and terrible and everything that could bring a grown man to his knees. And when she pulled away—he hadn't even the presence of mind to push her—her breath coming just as rapidly as his own.

"Do you know me now, Grey?" she asked softly. "Or do I need to wear a mask and pretend to be someone else while you pretend I'm me?"

Grey froze, a chill hand wrapped sharp fingers

around his heart. "There will be no more pretending, Rose," he informed her with more vitriol than he knew he had in him, especially where she was concerned.

"No more pretending," he repeated as he pried her arms from around his neck and pushed her away. "It's over, though scum that I am, I had hoped it might last a little longer. I suppose I should thank you for ruining the charade."

Chapter 7

Rose stared at Grey, the harsh lines of his face, the faint sneer around his mouth. She expected that he might be angry to learn her identity, but not like this. He didn't seem so much angry at what she had done, but rather that she had confessed to it.

"Which charade exactly have I ruined?" she demanded, suddenly very sober. "The one where you set out to sleep with another woman and pretend that she is me? Or the one where I pretend you might actually give a damn." She didn't normally use such language—it was unbecoming—but the situation seemed to call for it.

He cast a quick glance up the stairs. "Lower your voice, for Christ's sake." Then, he seized her by the elbow and pulled her roughly toward the first open door—the rose parlor. How appropriate that he choose the room with her name in which to put an end to all of their deceit.

Grey practically tossed her into the room before stepping over the threshold himself and shutting the door behind him. With four walls so close around them, his anger suddenly seemed a tangible thing, and if Rose were honest with herself, she was a little frightened of it.

His eyes glittered like pale, hard stones. "How could you do this?"

There was no point in pretending ignorance. "I had a suspicion that you might have feelings for me. I knew you often went to Saint's Row, so I aspired to be there on the same night." It felt good to confide. And, yes, her tone was more boastful than it should be, but she had been very clever and was proud of that fact. The only time she hadn't been clever was this evening. But then she hadn't been trying to impress him, she'd hope he'd sweep her up into his arms, carry her to his bed, and make love to *her*—not someone he pretended to be her.

"I have no interest in knowing how you came up with the plan, or how you managed to put it into motion. What I want to know is why you chose now to reveal yourself?"

That's what he was angry about? Not that she had tricked him, but that she had chose to reveal it?

"Because," she replied stubbornly, moving around the oak and cream brocade sofa. The more space between them the better. Space—and resentment—would keep her from sobbing. "I couldn't lie to you any longer."

A bitter smile twisted his lips, tugged the scarred flesh of his left cheek. "That is such a fucking lie in itself."

Her eyes widened. She'd never heard him use such language before. It was almost as fearsome as it was erotic. "It's not a lie! I could no longer continue with the foolish farce. It was an imprudent idea to begin with."

"I shan't argue with you on that point."

Rose scoffed at him. "You don't get to play morally superior with me, Grey. I may have been stupid enough to conspire against you, but you didn't even recognize someone you've known for years! If one of us must be the bigger idiot, I think it must be you!" Oh dear God. She covered her mouth with her hand. What had she just said?

Dark arched brows pulled together tightly over stormy blue eyes. "You're right," he agreed. "I am an idiot, but only because I allowed this ridiculous ruse past the point when I realized your identity."

Rose froze—like a damp leaf on an icy pond. "You knew?" And yet he continued to pretend . . . oh, he was worse than she by far.

"Of course I knew." He glowered at her. "Blindfold me and I would know the scent of your skin, the exact color and texture of your skin. Do you not realize that I know the color of your eyes right down to the flecks of gold that light their depths?"

Heart pounding, stomach churning in shock, Rose could only stare at him. How could he say such things to her and sound so disgusted? "When?" Her voice was a ragged whisper. "When did you know?"

"I suspected before but tried to deny it. The morning after we last met I took one look at your sweet mouth and knew there couldn't be two women in the world, let alone London with the same delectable bottom lip."

It hurt. Oh, she hadn't thought hearing him say

such wonderful things could hurt so much! She pressed a hand to her chest. "You suspected and yet you made love to me any way."

"Made love?" He snorted. "That's a girl's term, Rose. What you and I did . . . it was something far worse than making trite love."

Worse? How could he malign what had transpired between them. "So you regret it, despite your own choice to continue with the charade."

"What I *regret*," he growled, suddenly moving toward her, "is your sudden attack of conscience."

He was mad. She took a step back. "I don't understand you."

"If only you had managed to keep your guilt where it belonged." A ravaged smile curved his lips as he shook his head. "We might have continued on, with neither being the wiser, but now we must endure the rest of the Season together, knowing what we can no longer have."

"Then you admit you have feelings for me."

He laughed hollowly. "So many I can scarce discern them all."

It was a hollow victory at best. "If you care for me and I for you, then why can we not reveal our feelings? You have but to ask and I'm yours." Even though it meant breaking her promise to her father.

This time Grey's smile wasn't bitter, it was sad. "Even if it means never attending another ball? At least not with your husband? Even if it means having people whisper behind your back, pitying you for being married to 'Ruined Ryeton'?"

Rose opened her mouth, but nothing came out.

He saw her hesitation and grabbed it, but not before she saw the flicker of hurt in his eyes. "Being with me means more than being a recluse, Rose. You and your mother have already been touched by the scandal that surrounds me. I won't have people speculate that I will drive you insane like I did the lover who had me attacked—although the main suspect seems in possession of her faculties."

"I don't care about that," she insisted. But she did, a little. She couldn't help it. It was easy to say the words, but could she honestly survive that kind of scrutiny and cruelty when Grey wouldn't be there by her side through it? Could she go to balls and parties by herself and bear the malicious glances, or worse the pitying ones?

"You should. Your father did."

This was a night for revelations indeed. "What do you mean?"

Grey ran a hand through the thick waves of his hair. The rich fabric of his dressing gown parted to reveal a snowy white shirt open at the throat. She remembered how he tasted there, so warm and salty. When his gaze locked with hers, Rose was certain he could read her mind. She was also just as certain that he recalled the taste of her flesh as well.

"Before his death your father begged a promise from me. He made me swear that I would look after you and your mother."

"And you have," she insisted.

He held up his hand to prevent her from saying more. "And made me give my word that I would never touch you in any manner other than brotherly." Another rueful smile. "So you see, I preferred being able to pretend that I had kept my promise rather than face the truth of breaking my word."

He broke her heart, damn him. "He made me promise not to become attached to you," she confided, continuing with the evening's truthful trend. "It seems Papa saw something that neither one of us did."

"Oh, I saw it. I've seen it since you were eighteen years old and we danced together at some insipid ball. I don't remember where it was, or the day of the week, but I remember that you wore a pale tea-colored gown with Belgian lace, and that you had pearls in your hair."

She couldn't breathe. The tilt of his lips, the bleakness of his gaze, it was all too horrible. "And you wore a red cravat," she whispered. "I thought you looked so rakish in it."

"I was rakish," he admitted. "Your father knew that."

"You're not like that anymore."

The pity in his expression was almost too much to bear. "Only because I hurt a woman so badly that she wanted to see me dead."

"But—"

He closed the distance between them and cupped her bare shoulders in his warm hands. "She could be a friend of yours, Rose. Someone you've met and liked. Do you want to look at every woman over the age of five and twenty and wonder if she was the one who had my face sliced open? Because I won't lie to you. Despite the prevalent conjecture that Lady Devane must be the guilty party, there are easily twenty women who could have orchestrated the attack. And those are only the ones who made their hatred known."

Her stomach rolled. "I don't believe you."

This time his smile was kind. "My darling Rose. I was the worst sort of man, and in some ways I still am. The society you so dearly love made me into someone I don't care to remember, someone I would never want you to know. And I fear you would come to know him. The gossips wouldn't be able to help themselves."

"So you'd deny your feelings for me because you're afraid what society might say?" Her temper flared. "I never thought you for a coward, Grey."

He pulled her tight against him, so that she could feel his breath against her temple. Such torture to be held in his arms and not be able to kiss him, or touch him as she wanted. Even more terrible, was the inescapable feeling that this would be the last time he held her thus.

"I hate society. Society reviles me." He ran a hand down her back. "I've seen the look on your face before you run off to a ball or a tea. You love being around people. You thrive on it. I don't want to ask you to give that up. I *won't* ask you to give that up."

There it was, the final thrust of the knife. He wanted her. He cared about her, but neither went deep enough that he was willing to compromise for her as she believed she was willing to do for him.

And the salt in the wound was that part of her that agreed with him. "Thank you," she murmured, trying and failing to push her way out of his embrace. "Now I know where I stand."

One strong hand came up to cup her cheek, forcing her to look at him even though she'd rather eat glass. "You must have known this would happen, Rose. Otherwise, you wouldn't have gone to such extremes in the first place. Tell me, what did you honestly hope to achieve with tonight's revelation?"

Yes, what had she hoped for? "I do not know. Perhaps a balm for my guilty conscience. Or perhaps I'd hoped that you would beg my forgiveness for not recognizing me." This time she managed to free herself from his embrace. "Or maybe I hoped that my virginity and my heart might actually mean something to you."

She moved to walk away before hot tears could spill over her cheeks. She didn't mean to sound so foolish. She had engineered this situation herself, and had no one but herself to blame for its outcome. At least she should be adult enough to accept that.

Grey caught her arm as she tried to move past him. "Both are gifts I will treasure forever, you can be certain of that. No one has ever bestowed anything more precious upon me in the entirety of my life."

Damn him. The tears she tried so hard to stall slipped helplessly down her cheeks, scalding her flesh like hot, briny acid. She looked at him regardless, let him see the anguish on her face. "Obviously you have little regard for such gifts, sir, if you are willing to discount them so completely."

He flinched, but it was a meaningless victory. "We all, in the course of our lives, are given gifts we know we cannot accept, Rose. You are that to me."

Such beautiful and hurtful words she'd never heard before, and hoped to never hear again. She lifted her chin and blinked most of the tears away. "Thank you, Grey. That makes me feel so much better."

He didn't try to stop her this time as she brushed past him, but he obviously wasn't done with her, for he stopped her as she reached the door. "Rose."

She didn't turn, but straightened her shoulders. "Yes?"

"Go out and enjoy all the Season has to offer, and find yourself a man who will realize he is the luckiest man alive to have won you."

Hardening her expression, she cast one final glance at him over her shoulder. "Thank you, Your Grace. I believe I will do just that. Lord knows I won't find him here."

He was the biggest arse in England.

Of course Grey would only admit to a title of such distinction when alone and in the relative safety of his own home.

Safe. Is that what he was? When a woman as dangerous as Rose offered him her heart and body and he cried off like a simpering fool rather than take what she offered. He'd taken it willingly enough when he suspected the truth—when he'd be able to pretend she was someone else.

And now she knew the truth about him. That he had figured out her masquerade, and was diabolical enough to allow it to continue for his own pleasure.

Thank God she didn't know that he'd think of the gift she'd given him, the gift of her innocence, every time he thought about her future husband availing himself of her charms. Grey will always have been her first.

"Christ," he swore, heading toward the small cabinet where he kept a supply of spirits for guests. "I am not going to do this."

He found a bottle of scotch and poured himself a generous amount instead. He took a long swallow of the amber liquid, bracing himself against the potent burn as it slid down to his belly.

Once upon a time he would have said that Rose deserved this. This is what happened to innocent little girls who tried to dance with a big bad wolf. Years ago he would have shrugged, briefly lamented the loss of her body in his bed, and moved on to someone else.

He'd ruined her. Ruined her and dishonorably refused to do the right thing. History truly had a way of coming back and biting a man on the arse. Only this time he tried to excuse his behavior with the weak defense that he was doing what was best for Rose.

How could he have been so honest? He should have pretended outrage, but outrage had been his problem. He'd been so angry that she gave up so easily. They'd only had two nights together and now they'd never have another because by revealing herself to him she forced him to return to a damn code of morality where she was concerned.

It was all for the best, he told himself with another drink. Every time they would meet it would increase the risk of being found out. That kind of scandal was the last thing Rose needed her first Season since losing her father. The loss of her way of life and the loss of her father was more than anyone should have to suffer. She didn't need the taint of him running any deeper through her life than it already did. He might always have the satisfaction of knowing he had her first, but no one else would.

And yet, he was idiot enough to allow himself a brief moment of regret that he had to turn her away, a slight twinge of dismay that they hadn't been found out. Because then he would be forced to marry her and neither of them would have to feel so very guilty for betraying Charles's requests because the matter would be out of their hands.

Ah, he was so very good at bending things to his own rationale when he wanted.

He sat down on the sofa so he couldn't go after her. It was better this way. Hopefully she despised him now, would give up her foolish thoughts of him and go find a husband. Perhaps Kellan Maxwell would come up to snuff. The little shit.

A tapping on the window caught his attention and he turned to find his brother waving drunkenly at him through the glass with a ridiculous grin on his face. It was a sight he'd seen many times over the course of Archer's life.

Mentally rolling his eyes at his younger sibling, Grey rose to his feet and crossed the carpet to unlatch the window and open the large casements into the room. "What the hell do you want?" he demanded.

Archer grinned at him, all roguish intent and impish good humor. "I thought I'd find you all alone with your thumb up your arse."

Grey arched a brow. "What a charming way with words you have, brother. Did you sneak around the back of my house just to tell me that?"

"It's my house too," Archer argued with a slight weave. "Least when you're not here."

As a bachelor Archer had little choice in living arrangements. He could live with their mother and Bronte and never dare bring a woman or cronies home, or he could take a set of rooms at a lodging house—neither were appealing. Archer wanted a home, and now that he was back in London, apparently for good, he was looking for a townhouse to share with their youngest brother Trystan when he returned from America.

Until he found that dwelling, he divided his time between a set of private apartments, which he used to sleep and entertain, and Ryeton House, of which he was master when Grey wasn't in residence.

"Why are you here, Arch?"

His brother grinned. "I've come to rescue you. Now grab your coat and let's go."

"Go where?"

"To Whites, or Claridge's or Boodle's, or Chez Cherie's. It doesn't matter where we go. Come on, man!"

"Arch," Grey said with a self-deprecating sigh, "with the odd exception under the cover of extreme darkness, I haven't gone out in public in four years. Why would you think I'd go to a club, or even a brothel?"

"Because you need to get out," his brother retorted hotly. "You can't hide anymore. It's not seemly."

Hiding. Arch was the second person to accuse him of being a coward this evening. It was not a trend Grey cared for. "I'm not hiding. I choose not to go out into a society as poisonous as it is two-faced."

Archer rolled his eyes—and almost fell over. Only his grip on the window ledge kept him upright. "Nothing two-faced about Chez Cherie's. Just you'd rather sit here and play martyr."

"You're drunk." Grey moved to shut the windows. "Go the hell home and sleep it off."

A raised hand stopped him from shutting his brother out. "Wait!" Archer grinned foolishly. "I've got two lovely young ladies waiting in the hack. I know one of them would love to have the companionship of someone as lofty as you, Your Grace."

Grey was unmoved. "Two women has never been a problem for you before, I'm sure you won't have a problem entertaining both of them on your own." Archer's prowess was almost as legendary as Grey's own had been, only Archer didn't seem to inspire the same heightened emotions in his conquests—at least no one had tried to kill him yet. Perhaps his own tragedy had taught his brother the importance of discretion.

"One of them's a brunette," his brother blurted. "Tall, voluptuous, and with brown eyes a man could drown in."

Grey stilled. "Brown eyes," he repeated like an idiot. He was tempted, oh so tempted. But how could anyone ever satisfy him now that he'd had the real Rose?

Archer grinned. "Big brown eyes—like a spring foal. Good teeth too. Oh, and breasts a man could cheerfully suffocate between." He weaved a little. "Trust me, Grey. She's clean and tight as a virgin miss."

Thank God for Archer's drunken crassness. It

was that last remark, however true it might be, that slapped a little sense into Grey.

Rose was no longer a virgin and that was his fault. It didn't matter that he hadn't known that first night. Oh, who was he trying to fool. He had known. On some level, his soul had known. And yet he took her anyway, relieving her of the one commodity other than a fortune that a young woman had to recommend herself. How could he not when it was so prettily offered? Rose might have made a mistake in giving herself to him, but she'd planned it well in advance. She'd chosen him to be her first.

She seemed to want him for herself *only* as well—little fool. Was she trying to break his heart?

"Sorry, Arch," he said without much real remorse. "You are on your own tonight, old man."

His brother looked genuinely bewildered, the drunken sod. "But . . . big brown eyes?"

Grey grinned despite himself. "She is all yours. You can tell me all about it tomorrow." Grey's mother, sister, and Archer were joining them for tea. It should be a wonderful good time, especially when Rose's hatred had plenty of time to stew.

Archer looked delighted with the possibility of sharing his conquest, which only proved how inebriated his younger brother was. Archer might talk crassly and behave like a rake, but he wasn't one for kissing and telling.

"Good-bye, Arch. Your ladies are waiting."

That sent the other man off, and Grey closed the window as Archer stumbled off. He flicked the latch and returned to his scotch. He remained on his feet as he retrieved the glass and drained the contents.

He should go to bed. Things always looked better in the bright light of day. Plus, if he went to his own room he would be less tempted to go to Rose's, throw himself at her feet, and beg her to . . .

To what? Forgive him? Absolve him? Maybe to let him give her a good demonstration of the delights of gamahuching. Christ, he was pathetic.

He would do none of these things, of course. It was better that she resent him. Better that she stay away. It would be easier for him to find someone else. She asked more of him than he was willing to give—more than he could ever give. After all, if he knew anything about himself it was that he was not the kind of man who could make any kind of deserving woman a good husband.

He'd learned long ago that women tended to want loyalty from their men, that they wanted not only a man's fortune and his name, but his very heart and soul as well. It was this kind of greed, a woman wanting more than he was able to give that led to him sporting such a fetching scar.

It was that realization—justification?—that solidified the situation in his mind as he left the parlor. He had done the right thing by turning her away, rather than hauling her into his arms and promising her the moon as he had wanted. Eventually Rose would realize that, and know that by turning her away he'd been nobler with her than with any other woman he'd ever known.

Too bad, he reflected as he climbed the stairs to his rooms, that nobility couldn't keep a fellow warm at night.

Chapter 8

Rose managed to avoid Grey for the better part of the day on Saturday. She rose late and took breakfast in her room—toast and jam with a plate of steak and eggs and a pot of rich chocolate. Depressed spirits could diminish her appetite, but anger fueled it. And today she was angry. Not only at Grey, but at herself.

But she was not, she told herself, going to think about it. There was no point. She'd made a mistake, which she realized without Grey rubbing her face in it. And now the only thing left to do was move on.

The way she saw it, she had two choices. She could either pursue Grey and make an even bigger fool of herself, or she could throw all of her energy and efforts into finding a man she could like as much, or better than he. Perhaps she would be noble enough not to rub his face in it, but she doubted it.

Surely it couldn't be that difficult to find someone to love her? She wasn't an awful person, though she would freely admit to be willful and sometimes spoiled. Still, she was good at heart, and she was reasonably attractive with a large dowry. That had to be attractive to someone. The only reason she was so attached to Grey was because he'd been so good to her family, and he was the only man with whom she'd had more than one conversation in the last three years.

And so she would begin her search today.

After breakfast she climbed out of bed, poured a third cup of chocolate, bathed, and rang for Heather. By the time she finished dressing it was almost noon—time to meet Eve. The two of them, along with their mothers, were going shopping on Regent Street. It was exactly the kind of distraction Rose needed, made all the better by the knowledge that it would be Grey's money she spent. If that made her a rotten person, then so be it. She was happy to be rotten to the core. Her pride was wounded, her feelings hurt, and her heart broken. It mattered not that she was to blame for the entire mess, though Grey certainly wasn't blameless. If she had her own money she'd spend that, but she was a useless female and entirely dependent upon her benefactor and one day a husband. So, she would take advantage of Grey's wealth, and try not to think that he had taken advantage of her feelings.

He had known! How he must have laughed at her, the stupid little lovesick girl.

Rose shook her head. No more of that. Grey hadn't laughed at her. In fact, he'd seemed as pained as she was.

Right, too much thinking.

Taking up her hat—a large wide-brimmed affair trimmed with cabbage roses and ribbon—Rose used a pin to adhere it to her hair and then gathered up her paisley wrap and gloves. She wore a chocolate-rose walking gown with champagne silk piping and a high neckline. Her gloves were dyed to match as were her low-heeled boots. She looked rather smart, if she said so herself.

They arrived at Regent Street before the "fashionable" shopping hours of two until four in an effort to avoid the huge crowds that tended to block the street and make travel next to impossible. For many this was as much a place to see and be seen as Hyde Park, and it wasn't unusual to see a young lady and her chaperone stopping their driver in the middle of the street so the young woman could chat to a passing beau.

As early as they were, the street was still bustling with activity, the elegant shops with their stone fronts a constant flutter of *haute-ton* personalities, their footmen and maids laden with parcels.

Neither Rose nor Eve burdened their servants with such baggage. Rose bought some new perfume and gloves at Piver's, the famous perfumer who obtained medals for his work at the Great Exhibitions of '51 and '62. The scent was irresistible, and well worth the price. And the gloves perfectly matched the ensemble she intended to wear out with Kellan later that day.

And then, because they were so exquisite and obviously of superior French design, she bought two new fans as well.

Then, with their new accessories packaged and tucked in the back of the carriage, they braved the ever-increasing traffic to return home. They moved at a snail's pace, but Rose didn't care. She was too busy craning her neck for a glimpse of all the ladies who had come out simply to be noticed.

Eve and Lady Rothchild left them safely on the front step of Ryeton House, with a promise to see them Monday evening at Lady Carlyle's card party. Rose kissed her friend's cheek and then hurried inside with her mother to change for tea. Grey's family would be joining them. Were it not for that, Rose would feign a headache and stay in her room until Kellan came for her.

But since it wasn't in her nature to be so rude, she rushed up the stairs, quickly donned a yellow tea gown with Heather's help, put on matching yellow slippers and a pair of dainty gold earrings, and returned downstairs just in time to join everyone on the back terrace.

She just stepped out into the warm, grass-scented afternoon when a gentleman appeared at her elbow. "Lady Rose, you grow lovelier every time I see you."

Had it been a stranger who spoke she might have been flustered, but since it was Archer, Grey's younger brother, she merely grinned in response and offered her hand. "And your eyesight grows poorer every time you see me, sir."

He bowed over her fingers. "If I am blind it is only by your beauty."

She laughed at that, enjoying the good-natured sparkle in his bright blue eyes. He was so much more easy-natured than Grey, so much more full of life and flirtation. And yet, the family resemblance could not be denied even if Archer's features were a little thinner, a little sharper.

How would Grey feel if she found a replacement for him in his own brother? It was too low, even in jest.

"Careful with your flattery, sir," she warned teasingly. "I am trolling for a husband you know."

Archer's dark brows shot up in mock horror. "Never say!" Then he leaned closer to whisper, "Is my brother actually fool enough to let you get away?"

Rose's heart lurched at the note of seriousness in his voice. When she raised her gaze to his she saw only concern and genuine affection there. "He's packing my bags as we speak."

He laughed then, a deep, rich sound that drew the attention of everyone on the terrace, including his older brother.

"Will you by chance be at the Devane musicale next week, Lord Archer?"

"I will," he remarked, suddenly sober. "As much as it pains me to enter that viper's pit. I'm accompanying Mama and Bronte. Since there's never been any proof of what she did to Grey, Mama refuses to cut the woman. She's better than that."

Archer's use of the word "cut" might have been ironic, but what a relief knowing he would be there. "Would you care to accompany Mama and myself as well?"

He regarded her with a sly smile. "My dear, Lady Rose. Do you plan to use me to make my brother jealous?"

"Of course not!" And she was honest to a point. "I wish to use your knowledge of eligible beaux and have you buoy my spirits. If that happens to annoy your brother, then so much the better."

He laughed again. This time Grey scowled at the pair of them. Rose smiled and waved.

Archer tucked her hand around his arm and guided her toward the chairs where the others sat enjoying the day, the table before them laden with sandwiches, cakes, scones, and all kinds of preserves, cream, and biscuits. A large pot of tea sat in the center.

"What are you grinning at?" Grey demanded as they approached.

Archer gave his brother an easy smile, not the least bit intimidated. "Lady Rose has just accepted my invitation for both she and her dear mama to accompany us to the Devane musicale next week."

Grey stiffened. It was the slightest movement, like a blade of grass fighting the breeze, but Rose noticed. She'd wager Archer did too.

"How nice," he replied civilly, but Rose mentally winced at the coolness of his tone. He turned to his mother. "I'm parched. Mama, will you pour?"

And he didn't look at her again.

At half past four, Rose excused herself to go change for her outing with Maxwell. Grey watched her go with a clenched jaw. When she returned twenty minutes later in smart outfit of dark green corduroy, large feathered hat, and matching gloves, his teeth ground together. She looked gorgeous, of course. And it was all for Maxwell's benefit.

He had no right to be jealous, he knew that. Unfortunately, knowing something wasn't quite the same as feeling it. And a very vocal part of him felt that Rose belonged to him.

"I did not want to leave without saying goodbye," she said sweetly to his mother and sister. They both loved her, of course. They'd probably still love her even if they knew she'd seduced him.

Yes, because he was so much the wounded party in this case. Taken advantage of by a skilled and dangerous seductress whom he was obviously no match for.

Pull yourself together, Ryeton. You sound like a frigging little girl!

Maxwell arrived right on time, and cheerfully announced by Westford. Grey's entire face—from his scar to the forced smile he wore—began to ache at the sight of the younger man. Maxwell had to be nine and twenty at best. He was tall and dapper, and just charming enough so as not to seem threatening. It was a part Grey played very well at the same age, only he'd been a wolf masquerading as a harmless spaniel. He wasn't so sure the same couldn't be said for Maxwell.

He had no choice but to shake the man's hand and make small talk before watching him take Rose's arm and lead her away, both of them smiling like idiots.

No sooner had he sat down and begun to massage his jaw than his mother spoke. "She's such a darling girl, Lady Marsden."

Camilla beamed. "She's been a great comfort to me since my husband's passing, but then children always are, as I'm sure you'd agree, Your Grace."

His mother smiled sadly. It had been a decade since Grey's father passed and he knew his mother still missed him. She always would.

"I do, dear. I do." She took a sip of tea. "Young Mr. Maxwell would make a very good match."

Camilla's lovely face hardened just a little at the mention of Maxwell. Grey could have kissed her. "He was quick to abandon her the last time he courted my daughter, so I will have to reserve judgment until he's proven himself a changed man, no matter how well I wish to think of him."

"Very wise," Grey agreed, ignoring the look his brother slanted toward him.

"A few years can do wonders for a man's maturity," Archer remarked.

Grey shrugged. "Or not. Some men simply become overgrown boys and never face the consequences of their actions."

Archer smiled. "And some blame society and hide like scared mice for the rest of their lives."

Were they alone Grey might have hit him. But they weren't alone, and instead of giving into his anger, he was left with having to face how much hearing his brother say such a thing hurt.

Not only hurt, it made him deuced uncomfortable. He didn't say anything, and rose to his feet when the women began talking again. He walked toward the edge of the terrace, patting Bronte on the shoulder as he walked by. She flashed him a sweet smile, too young and too sheltered to see him for what he was just yet. To her he was her attentive, caring elder brother who liked to tease and spoil her whenever he could.

He did not look forward to the day that she would look at him differently.

Standing on the edge of the flagstones, Grey stared out at the garden sprawling before him. Perfectly manicured, it boasted several exotic shrubberies and flowers. Statues of gods and goddesses graced the grounds, still and unseeing as they loomed over the stone benches and hedges. He knew every inch of that garden, yet if he closed his eyes he couldn't conjure a single image. What flooded his mind was the memory of Rose sitting on a blanket on the lawn, reading her naughty book, asking him outrageous questions.

What were she and Maxwell talking about at this moment?

"I owe you an apology." Archer came to stand beside him, also looking over the garden. "I shouldn't have said what I did. It was very low of me."

Grey shrugged. "You've said worse."

"True, but those times I was right."

He laughed. "I'm not so sure you're not right now as well."

"You're many things, but I've never thought coward amongst them."

"That's because you're my younger brother. You're not supposed to have an accurate opinion of my strengths and weaknesses."

"And as eldest, I suppose you do have an accurate accounting of my strengths and weaknesses, Tryst as well?"

Grey turned his head with a brash grin. "Only your weaknesses. I haven't ascertained if you have any strengths yet."

Thankfully his brother laughed. "Bastard," he muttered.

"Undoubtedly." Then, with more seriousness, "I do know your weaknesses, Arch. You've a soft spot for a pretty face, especially one you think is in need of rescue."

Archer scoffed. "I haven't tried to play anyone's Lancelot since school."

"Be that as it may, I feel I should warn you away from Rose."

His brother stilled, arched a brow, and fixed him with a decidedly superior look. "Is this warning for my benefit or hers? Or perhaps your own?"

Grey frowned. "For the benefit of everyone involved. She doesn't need you to rescue her, and she'd only marry you because—"

"Because I remind her of you." He grinned at Grey's surprise. "Perhaps I do have an accurate understanding after all, brother."

Grey turned away. "Perhaps you do."

A hand came down on his shoulder. "Don't worry yourself. I have no intention of taking advantage of Lady Rose. Even if I did fancy her, I'm not foolish enough to pursue a woman obviously interested in someone else, and I'm too lazy to attempt to change her mind. Maxwell on the other hand . . ."

The ache in his jaw returned. "As long as he treats her as she deserves, I don't care. In fact, I wish him all the good fortune in the world." He could say that and actually mean it. "I promised her father I would see her happily situated. Her happiness is all that matters."

Archer fixed him with a pitying look. "If that

were true, old man, you would have married her already. Maybe you should ask yourself what could possibly be more important than her happiness. I'm fairly certain there's something, and it certainly isn't your own."

Speechless, Grey said nothing as his brother walked away. Instead, he stood and stared once again out into the garden, his fingers tracing the jagged line of his scar.

At five o'clock in the afternoon, the day had lost some of its heat, but the air in Hyde Park smelled of dry dirt, grass, and warm horse—an odor somewhat pleasantly carried on the soft breeze. Ladies wore hats and carried parasols to protect their delicate complexions from tanning, and would continue to do so as long as they were outside before the sun set.

Rose was no exception to this rule. As she leaned back against the cushioned leather seat of Kellan's vehicle, her face was well shaded by her lacy ivory parasol as well as the brim of her hat. Those and the breeze kept her from being overly warm and she was able to enjoy the ride for the pleasure that it was meant to be.

Rotten Row was crowded, but not so much as it would be at this time of day in another few weeks. It was still early in the Season and not everyone who was anyone had taken up residence in the city as of yet. Soon, however, it would be next to impossible to travel this well-trod path with any degree of haste. Of course, haste was the last thing on the minds of anyone present. The idea of coming to Hyde Park at this hour was to be seen. Haste was not conducive to that goal.

And Rose was more than happy to be seen today. Let everyone present gawk at her and Kellan and whisper what they would. Let them speculate as to whether or not he would renew his suit after several years. Rose did not care. Grey had told her to go out and find herself a husband.

Let it not be said that she was not good at doing what she was told—on occasion. Perhaps Grey would read about her outing in the society pages—if he read the society pages.

Beside her, Kellan sat straight and handsome in his dark brown coat and buff trousers. Not a speck of dust clung to the brim of his beaver hat, or his broad shoulders. His dark eyes were bright, with glints of gold when the sun hit them, and when he smiled at her, he flashed perfect white teeth that Rose envied and she fancied one of hers was rather crooked.

"Shall I assume from your expression that you are having a good time?" he asked as he held the reins confidently and easily in his gloved hands.

Rose smiled back. "I am. Thank you for inviting me."

Some of his humor faded as he directed his gaze back to the track before them. A gentleman went by them on a beautiful white mount, followed by a lady on a proud gray mare.

When Kellan spoke again, he kept his voice low, so that what he said was heard by her and her alone. "Rose, there is something I've been wanting to discuss with you."

Surprise—dismay even—clutched at her heart. Surely he wasn't going to propose so soon? And not out here in public! No, of course he wasn't. She was a fool to even think it.

And perhaps an even bigger fool to dread it as she did.

"Of course, Mr. Maxwell. You can say whatever you wish to me."

"You've always been so agreeable," he remarked with something of a rueful tone. "I don't understand why you haven't told me to sod off."

She couldn't help but chuckle. "Other than the simple fact that I would never say those words to anyone?"

He glanced at her, eyes sparkling. "Even so. I am humbled by your easy acceptance of me. I behaved abominably toward you years ago and yet you act as though nothing ever happened."

Rose twirled the handle of her parasol. "We cannot change the past, Mr. Maxwell. I reckon I would be a much happier woman if I could. No, all we can do is go forward."

His brow furrowed. "Does that mean you forgive me?"

She laughed again. "Yes, it does. I understand why you had to abandon your courtship after my father's misfortune and I do not blame you for it."

Kellan shook his head. "You are too good."

"No," she insisted with a sharp shake of her head. "I am not." Lord, if he but knew just how *not* good she could be! Of course, if they were married he'd realize that on their wedding night, wouldn't he? Or could she deceive him and make him believe she was a virgin? It wouldn't be right, but she would do it to spare his feelings, and keep her secrets. "But, I can be practical when the situation calls for it."

"Is that why you're here with me now?" he asked with amusement. "Practicality?"

Rose's smile was coy in reply. "Perhaps. Or perhaps I like giving the gossips something to natter about."

Kellan laughed aloud. "I've missed your wit, Rose. You always knew how to make me laugh."

"Yes." She twirled her parasol again. "You as well. I'm glad that we are friends again."

"Friends," he repeated. "Is that what we are?"

It had been a while since she'd flirted with a man without the benefit of a mask, but she thought she remembered how to do it. "For now."

They were smiling at each other as they passed beneath the thick shade of trees that lined the track, and Rose felt a stirring of hope in her breast. Her heart wasn't totally under Grey's control, and for that she was extraordinarily happy. It was possible for her to enjoy the company and attention of another man. No, she might not trust this man completely, but then she didn't trust Grey so much anymore either. In fact, she made herself a promise right then and there not to trust any man or his word until he had proven himself worthy.

Trust, like one's heart, was all too easily given and broken, and she was already tired of the disappointment that followed. Not that her life had been a particularly rough one, but thus far every man she trusted had let her down in one way or another, whether he meant to or not.

"Good day, Lady Rose, Mr. Maxwell." It was Lady Devane, perched on top of a white Arabian, a spirited gelding that perfectly complimented her blonde hair and blue riding habit. "It is a lovely day, is it not?"

"Good day, Lady Devane," Rose replied. "It is lovely indeed."

They made the necessary small talk, there was no way of avoiding it. Thankfully, the older woman directed most of her conversation toward Kellan, a fact that did not escape Rose's notice. Was it merely that they shared similar taste in men, or did Lady Devane see the entirety of the opposite sex as her own personal banquet?

Kellan, while perfectly polite, did not seem entirely unimpressed by the attention. Of course, what man would be? Lady Devane, while not breathtakingly beautiful, was something even more threatening. Lady Devane was interesting.

"I expect I will see you again soon, Lady Rose." Long sable lashes fluttered. "And Mr. Maxwell, I do hope I have the pleasure in the near future."

Rose watched with wry amusement as the woman rode off, her seat as confident as any man's. Several male heads turned as she rode by. She was simply the kind of woman who drew men to her.

"She's quite overwhelming, isn't she?" Kellan remarked with a smile.

Shaking her head, Rose had to agree. "I do believe she was flirting with you."

He shrugged. "She flirts with every man she meets. It's just her nature."

Her nature was not as harmless as he would make

it out to be, of that Rose was positive. "Be wary of her, Mr. Maxwell. I would hate to see you . . . hurt in anyway."

"Lady Rose, you have more than earned the intimacy of calling me by my Christian name."

"Perhaps," she replied with a teasing smile. "But you have yet to earn the intimacy of having me use it."

Kellan chuckled. "Well put. But tell me, what kind of danger could Lady Devane possibly pose to a gentleman of the world such as myself?"

His tone was light, but Rose could not find humor in the situation. She looked away. "I'm sure I have no idea. It is only woman's intuition."

She felt him glance at her. "It is more than that." He fell silent for a moment. "Dear Lord. Do you mean to say that she . . . Ryeton?"

Had she been so transparent or was he merely astute? Regardless, Rose's cheeks burned with the thought of betraying Grey. "I do not know. He has never condemned her in my presence, though I do know he suspects her."

Kellan muttered something under his breath that sounded profane. Rose wisely did not ask him to repeat it.

"I heard the stories," he commented. "There was speculation for several months until the scandal died down."

Rose kept her gaze on the track. She wanted to hear what he knew and yet she didn't want to know. "I imagine there was."

"Ryeton had quite a reputation back then. Everyone knew their wives, fiancées, even their daughters weren't safe around him."

She closed her eyes. No, she didn't want to hear this. "Am I to suppose that you believe he deserved what happened?"

"Of course not." He sounded genuinely affronted. "But then he never set his sights on anyone I held dear."

"Not that you know of," she remarked, because she couldn't help herself.

Kellan actually chuckled. "Well put. But I am grateful—and I think you should be as well—that Ryeton and your father were such good friends. The duke has much respect for you and your mother. I would hate to think of either you or Lady Marsden under the power of such a man if he'd decided to treat you as he did other women."

"Yes," Rose agreed, staring fixedly at a tree in the distance. "So would I."

Chapter 9

Monday evening found Grey in his study, a glass of brandy in his hand, his feet up on an ottoman as he sat in his favorite chair in front of a small fire in the hearth. In his hands he held the latest edition of *Voluptuous*, which he'd had Archer pick up for him. Surprisingly enough—or perhaps not so—this particular copy had come from the backroom of a prestigious bookseller.

Amongst the articles and essays, all of which touted to be directed at the "lady of class and experience" were erotic stories, poems, and advice on men. This advice ranged from how to flirt properly to how to best avoid wrinkling one's skirts during a public assignation. There was also a page's worth of instructions on how to give a man oral pleasure in the most satisfactory manner.

The article that most caught his attention, and the one he was currently reading—was titled: "*Coaxing Your Pearl from its Oyster, or A Lady's Guide to Instructing A Gentleman in the Ways of Her Pleasure.*"

It was all about teaching a man to give the most

pleasing oral delight. At first Grey thought it a bunch of foolishness, but as he read, he was forced to realize that at least once or twice in his sexual career a lady had made similar suggestions to him, particularly in his younger days when he made up for a lack of finesse with much enthusiasm.

Yet, if the woman, or women, writing this article were to be trusted, there were still things he could learn when it came to pleasing a woman. Since his pleasure in bed hinged almost entirely on his partner's enjoyment—age and experience had taught him that lesson—it would be in his best interest to continue reading.

Damn, maybe he should simply subscribe.

He was engrossed in a story about an older woman and a younger man satiating their mutual passions on a garden swing when a soft tap on the door interrupted.

And here he was with his rod half-mast like a randy young boy. These "ladies" certainly knew how to paint a vivid picture. He found the feminine perspective on shagging most illuminating—and arousing.

He shoved the magazine underneath the cushion of the chair opposite his. "Come in."

The door opened with a slight click. He rose to his feet when he saw that it was not a servant but Rose who crossed the threshold. She was dressed in an evening gown of dark plum that pushed up her breasts, cinched her waist, and emphasized the lush curve of her hips. She looked edible—ripe enough to burst with flavor on his tongue.

He'd like to try some of the advice *Voluptuous*

offered out on her. But that was hardly the honorable way to feel about a young woman under one's care. And he tried so very hard to be honorable now. Rose had destroyed that, reminded him of the cad he used to be. The desire he felt for her knew no respect, and therefore he would have to be all the more diligent.

"On your way to the Carlyle's?" he inquired. This was the evening they were to accompany his family to the card party.

She nodded. How in the name of God did her maid manage to keep all that hair on top of her head? She must have to use an entire box of pins. "Yes. Mama and I are waiting for the dowager and Lord Archer in the rose parlor." She flinched slightly at the mention of the room where their charade had come to an end. "Do you have a moment?"

"For you? Of course." He meant it. Whatever his sexual feelings for her, Rose was a very important part of his life. He would always be there for her, even when she was married to a man who didn't deserve her and didn't appreciate her willful, indulgent nature.

Not that he deserved her either, but how could he not secretly thrill that she had risked so much to be with him? True, she had manipulated him, but she never would have been able to do that without knowing his weakness to begin with.

As humbling as it was that she knew—or at least had some idea—of how deep his desire for her ran, it was rather freeing as well. He didn't have to pretend anymore. He merely had to resist. And he would resist. The motivation was standing before him, all dressed up to go out and be part of that living slime called society.

He refused to hold her enthusiasm against her. She was young and didn't know better. He prayed she never would.

She crossed the carpet, her skirts dragging softly. Each step brought her closer, her scent, her warmth. "I wanted to apologize."

His gaze lifted from her bosom. He remembered those breasts in his hands. "For what?"

"For deceiving you as I did. I misunderstood the nature of our relationship and behaved like a spoiled little girl. It was a terrible mistake and I hope you can find it in your heart to forgive me."

A terrible mistake? A mistake to be sure, but terrible? "There is nothing to forgive," he replied with a tight smile. "We were both at fault."

"Yes," she agreed with a smile of her own. "You are right. Can we be friends again?"

"We never stopped." At least that much was true. He might have played the fool, might have taken advantage of her, but he never ceased caring for her. He never would.

Rose practically sighed in relief. Grey had to struggle to keep his eyes on her face. "Good. I'm so glad you feel that way. Because I do so want your approval when I find the man I'm going to marry."

Grey's lips seized, stuck in a parody of good humor. "The choice is ultimately yours, Rose."

She waved a gloved hand. "Oh, I know that, but your opinion meant so much to Papa, and since he isn't here to guide me, I would be so honored if you would accept that burden as well as the others you've so obligingly undertaken."

Help her pick a husband? Was this some kind of cruel joke? What next, did she want his blessing?

She took both of his hands in hers. "I know this is rather premature, but next to Papa you have been the most important man in my life. I wonder . . ." She bit her top lip. "If you would consider acting in Papa's stead and giving me away when the time comes?"

He'd sling her over his shoulder and run her all the way to Gretna Green if it meant putting an end to this torture! "I would be honored." He made the promise because he knew whomever she married wouldn't allow him to keep it. No man in his right mind would want Grey at his wedding, let along handling his bride.

Was it relief or consternation that lit her lovely face? "Oh, good. I was afraid perhaps you wouldn't, given your fear of going out into society."

Grey scowled. Fear? Back to being a coward again was he? "Whatever gave you that notion?"

She looked genuinely perplexed. "Well, the other day Kellan told me how awful your reputation had become before your attack. I assumed your shame over that to be why you avoid going out into public now."

"You assume wrong." He'd never spoken to her with such a cold tone in all the years he'd known her. "I had no idea your opinion of me had sunk so low. And as one who has also been bandied about by gossips I would think you would know better than to believe everything you hear, no matter how much you might like the source."

Now she appeared hurt. Doe-like eyes widened. "My opinion of you is as high as it ever was! I'm simply trying to say that I understand why you choose to hide—"

"You think I'm *hiding*?" A vein in his temple throbbed.

Innocent confusion met his gaze. "Aren't you?"

"I avoid society because I despise it," he informed her tightly. "I would have thought you'd know that about me after all these years."

She smiled sweetly. "I think my recent behavior has proven that I don't know you that well at all. After all, I obviously did not achieve my goal in seducing you, did I?"

Christ Almighty. The girl knew how to turn his world arse over appetite. "There's no shame in being embarrassed, Grey. I know you regret the past, and I understand how difficult it would be for you to reenter society with that regret hanging over your head."

"Rose, I am not embarrassed, and I am not hiding. I shun society because I despise it. I hate the false kindness and the rules and the hypocrisy of it. Do you understand what I am saying? It is because of society that I have this." He pointed at the side of his face where the ragged scar ran.

For a second he thought she might chuckle, and honest to God he didn't know what he would do if she did. "Grey, society didn't give you that scar. A woman you treated with no more regard than your dirty stockings gave you that scar. You cannot blame the actions of one on so many."

His fingers tightened into fists at his side. "I do not blame all of society for her actions, of course not."

"How could you? You don't even know who it was, do you?"

"No." But he had suspicions. He was almost completely certain it had been Maggie—Lady Devane. He'd broken her heart the worst of them all.

"Of course you don't." Suddenly her eyes were very dark and hard. "I suspect it could be one of a large list of names, all women who you toyed with and cast aside."

A heavy chill settled over Grey's chest at the note of censure, and disapproval in her tone. He had known this day would come, when she would see him for what he truly was. He just hadn't expected it quite so soon.

"Yes," he whispered. "A long list indeed."

"So it's no wonder you would rather avoid society. I would too if I had no idea who my enemies were. It's certainly preferable to apologizing to every conquest and hope that you got the right one." She didn't say it meanly, or even mockingly, but there was definitely an edge to her husky voice.

"Is this what we've come to, Rose?" he demanded. "You've added your name to the list of the women I've wronged?"

She laughed then, knocking him even more off guard. "Of course not. I knew what I was getting myself into when I hatched such a foolhardy plan. No, your conscience need not bear the weight of me, Grey." When she moved to stand directly before him, just inches away, it was all he could do to stand his ground and not prove himself a coward.

Her hand touched his face, the slick satin of her gloves soft against his cheek. "I wish you would stop living under all this regret and rejoin the world," she told him in a tone laden with sorrow. "You have so much to offer it. I'm sure society would agree with me if you took the chance."

Before he could engineer a reply, there was another knock at the door. Rose dropped her hand just as her mother stuck her head into the room.

"Ah, there you are. Good evening, Grey. Rose, Lord Archer is here."

Rose smiled. "I'll be right there, Mama." When the door closed once more, she turned to Grey. "Let us put an end to this disagreeable conversation and put it in the past where it belongs. Friends?"

Grey looked down at her hand, extended like a man's. He didn't want to take it. In fact, he wanted to tell her what she could do with her offer of friendship and barely veiled insults. He wanted to crush her against his chest and kiss her until her knees buckled and her superior attitude melted away to pleas of passion. That was what he wanted.

She knew how to play him so very well.

He slipped his hand around hers. "Friends," he repeated roughly.

Her smile was bright enough to light up the room—and make him see stars. "Excellent! I'm so pleased. And now I really should go. I don't want to keep your family waiting."

His family. She was going out with his family. His

mother and sister, who would no doubt think her absolutely perfect.

Perfect for Archer, who his mother was determined to see married, now that she had given up all hopes for Grey. Or perhaps they'd want her for Trystan, although he was still living the life of an adventurous young man.

"Have fun," he encouraged with all the false enthusiasm he could muster.

She flashed a quick grin at him over her shoulder as she made for the door. "I'm sure I will. Your brother will see to that."

As far as parting shots went, it wasn't bad. By no means mortal, but deep enough to wound never the less.

Alone once more, Grey returned to his chair and pulled the copy of *Voluptuous* out from underneath the cushion of the other. He stared at it for a moment, contemplating finishing the article on pleasing a woman orally.

And then, with a snarl, he flung the pages into the fire, watching ash and embers fly up in the assault. The paper caught quickly, giving off a sudden bloom of heat.

Women, he thought as he watched the magazine's mocking text blacken and char.

He would be much happier in his misery without them.

It was a dangerous game she played. One that could easily end in more heartache. And yet, Rose couldn't stop herself, even though she'd all but given up hoping that Grey could ever love her.

She was hurt, embarrassed, and yet still determined. Her pride was wounded but not destroyed, and she was more than willing to put it aside to renew her efforts to bring Grey to his senses, to make him see that he was merely existing rather than living.

If that meant insulting him to make him see the truth, then she would, but she had to be careful that she didn't make him despise her in the process. Right now, with feelings between them as they were, that could happen far too easily.

And just as easily, she could come to despise him as well.

She should just accept defeat and move on, but she couldn't. Grey cared for her, and she lo . . . cared about him. In their world that was a rare thing, a wonderful thing. Shouldn't they give their feelings a chance? Instead, Grey withdrew from her. He could probably give her a hundred different reasons why they couldn't be together and yet not one of them would be the true one.

That he was afraid. Not so much of her, but of what life with her would mean for him.

"You are very quiet," Archer remarked as they walked together to the refreshment table. They'd just finished a game of whist and when Rose begged off from a second round, Grey's brother did the same.

"My apologies," she replied. "I do not mean to be rude."

"My brother doesn't deserve to take up so much room in that lovely head of yours."

She might have been insulted by his disparaging

Grey, or his familiarity with her, had she not been so surprised by the remark itself.

"You are impertinent, sir."

He grinned—a grin so much more roguish than Grey's. "One of my more charming traits. I did not mean offense, dear lady. Only that thinking about him will do you no good. The man is bent on punishing himself for the rest of his life."

Rose accepted the plate he offered her. "Thank you. Why would he wish to punish himself?"

"Because he's an ar . . . idiot. Sandwich?" He held up a cucumber sandwich caught in silver tongs.

"Please. I'm not certain I wish to discuss your brother with you, Lord Archer."

"Not even if I can help you win him?"

Rose's heart froze—no, it simply stopped. Her entire body went numb. She would have dropped her plate had Archer not swept it from her hand into his own.

"What makes you think I wish to *win* him?"

He flashed her a coy glance. "Please, Lady Rose. I've not made a career out of studying your sex to fall for your false innocence now."

Oh dear God. Had Grey told him?

"I've seen the way you look at him, and I've had to put up with hearing about you for the last four years—no offense."

Rose arched a brow as he piled food upon her plate. "None taken. I wasn't aware that I looked at your brother in a manner different from how I might look upon anyone else."

"Mm." He popped a small cake into his mouth, chewed, and swallowed. "That's just it. You try too hard to treat him like everyone else. It's obvious you care for him, and not just as the man who saved your life."

"Saved my life? How very dramatic."

He gave her a very serious look as he handed her the laden plate. "Where do you suppose you'd be right now if Grey hadn't taken you in? Certainly not here, with such good food and charming company."

Point taken. And now she felt simply awful for the way she had spoken to Grey earlier. She was such a cow.

"You shame me, sir." And worse, he'd made tears come to her eyes. Staring at her food—such a wonderful array he'd picked for her—she blinked them away.

He steered her toward a window seat where they sat in plain view of the room, but at least with a modicum of privacy. "My apologies, my lady. I did not mean to offend you with my plain and thoughtless words."

"Plain, perhaps. Thoughtless, I highly doubt it." She managed a small smile. "I don't think you do anything without thinking first."

Archer laughed, looking so much like Grey it hurt to look at him. "Were that but true. But I do apologize all the same."

"And I appreciate it. But you are right. I certainly would not be here were it not for your brother's generosity." She picked up a cake and took a bite, ignoring the sandwiches. At times like this, a woman wanted cake. Needed cake. Obviously Lord Archer knew this because most of her plate was covered with tiny frosted squares. Perhaps he truly had made a study of women as he'd claimed.

"And His Grace might not be in this world had it not been for you and your father." The words were softly spoken, but the lump that formed in Rose's throat was hard as rock. She swallowed, letting the sweet cake ease it.

She tried not to think of that night very often. How her father had brought Grey to their home because it was closer. She'd met them at the door, having heard the commotion as she lay in bed reading. Her mother had been slower to rouse, and so it had fallen to Rose to help staunch the blood while her father ran for a surgeon. He hadn't trusted a servant to do it, but he'd trusted her to take care of Grey. And she had. She kept pressure on the wound, and sat with him, holding his hand as the physician stitched it. For the next two days until Grey went home, she nursed him. She took care of him, even though her father told her it wasn't proper.

Secretly, Rose thought her father rather proud of her at that moment, for keeping her composure. He didn't know that she had sobbed herself to sleep over it. Or how she had prayed to God her thanks in sparing Grey's life.

"We merely called for the surgeon," she remarked absently. "Your brother was the one who fought so valiantly."

Archer's smile was wry, and a little rueful. "My brother was the one who got himself into that mess in the first place."

Her jaw tightened. "No one deserves that kind

of brutality, certainly not from a coward who gets others to do her dirty work."

He pointed a long, discreet finger at something across the room. "Hell hath no fury like a woman scorned, or some such rot."

Rose followed that accusing finger, and her gaze fell upon Lady Devane. "Are you certain?" she asked, returning her attention to her companion before the lady in question's curiosity could be piqued.

"As I can be," came the brusque reply. "That is what you have to compete with, my lady. The poison she injected is far more infectious and vile than the actual wound ever was. And the guilt he has taken upon himself is a far heavier load than your slender shoulders can bear."

She toyed with another cake, but couldn't seem to put it in her mouth. "So it is hopeless. Is that what you are saying?"

Archer smiled. "Nothing is hopeless, but if he means enough to you that you are willing to put up with him, then I will do what I can to help you."

"Why would you do that?" She took a nibble of delicious frosting as her heart thudded hard in her chest. "You don't even know me."

But what if he could help her convince Grey to rejoin the world?

He raised a cake of his own, the frosting stark white against the tan of his fingers. "Because you are the only woman with the exception of my mother and sister who knows my brother intimately and for some reason still likes him. That's good enough for me. Now, eat some of that cake I was kind enough to fetch you. I wouldn't want you to tell Grey I was a poor companion."

Rose's smile caught on her lips. "Are you suggesting I use you to make your brother jealous?"

Archer laughed. "My dear girl, it will take better men than me to drive Grey to action." His expression turned positively rakish. "But I'm as good a place to start as any."

Chapter 10

Grey dreamed about that night—the one that turned his life upside down and took him from being a man with a reputation for ruining others, to a man well ruined himself.

The dream was mostly memory, with his mind filling in blanks as it saw fit. He and Charles Danvers out at one of their clubs. Danvers feeling guilty for letting his financial situation get as bad as it had. Grey had felt certain his friend could turn things around with a few good investments.

Outside the club, both of them foxed, they'd staggered to their carriages. Grey remembered singing drunkenly to himself, but couldn't remember the exact tune. He never made it to his carriage. He was jumped by four, no five men who beat him to the ground. He fought back, but not good enough. He was too slow and there were too many of them.

On his back on the street. Cobblestones bit into his shoulders, cracked the back of his head as he struck them. Huge weight on his chest—a man. How many times did he hit him? Six.

Then, through blurred eyes he saw the blade glinting in the lamplight. He heard the man say something about ruining his "pretty face." The others held him as he began to struggle. And then he felt the jagged blade tear into his face. He yelled in rage and pain.

And then Danvers was there, wailing on them with his walking stick, shouting for the constable—anyone to help.

Grey's own coachman had come running. It had happened so fast no one had realized that he was the man being attacked until it was too late.

The dream followed what he remembered next, bits of the coach ride to Danvers's home. Rose, pressing cloths to his face. The surgeon stitching—then he passed out. But Rose had stayed with him. He knew this. She was there when he woke up. She had held his hand when the doctor tried to repair the damage.

He could see her so clearly, hovering over him like an angel, caring for and protecting him. She was so good at it—a surprise, given that she was a spoiled young woman. He tried to smile at her, but his face hurt. She touched his cheek, reached for something to the side.

Grey looked down and saw the knife in her hand. It was the same one they'd used to carve his face. His blood stained the blade. Terror cut through him as he met her gaze and saw the hatred there.

"You have no honor," she told him, her voice low and husky, like it was during their nights at Saint's Row. "You have no heart."

Grey couldn't move. He could only lay there and watch as she brought the blade not to his face, but to his chest, just above his heart. She smiled then, cold and deadly, not at all like his Rose.

And then she sliced him open.

He woke up with a cry that tore his throat raw as it caught there.

The sheets were twisted around his legs, pooled around his hips as he sat in the center of his bed gasping for breath, willing his heart to slow the hell down. He was still sitting there when the door to his room opened and the terror from his dream ran in clad in nothing but a nightgown, wrapper, and moonlight.

He'd seen her in far less, but he didn't think she ever looked so appealing as she did with her glorious sable hair trailing over her shoulders, her eyes wide with worry.

Worry for him.

"My God, Grey!" She fell onto the bed beside him, sitting so that she faced him. So that her hands could clasp one of his. "What the devil is the matter?"

"A dream," he replied roughly. "Nothing more."

"A dream?" Incredulity colored her tone. "It sounded as though someone was tearing the heart from your very chest."

He frowned. She'd heard? But it hadn't seemed that he'd cried out so loudly. Perhaps if her room was next to his she would have heard him, but she was on the other side of the house, where it was proper. Where he could think about her, but not touch her, not easily.

"Just a dream," he insisted. He listened for the

sound of approaching servants but heard nothing. "How did you hear me?"

Rose shook her head, sending waves of hair rippling. "I don't know. I couldn't sleep so I went down to the library for a book. When I came up the stairs I heard you."

And came running.

Grey tried to ignore the pinch in his chest. He looked at both her hands and then the door to his room. "Where's your book?"

She looked at him like she didn't understand the question. Then, understanding dawned. "In the hall," she replied. "I dropped it when I heard you shout."

"Scared I was suffering too much, or not enough?" he asked with a twist of his lips. He couldn't shake the image of her coming at him with that knife. The hatred in her gaze.

Rose released his hand and straightened her spine, putting a few more inches between them. It didn't matter how much physical distance she insisted upon, it would never stretch as wide as the emotional void that kept pushing them apart.

"I would never wish any pain upon you." Her tone was a stiff as her shoulders. "It's cruel of you to suggest otherwise."

"I know." But he didn't apologize. He couldn't. Let her think him cruel and unfeeling. It was the only thing keeping him from hauling her into his arms and burying his face in the peace of her hair.

He might have known she wouldn't be so easily chased away. No, she was going to sit there and make him face the hurt in her eyes—the hurt she tried so hard not to show.

"What was the dream about?"

He shouldn't tell her. A kind man wouldn't tell her. "I dreamed you had a knife and were about to carve me up like a rare beef steak."

Her sinful mouth opened, jaw dropping. She stared at him in horror. "Oh my God."

"Quite," was all he could think to say in response. He shouldn't have told her. There hadn't been any satisfaction in it.

And then the woman did the damnedest thing. She leaned forward and took his face—his ruined face—in her soft, slender hands, holding him so he had no choice but to meet her earnest gaze. "I would never hurt you, Grey. You don't have to fear me."

It took a second for her words to sink in, so lost was he in the sweet, melting chocolate of her eyes. "Fear you?" He reached up and grabbed her wrists, pulling her hands away from him. "Jesus woman, I'm not afraid of you!"

She sat there, wrists in his grasp, not bothering to pull free. She obviously didn't fear him. "What else could such a dream mean?"

Of all arrogant, idiotic . . . "Perhaps that I don't trust you?" he ground out.

The little witch—and surely she had to be a witch to have him as under her spell as he was—smiled kindly. "That's a lie, and we both know it."

She drove him insane. In fact, that was probably her plan. Drive him so stark raving mad that he didn't know up from down, arsehole from a hole in the ground. He had to get her out of his house—fast. "Woman, you try my patience."

Her smile never wavered, but she pulled free of his grasp. "Now that I believe. Never fear, Grey, you try mine as well. Now lay down."

His brow ached under the pressure of the scowl upon it. "What?"

Warm fingers pressed against the bare wall of his chest, sending a shock of awareness rippling through him. "I said lay down. I'm going to sit with you until you fall asleep."

"Like hell you are. Who the fuck do you think you are, my mother?"

She had to be red-faced now. Not from embarrassment, but from the shock of his language. But instead of maidenly indignation, he got a palm slapped hard against his breast. It stung.

"You stupid, rude man!" Both hands were on him now. "I'm only trying to be your friend. Now lay the hell down!"

The sound that rolled out of his throat was something between a growl and a chuckle. He'd made her mad enough to swear. Good, they were even. But when he grabbed her hands to push her away, his body did something else. He hauled her against him, and then rolled so that she was pinned between him and the bed, nothing but a few layers of insignificant cotton between them.

She actually protested, squirming against him like an outraged virgin. Her anger ignited his, and holding her arms above her head, he lowered himself so that his lips covered hers.

Grey kissed her without tenderness or finesse. He

didn't even try to be gentle as he ground his mouth against Rose's. Her sweet, full lips parted, allowing his tongue to slip inside, and as he tried to devour her, she offered her own hunger up in response.

She tasted like peaches, although he had no idea why. Sweet, juicy peaches. He drank her in, abraded the tender flesh of her jaw with the harsh stubble of his own. She didn't seem to mind. She had stopped struggling, the movements of her body now a languid dance against his. His cock was hard, demanding to be allowed inside the hot, luscious body he'd only craved more since he'd first explored it.

She was like no woman he'd ever known. She inspired compassion and fury at the same time, made him want to hold her tenderly even when he thought he might strangle her. How the hell did she do that?

Why didn't she fight him instead of pressing against him, whetting his appetite for her even more with the ripe sweetness of her body?

And damn it all to hell, how could a kiss make him want to toss aside the promise he'd made to her father and compromise what honor he had left? Because of this kiss, he was in danger of doing just that—and in danger of making love to Rose with her mother under the same roof. If he did that then he'd know he truly had no honor left.

If that wasn't a proverbial bucket of cold water, he didn't know what was.

Grey released Rose's arms and rolled off her. The sheets were still tangled around his hips, but now they stood up like a tent above his groin—damning evidence of his rock-solid cockstand.

"Get out," he rasped, throwing his arm over his eyes so he didn't have to face her. If he looked at her and saw hurt in her eyes, he'd never let her go. "Please."

The bed shifted slightly, sheets rustling. Her hand brushed his shin as Rose climbed off the bed. She didn't speak, didn't make a sound save for the pat of her bare feet against the floor as she practically ran to the door.

Only when the latch clicked shut behind her did Grey lift his arm and open his eyes. He was indeed alone. Good.

Tomorrow, he would find a way to discuss possible husbands for her with Archer, ascertain if his brother knew any men who might actually be good enough for her.

Then, because he knew it was the only way he stood a chance of getting any more sleep that night, and because his body demanded release, he slid his hand beneath the blankets and ruthlessly brought himself to orgasm.

And of course he thought of Rose the entire time. He thought of her after as well. In fact, she was the last thing he thought of before sleep finally claimed him once more.

This time he didn't dream.

Rose didn't try to avoid Grey for the next two days, it simply worked out that way.

Perhaps he avoided her and the chore of having to make ridiculous small talk in front of others while both of them remembered what had happened in his bedroom that night.

Regardless, it didn't matter if either of them tried to keep from seeing the other, that was what happened. The Season was in full swing now and Rose's social engagements were such that she was barely home for any longer than the time it took to change clothes.

This gave her almost no time to think about bringing Grey back into society, and even if she had the time to consider it, she had no idea how to go about making such a miracle a reality.

If it wasn't Kellan or Eve or Archer keeping her out and about, it was someone else. The invitations started pouring in on Monday, and hadn't stopped. She didn't fool herself into thinking it was her charming personality that had people vying for her condescension. No, it was Grey responsible for it. It would only be a matter of time before someone asked about him. They wouldn't be able to help themselves. They certainly had no trouble talking about him, even she had heard some of the whispers. Nothing too dire, but enough to wonder why these people had nothing better to talk about than a man who hadn't been out in society for years.

But she didn't worry about such pettiness this evening. Tonight, she had something far more pressing on her mind.

It was Thursday, and she was going to Saint's Row. Only tonight, instead of carrying a mask in her bag as she snuck off to meet Grey, she was attending a public function with her mother, Eve, and Lady Rothchild. A fundraiser for orphans, there would be all kinds of entertainment—just not the kind she'd originally intended to enjoy within the walls of the elite club.

Still, that didn't stop her from having Heather lace her into a pretty blue satin corset with tiny lavender rosettes on it, over top of which she donned a gown of teal silk with a square neck line and small sleeves that set wide on her shoulders. The bodice was snug, lifting her breasts but not making a shocking display of them, and the bustle lifted a cascade of ruffles that tumbled to the floor to train ever so slightly behind her. Accents of chocolate-colored bows and matching trim around the neck gave the dress warmth and kept the style from being too plain for evening wear. In her ears she wore simple topaz drops that her father had given her for Christmas the year before he died. It was difficult to believe that it would be three years this fall.

Three years since she'd looked into his warm brown eyes and felt the strength of his arms around her.

Tears prickled her eyes, and she wiped them away with the backs of her fingers. She was not going to think of her father with sadness.

But she couldn't help the guilt that crept down her spine. All her father had ever asked of her was that she stay away from Grey. He knew Grey was not the kind of man he wanted his daughter to be with. But would he feel the same way seeing the kind of man Grey had become? He wasn't the same skirt chaser he used to be.

But, she could hear her father's voice in her head, *was that because he'd changed, or simply because he no longer gave himself the opportunity*?

Rose wanted to believe it was the former, but she couldn't escape the realization that if she managed to make Grey confront his feelings for her—if she managed to win him—that she might end up hurt.

And why did she want him so badly? Because she couldn't have him? Or because he'd saved her life, as Archer put it? There had to be more to it. She couldn't be so shallow or so naïve. Surely the warm gestures, the consideration he gave both she and her mother, said something about his true self. There had to be more to her attraction than the way he looked at her, and what kind of man she thought he should be.

Because, if he was the man she wanted him to be, he would be here with her right now, instead of at home doing whatever it was he did at night when she was gone.

"Rose, it is your turn to have your fortune told." Eve was all enthusiasm as she took her by the arm and led her toward a colorful tent set up to one side of the grand ballroom. Swaths of bright fabric hung in exotic drapes and there was a curtain of beads in front of the entrance. There was a line outside, each lady holding a ticket that signified the order in which they would be seen.

Her mother was one of the ladies in the line, as was Lady Rothchild. "Do go, Rose. Perhaps she will tell you something wonderful!"

Forcing a smile, Rose let her friend lead her toward the tent.

"Ah, having your fortunes told, mam'selles?"

Rose turned her head to find a very beautiful and very cool-looking woman standing behind them. From the luster of her fair skin and her vivid hair, she could only assume that this was Vienne La Rieux, the owner of this club.

A woman who could take a business and make it so profitable—traffic in what had always been a male domain—had to be respected.

"Yes, Madame La Rieux," she replied. "Have you had yours told?"

"Ah, *oui*. Madame Moon informed me that I would soon meet a man who would turn my world upside down." She laughed, rich and throaty, as though she doubted that would ever happen.

"Perhaps she will see the same in yours," Eve suggested to Rose.

Madame La Rieux's eyes sparkled as they lingered a little too knowingly. "Or perhaps Lady Rose has already met him." Then she curtsied and left them to talk to the ladies in line.

Eve turned wide eyes to Rose. "She recognized you?" Her voice was a faint whisper.

Rose shook her head. "I don't see how. I think maybe she is just very astute." She took another step toward the tent. "What did this Madame Moon tell you?"

Her friend frowned slightly. "It was so strange. She said there was a man here tonight who was everything I could ever want, and that if I did not find him, my life would be empty and . . . tragic."

"Good lord." Rose dug in her heels. "I'm not going near this woman. It's all about men."

"We're women," Eve needlessly reminded her, giving her a shove toward the tent entrance. "Of course it's all about men. Now get in th . . . oh my."

Rose turned her head. Her friend was staring at someone on the other side of the room—a man. A handsome, lean, dangerous-looking man with the grace of a cat. A very predatory cat, and he was staring at Eve as though she was the sweetest, plumpest mouse he'd ever seen.

Perhaps there was more to this Madame Moon than she first suspected. One look at Eve's face and she could tell her friend was just as taken by this man as he by her. "Go," Rose whispered. And then loudly she said, "Eve, is not that Amanda Ross by the punch bowl? She said she had a recipe for a new face cream. Go get it from her, will you?"

Eve shot her a startled glance, because they both knew Amanda Ross was standing not two feet away from Vienne La Rieux, who was conversing with Mr. Dangerous. But as startled as her friend might have been by the encouragement, she also realized that both of their chaperones were in line to have their fortunes told and that she might never have an opportunity like this again.

"Of course," she replied loudly as well. "I will be right back."

And off she went. Alone, and the target of exasperated looks by the ladies waiting their turns, Rose ducked into the tent to face her future.

The interior of the tent was even more exotic than the outside. Rich reds, oranges, and violets greeted the eye as sumptuous velvet cushions, table linens, and the clothing worn by the mysterious Madame Moon.

"Good evening," the woman at the table said as she rose to her feet. "I am Sadie Moon. Welcome."

Rose had to struggle to keep her mouth from falling open. Sadie Moon was a tall woman—as tall as most men. She had a true hourglass figure with a tiny waist and flared hips. Her skin was like buffed ivory. Her thick dark hair was pinned up on top of her head, to allow a thick cloud of it to frame her face from beneath a huge, feathered violet hat. Her gown was a simple, unadorned design, but the same violet as her hat with a cherry underskirt.

She was like some strangely exotic bird, peering at her with all-too-knowing large eyes of blue, gold, and green. Fairy eyes. Rose didn't believe in fairies, but at that moment she could easily believe that Sadie Moon was not of this world.

"Lady Rose Danvers," she said dumbly, extending her hand. "A pleasure to meet you."

The fortune teller smiled. "Likewise." She gestured to the table. "Would you sit?"

Rose did as she bid, seating herself on the edge of the chair nearest the door. "I have heard wonderful things about your talent, Mrs. Moon."

The slender woman seemed to pause at the mention of her name. Or was it Rose's use of "Mrs." that stopped her? "Thank you, Lady Rose. I shall endeavor to live up to my reputation." She took the seat across the table. "Would you prefer cards, runes, or leaves?"

Rose smiled. "No crystal ball?"

Mrs. Moon's lips twitched. "It's broken."

She was an easy woman to like despite her strange appearance, or perhaps because of it. "I've never had my fortune told before, so what would you suggest?"

Odd, engaging eyes assessed her carefully, lingering on her face. "You are bold, impetuous, and willful." She made them sound like compliments rather than faults. "You have not the patience for cards or runes, which are open to much more interpretation. I would say leaves." With that she took a delicate china pot with a chip in the lid from the shelf behind her. She gently rotated the pot, no doubt to stir the leaves inside and then poured the fragrant mixture into a matching cup, its gold trim faded from being washed often.

"It smells delightful," Rose commented on a sigh. "What kind of tea is it?"

The fortune teller smiled. "My own special blend. Cream and sugar?"

After the tea was fixed, Mrs. Moon instructed Rose to drink it while thinking of a question or problem—even a wish. She was to drink it as far down as she could, even though it was very likely that she would get leaves in her mouth.

Once she had finished drinking, Rose turned the cup upside down on the saucer as she was instructed and turned it three times counter clockwise with her left hand. Then she pushed the cup and saucer across the table where it was picked up by Mrs. Moon, whose face was obstructed by the amazingly wide brim of her hat as she peered inside the delicate china.

"See the dregs on your saucer?" She pointed a long finger at the little wet puddles and piles of discarded tea leaves. "These represent the things you leave behind, the negative."

It just looked like tea to Rose.

"Tragedy. Grief. The wounds sting, but you are healing."

Rose couldn't speak. She could only stare.

Sadie Moon's hands were bare, she finally realized as she watched the woman pick up her cup and stare inside. The skin there wasn't as delicate as that on her face, the backs of her hands marred by tiny scars as though she'd been cut or burned occasionally over the course of her life. She hadn't started out as a lady, hadn't been born to the middle or upper classes, yet she spoke as though she had. She carried herself as though she had.

"I see a man."

Rose bit back a sigh. Of course she did. She seemed to see a man in every cup. And here she'd actually hoped that Sadie Moon might be as unusually talented as her appearance suggested.

"He hides himself. A mask. He keeps to the shadows."

Rose's heart rolled over her chest. "What else?"

"You want him," Sadie said, turning the cup in her palms. "You do not understand what you feel for him, or why he pushes you away."

"No." Rose was breathless. "I don't."

Those fay eyes locked with hers. "Because he loves you enough to give you up. He is all about duty and honor, but he is ruled by fear."

She was on the very edge of her seat now. "Yes. He's afraid of coming out of the shadows."

Sadie shook her head, the feathers on her hat bobbing. "That's only part of it. He's afraid for you."

"For me?" Rose's teeth clicked together. "Why?"

The fortune teller shrugged. "For that answer,

you will have to go to him. You have many men in your cup, Lady Rose."

Disappointed, Rose sagged a little. "For all the good it does me."

A bright grin flashed beneath that amazing hat. "The man who wants you but will not take you. Another who would take everything you offer and give what he can of himself—but it will not be enough. Another who wants nothing from you at all."

Grey. Kellan? And probably Archer.

"And your father." Sadie looked up, her gaze full of sympathy. "I am sorry for your loss. It's been . . . three years?"

"You could have read about him in the gossip rags," Rose replied uncharitably. Mrs. Moon had struck a nerve, seen too much of what she thought was hidden inside.

"I am used to being distrusted and thought a charlatan, my lady." There was an edge to the fortune teller's voice as well. No matter how used to it she was, it was obviously still a sore point. "Would the gossip rags know about the roses you have placed on his grave every week?"

How could she possibly know that? "You are frightening," Rose whispered, and she meant it.

Wide lips curved into a rueful smile. "I know." She moved to set the cup on the saucer. "My apologies."

"No!" Rose reached out. "Don't stop. Please. What else do you see?"

The cup hovered just over the saucer, but Sadie looked at Rose, not at it. "Only that this man you want and your father seem to have some kind of struggle between them. I can surmise only that your father has sway over you, and this man, even though he has passed on to the next world. What you want is obtainable, Lady Rose, but only if you are willing to give up and take control."

"That's . . . confusing, not to mention depressing."

The fortune teller laughed, a lovely rich sound that instantly brightened Rose's mood. "The most difficult choices are sometimes the easiest to make when the time comes. And sometimes, my lady, I am nothing more than a woman with a teacup. Your destiny is yours and yours alone."

That was exactly what she needed to hear. "Thank you, Mrs. Moon." She pushed back her chair and rose to her feet.

"Call me Sadie." She extended her hand. "And there's one more thing."

Rose accepted the handshake with a smile, hoping she would see this strange woman again. "What is that?"

"The man in your cup—the one who you say hides from the world?"

"Yes, what of him?"

Sadie smiled. "He's here."

Chapter 11

From where he sat in the box above the ballroom, Grey was able to watch Rose without her knowing.

The Duke of Ryeton, notorious rake and scoundrel, reduced to Peeping Tom. This is what Rose had brought him to.

It was exactly one week ago tonight that he'd made love to her for the last time. In this very building, in a room he canceled the reservation for just an hour ago.

The fundraiser was an annual event, for one cause or another. A group of ladies of a charitable event came up with the guest list and decided who would benefit from the money raised. Vienne La Rieux provided the location and the entertainment. Saint's Row was just exclusive enough that many people would cheerfully open their pocketbooks to get inside. They had no idea what went on in the private rooms of this building, and that was the way it would stay. Vienne was on the edge of respectability, and she struck him as the kind of woman determined to stay there. She liked being scandalous enough to be sought after, but was smart enough not to cross any lines.

It was all business.

That was how he should approach his relationship with Rose, but he'd never had much of a head for commerce. Oh, he knew how to work the land, take care of tenants and all that, but when it came to actual trade or investments, he let his brother Trystan take care of the rest. The estate made money and Tryst invested it, insuring that the dukedom and their family would go on being one of the wealthiest in England, while others fell beneath the wheels of progress. He wanted to leave something for his heirs. Only, they wouldn't be his heirs. They would be Archer's heirs, and Trystan's and Bronte's.

And Grey was fine with that. Resolved even. A man like him could never marry because he'd trust a rat before he'd trust a woman of his own class. And any woman beneath his class would have sense enough to know that he was hardly husband material.

Except for one, of course. He told himself he was there to find her a proper husband, but that wasn't the only reason, damn it.

The flap of the tent below opened and a familiar dark head emerged. He craned his neck forward, watching as Rose spoke to the garishly dressed fortune teller. He was too far away and the crowd below too noisy for him to make out what she said, but she was frowning.

And then she looked up. She looked right at him!

Grey jerked back into the shadows, heart pounding hard enough to bruise his ribs. Had she seen him? Slowly, he leaned forward, peering through the heavy curtains once more at the floor below.

She was gone.

His gaze raked over the crowd, searching for that familiar gait, the luster of her hair, but she wasn't to be found. Where the devil was she? Had she gone back into the tent? Or had she left?

He didn't see Archer down there either. Unease gave way to a disbelieving wave of jealousy. His brother wouldn't. Would he? After intimating that he knew Grey had feelings for Rose, he wouldn't honestly pursue her for himself? Grey would kill him if he did. Not that he would deny his brother happiness, but he would hack off his own foot to deny him Rose.

"The fortune teller told me you were here."

Grey's eyes closed as he stifled a groan. Caught. He hadn't even heard the door of the box open, he'd been so intent on finding her.

And she had found him.

He didn't turn around. He didn't need to. He could hear her coming closer. "I told her she had to be mistaken because you would never risk being seen with this many people about. I wonder how she knew?"

Grey stood, turning to face her. The lamps bathed her in a golden glow, warming her skin and casting glints of red in her hair. It made his chest hurt to look at her.

"Perhaps she told you what she thought you wanted to hear."

Rose inclined her head. "Perhaps. Why are you here, Grey?"

He could stop this right now and tell her he was

looking for a lover to take her place, but even he couldn't be that cruel—or that much of a liar. He could remind her that they had a rendezvous scheduled for this evening, but that would be cruel as well.

"I wanted to see you," he admitted roughly. He could have just as easily told her the husband-hunting lie. That would have been better for both of them. "Happy?"

She shook her head, little wisps of hair floating around her cheeks as she took another step toward him. He had nowhere to go, no retreat to be made with the chairs behind him and her blocking the exit. The only other choice would be to venture out further into the box and risk being seen by all below.

"No," she informed him tightly. "I'm not happy. What would make me happy Grey, is if you were to come down there with me."

His fingers went to his mask, snug and tight against his face. "That isn't going to happen." But his gaze flitted to the part in the curtains. He could see the crowd below, hear their laughter and conversation.

When was the last time he had a conversation with someone he wasn't a relation or employer to? Too long. Not since before the attack. He might not have had scores of friends, but there had been a few whose company he enjoyed.

"Why not?" She was a dog with a bone, for Christ's sake. She came to him, put those soft hands on his shoulders. "Grey, I'll be there beside you. There's nothing to be afraid of."

He grabbed her upper arms, hauling her tight against him so fast and rough her eyes grew as big as saucers. He'd scared her. Good.

"You need to stop talking to me like I'm a coward," he ground out. "I am *not* a coward."

She stared at him, the pulse hammering at the base of her throat. He wanted to kiss her there.

"All right," she said.

He should release her, but he didn't. If they were discovered together it would be the end of Rose's reputation. They would be forced to marry, and as much as he would delight in having her in his bed, he did not want to live with the resentment that was bound to follow.

"How many times do I have to tell you that I despise society, not fear it?" He ran his thumbs over the soft skin of her upper arms—the small expanse between her sleeves and gloves. "I don't . . . I don't like the man I was in that world, Rose. I'm better where I am."

It seemed to him then that she actually began to understand. She nodded her lovely head. "Did you honestly come here tonight to see me?"

He nodded. Christ, he wished he'd never said that. "I did."

She leaned toward him, bathing him in the subtle scent of her skin—so fresh and warm, like rain on a warm day. "Thank you."

Sweet lush lips brushed his as she came up on her toes, soft and terrible like the faintest touch of an angel's wing. He shivered. No woman had ever made him tremble with a kiss, let alone a kiss as half-arsed as that one was, and yet it was all he could do to remain standing and not fall to his knees before her.

And beg. Beg for her to light the shadows for him once more, to give him a glimpse of why he bothered to go on when life was such an empty drudge.

"You're not that man anymore, Grey," she murmured. "He never would have come to an event just to see one woman, certainly not one he'd already bedded. He would have already moved on to the next conquest."

He let go of her arms. She was right, and she shamed him with it. That she could have known what he was and still look at him as though he was the best man in the world.

"And he wouldn't have left a beautiful young woman alone when she was his for the seducing," he added, lightly tracing the curve of her shoulder with his finger. "But that's what I'm going to do, even though I'd rather haul you down onto the floor and fuck you on the carpet."

She gasped ever so softly at his crudeness.

"Good night, Rose." He moved past her to part the curtains and step out into the lamp-lit corridor. The last time he'd walked down this hall it had been on his way to meet Rose that first night. Now he was walking away from her.

But he had been tempted to stay—and not for the reasons he gave her. It wasn't that he wanted to screw her on the floor. He wanted to sit with her and talk. He wanted to hear all the gossip from below and have her tell him what the fortune teller had said. Why had she mentioned him in the first place?

And he wanted to take her downstairs and dance

with her in front of the entire gathering. He wanted to look at Lady Devane and have her see that she hadn't ruined him, not completely.

But he didn't do any of these things. He went home and drank himself stupid instead.

"Your brother is the most ridiculous, hardheaded, stupid man I know!"

Rose half expected Archer to chastise her. Instead, he took a second glass of champagne from the footman passing with the tray and offered it to her. "And you are surprised by this?"

"Astonishingly, yes." She took a long, unladylike swallow of the crisp, bubbly liquid.

"I'm astounded. Ah, here are two scoundrels you should know to avoid." His grin told her he considered them quite the opposite.

They were good-looking men, one tall and dark, the other almost as tall with brown hair and blue eyes and enough of the Kane countenance that she picked him for Grey's relation instantly. They met Archer enthusiastically, and then turned polite curiosity in her direction.

"Lady Rose Danvers," Archer said jovially. "May I present the Earl of Autley." The dark man bowed over her offered hand. "And my cousin, Mr. Aiden Kane?" The man who looked a bit like Grey smiled and took her hand next.

"It's lovely to meet you, Lady Rose," the earl said smoothly. "I hope you are enjoying your time in London?"

"Oh, yes," she replied. "Lord Archer has been a very entertaining companion."

"I don't doubt it," Aiden said with a grin as he clapped Archer on the shoulder. Some of his humor faded. "Tell His Grace we asked after him, will you?"

Rose straightened at the mention of Grey. There was something unsaid passing between these three men, something about Grey. Something she wasn't sure she wanted to know.

The gentlemen excused themselves very properly with her and in a considerably more familiar fashion with Archer and then left the two of them alone again.

Archer was not quite his usual self.

"May I ask what that was all about?"

Archer turned to look at her, his expression one of faint surprise, as though he hadn't expected to find her standing beside him. "Oh. Those two are Grey's oldest friends."

Rose frowned. "I cannot recall if he's ever spoken of them to me."

Her companion shrugged one shoulder. "He hardly speaks of them at all anymore, not that it's any fault of theirs."

And Rose understood his meaning. Like society and everything else, Grey had pushed his friends away as well after the attack. In fact, the only people he let anywhere near him were his family and her.

She wasn't quite certain she wanted to dissect the implications of that honor.

"Say, Lady Rose, you wouldn't happen to know the name of the lovely blonde standing next to Lord Ponsby, would you?"

"Hmm?" Distracted, Rose turned to look. "Oh,

that's Jacqueline Whitting. She's the daughter of the late Earl Monteforte. This is her first season."

Archer frowned. "No, not the girl—the woman with her."

Rose looked again as she drained her glass of champagne. "That's her mother, Lady Monteforte."

"Her mother!" Archer's jaw dropped. "She doesn't look old enough to be the chit's mother."

Rose shrugged. "Apparently she was quite young when she married the old earl."

"Must have been a babe," he commented, his gaze riveted on the beautiful woman. Then, he turned to face Rose. "Now, what did my brother do to earn your ire this time?—insist that you are better off with a boring young man who will love you for your dowry? Hang your puppy like that dastardly Heathcliff?"

The last was meant to make her laugh, she knew, and laugh she did. And when she was done, she was in a much better humor. "You have read *Wuthering Heights*?"

He nodded. "I have. Don't look at me like that! You do not believe me?"

"I believe you, but I must confess my surprise. You do not seem the kind of man who would read novels."

A sly smile curved his thin lips. "My dear girl. Who reads novels?"

"Mostly women, I would suspect," she replied, setting her empty champagne flute on the tray of a footman. Yet another passed with a fresh tray of full glasses and she took one of those.

"Exactly. If one wants to converse with a woman, one should have a variety of subjects at hand."

"But you only want to talk to them so you can seduce them."

"You shock and wound me."

Rose grinned. "Impossible."

Archer chuckled in return. "I do, however, have to wonder where Lady Monteforte's taste in literature lies."

He was a rogue and a scoundrel, but he was an honest one. "Why don't you ask her?"

"I just may—in a moment." Holding his half-full glass in his hand, he turned fully to face her. "I want to make certain you are fine first. What happened to put you in such a foul temper?"

"Grey was here."

He hadn't known, that was obvious from the way his eyes widened. "You lie."

Rose chuckled. "I saw him. I spoke to him. He said he came to see me. And then he ran out of here as though the hounds of hell were nipping at his heels."

Archer shook his head, an expression of disbelief on his face. "They tend to do that when Hades freezes over." Then he offered her a grin. "He braved being seen in public just to come here and see you?"

"He was watching from a balcony. I wouldn't have known he was here if the fortune teller hadn't told me."

His brows shot up. "And there's a story for another time. Look, Lady Rose, I know he's frustrating as all get-out, but you cannot expect Grey to change years of behavior in a week. You have to be patient—like waves lapping at a stone."

That was so very easily said. He wasn't the one being pressured to find a husband. He wasn't the one who felt as though everything she wanted was just out of reach. "You know, I suddenly find myself very interested in Lady Monteforte's literary tastes. Shall I make the introductions?"

"I will hang your puppy if you do not."

Rose grinned. He truly was the most charming of rascals. "How very fortunate for me then, that I do not own a puppy."

"For shame. Every young lady should have a puppy."

Rose made the introductions, and Archer wasted no time in asking Lady Monteforte if she cared to dance. For a moment it seemed the lady might decline, but then Rose offered to stay with Jacqueline and Archer offered the widow his arm. She hesitated before taking it.

Interesting. Rose had never seen a woman react so coolly to Archer's charm before. The Kane men were obviously losing their touch.

"How are you enjoying the Season, Lady Jacqueline?" Rose asked the younger girl when they were alone.

Little and fair with golden hair, wide blue eyes, and a reputedly large dowry, Lady Jacqueline Whitting was everything most Englishmen claimed to want in a bride. She also possessed a sweetness that Rose couldn't decide if she found refreshing or annoying.

"Oh!" the girl gushed. "It's been so exciting I can

scarce believe it's not a dream! Thank you so much for the kindness you showed me the night we met in introducing me to the other young ladies. I was so afraid I would never make friends, but you and Lady Eve made me feel quite welcome."

Speaking of Eve, where the devil was her friend? She hadn't seen her since she'd left her at Sadie's tent, when Eve went off to make contact with her mystery gentleman. What if her friend was in trouble? She'd never forgive herself for encouraging her.

But no—there was a familiar blonde head on the other side of the room. Her friend looked a little mussed, but otherwise unharmed. Her color was a little high, though.

Good God, what had Eve been up to?

"Is it true that he's the brother of the Duke of Ryeton?"

Rose's attention snapped back to the petite girl standing next to her. "Pardon?"

Jacqueline nodded at Archer, who was trying to engage Lady Monteforte in conversation as they waltzed. "He is the brother of Ryeton, is he not?"

"Yes. He is the next in line for the title." Now, why did she phrase it like that?

A faint blush colored the younger woman's cheeks. "I've heard his brother the duke is quite scandalous. Do you know him?"

The bottom of Rose's stomach seemed to drop several inches. "Yes. His Grace and my father were good friends."

Jacqueline whirled on her like a gust of summer wind. "Then, you must tell me if the stories are true!

I heard a lady once tried to drown herself because he spurned her affections. And that a mother and daughter once erupted into a public brawl over him! They say his face was quite ruined by a rejected lover. Is it true?"

Anyone else and Rose would have gladly imparted all she knew, but this was Grey, and talking about him like he was so . . . insignificant as a person was wrong. Shameful and wrong. He deserved better than this. "He was injured several years ago in an attack," she admitted. "I do not know the particulars."

Had a mother and daughter truly fought over him? *Oh, Grey.*

Jacqueline looked a little disappointed, but not totally dashed. "Do you know him?"

"For most of my life, yes."

"I hear he used to be quite handsome."

"He still is. Lord Archer and he look a fair bit alike."

Suddenly the young girl seemed to see Archer in a whole new light. "Is he as naughty as they say?"

Rose gave her a tight smile. "He's never been anything but kind to me." And now she understood why he strove to keep his distance, why he was so concerned that his reputation would taint hers.

It made her adore him all the more, and it broke her heart.

Jacqueline's full lips pouted slightly. "I do wish he came out into society. I fancy him rather like a hero out of a gothic novel, like Mr. Heathcliff."

How was that for a coincidence? This time Rose's

smile was more genuine. How many times had she thought of Grey the same way? "The duke would never hang a puppy though."

The girl shared her amusement. "I should hope not!" She giggled. "Still, I imagine him very dark and fierce."

He was neither of those things, but Rose didn't bother to correct her assumptions. She was struck—and rather cruelly, if truth be known—by the realization that she was guilty of doing the same thing Jacqueline was doing. She had made Grey into a hero of sorts because he saved her family in their time of need, and because she had been there when he was attacked. She'd seen his pain.

But the truth of it was, that he had been an awful man before the attack. He'd respected no one and cared about no one other than himself. She believed him to have changed, but how much of that was wishful thinking, and how much was fact?

The waltz had ended and Archer and Lady Monteforte were returning to them. Rose paid them little heed. "Will you excuse me, Lady Jacqueline? I see a friend of mine that I must speak with."

Of course the girl agreed and Rose turned and hurried through the crowd before Archer could claim her attention. She had to find Eve and find out what had happened with Mr. Dangerous. And then she had to go home.

She'd had enough of society for one night.

Grey wasn't quite drunk, but he was far from sober when Rose entered his study later that evening. His heart stuttered at the sight of her, but his head . . . his head couldn't take any more.

"I've been drinking," he warned her, just in case his sprawled posture and missing cravat wasn't enough indication. "And I refuse to dance this ridiculous dance with you any more tonight."

"May I have a drink with you?"

He glanced up. She stood beside the sofa where he half sat, half lay. She looked like someone who'd just lost her best friend or puppy or something equally as tragic.

He sat up. "Of course." Never mind that it wasn't proper. Who the hell cared? They were well past proper. He was simply trying to hold on to sane.

She poured herself a substantial glass of sherry and took a seat on the chair nearest him. He sat quietly, nursing the remainder of whiskey in his glass while she took several sips from her own.

"Do you remember my come-out ball?" she asked after a few minutes.

"Of course." And he did. "I remember telling you that you looked lovely in pink."

She smiled. "You danced the first dance with me so I wouldn't have to dance with Papa."

"You were afraid the other girls would laugh at you if you danced with your father."

"They didn't laugh at me for dancing with you."

"No." He chuckled and took a drink. "I wager they didn't."

Rose sighed. "They thought you were so scandalous, you know. All night I had girls coming up to me wanting to know about you. I felt very important."

He saluted her with his glass. "Glad to be of service."

"I think I fell a little bit in love with you that night."

Grey choked on a mouthful of whiskey. Coughing, he cursed himself for being stupid enough to relax his guard with her. "Rose . . ."

She held up her hand. "I'm not telling you this to make you uncomfortable, Grey. I wanted to tell you that you were a knight to me that evening—a knight on a big white horse. I didn't know much about your reputation, all I knew was that you made me feel grown-up."

He didn't know what to say. "And then?"

She smiled, but her lips trembled. "And then I caught one of the older ladies looking at me like she'd cheerfully rip my heart out of my chest and feed it to me. I couldn't understand why she disliked me when I didn't even know who she was."

"Do you understand now?" Why did he ask questions to which he did not want to know the answer?

"I do." She took another sip of sherry. Her lips were wet and inviting and he stared at them with such an intense longing in his gut he could weep. Drunken, crying men were always so very attractive.

"It was because of you," she continued, fixing him with an expression caught somewhere between distaste and pity—a mortifying combination. "She was jealous because you danced with me and not with her, I'm sure of it."

"Did you ever find out who she was?"

"Lady DuBarrie."

"Helena," he said with a rueful smile. "She was

unhappy in her marriage, I convinced her I could make her happy."

"Did you?"

He met her gaze with a hard one of his own. "Very. But not for as long as she would have liked. Greener pastures and all that." It was so difficult to look her in the eye and admit these things, but he would not shy from the truth. He owed her that. "Yes, she would have despised you for capturing my attention. And she would have hated you for being younger and more beautiful."

"I remember her being a beautiful woman."

"Only on the outside—like so many of us." Then he laughed bitterly, fingers going to his scar. "Well, not me. Not anymore, eh?"

She ignored that, dear girl. He couldn't stand her pity on top of his own. "Was she the one who tried to drown herself?"

"No. That was someone else." No need to mention names, not when the lady in question was still out in society. "Hard to believe that one man could cause so much trouble, isn't it?"

"It's difficult to believe it was you. You were so good to me."

He took a drink. "Only because you were the daughter of a friend. Were you anyone else I would have plucked you that first season." Just how much honesty did he owe her? Because surely this was a bit much.

She didn't look nearly as disgusted as she should have. She merely looked . . . disappointed. That was worse. Necessary, but worse.

"But you're not that man anymore," she reminded him.

Grey smiled, but there was little humor in it. "Who's to say? I really don't want to find out. Do you?"

She looked away, a frown knitting her delicate brow. He wanted to reach out and smooth that pucker away with his thumb, kiss her flesh smooth again. Hold her and tell her that he could be whatever she wanted him to be.

"I understand why you despise society," she said after a moment's pause. "I wanted to tell you that." She drained the rest of her drink and stood. She didn't quite meet his gaze.

"You do?" Color him astonished. He truly hadn't thought she'd ever see it.

She nodded, looking so remote and stiff—not his Rose at all. But she placed her hand on his shoulder as she walked by—a gesture of comfort? "I would avoid it as well if it reviled me as much as it reviles you. Good night, Grey."

And when she left him sitting there, drunk and about to get drunker, what little self-respect he had left got up and went with her.

Chapter 12

Archer arrived early the next morning. Grey was still asleep on the sofa in his study when he heard tapping on the window.

He opened his eyes and immediately regretted it as the sharp light of day pierced his brain. Squinting, he tried to focus on his brother, since he already knew who his visitor was. Only one person ever announced himself so annoyingly.

"Open the bloody window, Grey!"

Grumbling, Grey slowly rose into a full sitting position. His back and neck were stiff and his head felt as though someone had kicked it repeatedly from all sides. And his mouth! Christ, he didn't want to even think about what might have died inside it.

He staggered to the window, unlatched it, and swung it open. "What the hell do you want?"

Wide-eyed, Archer made a tsking noise. "Is that any way to greet your favorite brother?"

"You're not my favorite," Grey growled.

Unaffected, Archer easily adapted. "Is that any way to greet your second-favorite brother?"

Grey grinned, he couldn't help it. Archer had always had a knack for making him smile, just as he had a knack for pissing him off as well. "I'm hung over and feel like shite. What do you want?"

"You look like shite. What's this I hear about you making an appearance at Saint's Row last night?"

"Rose tell you that?"

"She did. I'm surprised you took such a risk just to see her."

Grey thought of her in that teal gown, the lights illuminating the luster of her skin. "It was worth it."

"Worth it, eh? So worth it you immediately came home and got sloshed."

"Something like that. And then Rose came home and I got even more sloshed."

Archer's expression turned to concern as he leaned against the window frame. "What happened?"

Grey shrugged. He'd already revealed more than he'd wanted. "Suffice to say she now knows what kind of man I am."

His brother snorted. "That girl has always known exactly what kind of man you are."

The words were plain enough, but there was a cryptic edge to them that had Grey puzzled. "What the hell does that mean?"

Arch shook his head. "Come to the stables with me. I want to show you something."

He looked down at himself. He was wearing the same clothes he'd worn last night and he was wrinkled beyond hope. Not to mention that he smelled like a distillery—an unwashed one at that. And his mask was up in his room. What if someone happened by and saw him . . .

He wasn't a coward. He just didn't wish to be seen looking less than his best.

An oath punctuated the early morning air. Grey was grabbed by the front of the shirt and yanked—hard. His only course of action was to brace one booted foot on the bottom sill to keep from falling.

Of course, that action only succeeded in making it easier for Archer to haul him completely out onto the lawn. He landed hard on both feet, the impact going straight to his ready-to-implode skull.

"What the hell?" Fist cocked, Grey punched his brother in the shoulder. "Jesus, man! What are you about?"

Archer punched him back. It hurt, and oddly enough it seemed to wake him up—clear the fog and some of the pressure surrounding his brain. "I'm trying to help you, you bugger."

"To do what?" Grey demanded. "Die?"

His brother grabbed his shirt again and began pulling him in the direction of the stables. Grey gave him a shove, breaking his hold, and almost tearing his own shirt in the process. "I can walk without your help, arse."

And walk he did. He fell into step beside his brother, irritation soon giving way to companionable silence. The morning breeze washed over him, carrying away the cloying odors of sweat and liquor, and refreshing him. It wasn't as liberating as a hot bath, or a bracing shower, but it would do for now. He could smell the flowers in the garden, beginning to open, hear the bees starting their daily work. Birds chirped happily, and in the distance, he saw a small rabbit hop into the garden hedge.

His father always said that things looked different

—better—in the bright light of day, and the old man was right. Grey didn't feel half so sorry for himself as he had last night after Rose left him. In fact, he felt almost . . . hopeful. It had felt good talking to her about his past, admitting to being the bastard he had been—and might still be given the opportunity. It had been strangely cathartic.

"I met someone last night," Archer said as they walked, the dew-kissed grass dampening the leather of their boots.

Grey glanced at him, squinting against the sun's still uncomfortable brightness. "Who?"

"Lady Monteforte. Do you know her?"

He thought for a moment. "Gorgeous blonde—a little cool-looking?"

"Yes, that sounds right."

He shrugged, a casual rolling of his shoulders to loosen the knots there. "I knew her a long time ago."

"You didn't sleep with her, did you?"

It was the exasperation—the readiness to accept it as fact—that made Grey stop, straighten to his full ducal height and face his younger brother with a scowl. "Contrary to popular belief, I have not screwed every woman over the age of twenty in England."

Archer raised a brow. "Only most of them."

Why argue? "Well, your Lady Monteforte was not one of them. She was virtuous and loyal to a fault, and as you know, I stayed away from such women." It was his one redeeming factor as a rake. He'd flirt, and take what was offered, but he never interfered with true attachment—never. And he tried never to cuckold a man who wasn't having affairs with other women behind his wife's back. At least those were two less sins he'd have to answer to someday.

His brother sighed in relief. "Good. I hate when I take a woman to my bed who has already been in yours. I feel like they're comparing us."

Grey grinned. "And find you lacking?" As much as he regretted some of his past, he was still a man, with a man's sexual pride.

If looks could kill, he'd be on the grass gasping his last. "I doubt it."

Still smiling, Grey turned his pinched gaze toward the stables. Christ, but the sun was bright. "What are you dragging me to the stables for again?"

"You'll see."

What Grey ended up seeing, once they entered the blessedly dim interior of the stables, was one of his dogs—Maz the Newfoundland—curled up on a bed of hay in one of the stalls. Curled up against her belly, were four of the most adorable puppies he'd ever seen. Coal black, silky and already big, even though they couldn't be more than five weeks old.

Grey grinned. He'd have to be a much harder man not to, and he'd always had a soft spot for animals. "I didn't know."

"Cute, what?" Archer squatted down beside the mother and stroked her massive head. Tongue lolling, she leaned into his touch.

Squatting beside him, Grey turned his attention to the puppies that were now awake and sniffing him with interest. Their little excited whimpers only served to tug harder on his heartstrings.

It was nice to know he still had heartstrings.

"You know," Archer remarked a moment later, when Grey was holding one particularly inquisitive pup in his arms. "Lady Rose has never had a puppy."

"What?" The notion seemed oddly inconceivable. What gently bred young woman of English descent never owned a puppy? Dogs were as much an aristocratic expectation as horses and a lengthy entry in Debrett's. Her mother had that quiet little terrier that kept to her rooms. He assumed the dog belonged to Rose as well. "Perhaps I should bring her out so she could pick one."

Archer smiled at him—almost proudly it seemed. "Why don't you pick one for her?"

Yes, that might go a long way in repairing the rift between them. While it was for the best that she gave up her romantic notions, Grey didn't want to lose her friendship. His life would be too pathetically empty without Rose in it.

He glanced at his brother. "How did you know?"

Archer hitched one shoulder. "It came up in conversation. I thought about getting her one myself, but then I met Lady Monteforte, and well . . . I wouldn't want anyone to get the wrong idea about my intentions toward Lady Rose."

Such as him, Grey realized as their gazes held. He smiled. "Of course not. Thank you for allowing me to take the credit."

Smiling, Archer cast a glance over the puppies vying for their attention. He already had his hands full trying keep two of them from climbing him. "Will you give her a girl or a boy?"

"Boy," he replied without hesitation. A massive,

loyal Newfoundland male to watch over Rose and protect her when he no longer could.

A strange, mischievous glint appeared in his brother's eyes. "An excellent choice. I wonder what she will name him?"

Rose woke that morning with a bit of a headache and the realization that she wasn't a nice person. She always thought she was, but last night with Grey she'd realized the awful truth. She was a judgmental cow.

It hadn't been her intention to insult him, but she'd done it all the same. At first she'd almost felt sorry for him, but after hearing the gossip—and then him not even trying to defend himself against it . . .

How could he have done those things? How could he have treated women so badly? And how could she, even after hearing it, still want to deny it?

Were you anyone else I would have plucked you that first season.

And no doubt then he would have moved on to someone else. The only reason he hadn't done that now was because he didn't go out anymore.

Or maybe he had moved on. Maybe, in the week and one day since their last night together, he'd bedded countless prostitutes. Maybe she had been just another conquest in a long and heartbreaking list.

Or maybe, she told herself when being maudlin started to become annoying, he was well aware of what people said about him and wanted to keep her as far from that as possible. Maybe, in that thick male head of his, he thought he was doing her a service by rejecting her.

Ridiculous, yes, but it was exactly the kind of thing an honorable coward might tell himself. Better to make them both miserable and keep up appearances than risk a chance of happiness and stir up the gossips. And perhaps his avoidance of society was for the best. People still whispered about his exploits of years ago. What would it feel like to stand by and watch him flirt with other women while the gossips speculated who would be next on his list of conquests?

And if she were an honest woman, which she was known to be on occasion, she could readily admit that hearing about his escapades had bothered her on so many levels. And, yes, it affected how she looked at him, how she thought of him.

But not, unfortunately, how she felt about him. Which either made her very generous, or very stupid.

She was also very hungry, despite the ache in her head. So, she climbed out of bed, rang for Heather, and set about getting ready for the day. She told her maid to tell Cook that she would like to take breakfast out on the terrace since it was such a lovely day and she doubted anyone would join her. Her mother had no doubt eaten long ago, and Grey was probably passed out somewhere if his condition of last night had worsened after her departure. She rather fancied him drinking himself blind after she made her grand exit.

Not that she wanted him to be miserable—she

simply wanted to think that her words and opinion mattered.

As she stepped outside onto the terrace, the morning breeze came to greet her, brushing her skin with a gentle warmth that promised to increase as the day went on. A small table had already been prepared for her, and on it was a selection of breads and jams, along with a plate of sausage and eggs. It was her favorite breakfast, as Cook well knew.

Rose barely poured herself a cup of hot, mouth-watering chocolate, when she saw Grey and Archer walking across the lawn. Archer was impeccable as always, but Grey was a mess. His clothes were the same he'd worn the night before, and obviously slept in. His shirt, open at the throat, revealed a glimpse of tanned flesh that made her heart twitch and her fingers itch to touch him. His hair was mussed, and stubble covered his cheeks and jaw, except where prohibited by his scar.

In short, he looked absolutely beautiful—a fallen angel. The only thing that made him remotely human was that scar, and she could easily tell herself he got that from battling the archangel Gabriel before being thrown out of heaven.

She squinted as she realized Grey held something against his chest—something that moved. Was that a puppy?

She jumped to her feet, and skipped down the few steps that took her down to the lawn. Lifting the skirts of her yellow morning gown, she hurried to meet them. "Good morning!" she cried. "What have you there?"

Archer smiled in greeting, but Rose barely noticed. Her gaze was riveted on the man looking at her with an expression so hopeful it neigh on broke her heart.

"I brought you something," he said, his voice low and strangely rough. "A gift." And then he held out his arms and offered her the sweetest face she'd ever seen.

"Oh!" What an idiot she must seem, her eyes welling with tears over a dog, but she didn't care. She let the tears come and slip down her cheeks as she took the warm, silky animal into her own arms, burying her face against its fur. "Grey, thank you!"

"He's too young to be away from his mother yet, but he's yours if you want him."

"Of course I want him! He's beautiful."

He ran a hand through the thick tangle of his hair. "I didn't know that you'd never had a dog before."

Rose cast a glance at Archer, who shrugged. "Telling my secrets are you, Lord Archer?" What else had he revealed?

Grey's brother shot her a sincere glance. "Only that one, Lady Rose. I did not think you would mind."

"And I don't." Turning her attention back to the squirming puppy in her arms, Rose was rewarded with a lick to the chin.

"He'll need to go back to the stables in a few minutes," Grey told her. "But you can see him whenever you like."

With her free hand, Rose reached out and took

one of Grey's. His fingers were so big and strong next to hers. She squeezed and then let go, letting him know with a touch just how much his gift meant to her. "I love him. Thank you so very much."

"What are you going to name him?" he asked.

Rose tore her gaze away from the pleasure in his, lest she do something stupid like kiss him in front of his brother. Instead, she cast a small, secretive smile at Archer. "Heathcliff," she replied. "His name is Heathcliff."

"Aren't these sort of theatrical performances better suited for a house party?" Rose asked Eve as they entered Lord and Lady Battenfield's drawing room, their arms linked.

"Yes, but rumor has it that Lord Battenfield is trying to woo Mrs. Terry with his knowledge of the theater."

"Mrs. Terry the actress?" Rose looked around the drawing room. "Is she here?"

"Of course not. Her running off with Godwin while still married made her quite scandalous. Still, Lord Battenfield is hoping she'll hear of his theatrical prowess and decide to succumb to him."

Rose arched a brow at her friend's choice of "succumb." "I gather, then, that Mrs. Terry is no longer with Mr. Godwin?"

"Heaven's no, but she is still married to Mr. Watts, the painter, although she left him years ago."

Rose sighed dramatically. "I can't keep it all straight. What does Lady Battenfield think of all of this?"

Eve giggled, and hugged Rose's arm to her chest. "Supposedly she's supported her husband's endeavors with great gusto, convinced that he'll publicly embarrass himself rather than win Mrs. Terry's favor. Honestly, I think he's a bit too drab for a woman as worldly as Mrs. Terry."

Rose slanted her an arch look. "Hmm. Be careful my dear, someone might mistake all this talk of succumbing and worldliness for experience on your part."

Her friend blushed and Rose had to bite her lip to keep from laughing. She could tease Eve herself, but she would never dream of calling unwanted attention to her.

While Eve hadn't given all the details—a fact for which Rose was grateful—she had imparted enough that Rose knew something of an intimate nature had happened between Eve and her mysterious gentleman. She hadn't pressed because Eve seemed as surprised that it had happened as she was. Quite frankly, she'd been shocked by the news. She never would have thought Eve as the type to risk ruination with an affair. Of course, many would say the same about Rose herself. And they would be wrong.

"Let's sit in the back," Eve suggested as they moved toward the rows of chairs set up before a makeshift stage. "No one will hear us if we laugh."

Rose chuckled now. "You are so bad."

They stopped long enough to point out to their mothers where they were going to sit, and then left the older women in the company of Lady Battenfield, as she and Rose's mother were old friends.

The drawing room soon filled up. Lady Battenfield must have invited a lot of friends to witness her husband's acting debut—or perhaps his humiliation. Rose and Eve watched other guests as they filed in and took their respective seats.

Soon, Lady Battenfield asked that everyone be seated as the play was about to start. Then, the lights dimmed, leaving only the stage area at the front of the room light. The play began.

Lord Battenfield came out in something that resembled a toga and showed entirely too much of his corpulent form. "Ladies and Gentlemen, tonight's entertainment will be a humble interpretation of William Shakespeare's *Timon of Athens*."

Rose joined the others in polite applause as she leaned toward Eve. "I'm sure I've never heard of this one. You?"

Eve shook her head. "I'm not much of a follower of the bard."

Shrugging, Rose settled back in her seat and waited. This was either going to be very good or very bad.

It ended up being the latter. The play seemed disjointed, although the blame for that couldn't be put totally on Lord Battenfield. His acting abilities were next to nonexistent, but he made up for it in sheer drama. Rose recognized some of his lordships "company" as various children of titled families. They seemed to be having a good time. But the play! In this case the play was *not* the thing. Neither it nor the people acting it out could seem to decide if it was a tragedy or a comedy and so the audience never knew whether or not they should laugh.

Rose was amongst them. Timon began the play as a posturing, wealthy character like many modern aristos, caring about nothing but money. Lord Battenfield played this with a naïve bravado that made it highly amusing. But then Timon lost his fortune and none of his former friends would help him. This should have been a serious moment in the production, but it wasn't. Finally, when Timon realizes the servant Flavius is his only friend and then seems to commit suicide in the wilderness, what could have been a poignant commentary on society became a joke when Lord Battenfield's death scene revealed that he was completely naked beneath the toga. It was just a glimpse, but Rose was certain she would be scarred for life.

She and Eve were trying to control their giggles when the curtains fell. It was then that Rose noticed her mother leaving the room, followed by Lady Battenfield. Her mother seemed composed, but Rose knew that look. She saw the tightness around her mother's mouth that meant she was trying very hard to hold back tears.

"I'll be right back," she told Eve, all her good humor gone. Holding her skirts so as not to trip, she strode from the room as quickly as she could without drawing notice, and as much grace as was expected.

Fortunately, she spied the back of her hostess as she disappeared into a room further down the corridor. It wasn't proper of her to give chase like this, in the lady's home, but what did propriety matter when her mother was involved?

The door was closed, so she knocked before opening it. If her mother wasn't there she would apologize. But as the door swung open, she saw that her mother was indeed there, and she was being comforted by Lady Battenfield who was saying, ". . . never would have allowed him to perform such a mockery had I known the subject."

"What's wrong?" Rose demanded as she entered the room. "Mama?"

Her mother was crying—something Rose hadn't seen since her father's death. It was as alien and strange as if the queen danced a jig at a common pub.

Lady Battenfield's expression was grieved as she looked at Rose. "I'm so sorry, my dear. The play . . . His lordship didn't know. He never would have performed had he known it would bring back unpleasant memories."

"Memories?" Seeing Lord Battenfield's naked thigh had brought back memories?

The lady nodded. "I will strangle him for reminding your mother of your father's tragic death."

But her father's death was an accident.

And then she looked at her mother's face and saw the horror there. No longer crying, she was looking at Rose with such terror and such . . . guilt.

Timon of Athens was rejected by his so-called friends. Timon lost his fortune and his pride. Those were unpleasant for Rose to think of as well, but not enough to drive her to tears. Not like this.

Timon of Athens took his own life.

Oh God. It was as though a great hand had reached in and wrapped icy fingers around her lungs. She couldn't breathe. Couldn't speak. And all her mother did was look at her, the awful truth in her tear-reddened eyes.

"You said it was an accident," she whispered.

Her mother straightened, pulled away from Lady Battenfield's comfort. "Rose, dearest—"

But Rose didn't listen. She yanked open the door and ran out as fast as she could. She ran through the great hall, not caring that people witnessed her distress. The gossips would be whispering tomorrow. No doubt the front page of the *Times* would herald the awful truth for all to hear.

Her father had killed himself. And if her mother knew it, so did Grey. Even Lady Battenfield knew.

Apparently the only one who hadn't known—other than Lord Battenfield—Rose thought bitterly as she ran into the night with tears streaming down her face, was she.

Chapter 13

It was raining.

Grey looked up from Trystan's letter as the first drops struck the panes of his study. Usually he liked the rain—the sweet smell of it in the garden often reminded him of Rose. But tonight it struck hard and with brutality—like Ophelia tossing herself from the tower to the waters below.

Suicidal rain. He obviously needed a change in locale if that was the bent his mind wanted to take. But where to go that his past wouldn't jump at the chance to bite him on the arse? Perhaps once the season was over and Rose well on her way to becoming another man's bride—if not already married—he would take a trip to America to visit Tryst.

Preferably, he'd board the boat to New York before Rose's nuptials. To hell with the request to act in her father's stead—as if she would even want him now. He might have a touch of martyr in him, but he wasn't a glutton for punishment. In fact, a visit to his younger brother would be the perfect excuse to avoid the wedding altogether, which was more than all right with him.

Rumor had it, according to Arch, that Maxwell

was planning to come up to scratch this time and actually propose to Rose. And if he didn't, there was some speculation that Aiden Kane might be a candidate as Lady Rose was said to have made quite an impression when they met.

Grey would slit his own throat before he let his cousin anywhere near Rose. Aiden was an unrepentant rake. Or at least he had been last time Grey had spoken to him, which had been years ago. Besides, Aiden would have to come to him to discuss particulars, and he doubted that would happen since he hadn't stepped foot in Ryeton House since Grey got his comeuppance.

It didn't matter that Rose was better off with someone else. That didn't mean he had to want to see it. He'd be pissed if she seemed happy and miserable if she wasn't.

He turned back to the letter from his brother as the fire in the hearth kept the dampness at bay. Tryst hoped to return to England sometime soon, possibly later in the summer. His business in New York had him very busy at the moment—which meant good things for the family fortunes.

It was just as well that his younger brother wasn't there, as much as Grey missed him. It was bad enough that Archer accompanied Rose everywhere he could. Of course, he was only doing what should have been Grey's duty. Trystan was a first-class flirt. All the little blighter had to do was bat the stupidly thick lashes that framed his impossibly blue eyes and women lost their reason as well as their knickers.

Of course, who had taught him that? He had Grey's way with women and Archer's wit. Or rather, he had the way with women that Grey used to have. And Tryst treated his lovers a damned sight better—or at least Grey hoped he did.

Thunder rolled in the distance as he rubbed his fingers over his scar. No one in America would have to know who he was. He wouldn't have to hide his face. He could go out, feel the sun on his face as he walked down the street—not just in his own garden. He could go to parties and dance. He could go to clubs and gamble.

Maybe, just maybe he could make some friends that weren't his immediate kin. Of course the scandal of his past would follow him, it always did. But these Americans didn't seem to care so much as the English did. Surely, he could find a little respite there.

Now, if only he wasn't a duke with responsibilities. He'd be on a boat by the end of the week. Archer would accuse him of running away, but Archer could go frig himself.

Grey smiled. He could leave Arch to take care of all of his ducal duties. That could be amusing.

A knock on the door interrupted his rare good humor. "Come in," he called. He didn't bother to don the mask that lay on the table beside him. It was evening and he was home alone. Unless an unexpected visitor showed up there was no need to adhere the leather to his face with the spirit gum that sometimes irritated his skin and was difficult to remove.

It was Westford, of course. "Begging your pardon, Your Grace, but one of the groomsmen just ran up to the house to say that Lady Rose is in the stables."

Grey frowned, his gaze jumping to the clock on the mantel. "She and her mother aren't due back for at least another hour."

"Apparently the young lady came home alone, Your Grace. By way of hired hack." The way the butler spoke one would think Rose drove the vehicle herself—naked. But that wasn't what had Grey on his feet.

Something had happened. Something that made Rose come home alone, leaving her mother behind. And instead of coming into the house and talking to him, or even going to her room to be alone, she had gone to the stables.

For a moment—and only one heart-stopping, gut-wrenching moment—he thought she might mean to take one of the horses out in this weather. The rain was coming down hard, the thunder rolling closer as flashes of lightning lit up the sky. But then he realized that Rose was not foolish enough to go riding in a storm.

She was with Heathcliff, her puppy.

He didn't claim to be an expert on women. Even he didn't have that much arrogance. But one thing he did know was that if a woman went running to an animal for comfort, then something awful had happened.

"Thank you, Westford. I'll take care of it."

The butler bowed his head and left the room.

Grey didn't bother going in search of a jacket, or even a hat. He was in nothing but trousers, boots, and his shirtsleeves as he threw open a window and jumped the short distance to the ground. His mother would certainly have something to say about the habit he was making of leaping out windows, but they were his windows and he was a duke, so he could do what he bloody well wanted.

Rain struck him like hundreds upon thousands of tiny, wet palms—slapping his face and shoulders as he ran toward the stables. His hair and clothes were soaked in seconds, water streaming down his cheeks and back. Thank God it was relatively warm.

By the time he reached the stables his hair was plastered to his head and his linen shirt was so transparent and stuck so closely to his flesh that he might as well not be wearing one at all.

He stood just inside the doors, dripping on the floor. The smells of hay and horse rushed to greet him but he ignored them as he slowly moved into the interior, down the wide corridor between the rows of stalls.

He heard sobbing.

Two young grooms stood on one side, obviously uncertain as to what they should do. Manners told them to be still and quiet, but duty dictated there was work to be done.

Grey made the decision for them, slanting them a quick glance and jerking his head in the direction of the back rooms. Twin expressions of gratefulness relaxed the youngsters' faces, and they bowed their chins as they set their tools aside and quickly disappeared into the darkness.

He watched them go before continuing on. Rose might have captured their attention with her obvious duress, but Grey wasn't going to let her become entertainment for his servants. Satisfied that they were indeed alone, he moved quietly toward the stall where the puppies were kept.

His heart broke at the sight that greeted him.

Rose sat on the hay, heedless of her beautiful gown. She looked like a princess—Cinderella forced to leave the ball, but not yet returned to her impoverished state. She had Heathcliff in her lap, holding him in her arms as she bent over his furry body, sobbing into his silky fur. The other puppies were snuggled against her, or trying to clamor up onto her lap as well. Their mother lay on her side, her head on Rose's foot, as though even she was trying to offer some kind of comfort.

Grey didn't say anything. He opened the door and entered the stall, closing the gate behind him so none of the dogs could get out. Then, he sat down across from Rose on the dry hay. The other puppies immediately ran to him, eager for attention. Heathcliff stayed in his mistress's lap, and old Maz kept her head where it was. Her only reaction to Grey's intrusion was a slight shift of her gaze.

He embraced the puppies, patting each of them as they vied for his touch, little tails wagging so hard their entire arse-ends waved from side to side.

"What happened?" he asked softly, after a moment's silence.

Heathcliff lifted his head at the same time Rose did. Her eyes were red and swollen, her cheeks streaked with tears. A piece of hay clung to her chin and stuck to her hair.

She looked beautiful. Achingly so.

"You're wet," she said, her voice thick. She wasn't

impressed with his arrival, that much was clear.

"I commanded the rain to stop before I left the house but it didn't listen." She didn't smile at his poor attempt at humor. "Why the tears, Rosie?"

She stared at him a moment, before returning her attention to her puppy. She ran her hand over his silky head. "Lord Battenfield graced us with a production of *Timon of Athens*."

Grey winced. "That's an awful play."

"Actually, it was fairly amusing until Mama left the room in tears."

He went still at the harshness of her tone—the sharp pain of it. Oh, shite. His gaze locked with hers. "Then what happened?"

Rose sneered at him, or perhaps it was his imagination, it was so slight. "Why didn't you tell me my father's death wasn't an accident?"

How was it possible to feel as though he'd been both kicked in the chest and relieved of a great burden at the same time? "He asked me not to."

Her fine brows drew together in an anguished frown. "You lied to me. I asked you if it was an accident you said it was."

He nodded. "Yes. I kept my word to your father and I lied to you."

She swiped at her eyes with the back of one hand. "How did he die? It wasn't a riding accident, was it?"

Grey shook his head. "No."

"How did he do it?"

"Rose . . ."

"Tell me, damn it!" she yelled. Heathcliff squirmed in her arms, but she held him close. "I deserve to know. Everyone else in London knows!"

She was right—not that everyone in London knew, but that she deserved the truth. "He poisoned himself. I found him as he was dying. It was too late to save him." It was suddenly very important to him that she know that. "I tried."

Fresh tears filled her eyes. Her hands fell limply to her sides. Released, Heathcliff looked around as though not sure what to do. He licked Rose's chin and jumped off her lap to join his siblings at his mother's belly. "I can't believe he'd leave us like that."

Grey hadn't been able to believe it either. He knew how much Charles loved his wife and daughter. "He said he was too ashamed to face either of you."

"So he thought leaving us alone would be better? That facing the scandal of poverty and suicide would be preferable to having him with us?" The fury in her gaze was blunted only by sheer, naked pain. "He left us to face the shame, and you to clean it up."

"He thought it was the best for everyone." And of course, it had been too late for Grey to convince him otherwise. He'd never forgive himself for that. Never. He almost hadn't answered his friend's summons that night—he'd been too busy sitting at home alone feeling sorry for himself as he often had in those days. His scar had healed by that time, but the scab had run so much deeper than just his skin. If he hadn't been such a prick, he might have gotten there sooner. Might have gotten there in time to stop Charles.

Rose laughed—bitterly. "And to think I called *you* a coward." Then her face crumpled and she began to sob in earnest. "My father was the greatest coward of all."

Grey rose up onto his knees, puppies scattering as he did so. He reached for her, drawing her into the circle of his arms as she cried so heartbreakingly hard. She was warm against his damp flesh, and she didn't seem to care that his clothing was wet. She clung to him as though her life depended on him, adding to the dampness at his shoulder with the hot salt of her tears.

She was killing him.

So when she raised her face, it seemed only natural to kiss her. To try to offer her whatever comfort he could. Her grief made him impotent, unable to imagine that he could do anything to ease it. His fingers bit into her waist as she held him, kissing him with a fervor that bespoke so much desperation.

When she jerked away, he let her. And when she hit him, he took it. But when she looked at him as though she didn't know who he was anymore, his heart cried out in confusion.

And when she jumped to her feet and ran from the stall, Grey didn't think about what was right or wrong, or what he should or shouldn't do. He listened to his heart.

He ran after her.

Rose didn't make it far. The rain made a soggy mess out of her gown, dragging it down around her shoulders, soaking the skirts so that they pulled at her like a dozen strong hands. The sodden ground was slippery beneath her flimsy slippers, and it only took one foolish misstep to send her sprawling.

She tried to catch herself, but her hands hit the grass hard and slipped out from under her. She hit the ground hard, her cheek striking the wet dirt. The pain, and the humiliation of knowing that Grey was right behind her and had witnessed her clumsiness, only served to make her cry once more.

If she could have kicked herself she would have. Inside, she sniffed, wiped away the water that threatened to drip off the tip of her nose, and began pushing herself upright.

"Rose!" Grey was suddenly there beside her. She couldn't make out his expression in the dark, but his tone was sharp with concern. "Are you hurt?"

"Only my pride," she replied honestly as he gently helped her to her feet. Blasted bustles and narrow skirts made it almost impossible for a woman to regain her footing.

But she didn't remain on her feet for long. As soon as he had her upright Grey swept her up into his arms and began striding toward the looming structure of Ryeton House, the lights of which looked so warm and inviting in the pouring rain.

"I can walk."

He ignored her.

"You should make me walk after behaving as I did in the stables."

"You were upset." He said it as though it was a fitting excuse.

She blinked against the rain. "I shouldn't have struck you. Forgive me."

"Think no more of it."

Her arms around his neck, her chest against his, Rose fought to control her body's awareness of his.

It felt so good to be held in his arms, to have him treat her as though she were fragile and delicate.

"You can't carry me into the house. The servants will see."

"I don't care."

"I do."

He said nothing, and she felt the stiffness of his body as he continued to carry her.

"Now what?" she demanded. "You play my knight errant because you think I cannot accept the truth about my father? Will you take me to your bed and fuck me because you feel sorry for me?" The word felt harsh and bitter on her tongue, but she wanted to shock him. She was angry because her father had practically forced Grey to take responsibility for her and her mother. She was a burden to him, one that he wanted to be rid of, even though he liked having her in his bed.

"Don't talk like that." His voice was tight as he stepped up onto the terrace. Ambient light from the house illuminated the sharp, wet angles of his face, and the disapproval in his gaze.

"That's what it's called, isn't it?" She reached for the handle of the French doors, accepting that he wasn't about to put her down. Fine, let the servants see. Let them talk.

He shot her a narrow look as he carried her over the threshold into the blessedly dry and warm interior of the house. "Not between us, Rose. Never with us."

Rose's throat was suddenly dry. How did he always know exactly what to say to confuse her even more? Just when she thought she knew what she meant to him, what he thought of her, he went and said something so undeniably wonderful that her mind began to whirl.

"Whatever you want to call it," she muttered, "I don't want it to happen just because you pity me."

"I don't pity you. I regret keeping the truth from you, and I'm sorry you found out the way you did, but I do not pity you."

"Good." Her jaw set mulishly. But if he didn't pity her, did that mean he wasn't going to bed her again? Because—oh God, she was awful—she *really* hoped he would. It didn't matter what lies she told herself, or how much she tried to be practical. She wanted Grey.

Oh, she knew that she would be another man's bride. Nothing short of a miracle could change that, but only in Grey's arms did she feel as though she truly belonged. It was foolish really, because he didn't want her—not permanently.

Thankfully none of the servants were milling about, so they didn't witness their master carrying her through the hall and up the stairs as though she weighed no more than a child. No one saw how the two of them were soaked to the skin, or how she was covered in dirt. That was good, because they might wonder how she got to be covered in dirt and that would lead to speculation.

And God knew she couldn't afford any more scandal in her life at this juncture. It was amazing that others accepted her into their homes as it was. Still, it had been years since her father's death, and even more since Grey's attack. Perhaps now she was considered interesting—a tragic creature touched by scandal but never really of it.

He carried her all the way to her bedroom, where poor Heather sat by a low fire reading a book. The maid jumped to her feet as the door opened, and looked suitably horrified to see the Duke of Ryeton stomp into the room with Rose in his amazingly strong arms.

"Run a hot bath," he ordered as he gently set Rose on her feet. "And have Cook send up tea."

Heather bobbed a deep and somewhat frantic curtsey. "Yes, Your Grace. Right away."

As the discomposed maid scurried off to do his bidding, Grey set his hands on Rose's shoulders. His strong fingers tugged until she turned to face him. It was difficult to meet his gaze in the bright light, especially after all that had transpired between them. She felt raw under his scrutiny. Chafed and brittle, on the verge of tears or laughter, or perhaps both.

He cast a quick glance over her shoulder as the sound of running water came from the adjoining bath.

"I'm sorry I wasn't there for you." The faded blue of his eyes shone with sincerity, and regret.

"Which time?" She wasn't trying to be snide or cruel, just curious.

A ghost of a smile curved the unforgiving lines of his lips. "Tonight."

Good lord, she couldn't swallow, her throat was suddenly so tight. Did he actually mean that he wished he had been at the Battenfields'? Out in public? For her benefit?

"Lord Battenfield's thespian endeavors would no doubt make you reconsider, but I appreciate the sentiment all the same. Thank you."

He regarded her for a moment, with an expression she didn't even bother trying to decipher. She was simply too tired to puzzle out what was going through his head. And yet, if he hauled her against him and sucked the tongue right out of her head, she wouldn't put up a fight. Not now.

"Good night, Rose."

"Good night, Grey." There was still so much left unsaid, but she wouldn't know where to begin, and right now she just wanted to sink into a hot bath and then climb into bed and forget this night ever happened.

No doubt the gossips would be buzzing about it tomorrow. The mere thought was enough to make her want to hide under her bed and never come out.

He left her with a chaste kiss on the forehead. As soon as the door clicked shut behind him, Heather appeared once more to assist her in disrobing. Once she was naked, she dismissed her maid. The girl was obviously concerned about her, and Rose appreciated it, but she wasn't in the mood for companionship or friendship wrapped in servitude. She wanted to be alone.

She soaked in the clove-scented water until it began to cool and the tips of her fingers were like prunes. Only then did she climb out, dry herself with soft towels, and then slip into a nightgown and wrapper. She shivered as she slipped her arms into the sleeves. Heather had left it warming by the fire for her and it vanquished any thought of chill remaining in her bones.

Tea waited for her on the small round table by the chair near the fire. Rose poured herself a cup and sat down to drink it. She thought of picking up her book, but her mind was too restless to read, yet too numb to think. She sat in the comfortable chair, her feet tucked up beneath her, sipping the sweet, hot tea.

The soft knock that came upon her door a few minutes later was not unexpected. "Come in, Mama."

And it was indeed her mother. She came into the room, her shoulders bowed, her face looking ravaged and aged far beyond her years. Any thoughts of harboring a grudge went up the chimney at the sight of her. She looked devastated. And yet, unlike Rose, she'd stayed behind at the party, facing those who would whisper about her. Her mother might be a liar, but she was no coward. Rose would do well to aspire to the same. Her mother never ran away from anything.

Rose smiled. "Would you like some tea?"

Chapter 14

"I should have told you," her mother readily admitted a few sips into her tea. "I'm sorry."

They sat together at the hearth, cups in hand, sharing a footstool as they tried to ease the tension between them.

"I appreciate that," Rose replied, finally daring to look at her. "Why didn't you?"

For the first time since sitting down, her mother looked at her. Her dark eyes were bright with regret and sorrow. "I knew how dearly you loved and respected your father. I did not want to change that."

Rose nodded. She understood. She didn't agree with what her mother had done, but she understood.

"Is it true Grey found him?" It wasn't a question she truly needed to ask. She already knew the answer.

"Yes. I can still remember the horrible anguish on his face when he came to fetch me."

God. Poor Grey. Poor Mama. "I'm sorry you had to go through that alone, Mama. Had I known I could have comforted you."

Her mother reached over and patted her arm, a sage smile curving her lips. "You did, my darling. You did."

Her mother didn't stay long—there wasn't any reason. Rose forgave her, of course. There had never been any doubt of forgiveness. The moment her mother acknowledged that she should have told her, it didn't seem so awful anymore.

The concealment had been done out of love. An attempt to preserve Rose's love for and good opinion of her father. The truth didn't make her love him less, but it did change the opinion she'd always held of him. She used to think him so strong. Now she knew the truth.

Of course what her father had done was awful, but she wasn't going to hold that against her mother. If she was going to be angry at anyone, it was her father. How dare he go and leave the two of them like that! Making them face the scandal of both his ruination and death. And how could he force his dearest friend to pick up the pieces and take on not only his widow, but his daughter as well?

Knowing all that she did now, Rose couldn't help but wonder why Grey wanted her in the first place. How could he be attracted to her given how little choice he'd been given in having her dumped into his lap?

He could have turned them away, but he hadn't. He could have simply given them money and forgotten about them, but he hadn't. He'd done so much for them, and until now Rose had thought that maybe she might someday repay him for all he'd given them. Now she knew that would never happen. There was no way she could repay his friendship.

Knowing that made it so much harder to resent him for not braving society, especially since she was now made to realize what a coward she could be as well.

It was after midnight. She was alone in her bed, unable to sleep. She was restless, and uncertain. She couldn't shake the feeling that there was something she had to do—an itch just under her skin that she couldn't satisfy no matter how hard she scratched.

There were amends to be made.

Rose slipped out from beneath the blankets and donned her wrapper. Barefoot, she crept from her room and padded softly down the corridor, into the opposite wing to Grey's chamber.

She knocked quietly, even though there was no one else in that part of the house to hear or see her scandalous behavior. Though, it didn't feel scandalous to go to Grey. It hadn't felt scandalous to seduce him either.

He answered within moments, opening the door to face her in nothing but a pair of dark trousers and an open dressing gown of dark blue paisley. "Rose." He didn't sound surprised. He didn't sound disappointed either. More like he had hoped she would come but he expected her to have the sense not to.

"May I come in?" she asked in a low voice.

He glanced past her into the corridor. Rose didn't have to look to know that it was as dark and empty as it had been two minutes earlier. "It isn't proper."

She smiled slightly. "Does that really matter?"

Grey didn't reply, but he stepped back to let her enter.

"I spoke to Mama," she told him as she moved into the rich warmth of his bedroom. "I'm not angry at her, if you were concerned."

"I wasn't," he replied bluntly as he closed the room, sealing the two of them away from the rest of the world. "I knew you would make things right."

Rose turned. Clasping her hands in front of her to keep from fidgeting, she forced her gaze to his. "I feel as though I need to make things right with you as well."

He shook his head. The lamp light cast reflections in the dark waves of his hair. Was that silver she saw at his temples?

"You don't."

Her hands were fists now, tight at her sides as she walked toward him. "No, I do. You had Mama and I forced upon you and yet you've been so good to both of us while I've been a complete hellion toward you."

He smiled at her choice of words. "*Hellion.* I wouldn't have chosen that particular description, but all right. I've never viewed either you or your mother as a burden, I want you to know that."

It was difficult to believe, but she wouldn't argue that point right now. "I've been awful to you, and for that I'm sorry. I shouldn't have seduced you as I did."

Amusement softened his features. "I was a willing participant."

"But not anymore," she reminded him, succeeding in wiping all humor from his face. "Not since the masquerade ended."

He looked way. "No. Not since."

Another tentative step. "I thought only of my own wants and I deceived you, knowing you'd do the honorable thing and refuse me if you knew the truth."

His gaze locked with hers. "I knew the truth the second time. I think I knew it that first night. Rose, I simply didn't want to admit it."

She frowned. This wasn't a new revelation, but they hadn't really discussed it before. "Why? What is there about me that makes me the least bit desirable?" She wasn't fishing, she truly wanted to know. Right now she didn't feel very attractive.

There was no joy in the laugh that seemed to catch in his throat. He closed the scant distance between them, taking her face between the warm hollows of his palms.

"Foolish girl. You are everything that is good in life. Don't you know that?"

She would have shaken her head were she not afraid that he would release her. "No. I'm manipulative and spoiled. And I think only of my own happiness."

"You are good and sweet and true." His thumbs brushed the apples of her cheeks. "Everything I am not. Everything. I want you so badly I may go mad before the Season ends."

Breath caught in her throat, unable to squeeze through the tightness there. "I don't feel good or sweet or brave. I feel awful, Grey. Just awful." She wrapped her hands around his wrists. "My father doted on me, never denied me or my mother the smallest whim. He lost his fortune because of us. He took his own life because of us."

He pulled her against his naked chest, but not before she saw the anguish in his expression. He was warm beneath her cheek and she slid her arms around his narrow waist, closing her eyes in bliss. This was safety. This was home.

"Your father, God rest his soul, died because he didn't have the smallest inkling as to how to handle his affairs, not because of anything you did. And he died because he would rather give you up than have to face you. That was his fault, not yours."

Tears leaked from her eyes, searing her cheeks. She'd cried so much that night her eyes actually ached, but she couldn't seem to help it. "He told me to stay away from you."

Strong hands roamed her back in the most comforting fashion. "You should have listened."

Rose raised her face to look at him. "But then I would not have known what it was to be truly happy."

Grey's eyes widened, and for a moment he looked young and vulnerable. "Don't say that. I've made you miserable."

She smiled sadly. "True, but those nights with you at Saint's Row? That was happiness for me. The most I've ever known."

His mouth opened and she pressed her fingers against his lips to close them. "You don't have to say anything. I already know it's not what I want to hear."

Grey frowned, and reached up to move her hand from his face. He held her fingers within his. He gave off more heat than the fire she'd dried herself in front of earlier. Heat that went straight to her bones, right to the very center of her being, radiating out into her limbs. There was nothing seductive about their embrace and yet she ached inside, that wet and willing part of herself desperate to take him inside once more. She wanted to claim him, mark him.

Ruin him for anyone else.

"I was happy too," he said softly. So softly she wouldn't have known it was him who spoke were she not watching his beautiful lips as they formed the words. "God help me, you make me forget every vow and promise I've ever made."

Heart pounding, Rose didn't resist as he dropped her hand to thread his fingers in her hair, pressing against her scalp. "You make me feel like someone else," he told her gruffly. "A good man. A worthy man, and not a selfish bastard too corrupted to ever be loved."

Her eyes burned, but Rose managed to hold the tears at bay. She bit her lip, staring at him, she knew, with her heart in her eyes. She didn't care. "You are a good man," she whispered. "The best I know." Who else would cut himself off from almost all contact with people simply to keep himself from returning to a way of life he wanted to leave behind?

"You shouldn't say things like that."

"Why not? I believe them."

"Because when you say them, *I* want to believe them." And then he lowered his head and captured her mouth with his own.

* * *

She didn't hit him this time, didn't try to pull away. It wouldn't matter if she had—Grey had no intention of letting her go.

It was folly to kiss her, even more so to go any further than that, but he was beyond caring. Nothing felt more right than holding Rose in his arms, kissing her lips, feeling her body yield against his.

She tasted sweet, her mouth hot as she let his tongue inside. Grey's fingers massaged her scalp as his lips moved lazily against hers. Hunger built inside him, demanding that he satisfy the craving his body had for hers.

Rose was all softness and ripe curves in his arms. So trusting and giving. He'd known that about her years ago when she'd looked after him after the attack. She'd heard the stories about him, seen him at his worst and yet she wanted him. What redeeming qualities she found in him, or how she'd found them, remained a mystery to him wrapped in the fear that she saw him as something he wasn't—a man he could never be except in her mind.

And yet, those fears didn't keep him from kissing her as though it was his last day on earth. And when her strong, slender hands roamed over his back in a gentle caress, he groaned against her mouth.

Those same hands slid around to his front, parting the opening of his robe to settle softly on his torso. Christ, her touch was like the sweetest agony. Nimble fingers caressed him, explored him, sliding up to push the fabric from his shoulders. He released her long enough to let the dressing gown fall off his arms. It pooled at his feet in a warm heap.

Rose touched him like he was a marvel of nature—something wonderful she'd never seen or experienced before. That was heady stuff, even for a man as experienced as he was. Women had treated him as a favored lover before, but none had ever made him feel as Rose did. Perhaps if one had, he wouldn't have moved aimlessly from lover to lover searching for that elusive emotion.

An emotion he refused to name at this moment.

His naked arms closed around her, pulling her lush body against his. She was wearing too many layers, but he would remedy that soon enough. He kissed a trail from her forehead to temple, cheek and jaw, tasting the delicate salt flush of her skin. His hands slid down to cup her full, round bottom, squeezing the succulent cheeks. He was going to kiss her there, where her thigh met her ass. He was going to kiss her in so many different, delicious places until she begged him to shove his cock inside her.

He wanted to hear her cries as he made her come, wanted that surge of masculine power knowing that he had given her pleasure no other man ever had. And for tonight he would let himself believe that no man ever would ignite her blood the way he did.

This one last time. Just this once and then he'd let her go.

"Undress me," came her whispered command.

Grey shuddered at the seductive throatiness of her voice. He was powerless against it, not once thinking about disobeying her every whim. Holding the molten chocolate of her gaze with his own, he brought his fingers up to the sash of her wrapper, giving it a tug that sent it floating to her sides.

Easily, the heavy garment slid from her shoulders and dropped to the floor, leaving her in a thin nightgown of fragile peach satin that clung to her curves, hinting at the delectable flesh beneath. Her nipples stood, rosy and tight beneath the fabric, begging for his touch. And touch them he did, dragging the pad of his thumb over one sensitive peak as his other hand pulled the strap down her arm.

"I could look at you forever," he admitted roughly as the gown joined her wrapper on the floor.

"Looking is very good," she replied, kicking the garments aside with a flick of a slender foot. "But I would much rather you touch."

There was no artifice in her tone, no knowingly seductive notes—only an honesty that shook him to his soul.

He picked her up and carried her the few steps to his bed. He placed her naked body on the sheets and stood back. He took his time studying the lush splendor of her as he opened his trousers and pushed them over his hips and thighs. When he straightened, the full length of his arousal jutted in front of him, revealed to her bright gaze as her nakedness was to his.

"Are all men as beautiful as you are naked?" she asked with a hint of a smile.

Grey grinned back. "No," he replied. "I am an exceptional specimen of manly perfection—how the hell should *I* know what other men look like naked?"

Rose shrugged as she chuckled. "You stand a better chance of knowing than I would."

He climbed on the bed, easing his body onto the

sheets beside her. "I cannot tell you. All I know is that I've never seen a woman as beautiful as you." He kissed the tip of her adorable nose as he placed his palm on the gentle curve of her stomach.

Soft pink suffused her cheeks. "You lie."

He shook his head, solemn as the grave. "Not about this." And then he kissed her again, because he didn't want to risk ruining the moment with silly chatter.

Or risk saying something better left unsaid.

Grey couldn't get enough of touching her. He could barely keep his hands in one spot for longer than a few seconds, he was so anxious to explore every silky inch of her. Finally, he braced himself on one forearm and slid the other hand between her thighs. He could wait no longer to feel her slick, wet heat.

Rose parted her legs for him, giving him full access to the sweetness between. He eased a finger into her, groaning as her body clutched at him, welcomed his intrusion. His thumb slid between her damp folds, finding the hooded nub that stiffened at his touch. Her hips lifted, heels digging into the mattress as she whimpered against his lips. Christ, it was music to his ears.

He kissed her jaw, her neck, and shoulders before lowering his head to her breast. He closed his lips over one puckered nipple, drawing it deep into his mouth with a gentle pressure and a sharp flick of his tongue. She gasped and writhed beneath him, thighs spreading even wider as he worked his finger in and out of her.

"This is frigging," he growled as he lifted his gaze

to her heavy one. She looked like Aphrodite—a goddess of desire and pleasure. "They do this in those stories you like to read, don't they?"

She nodded. "Yes," she whispered, arching her hips once more.

He smiled. "Would you like a little gamahuching, Rose?" Personally, he thought the term ridiculous, but he loved the heat ignited in the depth of her eyes when he said it.

"Yes." Her voice was little more than a strangled whisper.

Grey flicked his tongue over her nipple. "Say please."

Rose gasped. "Please."

Smugly, Grey was about to slide downward when he heard a ruckus outside in the hall. He barely had time to register the sound of voices before the moment was shattered.

The door burst open, and Grey reacted without thought, trying to shield Rose with his body. He lay on top of her, bare arsed as four men stormed into the room.

"Grey, we have a problem. Bronte has—oh, shit."

Grey looked up, glaring at his brother over his shoulder. Oh shit was right. Archer wasn't alone. Westford was with him, along with two men Grey didn't recognize. An older man, obviously of the upper middle class, and a younger one of similar rank.

Shit. Shit. And more shit.

His brother was already trying to steer the strangers out of the room, but the damage was done. Westford obviously recognized the woman beneath him, as did Archer. It wouldn't take much for the other men to put it together either, especially since they could easily see Rose's hair and part of the lower portion of her face. A social meeting with the Duke of Ryeton's charge and they'd put it together.

There was no escaping it now.

He was going to have to marry Rose.

Chapter 15

When scandals came, Grey realized, they arrived not as single spies, but in battalions.

"Bronte did what?"

"She eloped," Archer informed him as he poured drinks for the four of them. "With Lord Branton's oldest son."

Lord Branton was the older of the two men sitting across the room on the sofa—glaring at both Grey and Archer. The younger was another of his sons. "Where is Mama? Does she know?"

"Of course she does. It was she who discovered our sister's absence. Thankfully she chose to remain behind at the house. I hate to think of her walking in on your bare arse as I did. What the hell were you thinking?

Grey glared at him. "Not that someone might waltz into my private chambers without so much as a frigging knock."

"Jesus, Grey," his brother leaned close, making sure they weren't overheard. "She's under your protection."

"And now she'll be my wife." The *she* in question was hopefully in her own bed, and hopefully asleep. No need for both of them to be awake and frustrated over what had been interrupted between them.

Or was Rose lying in bed thinking of their bodies entwined? Did she fantasize about having him inside her? Were her fingers working between her round thighs, sliding through moist heat to relieve the ache?

Frig. Just what he needed—a cockstand in the company of strangers—and worse, his brother.

"Do you love her?"

"Since when have I had to love a woman to fuck her?" Yes, he was deliberately dodging that question. It made him decidedly uncomfortable. More so because just a few hours ago he'd told Rose to never use that term in reference to what happened between them. And now he was because he was too embarrassed to admit the truth to his brother.

"You're not simply bedding her, you're going to marry her."

Grey shrugged. "Our kind doesn't care about love, Arch. It's a decent enough match. And now Mama can stop worrying that she'll never have grandchildren."

Archer straightened. "That's cold, even for you."

It was the "even for you" that needled. "Gone romantic on me, have you? Must be that lovely widow you've been pining over."

Arch colored, his lips tightening, but he said nothing.

Grey inclined his head toward his unexpected guests. "Shall we forget about my rash behavior and concentrate on our sister's instead?"

His brother took Lord Branton and his son a glass of scotch. Grey followed with similar glasses for himself and Archer. When they were all seated, Grey spoke: "Why did your son feel the need to whisk my sister away, Branton? Does he have ruination or marriage on his mind?"

Impugning the honor of a man's favored son might not be wise, but Bronte was the daughter of a duke, and therefore, a prize. And Grey was in no mood to play polite. The man had interrupted his making love to Rose—something he could cheerfully strangle his impulsive little sister for being a part of.

Branton's lean cheeks flushed, but he retained control of his emotions. "I am certain it is marriage Alexander intends, Your Grace. He is very much in love with your sister."

Grey arched an imperious brow. "Really? Then why have I never met him? Why has he not come to me to ask for my sister's hand?"

It was the boy who spoke, glaring at Grey with all the defiance of a loyal brother. "Perhaps because society believes you to be some kind of monster, Your Grace. Perhaps because your sister thought you would never agree to the match."

Branton admonished his son, but Grey didn't listen. He turned to Archer instead, who stared at him with a steady, yet sympathetic expression. It didn't bother him what society thought—not really. What bothered him was that it seemed his baby sister agreed. How could she have thought that he would ever deny her happiness?

"Lord Branton, does Alexander have sufficient funds to marry my sister?"

The man nodded. "We are a wealthy family, Your Grace. The bulk of my fortune may have come from trade and investments and hard work, but I'll not apologize for it. Our family can trace its roots back to the Conqueror, and while we have skeletons the same as every other family, we've not been scandalmongers."

Unlike the Kanes was the part left unspoken.

"And you are convinced that he loves her?" The emotion might not need to be present in order for him to marry Rose, but it would be a part of Bronte's marriage, even if it killed him.

The older man nodded, face set with conviction. "I am."

Grey raised his glass and swallowed the potent liquor with one gulp. Then, he rose to his feet. "Then let us bring them back to London where they can have a proper wedding and I may give my sister away. Arch, have the carriage readied. I have something to attend to before we depart."

Of course Archer knew what he meant. To Grey's surprise, his brother acquiesced without argument—or smart-arse retort.

He left the men to fend for themselves for the time being. Perhaps he should have lit a fire under them and the servants to have a carriage ready so they could go tearing off into the night, but they would find them. And even if they had already eloped, Grey would make sure his sister had a proper wedding. And damn it, he would be there to walk her down the aisle, and society be damned.

He had promised Charles that he would give Rose the same kind of wedding, that he would see her married to a good man who would love her. He'd never intended to be a liar in that matter, but he was and he didn't even have the decency to feel that badly for it.

Although he was certain the day would come when he did.

He took the stairs two at a time, each stride long, silent and even. Camilla had stuck her head out of her door at the commotion earlier, but Grey told her to go back to bed—all was well. Fortunately, her daughter had been wise enough to remain in his room, anticipating that her mother would be curious.

She was in his room still—not in her own as he'd thought—clad in his dressing gown as she paced the carpet. When he raised a brow at her choice of clothing when her own was on the floor, she blushed so very becomingly and smiled. "It smells of you. Do you think me foolish for wanting to feel as though a part of you is with me?"

Foolish? Never. Dangerous, yes. She had his heart pounding so hard he thought it might break his ribs. "I think that if I didn't have to chase down my sister I'd finish what we started earlier."

Her breath hitched. "When will you be back?"

"I don't know. Before dinner I expect. That will give you plenty of time to decide how to tell your mother that we are to be married. If you want we can tell her together."

She stared at him as though he'd sprouted two heads and it was all her fault. "Surely we don't have to take such drastic action."

Surely the consequences of their affair couldn't

have escaped her? She had to know they had no other recourse unless she wanted to face ruin and he would not be responsible for that. "Rose, we were seen together naked and in my bed by my brother, my butler and two men who are about to become intimately acquainted with this family. We must marry."

She frowned, delicate brow pulling in a manner that made him want to kiss it smooth and promise everything would be all right. He'd do his best to make her happy.

Yes, he would willfully lie to ease her burden.

"But, you've sacrificed so much for me and Mama already." Christ, she wasn't going to cry, was she? "It doesn't seem fair that you be forced to marry me because I made the mistake of coming to your room."

"Is that what it was? A mistake?" His head swam and his heart felt strangely tight. Hadn't she told him earlier that she wanted this? Perhaps she hadn't come right out and said it, but he had thought it was obvious.

Her eyes widened, big brown circles that stared helplessly at him. "You aren't the least bit angry with me, are you?"

"No," he replied. "Strangely enough I'm not angry at myself either, although I could strangle Bronte's future father-in-law for arriving when he did."

Rose glanced away, but not before he saw the flash of desire in her eyes as she remembered what he was about to do to her before they were interrupted. "Yes, I could strangle the poor man as well."

Sweet God, were it not for Bronte he'd throw her on the bed right now and screw her senseless.

"When I return I will procure a special license for us to marry."

Her gaze flew to his. "Grey—"

He could not bear to have her refuse him now. "We will be wed. And then we will continue what we began tonight—no interruptions."

And just in case she didn't believe him, he took her by the arms and hauled her roughly against his chest, lowering his head to bruise her lips with his own. She was his now. Or at least, she soon would be.

Till death do them part.

As he left her to rejoin the men downstairs, he found himself wishing to live to be a very old man.

"I have a confession to make."

Rose looked at Eve as they sat together on a blanket in the stall with Heathcliff and his siblings. "That makes two of us. You first."

A vision of English loveliness in a pale green gown, Eve leaned close and whispered dramatically, "I went back to Saint's Row last night."

Rose blinked. "Whatever for?" She was a little hurt that her friend snuck off without her, and also concerned that Eve had taken such a risk. Her own risk had landed her somewhere between elation and despair—a horrible place to be, one she would not wish on anyone.

"To see if Dae was there." Eve's gaze dropped to the puppy sleeping in her lap. "I told myself that if he was, and if he wanted me I would run away with him rather than accept Gregory's inevitable proposal."

Well, this was certainly a turn of events. Eve had always seemed so content with her future marital expectations. "Was he there?"

"No." She looked so deflated. "When I encountered Madame La Rieux, she informed me that he had been called away to Japan of all places. Then she showed me a private exit from the club. Rose, my father was there!"

Rose took her friend's hand. Thank God her friend hadn't been found out. "I'm very grateful to Madame La Rieux for coming to your aid, but I am sorry you didn't get to see your gentleman again. Would you truly have jilted Mr. Gregory for him?"

"In an instant." Eve met her gaze with a confused one of her own. "Gregory was with my father. They were there with women I didn't know. Young women."

Two disappointments—or three if one wanted to split hairs—in one night. Poor Eve. Rose gave her a hug. "I'm so sorry, dearest."

Eve shrugged then, gently pulled out of Rose's embrace. It was obvious her friend did not want comfort—no doubt because she was trying so terribly hard to keep from falling apart. "I shan't expire from it. What is your confession?"

"Last night Grey and I were caught together and now he insists we marry."

Eve's eyes were huge blue saucers. "Define 'caught.'"

Rose stroked Heathcliff's silky ears. "Naked and in bed—that sort of caught."

Her friend looked positively scandalized—and gleeful. "No! Who caught you?"

"His brother Archer and a servant." She purposefully did not mention anything about Bronte's situation. As much as she trusted Eve, she could not be certain that none of the grooms wouldn't overhear. And since most of the household probably knew about her and Grey by dawn, it didn't seem so important to keep her own council in that regard.

"I have no doubt that your maid is getting every sordid detail—and possibly embellishment—belowstairs as we speak."

Eve frowned. "Do you think Ryeton's servants would be so cruel as to discuss you openly?"

She rolled her eyes. "They would never in a million years do anything to intentionally hurt me or Grey, but there's bound to be talk. It's that affection for both of us that makes their lips loose. I swear one of the footmen grinned at me this morning as I took breakfast."

Her friend chuckled sweetly, laughing even harder as one of the pups came up on its hind legs to lick her chin. "At least you will have dedicated servants, if not indiscreet ones."

Rose had to smile—it was that or burst into sobs. "At least."

But Eve was too observant. "I thought you would be happy to be marrying Grey. You've had feelings for him for years."

"I have." It was easy to admit it. She'd never tried to conceal her feelings from anyone but Grey himself. "But he's marrying me because we were caught, not because he loves me."

"Do you love him?"

She hesitated. Did she care if anyone overheard what she was about to say? No. "I do, and, no, I haven't told him how I feel. I couldn't bear his reaction."

Eve's face was a study in pity. "But perhaps he does love you and is just afraid to tell you."

Rose laughed aloud at that. "The only thing Greyden Kane is afraid of is facing his past. No, if he loved me he'd tell me. At least he would if he recognized the emotion."

"You are very harsh on a man you claim to love."

She shrugged—there was no real censure in her friend's tone. "I know him, Eve. And that includes knowing his faults yet loving him anyway." And that was why it hurt because she did know him, and she knew that given a choice, he would not marry her.

Despite this knowledge, she loved the idiot regardless. All she could do was hope that one day he could love her in return, that the desire and friendship he felt for her would grow and mature.

But she was terribly afraid that just the opposite would happen, that he would resent her for trapping him into marriage—one more mess of her family's making that he had to fix.

"If you love him then you should trust that he will not disappoint you."

Sage advice indeed. "It's not him disappointing me that I'm worried about."

"Oh, my dear friend."

Rose lifted her chin resolutely. "Let us speak of it no more. It is done and I will make the best of it.

What are you going to do now that your gentleman is gone?"

Eve reached over to pat Maz. The old girl's tongue lolled in gratitude as long fingers combed through her thick fur. "I fully expect Gregory to propose before the end of the Season. He'll want our wedding to happen just before everyone retires for the country—the social event of the year, you know."

She sounded so resigned. Rose had never understood how her friend could be happy having her future planned out for her. Now she realized that Eve wasn't happy, she merely accepted her fate. It was a good match, even though Mr. Gregory wasn't titled. A match to which she could offer up no opposition except that she did not love her future groom.

That simply wasn't a good enough reason not to marry amongst the aristocracy.

"You do not have to marry him, Eve."

Pale blue eyes locked with hers with a ferocity that startled Rose. "Yes, I do. He could very well be prime minister someday—and he has chosen me to stand beside him. I may not love him, but I doubt I shall ever find a man who holds me in as high regard as Bramford Gregory. I would be a fool not to marry him. Just as you would be a fool to turn down the man you love."

When Eve decided to make a point, she did a fine job of it. "You have a wonderful knack for putting things in perspective, my dear. You make me feel quite intellectually inferior."

The blonde girl grinned. "You see? I'm already learning to become a politician's wife."

They shared a chuckle and then set the puppies closer to their mother. It was almost luncheon, and time to return to the house. They brushed the straw from their skirts and gathered up the blanket, laying it over the side of the stall for the next time Rose visited Heathcliff.

Rose blinked as they walked out of the stables. Inside had been somewhat dark, but outside the day was bright and cheerfully sunny—the kind of day it should be when a woman realized she was going to marry the man she adored.

Honestly, if Eve asked her why she loved Grey, she wasn't certain she would be able to answer. There were so many things she liked about him—and probably just as many things that she did not. But when it came right down to it, he was her favorite man in the whole of her life. Not even dear Kellan had ever come close to holding so much of her regard.

Kellan. Oh, dear. He hadn't proposed, but he had paid enough particular attention to her that people had noticed. She hoped he wouldn't be too angry with her. Hoped that he wouldn't be hurt by her engagement to Grey. She had come to think of him as something of a friend and she would hate to lose that.

As they walked toward the house—standing so stately and elegant in the afternoon sun—the dark green grass pulled gently at the hem of her gown, swished against the sides of her boots. The breeze carried the scent of flowers, a lingering dampness from the rain the night before, and the sounds of carriage wheels and hooves from the street beyond—the only reminder that they were in town and not the country.

Rose tipped her head back, so that the brim of her bonnet could no longer keep the sun from her face. It truly was a beautiful day.

"You'll be mistress of all of this soon," Eve remarked, breaking their companionable silence. "This and all of Ryeton's other properties. Rose, you are going to be a duchess!"

Her friend's excitement was contagious—and terrifying. "I hadn't thought of that," she admitted with a wry grin. "Imagine that. Do you suppose people will try to curry my favor?"

"Undoubtedly. Your slightly scandalous past will only add to your popularity."

Slightly scandalous. That was a nice way to word it. Although she had no doubt that Eve referred only to her relationship with Grey and not her father, the truth about whom she'd shared with her friend earlier. Of course Eve hadn't passed judgment. She'd simply listened, sympathized, and offered a strong shoulder, everything a true friend could.

"I think a good duchess always courts a bit of scandal," she quipped. "All the interesting ones certainly did, historically speaking."

Eve agreed. "Have you told your mother yet?" she asked after a small pause.

"Good grief, no!" Rose chuckled hoarsely. "Grey said he'd tell her with me and I plan to hold him to it."

"You're acting like a wife already."

"Yes," she allowed as the reality of the situation suddenly seemed to come crashing down upon her. "I suppose I am."

Grey had asked—no. Grey had *told* her that she was going to marry him. And he wasn't angry about it. In fact, he seemed eager to have the union performed as quickly as possible. Perhaps that was to avoid as much scandal as possible, or perhaps it was because he genuinely wanted to marry her.

Lord knew, she was anxious to have her wedding night arrive. To think that they would no longer meet in secret. There would be no more need for masks or skulking about. She could spend the night in his arms without worrying about leaving the next morning. She wouldn't have to worry about being seen.

They would be husband and wife. Forever joined for better or for worse. Surely it would be for the better.

God, please don't let it be for worse.

Chapter 16

After more hours in a carriage with Archer than he ever wanted to experience again, Grey returned to Ryeton House. All he wanted to do was find Rose, climb into bed with her, and sleep for the rest of the day. Honestly, sleep. Entwine his legs with hers, sink into her arms, bury his face in the sweet warm hollow of her neck . . .

"You coming?"

Grey blinked and turned his head. He was standing in the drive with Archer and the others watching him expectantly.

Archer shook his head, clearly exasperated. "Are we going inside, Your Grace, or shall we conduct our business on the street for all Mayfair to witness?"

"Inside," he mumbled. Could he be any more of an idiot? He walked toward the door, the others falling into step behind him. Archer took Bronte's arm and led their pale, scared-looking sister into the house. Grey hadn't had much of a chance to talk to her, to let her know that everything would be fine. She probably thought he was going to rant and rave and tell her she could never see Alexander again.

Truth be told, ranting and raving was tempting. And a little fear was a small price to pay for what she'd put him through—and for thinking so ill of him to begin with. When had he ever given her reason to think him a monster?

He rubbed a hand over his face as he entered the house.

Christ.

He wasn't wearing his mask. He'd left the house in the company of strangers and traveled across half the country without the supple leather protecting him from curious gazes and whispers.

Westford was there to take outwear and ask what he could do to be of service. Grey asked him to send a light repast to his study, as his guests might be hungry. Then he led his little silent group across the great hall into the one room in the house where he felt in total control.

His sister stood by the chair where her lover sat.

"You may sit, Bronte," Grey said softly.

Her stubborn chin jutted defiantly. "I'd rather stand."

Grey shrugged. "As you wish." But he wanted to ask just what she thought remaining on her feet would accomplish.

Drinks were poured—brandy for the men, sherry for Bronte. The housekeeper arrived a few moments after with a platter of meats, cheese, and bread. Lord Branton dove in without prompting.

Grey snatched up two slices of sharp cheese and hitched one hip on the corner of his desk. Half standing, half sitting, he regarded his company—particularly Alexander. He was perhaps in his mid to late twenties. A tall, handsome lad with obviously more balls than brains.

"Lord Kemp," he began, addressing his future brother-in-law by his country title. He waited until the younger man looked at him to continue. "Your father assures me that you have genuine feelings for my sister. Is that true?"

The young man nodded his dark head. "I do, Your Grace. I love her."

Direct eye contact. That was a good sign. "I wouldn't let her go for less. Here's how the rest of this romantic drama is going to play out—the banns will be read for the next three Sundays at St. George's. After that, you and Bronte will be married in a small, intimate ceremony of close friends and family."

The young lovers exchanged startled, and delighted glances. On the social scale, Alexander Graves was beneath Bronte, but Grey didn't give a rat's arse what the society matrons thought. Bronte might eventually feel the sting of her choices, but those would be her consequences to bear.

"Also, Bronte has a dowry of forty thousand pounds." It was gauche to discuss money so openly, but the company would undoubtedly pardon him. "She also has a fortune of her own made through investments. The dowry will be yours, of course, but Bronte will retain full control of her fortune—and I will continue to oversee those investments for her." Well, Trystan would.

His sister obviously took offense to this. "Grey, I am old enough to decide what I do with my own money."

He slanted a narrow gaze at his beautiful sibling. He wasn't angry at her. He was hurt, damn it. "And I want to ensure it stays that way."

She flushed, but she said no more. Alexander reached up and took her hand. "I don't need your money, my love. And your brother merely shows his own concern and love for you by wanting to ensure you have financial independence."

Much of the flush bled from Bronte's cheeks. *Well done, Kemp.* Perhaps this marriage might work after all.

"Lord Branton," Grey spoke, turning his gaze away from the happy couple. "Would you like to say anything?"

"I would like to offer the newlyweds the family home in Essex until they find a domicile of their choosing."

Grey's lips curved. "You are very generous, sir." And wanting to show his own wealth and property—that was all right. The man made it clear on the search for the missing lovers that he was heartily embarrassed by the entire situation. Grey tried to ease his mind, but he'd obviously not been as successful as he had hoped.

"And I would like to apologize, Your Grace." It was Alexander who spoke. He rose to his feet and faced Grey without flinching. He was tall and lanky, with a good breadth to his shoulders and a straightness in his spine that spoke well of the man he was to become.

"Kemp?"

The younger man cast a loving glance at her before turning his attention back to Grey—and

Archer as well. "I hope you will forgive me for my impulsive behavior. I thought only of having Bronte for my wife. Had I thought with my head instead of my heart, I would have seen that reason and spoke to you before acting so rashly."

Grey had to grin. *Before* acting so rashly. The young pup had no trouble looking him in the eye and telling him that he would have whisked Bronte away if he'd forbade the union. That might have made for an interesting morning.

"Apology accepted. Now, I think perhaps we would all like very much to bathe and rest. Branton, perhaps you and your family would care to join us for dinner tonight? We will celebrate the coming nuptials."

Despite the short notice, the earl nodded. "We would be honored, Your Grace."

"Excellent. Now, if you will excuse me, I have to obtain a special license."

Bronte frowned. "I thought you wanted the banns read."

Grey grinned, unable to resist giving her a shock to make up for the one she'd given him. "Oh, it's not for you, dearest. It's for me."

And then he left her with her mouth gaping.

Grey returned later that day from procuring the special license at Doctor's Commons just in time to dress for dinner. Well, he hadn't actually procured the license. His solicitor did while Grey waited in the carriage. He had no desire to feed the gossips anymore than he had to.

The day wasn't about to get any easier. He did not relish the idea of having to face Camilla and tell her that his promise to her husband was well and fully broken. Not that she knew he'd ever agreed to keep his debauched hands off of Rose, but he knew and that was bad enough.

When he entered the drawing room just before eight, he found Rose already there. Her mother had yet to come downstairs. The Graveses and his own family had yet to arrive as well.

A few moments alone with his betrothed. How unexpectedly uplifting.

His fiancée rose to her feet when he walked in. "I understand from the bustling of the servants that we're having company for dinner tonight?"

"Good evening to you too." He smiled. "Yes. Bronte's fiancé and his family will join us, along with my own bunch."

"I suppose we will announce our engagement as well?" Rose clasped her hands before her, as though she wasn't sure what to do with them. As Grey approached her, each step measured and slow, he thought of several tasks he'd like to give those nimble fingers.

"Yes, though I have no desire to steal Bronte's thunder." Was she embarrassed to face the men who found them together? She had to be. He would do everything he could to keep attention from her. And if one man so much as *looked* at her with censure in his gaze . . .

"Do you like her betrothed?"

"He seems a decent sort, yes." He was almost to her.

She swallowed, delicate throat constricting. "That's good. Did you tell her about us?"

"Sort of."

It was nice to see the anxiety in her features give way to something else—curiosity. "Sort of?"

"She knows I went for a special license. I imagine Archer informed her of my choice of bride. No doubt she and Mama will want more details than I plan to give. I fully expect to be exhausted by the pair of them by the end of the evening."

Rose's lips curved. "What would the *ton* do without us to feed them scandal broth?"

Grey returned her grin. "The lot of them would starve."

They chuckled, and as the humor faded, Grey tilted his head to look at her. "You look beautiful tonight."

She flushed, pleasure lighting the dark depths of her eyes. "You don't have to say such things."

"I know I don't, but you are my fiancée and it's perfectly acceptable for me to voice my thoughts aloud. It's rather refreshing after keeping them to myself for so long."

That got her attention. One of her fine, high brows twitched. "How long?"

He grinned. "Since you were old enough for me to think such thoughts without being lecherous."

They stood no more than six inches apart. Close enough that he could see how amazingly flawless her skin was—not a freckle in sight. Close enough that she could see every twist and knot of his scar—and yet she barely glanced at it. Her gaze was riveted on his. She didn't care that he was disfigured—at least not on the outside. Not on the inside either, so it seemed.

"I've never been a good man," he confessed—a little more hoarse than he liked—"but I promise to be a faithful husband." It was the best he could offer, because as much as he would like to be the man she wanted, it wasn't going to happen.

Her smooth brow puckered. "I haven't actually consented, you know."

"Rose, we have to marry."

"No." She raised sparkling eyes to his. "I want you to ask me to marry you—not demand it. I don't care if it has to be done. I want to feel like I have a choice."

"If you did have a choice, what would it be?" He was on dangerous ground with her, inching into territory better left unexplored for both their sakes.

Rose smiled, and everything was right with the world. "Ask me and find out."

His hands came up, seemingly of their own volition, to cup her face. She was so delicate, yet so strong. Her entire world had been turned upside down, and yet she faced him with a teasing glint in her eyes and a soft flush of color in her cheeks.

"Rose Danvers, will you do me the extreme honor of becoming my wife?"

Were those tears dampening her eyes? And was it joy or sorrow that put them there?

"I will."

He knew that they had to marry regardless, but hearing her say those two little words was like someone kicking his heart through his ribs. It hurt, but there was such unfathomable joy that came with it—such terrible happiness that Grey had no idea what to do with it. He'd never felt anything like it before.

Holding her face, he lowered his head and hungrily claimed her mouth with his own. Her lips parted for his tongue as her fingers bit into his arms. A trickle of warm wetness brushed against his thumb. She was crying.

A sharp gasp came from the open door. "What the devil is going on here?"

The kiss and its magic were broken. Rose stepped back, and Grey dropped his hands, but he wasn't willing to let her go just yet. He placed one arm behind her back, holding her close so that they faced her mother together.

Camilla did not look happy. In fact, she looked like any mother would to walk into a room and find her daughter being molested.

"Mama," Rose began. "It's not what you think—"

"It is exactly what you think," Grey countered, drawing his friend's stormy and narrow gaze. "I have asked Rose for her hand in marriage and she has accepted. I regret that you had to find out this way, but I was too overcome with joy to contain my feelings."

He could feel Rose gaping at him. He didn't look at her, not because the words were a lie, but because they were all too damnably true.

"I do hope you will give us your blessing, Camilla." She might not approve based on his past or his age—though it was only a ten-year difference. Grey mentally crossed his fingers that she would consent, because it would make any rumors she heard about them much easier to ignore.

The older woman's green eyes filled with tears as she covered her mouth with her hands. "Oh my, this is wonderful!"

Grey hadn't realized he'd been holding his breath until it rushed out of his lungs. Camilla apparently didn't have the same apprehensions her late husband had.

Rose clutched at his arm, as though she couldn't believe it and needed help to remain upright. Her attention, however, remain fixed on her mother, who was now coming toward them with her hands outstretched. Grey took one, Rose the other.

"I am so happy for both of you," she announced with a sniff. "I admit, I thought this might happen. I have seen how the two of you look at each other."

It occurred to Grey to point out that there was a difference between love and lust, but he wisely kept that opinion to himself. Then, he remembered that Charles Danvers had never even looked at another woman let alone broken his wedding vows by sharing another's bed. Perhaps Camilla understood something he did not.

Rose and her mother embraced. Grey didn't listen to what they said, but it was something that made tears run freely for both of them. As the two women held each other, Camilla looked up and locked her gaze with his. She looked genuinely happy.

Grey inclined his head, returning her smile with a faint one of his own. Perhaps for some, love and lust went hand in hand.

What a thoroughly charming, if naïve, idea.

* * *

It was Thursday, May 31. Her wedding day. Rose awoke and met the bright morning sun with a mixture of apprehension and anticipation.

Birds sang, the breeze blew, and there was nary a cloud in the sky as she peered out her window at the garden below. The servants had set up an arbor there, near the fountain, and a few chairs sat on the thick green grass.

Not many guests had been invited. She'd always thought her wedding would be a kind of storybook affair, at St. George's with attendants and a flower girl and white doves flying overhead. Silly, perhaps, but it was still a little sad letting go of the fantasy.

At least the groom was right, she allowed, turning away from the window. And while she might not be able to lay claim to his heart, she could be reasonably certain of his liking for her, and that it wasn't simply desire or duty that led to their union.

Love could grow. That was what she told herself, but it didn't ease the shadow of dread hanging over her heart and dimming the sun on this beautiful day.

She turned her thoughts to happier affirmations as she rang the bell for Heather. She was going to be a duchess, something every girl dreamed about as a child. She was going to have a husband she adored, family she enjoyed. And tonight, she would go to Grey's bed without the thought of scandal or the fear of being caught. She'd be a liar if she said that the thought of having him make love to her for the rest her days wasn't enough to put a smile on her face.

If she closed her eyes she could almost feel his

hands on her skin, his fingers probing, touching her in all the right places. His mouth, burning a moist trail from her head to her toes—oh, and the things in between!

A soft knock on the door pulled her from her carnal thoughts. Her cheeks were hot as she called out for her maid to enter.

But it wasn't her maid. It was her mother—already dressed for the ceremony in a pearly lavender satin gown. Rose's eyes filled at the sight of her. It was the first time she'd seen her mother out of black since her father's death.

"I thought we could breakfast together," her mother said, closing the door behind her. "I'd like a little while longer to enjoy you as mine alone."

Rose wiped at her eyes. "You're going to make me cry."

"Well, then it will be your husband's job to make you smile."

Rose blushed again, remembering where her smile had come from just moments before. Her mother laughed softly—a lovely sound. "Do we need to discuss what happens on the wedding night, my dear, or have you thoroughly educated yourself by stealing my magazines?"

"You knew?"

Camilla frowned, but there was no anger in it. "Do you think I'm a fool? Of course I knew. At first I thought I should stop you, and then I realized that I didn't want you going to your marriage bed as frightened as I was." She shrugged. "I suppose there are some who would think that awful of me to let you read such things, but I've never been very good at playing the hypocrite. You're not frightened are you?"

"No, Mama."

Her mother nodded, then sat on the edge of Rose's unmade bed and regarded her with a gaze that was strictly maternal. "Are the rumors I've heard true, Rose? Were you and Greyden found in a compromising position?"

"We were." There was no point in lying. "I'm sorry, mama."

Her mother waved a hand. "You wouldn't be the first to be sent to the altar this way." She folded her hands in her lap. "As long as you want this marriage, Rose, I'm not the least bit concerned about how it came to pass—although a little more discretion might have been preferable."

"I do want it. Very much. I love him."

Camilla sighed into another smile. "I know. I believe he loves you too."

Rose shook her head. "He has yet to say it."

"Men always feel it long before they say it, my dear. They're a little slow that way."

She laughed, just a little—enough to ease the tension from her shoulders. "Thank you for being so understanding, Mama. It means so much to me."

Her mother stood and came to her, taking both of her hands in hers. "I suppose I could rant and give you a good head-reading, but no good ever came of that. You've made your destiny and now all that's left is to follow through. My main concern isn't that you never give the gossips something to natter about. My only concern is your happiness, and I think Greyden makes you happy."

"He does." She frowned. "And oddly miserable at times."

She was pulled into a warm, sweetly scented embrace. "That's love, dearest. Welcome to it."

Heather had arrived, so after sending her downstairs to ask Cook to have breakfast sent up, Rose bathed and allowed her maid to start working her magic while she and her mother nibbled on warm croissants with strawberry jam and sipped delicious cups of chocolate.

Her wedding gown was pale ivory silk with tea-dyed lace at the neckline, bustle, and hem. Mr. Worth himself, while not the designer, would have to approve of the fine detail in the embroidery that covered the bodice and circled around her hips.

Heather gathered her hair up in strips, curling it with tongs and pinning it in place until the back of her head was nothing but a neat nest of smooth curls. A large pearl and gold comb slid into place behind the mass. Matching pearl drops and a multi-strand choker completed the look. The pearls had been her mother's, and before that her grandmother's. And now they were Rose's, to be passed on when she had a daughter of her own.

Children. Good lord, she could barely believe she was getting married! Thoughts of children could wait.

Ivory slippers and a bouquet of orange lilies, white orchids, and tea-colored roses completed the ensemble. The flowers were perhaps a bit much, but Rose thought them pretty.

"Everyone is here," her mother announced, turning away from the window to bestow a broad smile upon her daughter. "I wish your father was here to see you."

The mention of her father killed some of Rose's joy. "He wouldn't be happy to see me marrying Grey."

Camilla's brow tightened. "Nonsense. Grey is not the same man he was back then. And your father would only want to see you happy."

Rose wasn't quite certain her father would agree with that assessment of Grey, but it really didn't matter, did it? Her father was gone—had taken his own life. And Grey, regardless of what her father had thought of him, had stepped in and cleaned up Charles Danvers's mess.

"Shall we go down?" Her mother offered her arm. "No doubt your groom is anxious to claim you."

They walked down the stairs together, through the hall. Rose's heart pounded rapidly, and her fingers trembled as they clutched the stems of her flowers. When they reached the glass terrace doors, music began to play. Startled, Rose peered through the glass and spotted Grey's sister Bronte playing a harp near the arbor. Of course he hadn't hired musicians. She wasn't bothered by that, however. It was much more intimate to have Bronte play.

"Ready?" her mother asked.

She took a deep breath, held it, and then slowly exhaled. "Ready."

They stepped out onto the terrace, and the few guests present turned to watch her. Grey's family smiled at the sight of her—and Archer made her smile with an exaggerated wink.

Eve was there as well. Dear, wonderful Eve. She was actually crying a little, dabbing her eyes with a lacy handkerchief as Rose and her mother drew near.

And then, she saw Grey standing near the vicar beneath the arbor, and her feet moved toward him without being told. Her mother sat down beside Eve and Rose made the rest of the journey on her own.

He wore a stark black jacket and trousers with a crisp white shirt and a cravat the same tea-color as the lace on her gown. In his lapel was a single orange lily. His thick hair was brushed back from his handsome face. And, yes, that was a little silver at his temples. His strong jaw was freshly shaven, and she could smell the faint scent of his shaving balm.

Perhaps the most wonderful thing was that he had chosen not to wear his mask. It was mostly family present, but to show his scar in front of Eve meant so very much to her.

His pale blue eyes seemed to smolder with heat as she approached, filling Rose with feminine pride. Perhaps he didn't love her, but he looked at her as though she was the most beautiful woman on earth, and for now that was enough.

He didn't speak as she came to stand beside him, which was just as well because she doubted she would be able to form a reply. He simply took her right hand in his left and gently squeezed.

Three weeks, Rose realized as the vicar began to speak. It had only been three weeks since that first encounter between them at Saint's Row. In fact, it was three weeks to the very day.

If that wasn't a happy coincidence—surely a good omen—she didn't know what was.

"Do you, Rose Elizabeth Danvers . . ." Rose tried to listen but it was so difficult with Grey watching her as he was. It was only when Grey smiled that half-smile of his that curled her toes and made the base of her spine tingle that she knew the vicar had asked her that very important question.

Smiling, she glanced at the old man before returning her gaze to Grey's. "I do," she replied. "I certainly do."

Chapter 17

It wasn't the wedding she deserved, Grey thought as he sat at the table, eating luncheon with his bride and their guests, but no one would ever know that from looking at her.

Rose hadn't stopped smiling since the ceremony. She was smiling now as she chatted with his mother. Was he alone responsible for that smile? That was too heady to contemplate. And far more responsibility than he was comfortable assuming. If he could make her smile so wonderfully, then he could take it away just as easily.

He never wanted to be the man who broke Rose's heart, and it killed him knowing that he was going to disappoint her very badly one day. It was unavoidable, he could only hope that it was a long time in coming.

And that she might forgive him for it.

It would be easy to think that she had tricked him somehow. That marriage had been her goal since she first sought him out three short weeks ago. But that wasn't fair. He was too smart to fall for such a ploy. And Rose could never be that devious.

As if sensing that she was the object of his

thoughts, his wife turned her attention—and that amazing smile—to him. Grey raised his glass to her, hoping that his gaze told her all the things he could not until they were alone.

He was not disappointed. The smooth apples of her cheeks brightened with the sweetest shade of pink that filled his head with thoughts of rubbing the rough of his jaw against her bottom cheeks until they turned a similar hue. And he would—just as soon as they were alone.

For now he would have to be content with watching her and being grateful that he didn't have to stand up any time soon.

Luncheon—instead of the traditional breakfast—was a drawn-out affair full of conversation and joviality. Even Grey experienced a lightness that he hadn't felt for some time. And when Archer raised his glass and toasted to his and Rose's happiness, it brought a lump to Grey's throat that refused to budge even after the cake had been cut.

He thanked his brother for it when he walked his family to the door later.

"I meant every word of it," Archer replied, giving him brief, fierce hug. "Even though you don't deserve a woman as fine as yours."

Didn't Grey know it.

Rose's mother was the last to go, departing several hours after the other guests as she was returning to the country not only to give the newlyweds time alone, but because it was where she felt most comfortable.

Seeing the tears in his wife's eyes as she bid farewell to her mother, Grey promised that they would join Camilla as soon as the Season was over.

And sometime he would have to take his wife on a wedding trip. It was only proper. Perhaps they could go to New York and visit Tryst. She deserved a trip. She deserved a husband who would show her the world and all the wonders of it.

Once the carriage bearing Camilla was gone, Grey offered Rose his hand and led her into the house. "I have a wedding gift for you."

"You do?" Myriad emotions crossed her features, the last of which was dismay. "I don't have anything for you."

He squeezed her fingers. "You are gift enough." And he meant it. There was nothing she could give him that he wanted because he already had the one thing he'd most desired—her.

Inside he directed her to his—their—bedroom where he poured them each a glass of wine and pulled her down onto the bed beside him. It was nice, this companionship between them, this ease that marriage had created now that they no longer had to hide their regard and desire.

"Do you want to know what your gift is?" he asked as she snuggled into his side.

"Yes." Her eager brown gaze rose to meet his, accompanied by a shy smile. The sight of her took his breath away. He was unable to help himself, and lifted the back of his fingers to caress her cheek.

"Look behind the pillow," he instructed, taking her glass of wine from her to free both her hands.

She turned, giving him the opportunity to admire the snug fit of her bodice as it hugged her sides and the curve of her pretty breast. When she faced him once more, she had a magazine in her hands. "*Voluptuous?*"

Grey smiled at the naughty light in her gaze. "A full subscription. Perhaps you will discover between the pages other activities you would like to sample with me."

It wasn't much of a gift, certainly not an expensive one, but Rose embraced him as though he had given her the world—and he had the wine stains on his cuffs to prove it. "Thank you!" She kissed his cheek. "Oh, Grey, thank you so much!"

"It's only a magazine, Rose, but you are welcome."

She pulled back so that he could see her face, the delighted flush in her cheeks. "It's not just a magazine. It's a gesture of . . . trust and respect. Do you know how many husbands would forbid their wives to read such literature?"

Yes, he did, and he would hardly call it literature. "I'm of the opinion that a husband can only benefit from his wife reading this kind of material."

A coy, seductive—wonderfully wicked—smile curved her full lips. "Perhaps we will both benefit."

He could shag her senseless right then and there. He gave her back her wine instead, and positioned himself with his back against the headboard. He tugged her close, turning her so that she sat with her back against his chest. "Read to me."

She looked horrified at the idea. "What? No, I couldn't."

Grey trailed his fingers down the side of her neck, smiling smugly as she shivered. "Read it. Please."

Her fingers trembled slightly as they parted the pages. "What would you like to hear?"

"A story," he replied, brushing the tip of his finger along the curve of her ear. "Something that will take a while." Because the longer she read, the longer he could touch her at his leisure.

" 'Lady Jane's Confession,' " she read, her voice a little huskier than normal, " 'Or, An Adventure in Lust.' "

Grey gently pulled a pin from her hair and set it on the bedside table. "Sounds interesting."

He listened with one ear as his bride began to read in that sweet, rich voice of hers. There was a slight tremor to her words—anticipation perhaps? As she spoke, he plucked each pin from her hair until he was able to comb his fingers through the thick, silky strands, draping and arranging them over her right shoulder so that the left side of her neck was left vulnerable to his attentions.

" 'Oh! I cried as my lover slid two fingers into my dewy chasm, awakening the most voluptuous of feelings within me. Gently he moved his hand in and out, frigging me with the most maddening patience.' "

Passion quivered in her tone, sending a bolt of lust straight to Grey's groin. His cock stirred, hardening quickly as she continued to read. He bowed his head, brushing his lips along the curve of her ear, dampening the delicate flesh with the tip of his tongue. Rose shuddered against him, her breath hitching. But she never faltered.

" 'I was ready to spend, writhing beneath the force of his ministrations, when suddenly he fell between my splayed thighs and took my aching little clitty into his mouth, forcing me to erupt in such sensation that I thought I must have lost all reason.' "

Christ.

He slid his hands up her sides, around to her front to graze her breasts, the round swells just above the neckline of her gown. The fingers of his right hand eased inside her gown, manipulating the flesh inside her snug corset, until he found her hardened nipple, blunt and tight against his hand.

Rose gasped, arched her chest against his touch. His cock swelled in response. And the fingers of his other hand slid around to her back, to fumble with the row of tiny buttons that kept him from her bare skin.

"Keep reading," he commanded. Did she hear the rasp in his voice? Did she know how badly he wanted her? How much she excited him by reading such explicit words aloud?

" 'I regained my senses to find my lover hovering over me, his thick cock in his hand as he guided the large purple head of it to my quivering cunny. He thrust his hips and filled me with one stroke, forcing me to cry out at the rapture of his intrusion.' "

Buttons undone, Grey pulled her gown from Rose's shoulder, immediately fastening his mouth on the sweet flesh there. He pinched her nipple with his other hand. She was so responsive, rounding her spine to push her breast against him. Her legs moved beneath the narrow skirts, and he could see her thighs pressing together. Did it ease the ache, or make it all the more intense?

Suddenly, he knew what he had to see. Removing

his hand from her corset, he pushed her gown down to her waist before moving so that he could pull it over her hips and toss the froth of fabric to the floor. She was left in her corset, drawers, and stockings. He removed his own shirt—male pride swelling as well as his prick at her frank and open appreciation of his bare skin. His shoes and stockings went as well, so that he was left in nothing but his trousers as he returned to his previous post behind her on the bed.

"I want you to keep reading," he murmured against her temple, taking her right hand in his and guiding it to the cotton-covered juncture of her thighs. He nudged her legs apart with his own hand, sighing at the dampness that warmed the slit in her drawers. He drew her fingers down to that void in the fabric. "I want you to touch yourself while you read."

Her flawless cheeks must have turned four different shades of crimson at his wish, but Rose didn't remove her hand. She slipped nimble fingers inside the flimsy garment, spreading the opening wide so he could see the dark curls beneath, a hint of tender pink flesh. Grey watched with held breath as she parted the lips of her sex and slid a finger inside. Her breath hitched.

God almighty, she was going to be the death of him. He moved his hands to the hooks of her corset as she began to read once more. The little minx had a much stronger voice this time, as though she knew the power she had over him.

" 'Within minutes I experienced the familiar swell

inside me and I spent again with a great flood of juices and a most enthusiastic cry.' "

Her corset joined her gown on the floor, leaving nothing but her short chemise between his hands and her full breasts. He cupped them in his palms. They were heavy, with tight tips that begged for his mouth. Soon enough he'd taste them. Right now this torture was too exquisite to end just yet.

Rose's breath was becoming shallow as she read, her fingers working quickly between her thighs. Grey watched, dry mouthed as she pleasured herself. She reclined against his chest, legs splayed, the scent of her arousal drifting up to tease him like the sweetest, faintest spring breeze.

" 'But my lover was not done with me just yet. His member still stiff within me, he bade me to roll over, so that my belly rested on the pillows he'd placed beneath me. I half lay, half knelt before him, the round globes of my bottom lifted. He caressed them with his hands and then I felt his mouth on the right cheek. He licked me and nipped at me like a stallion at a mare. His tongue slid b . . . between my nether cheeks, touching me where no other man ever had before, awakening within me new sensations of such voluptuousness that I cried out at the sheer—*Oh, Grey*—joy of it.' "

Rose's shoulders pressed into his chest as she lifted her hips to her own hand. Grey lowered his mouth to her shoulder, simulating on that delicate skin what the lover in the story did to his woman. He squeezed her breasts, pulling open the fragile cotton to claim the naked swells as his own, pinching her nipples and rolling them between his fingers. She gasped at the force he used, but didn't ask him to stop. In fact, she pushed her chest against his hands.

"'He slipped the massive monster between his legs into me from behind, awakening my already replete quim in the most delicious fashion. He took me like an animal, pressing his chest to my back and stroking my aching clitty with ruthless strokes until we spent together in a symphony of delighted cries.' Ah! Grey, *ohh*."

Eyes closed, Grey held Rose tight against him as orgasm washed over her heated body. Her cries awakened something long dormant inside him, something so long forgotten he had no idea what it was, he only knew that it felt as though someone had punched him in the stomach and made him like it.

He plucked the magazine from her lax fingers and set in on the bedside table. Then he shifted her in his arms so that her chest was against his. Her eyes were molten, lazy pools of the richest chocolate. Her face flushed and dewy like the petals of her namesake. And those lips—those succulent, arousing lips—were parted, waiting for his kiss, unknowingly inviting his cock.

"I liked watching you make yourself come," he whispered. "I think you liked it too."

She stared up at him, the coyest of smiles lifting her lips. "I liked knowing you were watching." And then his natural seductress brought her fingers to his lips—the same fingers she'd used to pleasure herself.

Lying with Grey, feeling the hardness of him against her hip, Rose experienced a surge of feminine power she'd never known before. His eyes darkened to a stormy blue as she pressed her damp hand to his mouth. And then his lips parted, enveloping her fingers in wet heat. His tongue licked her from knuckle to tip, swirling slowly from top to bottom, as though he wanted to savor every taste.

Her body throbbed in response, moving to press against him. She couldn't look away from the desire in his eyes, the shaded and highlighted lines of his rugged face. The lighting was such that she could barely see his scar, but it didn't matter. His scar had never mattered to her. She thought he was beautiful.

How amazing to be able to look at him this way without any masks between them. To lay with him, knowing that soon he would slide his hardness inside her and know that it was indeed her he claimed. She could clutch the muscular curves of his buttocks and have him know it was her fingers that held him. She could take his erection into her mouth and watch him watch her, knowing that he thought of no one else—that she was fulfilling his fantasy as much as her own.

It was empowering. It was amazing. And it made her feel so naked and vulnerable it was almost unbearable.

He released her fingers and lowered his lips to hers. She could taste the faint musk of herself on his tongue—not unpleasant at all. She wasn't the least bit shamed by it. In fact, she tangled her tongue with his, rejoicing as he groaned into her mouth.

When he broke contact with her lips, he continued the kiss down her neck and chest to stop at her breasts. Body tight with need, Rose waited, humming like a string wound too tight as Grey's lazy tongue lightly circled her nipple—teasing but not quite touching.

He did this with the other one as well, making the peak so hard it was almost painful, but he didn't give her the relief of his mouth.

"Wretch," she ground out, hoarse with need.

Suddenly her nipple was in his mouth, assaulted by the wet whip of tongue, the hot suction of his lips. She cried out, arching into the pleasure/pain as his teeth joined the torture. It hurt, but it felt so good! Between her legs she felt a flood of humidity with a pulse of need that made her rub herself against his side like a cat in heat.

When Grey's mouth left her breast she moaned, but then he was moving downward and all thoughts of protest died in her throat when she realized what he was going to do.

Wanton that she was, Rose raised herself on her forearms to watch, tingling all over in anticipation.

Grey kissed the damp curls between her thighs. Rose's hips jerked in delighted response. He chuckled, bathing her in warm breath that raised gooseflesh all over her body and sent a shiver down her spine.

Another maddening and somehow chaste kiss. She wanted more. She knew there was more. She tried to arch her hips, but he had her hips in his strong hands, holding her immobile on the coverlet.

Up on his elbows, he raised his gaze to hers, so

smoky and hot and slightly shuttered with heavy lids. He had the loveliest eyelashes.

"What do you want me to do, Rose?" His voice was so deep. So sultry, it drew the heat of her to him—right to where she ached to clench him deep inside.

Rose was too far gone to care about shame or propriety. And she was just experienced enough to know that maidenly reserve—especially with this man—was just plain foolish.

She lifted a hand to trail her fingers through his thick hair with a gentle caress. "Taste me," she commanded. "I want you to lick me like I've read. I want your tongue inside me."

Was it possible for a person's eyes to turn to molten silver? That's what seemed to happen to Grey's at her words. The hottest silver, with a hint of blue.

He didn't speak. But still holding her gaze, he removed one hand from her hip and used the fingers to part the lips of her sex. The air was cool against her heated flesh, awakening yet more need, heightening her already gargantuan arousal. Rose watched, torn between his eyes and his mouth as he slipped the firm length of his tongue inside her. His stubble abraded her thighs and the sensitive flesh where her bottom met her legs and she didn't care. It felt so good as he made love to her with his mouth—and when his tongue slid up through the delicate folds to find her "clitty" she fell back on to the bed with a desperate cry.

She was still sensitive from the orgasm she had given herself and she came again very quickly against his tongue, fingers still tangled in his hair, holding his head between her thighs as waves of heat and pleasure ripped through her.

He gave her a moment to recover, kissing his way back up her body. This time she met his lips eagerly, licking the salt of her body from his mouth.

She slid her hands between them, unfastening his trousers. Then she pushed the finely made garment over the lean lines of his hips. His flanks—slightly concave—were like silk over steel, the curve of his buttocks as firm and delicious as she remembered. Grey pushed up onto his hands, making it easy for her to undress him. When her arms reached their limit, she used her toes to seize the light wool and pulled them down his long legs. He kicked them onto the floor.

She pushed at his chest and he let her, rolling easily onto his back in the middle of the huge bed. Rose came up to straddle his thighs. Her hair hung wildly around her shoulders. Between her legs she was soaked and she could smell her own musk, and yet Grey looked at her as though she were an angel come to earth.

"Beautiful, perfect man," she whispered, not caring that she said her thoughts aloud.

His fingers gripped her thighs. He was so strong and yet so gentle. So fierce and yet so tender. No wonder the women in his past had become so enamored with his lovemaking. He could make a lady a whore and a whore a lady—or a combination of the two and treat both accordingly. The perfect lover who knew when to make love and when to . . . what was the word? Ah yes, *fuck*.

Leaning down, she kissed his firm lips, nipped at them with her teeth, laughing softly when his fingers bit harder into her legs. She kissed the whisker-roughened skin of his jaw, the smoother, almost fragile flesh of his neck, sucking where heat and salt mated at the base.

Down his chest she moved, tasting him with lips and tongue. She toyed with his flat nipples, ran her tongue between the bones of his ribs, down to his shallow navel. He was muscle from shoulder to ankle—perfect just like the sculpture of David, only more so for his humanity.

When Rose reached the jutting length of flesh between his legs, Grey pushed himself up so that he was leaning against the headboard.

She flashed a teasing gaze at him. "What do you want?" she asked, mimicking what he had done to her earlier.

He grinned, not knowing the meaning of shy. "I want you to suck my cock."

It wasn't difficult. Rose simply did what she wanted, and Grey's moans let her know if she was doing it right. When his hand came down on the back of her head, she knew she was. She licked the long, thick length of him, slid her mouth all the way down until she felt the tip in the back of her throat. She grazed him lightly with her teeth, applied a sucking pressure with her cheeks. And when he arched his hips, she sped the up and down motion of her head until he pulled her hair, fingers biting into her skull, a hoarse cry tearing from his throat.

Wiping her mouth, Rose came up on her knees. Grey was slumped against the headboard, but his gaze was on her. Never had she seen such an expression on his face. It wasn't anger, though it was certainly fierce and a little frightening. And it wasn't humility, though there was some humbleness there as well. So when he suddenly reached out and wrapped his hand around the back of her neck, Rose didn't know what to do. Then he hauled her against him so roughly she couldn't catch herself, and landed hard against his chest. He didn't even seem to notice, and then his mouth was ravaging hers and Rose didn't care either.

She had enjoyed giving him pleasure, had felt an undeniable power as she did it, but it meant something to him that she had done that for him—something she was either too inexperienced or too dumb with desire to comprehend.

She sat on his lap, thighs locked around his hips as he kissed her with such hunger she was helpless to respond. All she could do was take it, and let him take his fill. She could feel him hardening again beneath her and she delighted in it. He wasn't done with her, not yet. He wouldn't be done with her until he'd emptied all the emotions swirling inside him, until he'd exhausted the fire within them both. Rose welcomed it. She would take whatever he wanted to give her, and give whatever he commanded of her.

She lifted her hips, reaching between them to brazenly guide the head of his shaft to the entrance to her body. The stories in *Voluptuous* didn't do this part of it justice. There were no words to describe the nudge of delicious invasion, the exquisite stretch of being filled, the completion of having him fully and totally inside her. Slick friction was only part of the pleasure. Staring into his eyes and seeing how much he wanted her was more. Feeling the tension in his body as he clung to her, knowing she would be bruised in the morning and would be glad for it, was only another component of this amazing act. How could she possibly describe it when she didn't wholly understand it? No one could.

They moved slowly, Rose rising up and down on Grey's lap as their gazes held. She could scarcely breathe under the force of those eyes. Couldn't think. She could only feel and the pressure of it filled her heart near to bursting. Such pressure in her chest, such an ache in her throat. She closed her eyes, tried to squeeze it all away.

"Look at me," Grey commanded, holding her hips so that she was poised above him, the head of him just inside her slick walls. She wanted to bear down, but he wouldn't let her. "Open your eyes and look at me."

How could she deny such a plea? Even if she had the will, her body did not. She opened her eyes, heart pinching at the vulnerability in his. He didn't understand why she closed her eyes. He thought it was because of him.

Sinking down to fully engulf him once more, Rose gently churned her hips, stoking the fire within herself, fanning the flames that begged to burst out of control. She leaned into him, pressing her breasts against the hard wall of his chest. The crisp hair there rubbed against her nipples, making those muscles inside her clutch at him with even more desperation.

She pressed her lips to the scar that ran almost the

entire side of his face. The skin was warm, satiny. She ran her mouth the length of it, pressing gentle kisses to the once-ravaged flesh. Grey's hands released her thighs to slide around her back, holding her close with the combined strength of his arms. Was that a sob that just brushed her ear?

Rose wrapped her arms around Grey, quickened the pistoning of her hips as her tumultuous emotions threatened to erupt. "You are the most beautiful man I know, Greyden Kane," she whispered. "And it has nothing to do with your face."

Suddenly she was flung backward onto her back. Grey's body still joined with hers, he grabbed one of her thighs and lifted it, pressing her knee to her chest as he thrust hard. His other hand was beneath her neck, holding her head still as his mouth claimed hers in a kiss that was as beautiful as it was brutal. He slammed himself into her willing—welcoming—wetness, thrusting so deep. So deep.

Rose clung to him. She wrapped her other leg around his back and lifted her hips to accept the ferocity he offered. Oh, God. It felt so good. If he didn't give her what she wanted soon she wasn't going to survive. She wanted . . . she needed . . .

"Grey!" It wasn't a warning of her oncoming climax—it was a plea that he join her. That he finish this the only way it could end for either of them without leaving them bereft.

He didn't disappoint her, and that meant more than either of them would probably ever admit. One last, violent thrust and his cry mixed with her own. They came together, clutching each other tightly as orgasm tore through them both, leaving them boneless and mindless in its wake.

Afterward, too satisfied to do anything but lay there after Grey drew the coverlet over them, Rose nestled against his side, her thigh draped over his.

"I love you," she whispered, once she'd regained the power of speech.

Grey said nothing.

When she raised her head to—rather bravely, she thought—look at him, she found him with his eyes closed, face turned slightly toward her, lips barely parted. He was asleep. Obviously, she thought as she eased herself down beside his warmth with a wide yawn, he hadn't heard her confession.

Chapter 18

"I do."

"You are the most beautiful man I know."

"I love you."

Grey heard the words, spoken in Rose's honeyed voice, echoing over and over again in his head. He'd been told similar sentiments in varying degrees and manners over the years, all by different women. Some of them had truly meant what they said, while others told him what they thought would garner them the brunt of his favor. Regardless, he'd never heard as much sincerity in all those other times combined that he'd heard from Rose last night.

Rolling onto his side, he tucked his arm beneath his head and watched his wife sleep. His wife. His beautiful, surprising, sensual wife. The last thing he ever thought or wanted to be was Rose's husband, and yet here he was. And if someone—a fairy godmother or some other magical being—offered to undo it all and return him to the life he had a month ago, he wasn't sure he'd agree. In fact, he was certain he wouldn't.

He should feel guilty for that, he knew. He had promised Charles Danvers that he would stay away from his daughter and he had willfully and recklessly broken that vow despite the best of intentions. However, Charles Danvers had made many promises as well, promises he broke when he took his own life. So if his old friend's ghost ever did come a-haunting, Grey would feel reasonably justified in telling him to sod off.

Rose stirred slightly, rolling to her side so that she faced him. The dark fringe of her lashes lay soft upon her cheeks. The pillow pressed against her face, giving her a childlike appearance. Her full lips parted slightly on a sigh and remained open. Grey smiled, wondering if she was going to wake up in a puddle of drool. He didn't care if she did. He didn't care if she snored—which she didn't—or if she talked in her sleep. None of these things could ever be a flaw in his eyes.

In fact, he didn't know what she would have to do to make him think her anything less than perfect.

And she loved him. Christ. What was he going to do about that? Eventually, she was going to ask whether or not he loved her. And what would he say?

Did he love her? He'd always thought of love—when he wasn't being cynical about it—as something honest and selfless. He never really had any trouble with honesty. Many people would say that he was sometimes *too* honest. But selfless? Even he had to allow that he was probably the most selfish person he knew.

He brushed a lock of hair back from her face. Rose's nose twitched but she didn't wake. Meanwhile, outside dawn was just raising her radiant face.

It promised to be a bright and sunny day. Birds were already singing and he could hear the groundskeepers and gardeners begin their daily work. Normally he would sleep through it all, but they'd retired so early the night before that he was wide awake and sorely tempted to wake Rose just so he'd have someone to talk to.

Normally he'd simply get up and go about his business. If he were in the country he'd saddle his horse and go for a ride. Given the hour, he probably could get away with doing the same in London, but a tear through Hyde Park wasn't the same as riding hell bent for leather over his own vast estate.

Besides, he'd have to leave Rose to do that. And that simply wasn't an option.

God must have taken pity on him, because it was at that moment that the woman beside him opened her eyes. They were glazed and somewhat unfocused, but Grey grinned at the sight all the same. She closed them again, rubbed them with her fists and then looked at him once more—slightly more aware.

"Good morning," he said.

A slow, bright smile curved her lips. "It's hardly morning. It's still dark out."

It was bright enough for him to see her face, and that was all he needed. "Close enough."

She rolled away from him and threw back the covers. Naked, she strode across the room.

"Where are you going?" he demanded, bolting upright. Was that fear causing his heart to race like that?

Rose shot him a sheepish glance over her bare shoulder. "Morning constitution," she replied and slipped into the adjoining bath. The door clicked shut behind her.

Grey fell back against the pillows, cursing himself for being such an idiot. Had it been so long that he'd forgotten what it was like to wake up with a woman? And what the hell had he thought she was doing? Running away from him without a stitch of clothing?

He rubbed both hands over his face. He was an idiot. She'd made him an idiot.

She returned but a minute or so later, climbing back into bed and snuggling against him. She felt good—like warm satin against his skin.

"What are we going to do today?" she asked brightly.

He trailed his fingers down the supple length of her arm. "What would you like to do?" The question left a slightly bitter taste in his mouth. Was it going to begin already? She'd suggest going out and he'd say no. Or she'd want to have a party and he'd say no. He'd thought it would take longer than this for her to regret marrying him. Not that he'd given her a choice.

Selfish.

A baby-fine cheek rubbed against his shoulder. "I would like to stay in bed all day. Can we?"

He stilled. "Do you mean that?"

Her head lifted and she met his gaze with a cheeky one of her own. "I do. I want your full attention for the entire day."

Grey grinned and rolled her onto her back, easing himself between her splayed thighs. "I think that can be arranged."

Thank God it seemed his bride was a little selfish too.

Rose never would have fancied Grey the kind of man given to enjoying picnics, but there he was, lounging on the blanket beside her. Propped up on one elbow, his long legs stretched out, he popped a grape into his mouth and chewed thoughtfully, his gaze seemingly fixed on the fountain just a few feet away from them at the front of the garden.

He looked good in the sunlight—so rugged and hale. The scar only served to give him a dangerous edge, one that she found dastardly appealing. Without it he would be a devastatingly handsome man, but honestly she thought she preferred him with it. It kept him from being too perfect.

He didn't wear his mask as often anymore. But then, he never had worn it much around home from what she could remember. Only at Saint's Row, when there was a chance of being seen.

Perhaps he liked the air of mystery it gave him. Perhaps it attracted women drawn to an anonymous lover. Well, there would be no more of that!

Or perhaps he only wore it when he wished to hide.

"Ruined Ryeton." What drivel. He wasn't ruined. He was merely . . . damaged. An awful thing to think of one's husband, no doubt, but ruin couldn't be repaired. Damage could.

Now, if only she could sort out just how to make that happen, all would be perfect.

He wasn't a monster as he seemed to think. She remembered him wanting her to look at him while they made love the night before. The vulnerability in his eyes as he looked at her. He had been as affected by their union as she, so much so that it was difficult to meet his gaze after revealing so much of herself. Perhaps that was why he seemed to find the fountain so fascinating as well.

She didn't try to push him into conversation. She was happy to sit there, nibbling on the banquet Cook had prepared, and watch him. He watched her when he thought she wasn't looking. What did he think when he looked at her? Regrets? No, she couldn't see any of that in his expression. He looked at her as though he couldn't quite figure her out. And oddly enough, sometimes she thought he looked at her as though he was a little frightened of her.

But that was just foolish. Wasn't it?

"When Heathcliff is old enough to leave his mother, I would like to bring him into the house. Is that agreeable to you?"

Palming a bunch of grapes, Grey turned his head to smile at her. Oh, that smile. "Of course. He's to be your pet and friend. I expect him to become one of the family."

One of their family. The thought caught the breath in her throat. They would have a family someday. She could be pregnant now for all she knew—last night they hadn't used a condom. Was it wrong to hope that she wasn't with child? Of course she wanted to be a mother one day, but not right away. She wanted time with Grey first. After years of wanting him to notice her, she wasn't keen on the idea of sharing his attention with an heir.

So, of course, Rose decided this would be a good time to discuss such matters. "I would also like to know if you know ways to prevent pregnancy."

He choked on a grape. She lurched toward him, but he coughed and spat the villainous fruit on the grass. He wiped at his watery eyes with the back of his hand as he turned his face to her once more. "That will teach me not to chew sufficiently."

Rose smiled shakily, her heart skipping. "You scared me." What if he had choked to death right there in front of her?

She couldn't even begin to contemplate life without him.

"You stunned me. That's not exactly something you bring up out of the blue." His eyes twinkled. "Was it the mention of your puppy? Are you frightened of having a litter?"

When he looked at her like that—like they were friends and so much more—it made her insides feel like leaves blowing in the wind. Her gaze slid to her lap. "I would like us to have some time together before we have children."

Some of the tenderness drained from his expression. "I should have taken precautions last night. I'm sorry. I didn't think of children, only . . ."

"Only what?" If it made his eyes warm like that, she wanted to know what he'd been thinking.

His gaze locked with hers, so sharp and hot. "I thought only of how it felt to be naked inside you."

A hard throb pulsed low and deep inside her, bringing sexual awareness speeding to the surface. It had been different without the "French Letter." It had been better than the times at Saint's Row, even though she wouldn't have thought that possible. But that difference wasn't entirely physical, she knew that. "And how did that feel?" Lord, was that warble really her voice?

Grey regarded her from beneath heavy lids. "Like heaven."

Dear God, the man knew exactly what to say to her. She was already leaning toward him, pulled by some invisible string. "Really?"

He reached out, cupping her jaw with his warm hand. His thumb brushed her lower lip, pulling it just a little. "Really. And if we weren't out in the open I'd show you."

"I'd let you," she replied breathlessly.

The air between them seemed to crackle. If lightning struck the ground between them it wouldn't surprise her.

Grey rose to his feet and held out his hand. "Come with me."

Rose put her hand in his, letting him help her to stand. He kept hold of her hand, twining their fingers together as he drew her into the garden.

"Where are we going?" Rose asked, heart beginning to thump in earnest. Her skin was tingling, tightening in all the right places.

"You'll see."

He led her to a small stone shed deep in the garden. It was covered with ivy and flowering vines, its windows stained glass like a chapel's. The door opened easily, and Grey led her inside.

It was obviously the gardener's shed, but instead of being dirty like she expected such a place would, it was neat and tidy. Not a cobweb or bug to be seen. The air smelled of earth and grass, sweet and warm.

Grey closed the door and propped a shovel under the latch. Then he turned to face her.

Knees shaking, Rose let him pull her into his arms, wrapping her own around him. She didn't protest when he lifted her and set her up onto the smooth wooden table, and she didn't utter a sound when he lifted her skirts and slid his hand beneath.

But she did gasp when she felt his fingers against her inner thigh.

"You're not wearing drawers," he accused softly—amused.

She smiled slyly. "I thought perhaps it might be better if I didn't."

He chuckled, the fingers of his other hand going to the front of his trousers as he stroked her naked flesh. "Darling Rose, you are the loveliest surprise I've ever been given."

Given. As though she were a gift. Her chest tightened. And then he took her hand and guided it to the thick length of his erection and she forgot all about sentimentality. He felt like hot, hard satin against her palm and fingers.

"Stroke me," he commanded.

Feeling naughty as he jerked in her hand, Rose leaned forward to lock her gaze with his. "Wouldn't you rather be inside me? Feel me wet and hot around you?"

His eyes widened and he groaned, wrapping his own hand around the one that held him. She could feel him pulsing against her palm. It aroused him when she talked like that. Good, because it aroused her as well. She was already squirming, ready to beg for his fingers inside her.

"I will be inside you," he growled, sending a shiver down her spine. "Later. Right now, I'm going teach you other ways we can please each other."

The hand over hers began to move, showing her how to handle him, what felt good. Beneath her skirts, his fingers climbed higher, finally touching the damp curls at the apex of her thighs. He parted the lips, found her clitoris with his thumb and slid a long, broad finger into her welcoming wetness. Then a second.

And like the night before, their gazes locked, making Rose tremble in places she didn't know existed.

"You are so tight," he murmured. "Hot and wet. You taste so good like salt honey. Did you like having me eat you last night?"

He could bring her so close to the edge simply by talking. Rose lurched forward as his fingers curved inside her, finding a spot that made her clench her thighs in delight. "Yes." She gasped, moving against his hand. Then she brushed his ear with her lips and whispered, "Did you enjoy spending in my mouth?"

Apparently she wasn't the only one inflamed by words. His free hand grabbed her by the back of the head and held her while his mouth plundered hers. His fingers were ruthless inside her, his thumb almost brutal in it strokes. Sensing the violence of his need, Rose quickened her hand as well. Her finger wrapped tight as she roughly moved them up and down the length of him. A little slip of moisture from the head moistened her palm, lubricating her ministrations. Grey groaned in her mouth and she knew he was close. So was she.

She came first, but only by a second. As soon as she cried out against his lips, her internal muscles grasping at his fingers, Grey stiffened. He pulsed in her hand, emptying himself onto the table beside her.

He withdrew his fingers from her, but didn't move away. He stood at her knee, his forehead resting against hers and pressed a handkerchief into her hand. She didn't really need it, but she wiped what little stickiness there was away. Then he used it to wipe the evidence of their tryst from the tabletop.

"Thank you," Rose murmured. "That was delightful."

Grey chuckled, flashing a lopsided grin that made his eyes sparkle like aquamarines. "You make me feel . . ."

"Yes?"

He shook his head, surprising her with the degree of awe and self-consciousness in his expression as he drew back, and helped her down from the table. "That's it. You make me feel."

Rose smiled and kissed him. It wasn't exactly a declaration of love, but he was getting closer.

It would do for now.

Like all good things, it was inevitable that their perfect day come to an end.

Grey and Rose were in the library after dinner, sharing a glass of wine as they lay on opposite ends of the sofa reading. Rose had her feet in Grey's lap and he rubbed them with one hand as he perused the newspaper he hadn't gotten around to reading that morning. Likewise, Rose was reading her mail.

It was said mail that brought reality crashing down around them once more.

"Hmm," she said.

That was all it took for him to jerk his head up and turn his attention to her. Never mind that there were Indian uprisings in America or unrest and fighting in Turkey. "What?"

She glanced at him over the top of what appeared to be an invitation. "Oh, just an invitation to a party next week."

She was as transparent as water, God love her. "If you would like to go, you should accept." He forced a smile, even though dread crawled up from his stomach and left a bilious taste in his mouth.

There was no surprise in her expression. A little disappointment, but nothing at all what he expected. "I didn't think you would want to come."

What did she mean by that? Of course he didn't want to go, but she made it sound so . . . cowardly that he didn't. Or rather, that was how it sounded in his ears. Although, if he was pressed he would admit that there was nothing in her expression or tone to support that theory.

"That doesn't mean that you should not go if you wish."

She seemed to ponder that for a moment, then

flashed him a mischievous grin. "I would like to see what it is like to be received as a duchess."

How could he not chuckle at that? How could he not be acutely relieved that she didn't press or pout?

So why was he strangely dissatisfied all the same?

"Then we shall have to make certain you are dressed like one. Would you like an appointment with Mr. Worth? I'm sure he can be persuaded to have a new gown ready for you in time."

Her eyes widened in delight. "Do you think so?"

"I would bet on it. Remind me to show you the combination for the safe in our bedroom. The Ryeton jewels are yours now."

If she grinned any wider her face would surely split. "Our bedroom. I like the sound of that."

Grey shook his head with a smile. She was more excited about sharing his bed than she was about diamonds. Interesting, funny girl.

The humor faded from her eyes.

"What's wrong?" He kept his voice calm.

Her brow puckered ever so slightly. "What should I tell people if they ask about you? Before I could plead some kind of ignorance, but as your wife . . ."

She shouldn't have to ask these things. It shouldn't be a burden for her to bear. "Tell them I'd rather slit my own throat than associate with them."

Rose looked horrified at the thought—so much so that Grey's heart pinched. She really was adorable. "Or, you could tell them that you have thoroughly exhausted me in bed and I am unable to draw the strength needed to rouse myself."

That brought a sparkle back into her eyes. "I rather fancy that. It would certainly set tongues wagging, wouldn't it?"

It certainly would, Grey allowed with a mental grimace. Unfortunately, wagging tongues wasn't something Rose was going to be able to avoid as his wife. People were going to talk—to her and about her.

"Rose, you might hear things about me—"

"I don't doubt it. I've already heard about your legendary escapades."

This time the grimace showed. "I hate to admit it, but some of those stories are true."

She arched a brow. "I wager a great deal more than 'some'."

Adorable and cheeky. "I . . ." He scowled. Christ, he was an idiot. "I would hate for you to be hurt by gossip, however factual it may be."

To his surprise, Rose set her correspondence aside and leaned forward to place a long, slender hand on his thigh. "These stories, they're about your past, correct?"

He nodded. "Yes."

"I believed you when you told me you would be faithful to me. Did you lie?"

"Of course not!" If he didn't deserve to be asked, he would have demanded an explanation. "I may not be a saint, but I'm not a liar." Not generally. Not in that respect.

She shrugged and took up the glass of wine from the table in front of the sofa. "Your past cannot hurt me, Grey. I'm sure there are things you have done that would . . . unsettle me, but you are mine now, and mine alone. I will endeavor to have faith that you are made of better stuff now, and ask that you believe that I am not as spleeny as you may think."

"Spleeny is not a word I would ever use to describe you," he replied. Amazing perhaps. Incredible. Shaggable—if that was even a word.

She smiled, took a sip of wine and placed it on the table. Then, she moved to slide her body up his. "Have you ever made love in this room, Grey?"

"No." He hadn't. He had in the front parlor, and in the music room, the blue drawing room, and once in the pantry, but never in this room.

His naughty wife grinned. "Neither have I."

His laughter was cut short as she kissed him. And as her curious fingers found their way to the hard ridge in his trousers, he actually felt hopeful. Maybe being married to him wouldn't be so horrible for Rose after all.

He could always hope.

Chapter 19

Grey kept his word. He not only showed her the Ryeton jewels, he handed them over for Rose to wear as she wished. The stones were amazing, the settings exquisite. She wore a parure of diamonds—and nothing else—to bed that same evening just so Grey could watch her sparkle.

She wore those same diamonds to the party at Lady Frederick's the next week. They went divinely with the silver and black Worth gown she wore.

He also kept his word and didn't attend the party with her—not that she ever imagined he would. And it was just as well, since Rose knew she would have to face Kellan—something better done alone.

But even if it weren't for Kellan, she wouldn't be upset with Grey for not being there with her. She knew how stubborn he was when she married him, and didn't expect him to change overnight. She also was beginning to get a good idea of why he chose to hide away from society.

At first she thought it was because of his scar, and that people would talk about what had happened to him, but Rose suspected that a larger component of her husband's reclusiveness lie in the "hypocritical" nature of society he'd gone on about in the past. She suspected that Grey feared returning to the world that once coddled and kowtowed to him, would cause him to revert to his once abhorant behavior.

Personally, she didn't believe that would ever happen. He had changed too much and become too good to ever be that man again, but she would be lying if she didn't admit to feeling some trepidation herself. She couldn't bear to lose him.

But other than that, she refused to think about whether or not he would ever accompany her socially. It was too depressing.

So here she was, arriving alone at Lady Frederick's. It felt odd to attend a party alone, without chaperone or some kind of supervision. She was a married lady now, and needed no one looking after the preservation of her virtue.

Not that it had worked when there had been someone doing just that.

"Good evening, Your Grace."

Rose paused on the wide steps. Holding her skirts so they didn't collect drag, she turned to see a beaming Eve coming toward her as Lady Rothchild alighted from the carriage.

"Eve!" Rose cried, holding out her arms for an embrace. "How good to see you!"

"You're so beautiful," Eve told her as she hugged her. "Marriage obviously suits you."

Rose couldn't help but blush a little—either from the praise, or the memory of all the things she and Grey had done to each other in the short week of their marriage. One week and a day to be exact.

"You know, I believe it does," she replied, stepping out of the embrace.

Eve's smile turned hopeful. "In two months we shall see if it agrees with me as well."

Rose cast a brief glance at Lady Rothchild who had yet to join them, then turned her attention back to her friend. "Gregory proposed?" She wasn't surprised as it had been expected, but she had thought her friend would share the news with her in a more private setting.

The blonde nodded, the moonlight turning her hair silver. "We have yet to affix an exact date, but shortly after Parliament dissolves, I expect to become Mrs. Bramford Gregory. They say Victoria plans to bestow a title upon him, you know."

Rose's brows drew together. She couldn't tell if her friend was happy or not. "What about your mystery gentleman?"

Eve shrugged and looked away. "He's gone. Gregory is here, and my family has expectations of me." Her gaze locked with Rose's once more. "It's a good match."

Which of them was she trying to convince? Rose nodded. "Of course it is. And Gregory adores you. I've no doubt you will be very happy."

Her friend only nodded. Anything else she might have said was left silent as Lady Rothchild met them. There was a hint of censure in the older woman's gaze as she regarded Rose. Of course, she didn't say anything. Rose knew Lady Rothchild liked her, she always had, but she obviously did not approve of Rose's marriage—or the manner in which it came about. And it was obvious that she did not want her daughter touched by scandal.

Of course, a little scandal could be a good thing, and actually improve one's social standing. Everything in moderation. What a strange world it was.

Rose greeted the countess with polite ease, starting a little when Lady Rothchild dipped a slight curtsey. That was right. She was a duchess now. Regardless of what Eve's mother thought of her, Rose's rank was higher.

That was enough to put a big grin on her face.

The three of them entered the house together, and when they reached the ballroom, the footman there announced them. It wasn't Rose's imagination—when her name and title echoed across the room, a silence fell, followed by a hushed buzzing as she stepped across the threshold.

Whispers. They were whispering about her.

She couldn't stop the flush that spread across her chest and up her neck to her cheeks, but she held her head high as every set of eyes watched her entrance. She even managed a slight smile. Some people watched her with contempt—although those were few. Others watched her with interest or thinly veiled pity. And there were those, of course, who seemed curious—those were the ones to watch. Those were the people who would speculate over every little tidbit until they found a story they could believe and, of course, share with others.

Gossips.

Surely all these whispers couldn't be over her marriage to Grey? They weren't the first couple to have been caught together and then married. Certainly a few of the guests present had similar origins for their unions.

Of course, they were the first to fall this Season. Bronte's erstwhile elopement had been reined in and stifled, so Rose and Grey would be all the rage until someone else gave them something to talk about. Wonderful. With any luck someone would do something scandalous soon.

Eve stepped forward, chatting gaily as though nothing was amiss. Of course, Rose knew better. Her dear friend was simply trying to distract her, and Rose loved her all the more for it.

"Good evening, ladies," came a familiar male voice.

Rose turned and saw Kellan standing beside them. He looked very dashing in his black and white evening dress, his gold cravat lending a touch of boldness to the otherwise stark ensemble. He didn't look the least displeased with her. In fact, when his dark gaze met hers, Rose thought he looked rather concerned.

"Mr. Maxwell," she greeted with a smile. "How lovely to see you."

He offered his arm. "May I escort you to the refreshment table, Your Grace?"

Right now a friendly face was just what she needed. Rose slid her hand around his arm and asked that Eve and Lady Rothchild excuse her. Then, she allowed Kellan to direct her across the room.

"I must confess I'm surprised that you are speaking to me," she told him softly as they walked. She was keenly aware of many eyes watching them.

There was nothing but friendship in his expression. "Have you wronged me in some way?"

"I thought . . ." Heat rushed to her cheeks. "I was obviously mistaken."

His free hand patted the one she had on his arm and chuckled. "Forgive my impertinence, dear lady. Allow me to ease your conscience. While I might have had certain notions as to where our friendship might head, I never had any expectations. Nor do I feel that you led me to believe otherwise. You may rest easy on that account."

It was all she could do not to sigh in relief. "Oh, I am very glad to hear that."

At the refreshment table, he poured them each a glass of punch, and then pulled her aside, through the balcony doors and out into the night where they might talk with more privacy. But, gentleman that he was, he made sure they stayed in the light, where anyone might see them.

"Rose, forgive my familiarity, but I must speak to you."

There was something sharp in his tone that had her brow furrowing. "You may speak freely with me, Kellan. I hope you know that."

Her use of his Christian name seemed to comfort him. He gazed down at her with eyes as black as the night around them but twice as bright. He was a lovely man, but her heart belonged to pale blue eyes and sardonic lips capable of great tenderness.

"I want you to know that if you are ever in need of a friend you can come to me. I will always make myself available for you."

Rose's frown deepened. "I appreciate that, but

why do you say this? Is there something you know that I do not?"

He angled himself so that his back was partially toward the house. No one watching could see his face, or attempt to discern what he was saying by watching his lips. "I will be blunt. Rose, I know what Ryeton is like. I've seen how he treats women." He held up his hand when she would interrupt. "I do not wish to speak ill of your husband, whom I know you care for dearly. I only want you to know that if you ever find yourself in the position of needing protection, I will give it."

"Protection?" Rose repeated dumbly. Obviously he wasn't offering her a carte blanche—not with an expression so tormented. "If I didn't need protection before, why should I need it now?"

His eyes darkened, if that were possible. "Before you had your mother to watch over you. I just want you to know that *if* you ever need to leave your husband's house, if you should find yourself in some kind of personal danger, you can come to me. I cannot say it any plainer than that without casting aspirations upon the duke."

Rose gaped at him, and there was nothing refined about it. Her jaw dropped and her eyes were so wide and unblinking they began to itch. Finally, she managed to close both. "I'm touched by the gesture, but I have nothing to fear from my husband." The fact that he thought she did irked her.

Was that the reason for all the whispers, people felt sorry for her?

"Of course." He didn't sound convinced, which irked her even more. How dare he presume to know

Grey better than she? How dare he assume Grey to be a scoundrel of such low account!

Her temper would not be denied, though she struggled to keep a tight rein on it. "Do you honestly believe I would have married him if he were the kind of man I should fear?"

Kellan glanced away. "I do not know the exact circumstances of your marriage, only what I have heard and I place little trust in them, but the duke would not be the first man to overwhelm a young lady with his attentions."

A snort of disbelief tore from her throat. "Trust me, Mr. Maxwell." No more Christian name familiarity for him! "Greyden Kane has never had to 'overwhelm' anyone." He was overwhelming enough on his own.

It was too dark to tell for certain, but she thought Kellan might have flushed. "Since we are speaking plainly, I must express my surprise that you would fall so readily into the clutches of such a man."

Rose's eyes narrowed and she took a step toward him as the flames of anger leaped to life within her breast. "By 'such a man' you refer, of course, to the duke. The very same man who came to my father's aid when his so-called friends abandoned him. The same man who took my mother and I in after my father's death and kept us from a life of poverty and no prospects. The very man who was a friend when others—including you—turned their back." Rage tightened her jaw and clenched her fingers into fists. "I would rather fall into his 'clutches,' Kellan, than depend on your friendship, which has proven itself far less palatable than this swill Lady Frederick calls punch. Excuse me."

She shoved the glass into his hand, not caring that some of the sugary liquid splashed over his fingers. And then she whirled on her heel and left him standing alone, and went back inside to face the stares with as much dignity as her anger would give her.

"How is marital bliss treating you?" Archer asked as he and Grey sat together in the matching wing-backed chairs in Grey's study, chatting over a glass of brandy. "Blissfully?"

"It's all right," Grey repeated—without as much enthusiasm as he should have.

Archer frowned, dark brows pulling together over his bladelike nose to give his usually convivial face a fierce appearance. "It's not yet been a fortnight and it's 'all right'? That's rot, Grey."

Instead of sighing, or perhaps slapping his brother in the head, Grey drained his brandy and reached for the bottle to pour himself another. "I'm not discussing my marriage with you." What he wasn't going to discuss was that his beautiful wife had changed somehow and he blamed himself for it.

He couldn't quite put his finger on it, but ever since Rose had gone to the party at Lord and Lady Frederick's, she had begun to spend more and more time at home. Granted, as Archer so eloquently pointed out, they hadn't quite been married a full two weeks, so perhaps he was just being unreasonably suspicious.

Still, Rose seemed to be more selective over her invitations. When she wasn't with him—and he wasn't complaining about her wanting his company—she attended events that were smaller, more intimate. And she spent a great deal of time with her good friend, Eve Elliott.

"I think the gossip has been hard on Rose." There, he said it.

Archer's expression was something of a mocking grimace. "You *think*? Even you are not that obtuse. Of course it's been difficult on her. I heard the entire gathering went silent and then started whispering when she walked into the Fredericks's soiree. No one's surprised that you bedded her, they're all amazed that you married her. All of London's wondering what's so special about her while you hide your face like a guilty man and feed the speculation. Christ, the entire *ton* thinks you're like the beast in that fairy tale."

Except the beast eventually turned into a prince once again. That wasn't going to happen in this case. He'd never been a prince and never would be.

And of course, Rose hadn't told him about the party. If he'd known . . . What? What would he have done? By then the damage had happened. There was nothing he could do to change it.

Still, he felt damned rotten knowing what his reputation did to her. He could only imagine what they said, the speculations they snickered over.

Grey sighed. "If I showed up at one of these parties it would only make it worse."

"How could anyone knowing you have the bollocks to face them make things worse?"

"Because Rose would know that at least half of the women there have shared my bed. She would know that the men despise me. She would know what a . . . *'beast'* . . . arse I was. Am."

Archer shook his head before raising his glass. "I think she knows all of that already. Seems she likes you regardless. Do you think she's a little, you know, touched?"

For a second, Grey's temper flared. Until he saw the amusement glittering in his brother's bright blue eyes. He laughed. "She has to be for marrying me, don't you think? Personally I'm grateful for it."

Archer smiled. "I'll have Mama invite her to the theater Tuesday night. A little family support will help. Plus, you know how Mama is. She'll force others to bend to her will with a gentle smile on her face."

That was indeed true. "Thank you. I'm sure Rose will appreciate the gesture."

His brother took another quick sip of his drink, his gaze dropping. "There's something else."

Grey frowned. "About Rose?"

"About Bronte." Archer seemed to have trouble meeting his gaze. "About the wedding."

It was still weeks away. The last of the banns would be read this Sunday. "What of it?"

"She's asked if I would walk her down the aisle."

Grey schooled his features, but it was hard. Christ, that hurt. All the more because he had expected it. He had suspected that his sister would be embarrassed—perhaps even ashamed of him. And he would never want the taint of his past to ruin what should be the most wonderful day of her life. But thinking she wouldn't want him to stand for their father, and finding it to be true were two different things.

"Well," he said. His voice was hoarse and raw. "That is certainly her decision and I will honor it."

"It's not her, Grey, it's Lady Branton. Bronte only wants to please her new in-laws."

Grey forced a smile. Archer might wish that true, but he heard the lie in his brother's tone. His sister hadn't been hard to persuade. "Of course she does. It's no matter, Arch. You'll do a much better job of it. You are much more graceful than I am."

Archer regarded him with such a sorrowful, guilty expression that Grey had to blink and look away. There was a strange burning feeling behind his eyes.

"You wanted to do it, didn't you?" Archer asked quietly. "You were going to stand up in St. George's and say to hell with all of them for her, weren't you?"

He could do little more than nod. He should have cared more about his family. Should have thought about how his actions and scandals would reflect upon them. As the head of the family he should have taken better care of them.

His gaze lifted, meeting Archer's. "I'm sorry," he murmured.

It was as though the younger man knew exactly what he meant and heard all the other things he wanted to say but couldn't put into words. "I know. I'll talk to her. Once she knows—"

"No!" Grey's head jerked up, eyes burning now

with something he recognized—determination. "You'll say nothing. You will escort her to her groom as she asked. Do you understand me? Say *nothing.*"

His brother's displeasure was obvious, but he nodded in agreement. "Fine. I won't say a word. You're an arse for forcing me to do this, though."

That he was an arse seemed to be the general consensus of the day.

"You will be making our sister's wedding all the more pleasant for her. There's no shame in that, Arch." What was next? Would Bronte ask him not to come at all? Because he knew why Lady Branton hated him so badly, and she might not stop at denying him the pleasure of giving his baby sister away on her wedding day. How far could a woman scorned spread her influence over an impressionable young woman? Bronte loved him, but she loved Alexander more—and she knew Grey would do whatever she asked.

Well, Georgiana—Bronte's future mama-in-law—would be in for a surprise if she thought she could deny him the joy of seeing his sister happily married. If Bronte asked him not to attend the wedding, Grey would go straight to the source. She'd back down in an instant if she thought he might tell her husband about that time at Drury Lane when Grey had fucked her in his private box during a staging of *Othello.*

If memory served, the lady in question came like a banshee during Desdemona's death scene. Grey had to smother her screams with his hand, laughing as he did so.

The memory left a sour taste in his mouth. There was no sweetness in shame, and that was what he felt when he thought of his past. He was not a nice man. Certainly not the beautiful man Rose thought him to be.

But then, what did an innocent like Rose know about men? Perhaps a little more than he wanted to credit her with. Her naughty magazines might not spend much time dealing with human emotion, but they did spend a great deal of time revealing just how much men were led by their pricks.

Archer finally relented and agreed not to say a word to Bronte or Alexander about any of it. And then he took his leave, having made plans to call on Lady Monteforte.

"Does Lady M know it is her you are determined to have?" Grey asked as he walked his brother to the door.

Archer grinned. "I'm not sure. I suspect she thinks I'm trolling after her daughter. Either that or she's afraid of my manly allure."

Grey laughed aloud—a large guffaw that felt good as it tore from his throat. "No one in their right mind would be afraid of a runt like you." Of course it was a joke. Archer was leaner than Grey, but he was the same height if not a little taller.

"The ladies are," Archer lamented. "They're always afraid that I'll ruin them for another man."

"I'm sure you would at that." Grey pushed his brother out into the drizzly afternoon. "Go frighten hapless women and leave me alone."

When his brother finally made his way down the

steps to his waiting mount, Grey went in search of his bride. He found her through the aid of the housekeeper, who informed him that she was in the stillroom sampling some soaps and creams her lady's maid concocted.

She was a delicious mess. Her gown was rumpled from God only knew what, and bits of hair had escaped the chignon on the back of her head, to wisp around her dewy face. Pots bubbled on the stove, filling the room with the scent of flowers, cloves, and other olfactory delights.

"Smell this," she commanded when he entered the room. She shoved a small jar under his nose. "Do you like it?"

It smelled something like bay rum, only richer. "I do."

"Good. It's a new shaving soap for you." She set it down on the counter and brushed hair back from her face. "Has Archer left already?"

Leaning his forearm on the counter, Grey smiled at her as he leaned closer. She really was the most delectable little thing. "He has."

She returned the smile with a half one of her own. "So you were bored and decided to come looking for me?"

He trailed a finger over the exposed part of her upper chest. "Something like that."

Blushing prettily, she brushed his hand away, but not before giving his fingers a squeeze. "Well, I'm busy, so unless you want to help Heather and me in our endeavors, you will have to find some way to amuse yourself."

Grey sighed. "All right, I'll go, but only because I'm likely to ruin whatever beautification potions you two lovely witches are brewing."

Behind Rose, the maid Heather giggled. Grey grinned at Rose's wide-eyed disbelief as she looked at first her maid and then him. "Have you always charmed women so easily?"

Grey's humor faded. "I'm afraid so." And then softly, "If it offends you . . ."

She shoved her palm into his shoulder. "Don't be an idiot. Flirt with my maid all you want. But I don't want to hear anything from you when I smile at the footmen."

God she was amazing. He slipped his arms around her, not caring that the maid could see, even though she made great pretense of not looking. "Are you going out tonight?"

Rose pushed against his chest. "Grey, I'm all sweat and grime."

"I don't care. Answer me, are you going out?"

She arched a brow. "Are you trying to get rid of me?"

"No." He held her gaze as he lowered his head, but he didn't kiss her. He simply let the words drift across her sweet lips. "I'd keep you here every night if I could."

She shivered delicately. Christ, he could kiss her. He could make love to her right there. "All you have to do is ask."

"I won't have you give up your society for me."

Something flickered in her dark eyes. "It wouldn't be much of a sacrifice."

Because of the gossip? How long before she began

to resent him for it? He could just push her away and be done with it—tell her to go out and find herself a lover, but he would rather carve up the rest of his face than do that.

Instead, he took the coward's route. He didn't ask for an explanation. He didn't want to know what she'd heard about him or what they'd said about her. He simply smiled and decided to take advantage of what time he had left. Because he loved having her with him, and spending what had always been lonely hours in company better than any he might have deserved or ever wished for.

"You are sweaty and grimy," he murmured in his most seductive tones. "And now I find I am as well. Shall we meet in the bath in, say, twenty minutes? I'll scrub your back if you'll scrub mine."

Of course, when she joined him later, and their naked bodies came together in the hot, soapy water, all thoughts of scrubbing disappeared. And so did—for a brief while—all of Grey's misgivings.

But he knew they'd be back.

Chapter 20

Surely nothing awful could happen at a tea party?

This was Rose's hope as she took a seat beside Eve in Lady Rothchild's parlor. She sipped at a cup of tea and nibbled on the various and delicious refreshments offered by her best friend's mother.

They discussed books and charities, music and theater. Conversation was kept very polite and bland given the youth of some of the ladies in attendance. In fact, it was downright boring, but Rose happened to like boring.

At least no one was looking at her as though she'd sprouted horns. No one had whispered when she walked in. That was definitely a good thing. Perhaps Eve was right and the whole scandal of her marriage was already blowing over, making way for some other juicy tidbit.

She ran her palm over the blue velvet of the sofa where she sat. This was where she and Eve often gathered over the course of their friendship to discuss their dreams and hopes for the future. Rose could remember sitting in that very spot as she informed Eve that she wanted to marry the Duke of Ryeton. Eve had thought her mad, of course, but supported her regardless. And Eve had wanted to marry a spy—a rakish one at that. Of course, he would give up his rakish ways for her. Rose had deemed it a perfectly sound plan, and they laughed.

How odd that Rose had achieved her goal. True, it might not have happened the way she dreamed, but it had happened regardless. And though the gossip distressed her, she wouldn't give Grey up. Was it really so amazing that he'd married her? Surely not.

As for Eve, she was going to marry a politician. A man who might someday be prime minister of their great country. Perhaps in his youth Bramford Gregory had engaged in intrigue and rakish endeavors, but he had kept them well hidden, except for being seen at Saint's Row with an unknown woman. His future wife would probably never know if he'd given up his vices or not. Poor Eve. She hoped her friend would find happiness.

Eve turned to her. "Excuse me for one moment, Rose. Mama has asked me to check on the scones."

Rose nodded. "Of course."

No sooner had her friend departed than an elegant blonde woman approached. Rose knew who she was though they'd never been introduced. "May I sit with you?"

The woman had a beautiful, almost icy look to her, with sharp cheekbones and a top lip wider than her bottom. Very striking, but there was something in her blue eyes that made Rose like her. She had the look of someone who didn't suffer fools.

"Of course."

The woman offered her hand before sitting. "I'm Lady Madeline Monteforte."

Rose could see how Archer would be attracted to this woman, most men would be. She could also see that he would have a difficult time catching her. This woman had the look of someone who hid any vulnerable aspect of herself away where no one would ever find it, and that included her heart.

That realization that Archer would have to rely on more than charm made her smile. "It is lovely to meet you. I am Rose Danvers Kane, Duchess of Ryeton."

Madeline smiled at her, her eyes crinkling at the corners. "Yes, I know. Your husband is brother to Lord Archer Kane, is he not?"

Ah-ha. "Yes, he is. Do you know my brother-in-law?"

The lady's cheeks didn't so much as pinken, but her eyes took on a brightness that made Rose bite the inside of her mouth to keep from smiling. Yes, she was a cool one. "I do. I wonder if I might be so bold as to inquire into his character?"

Rose raised both brows. "I should think he is exactly as he has presented himself to you, Lady Monteforte."

Now the woman flushed slightly. "Forgive me. I mean no offense to your relation, but you see, I believe Lord Kane might have developed an interest in my daughter, and I want her to be happy in her choice of husband."

An interest in her daughter? She couldn't be that blind, could she? Or had Archer somehow managed to make a royal mess of things? "I assure you, that Archer Kane is one of the best men I know." And that was the truth.

Madeline smiled. "Thank you. You have no idea how much that lightens my heart to hear you say that."

Did it? So why did Rose get the feeling the lady was disappointed? Had she been hoping to hear that Archer was something else? The kind of man unsuitable for a young woman, perhaps? The kind of man better suited for a mature woman who knew exactly what she wanted?

Oh, wait till she told Grey!

She missed him. Of course he couldn't be there with her at a lady's party, but even if it wasn't just for ladies, he wouldn't have come. This was the way it was going to be for them. If she wanted to attend an event she would have to go alone.

She was going to have a lot of lonely evenings in her future.

"Perhaps you and your daughter would come to call at Ryeton House someday, Lady Monteforte? I would so enjoy the chance to get to know you better." And to have Archer come to visit.

"That would be lovely." She seemed to mean it. Either this woman cared little about scandal or she had yet to hear it. She would have to be very open-minded to consider allowing her daughter to marry into the Kane family. "Thank you for the invitation. And now I see Lady Eve has returned. I will give her back her seat. Good day, Duchess."

Eve stopped to speak to another lady, and Rose, noticing the platter of cucumber sandwiches on the buffet, rose to her feet to get herself a plate. As she made selections from the various platters, she came up behind a trio of women who did not seem to notice her.

"The duchess is either incredibly brave or incredibly naïve," one said to her companions. "To constantly put herself in the company of her husband's former lovers."

Rose froze. She should walk away right then, but she couldn't. Her feet seemed rooted to the spot.

"Never mind that. How on earth did *she* manage to do what countless others could not? She's no comparison for Lady Devane's elegance or Merriam Bellforte's beauty."

"Perhaps she isn't as innocent as we've all been made to believe."

The third woman snorted. She looked bitter and mean. "Ryeton needs an heir. Since he's a social pariah, his choices of a bride are limited. No doubt he chose his bride based on convenience and desperation."

"She does owe him a great debt."

The bitter one spoke again. "Don't make her out to be a martyr. It's not that difficult to spread one's legs when there's a title and a fortune involved. Ryeton's prowess is legendary. I doubt she suffered."

The three of them giggled. And then one of them looked up and met Rose's gaze. At least the woman had the grace to look horrified.

Her stomach churning, Rose turned away. She forgot about her plate and the cucumber sandwiches and stiffly made her way back to Eve. She had to leave.

Of course, she was intercepted by two younger women who stepped directly in front of her. It would have been rude to brush past them, and Rose tried never to be rude.

"Pardon me, Your Grace. May we ask you a question?"

No! Couldn't they see that she was about to die of mortification? "Of course."

One of the girls was Jacqueline Whitting, Lady Monteforte's daughter. "We've heard that your husband, the duke wears a mask," she said. "Is that true?"

Was she about to become the butt of a cruel joke? Because it was one thing to have to take a higher path when a full-grown woman made remarks, but she had absolutely no intention of letting some little chit insult her. "It is."

The other girl—Priscilla something—practically swooned. "How romantic! Just like the hero in *La Mascarade de la Peau*!"

"The Masquerade of the Skin?" Where had she heard that title before? Her eyes widened and the girl blushed scarlet. *Voluptuous.*

Rose leaned forward to whisper conspiratorially in the younger woman's ear. "Indeed."

The two exchanged excited and embarrassed glances, giggling the whole time. No, Archer would never be interested in this girl, if for no other reason than she was a girl. Despite her choice of reading material, Jacqueline was an innocent, and Archer had no patience for that. But whoever did end up winning Lady Jacqueline's hand was in for a few surprises.

And that was as far as Rose wanted to think upon it.

When Rose left them, she felt strong enough to continue at the party. She wasn't going to let those women know they'd driven her away. And when the one who had seen her caught her eye and smiled ruefully, Rose managed a tight smile in return. Being contrite didn't change what had been said.

". . . And then Lord Benning forbade me from ever going back there!" Lady Benning announced to the shocked group hanging on her every word. Rose resumed her place beside Eve. She looked at her friend, hoping to glean some idea of what she had missed.

"I cannot believe that." It was one of the women who had talked about her earlier. This one didn't look the least bit contrite. In fact, she looked indignant, as though Rose was the one who had done wrong by overhearing her mean remarks. "What about you, Your Grace? Does your husband dictate where you can and cannot go?"

The woman looked as though she expected to be proven right.

"My husband would never do that." Rose informed her coolly. "Although there will always be *unsavory* characters at any social gathering, my husband trusts me to decide the ones I wish to attend."

The woman flushed, and Rose felt a certain amount of satisfaction in knowing that her barb had struck a nerve. "If that's true, he must have changed immensely since the days when we were acquainted."

Ahh. Now the claws came out. No wonder the woman had made such vile aspirations earlier. She was jealous.

"He has." Rose held the other woman's gaze, not caring a whit for how she said the word "acquainted." This woman had slept with her husband, and oddly enough she wasn't the least bit jealous. She did, however, feel sorry for the woman because Grey *had* been a different man back then. "My husband is very attentive and courteous to my wishes. I couldn't be more *satisfied* with my situation." Oh God, had she actually said that? The innuendo practically stood up on its own and waved to everyone in the room.

What was it about Grey—no, about this woman—that made her feel as though she had to defend her marriage, and brag about her sex life? It was just so petty.

"You were once a *friend* of the duke's, were you not, Lady Devane?" The woman—whose name Rose could not remember—slanted a devious glance in the blonde woman's direction.

Everyone looked at Lady Devane, because everyone knew the rumors and everyone wanted to see not only Rose's reaction, but Lady Devane's as well. Vultures.

Eve pressed her knee against Rose's, giving her some well-needed support.

"I was, Lady Gosling," Lady Devane replied smoothly. "But that was a long time ago, back when he was a man who never thought to marry." She smiled at Rose. "And then he met the one woman who could tempt him. I believe you must be an extraordinary woman, Your Grace."

Rose could have kissed her, for in that one moment, the woman who could have easily become her enemy proved herself a friend. And not only a friend, but she let every woman in that room know what she thought of their vicious tongues.

"Thank you, Lady Devane." Rose flashed a genuine smile. "But I feel that I am the fortunate one."

Lady Gosling—what a ridiculous title!—said nothing. Tight-lipped, she turned away and went off in search of other prey.

Yes, Rose thought, as Eve discreetly squeezed her hand and whispered, "Old hag," she was fortunate. But Grey was obviously the smarter of the two of them, because he had enough sense to stay the hell at home.

Dawn had yet to raise her sleepy face when Grey woke. Outside it was dark, the street lights the only illumination in the gloomy, rainy early hours.

Beside him, Rose slept deeply and peacefully, face adorably smooshed as she burrowed into her pillow. But unlike other mornings, he wasn't content to lie abed and stare at his wife.

His wife who had been spending more and more time at home as of late. While he'd love to think that it was devotion to him that kept her from parties and balls, he knew it was something more. Rose loved parties, loved dressing up and going out. She craved social interaction, and the loss of such activities was beginning to show.

His happy girl no longer seemed happy. No longer seemed to be the young woman whom he thought could make anything she wanted a reality simply by force of will.

And it was all his fault.

She didn't talk to him about it. In fact, he was pretty much convinced she bold-faced lied whenever he asked. And that could mean only one thing—that he was the reason she no longer showed her face in society. Other than visiting with Eve Elliott, and the odd caller she received here at the house, she saw no one.

And last night, he could have sworn he'd seen resentment in her eyes when he asked if she had plans for the evening, as he asked almost every evening. He was only curious. For a while, she would tell him about the parties she attended, and he enjoyed hearing about them. Now that there weren't any parties, there were no stories, and he missed them.

He slipped out of bed, careful not to disturb her, and hurriedly pulled on a shirt, trousers, and stockings. He grabbed his boots from beside the door, his mask from the dresser, and crept from the room like a thief or a guilty lover.

Perhaps he was a little of both. Somehow he had managed to steal Rose's joy for life, and he felt terrible about it. But he had no idea how to give it back.

That guilt—that restless unease—was what kept him from sleeping and weighed on his conscience. It was what drove him downstairs at this ungodly hour, into his mask, and out the back.

The air was thick with mist, dampening his hair and clothes with the lightest touch as he strode purposefully toward the stables. His heart huffed against his ribs, half terrified, half excited about what he was about to do.

The stables were deserted of course. The grooms wouldn't be up for at least another hour, and that was all right. The fewer servants around to witness his behavior the better—it would keep chaos and gossip to a minimum.

He saddled his horse—a great sable gelding he called Marlowe—and swung himself onto the animal's strong back. Gathering the reins, he set his heels to the horse's sides and let his eager mount carry him out into the dark.

It was obvious Marlowe was thrilled to be out. He was sadly underused while in London as Grey rarely rode him. A blatant abuse that Grey was about to rectify—at least for today.

A discreet cantor took him down the street to Hyde Park corner. Once safely inside the park, where there was little risk of encountering traffic or the odd pedestrian staggering home in the waning hours, Grey allowed Marlowe his stride. Hatless, and in his shirtsleeves, he bent over his mount's back and reveled in the feeling of the wind and rain in his hair. Against his skin.

He was free. And he didn't care that anyone might see him. Grey's heart soared. Sweet Christ, but this felt good.

He rode until the sun began its slow ascension, and then steered a sated Marlowe toward the gate. He passed a gentleman on the way out. He didn't recognize the man, but it was apparent the man knew him. Grey held his breath for a split second—wondering if he had cuckolded this man, and if he might try to confront him. An irrational thought, but it was there all the same. He didn't mind confrontation, the skirmish with Martingale at Saint's Row proved that. What he wanted to avoid was the possible scandal. Rose didn't need more of his mess to contend with.

The man merely tipped his hat to him. Grey nodded in response, and then the stranger was gone.

Well, he allowed, as the tightness in his chest relaxed somewhat, obviously not everyone in London thought him the spawn of Satan.

He arrived home, shirt clinging to him, hair stuck to his head, just as the grooms were going about their morning work. To say that they were surprised to see him was an understatement.

Grey grinned at them. "Good morning, gentlemen." He left Marlowe in one young lad's capable hands and jogged back to the house, hungry for breakfast and eager to see his wife.

She was still asleep when he bounded into the bedroom, but the noise of his arrival woke her.

Stretching, she sat up against the pillows and regarded him with bleary eyes. "Where have you been?"

"I went for a ride," he told her with that idiotic grin that refused to leave his face.

She squinted, rubbed her eyes. "You went for a ride?"

"Yes." Somehow, though he hadn't envisioned her response, he'd thought it might be more enthusiastic.

Instead she frowned. "In your shirtsleeves in the

rain, with no hat, no cravat where anyone might have seen you, and yet you won't attend a party in full evening dress with me?"

Grey blinked. "I thought you'd be happy." Hell, he was happy. Or rather, he had been. He'd felt so light and joyous. Now, he felt as though he had done something wrong.

"Happy?" She choked on the word, pulling herself upright. She looked so young and so angry sitting there with her hair tumbling in a loose mess around her shoulders, the sheets pulled up to her chest. "Since my arrival in London I've had people stare at me, whisper about me—and you. I've heard women discuss your body in manners that hint at obvious personal knowledge. I've weathered innuendo, pity, and cruel jokes while you hid away in this house. And now you expect me to be happy that you have given the gossips more fodder to use against me? Now everyone will be talking of the wild Duke of Ryeton who rides around Hyde Park half naked. Of course, Grey. I'm happy. Good for you."

He'd never seen her like this. Never known such venom existed inside her. And yet, he couldn't quite fault her for it. That understanding, however, didn't stop his emotional reaction. "You knew what I was when you agreed to marry me. I've never tried to hide my past from you."

"No, but you never shared the full extent of it, have you?" She came up on her knees, looking so deliciously rumpled in her thin nightgown with her hair hanging wildly around her shoulders. "Is there a woman in all of England over the age of five-and-twenty that you haven't fucked and who doesn't despise you for it?"

"My, my. What an enlightening vocabulary you've developed, Your Grace. Your father would be so proud of how easily vulgarities slip from your lips." The moment the words left his lips, he wished he could take them back.

Rose blanched. "Don't you dare bring my father into this. He told me to stay away from you."

"A warning you willfully ignored, because *you* wanted to 'fuck' me, to use your own word. Don't blame me for that, Rose. You came looking for me. I would have continued on doing my best to avoid you."

"If you think so lowly of me, why did you ask me to marry you?"

"I don't think lowly of you." How could she possibly think that? "I simply want you to realize your own culpability in our marriage. Although, I would like to think there's more between us than fucking." It was the kind of word once you used it, it was so easy to use again and again.

She sank onto the bed. "I don't know what we have. I thought . . . but now I don't know. I feel like I don't know you."

Grey's fist went to his chest, to where his heart lay broken. "Perhaps that's because you've changed me. Two weeks ago I never would have ventured out into Hyde Park, whether there was chance of being seen or not. But this morning I went, Rose. I was seen and I didn't care. And I think that must be because of you."

Throwing back the covers, she climbed out of

bed. She was scowling, practically twitching with anger. He only understood part of it, but he knew that she blamed him for her own discontent. She blamed him for everything at that moment, and he didn't know how to fix it.

"And I should praise you for that? Perhaps pat myself on the back? My God, Grey! The man who saw you no doubt recognized you and thinks you were there to meet someone. Or that you were just coming home from being out all night. The next time I go to a party—alone—I'll have to face that speculation. All my insisting that you are not a lothario will be reduced to naught. And as usual, you won't be with me to help me weather it. I'll be left to defend your honor and my own, so you'll have to excuse me if your jaunt this morning, and my apparent responsibility for it, doesn't fill my heart with joy. Now, if you'll excuse me, I'm going to go sleep in my own bed. I'm tired."

Grey watched her go feeling somewhat shocked and mystified. He also felt stupid and angry and sad.

He sat down on the bed and rubbed his face with both hands. He'd known he was going to be a disappointment to Rose. He'd known that she would come to resent and despise him, just like every woman he'd ever touched.

He just hadn't thought it would happen so soon.

Chapter 21

How would she fix the debacle she'd made of her marriage? That was the question Rose pondered as she walked the gravel path that meandered through the garden, Heathcliff dozing in her arms. His furry little body was warm against her chest, providing a solace and comfort she thought perhaps she didn't deserve, but needed regardless.

She was still hurt and angry with Grey though days had passed since he'd told her about his sojourn to Hyde Park. He'd never repeated the outing—or if he had, he'd wisely kept it to himself. As much as Rose wanted him to find the courage to leave the house and rejoin the world, she wanted him to do it with her. Surely that wasn't so wrong?

Meanwhile, her nasty response to his previous attempt undoubtedly left him loath to repeat the experiment and she cursed herself for it, even though she continued to feel the sting.

It made no sense, she allowed, rubbing her chin along Heathcliff's silky head. She should be pleased, but she wasn't. He had wanted her to be happy about it, when all she could think about was the one man who had seen him. The one man who was bound to mention to friends who he had seen. Some might doubt him, but others would believe and they would talk about the state of the duke's clothing, the mask that he wore. And if Rose ever managed to find the spine to show her face in public again, they would whisper about it. Some would even ask her about her husband's behavior—and wonder why he could trot around the park but not join her in society.

And then they'd talk about his attack, and they'd speculate some more. And someone would mention that perhaps he was coming home from shagging a mistress or a whore because his sexual desires, his "legendary" prowess was too much for his wife to endure or satisfy.

Yes, she should be happy that he'd left the house; but, damn it, he shouldn't have become a recluse to begin with!

It was embarrassing to have their relationship discussed so. She was humiliated and ashamed.

Ashamed of the man she liked better than all others. The man she fancied herself in love with. How was that even possible?

And she loathed herself for feeling this way, for thinking so lowly of Grey, who had shown her nothing but kindness and passion. Who had done nothing but try to please her and make her happy in the years following her father's ruin and death. Anything she'd asked for—though, she'd made few requests—had been granted. Even things she hadn't dared voice aloud, he'd seemed to know and answered.

Yes, she had known about his past when she pursued him. She'd known the depth of the stain on his reputation, but her feelings made her look beyond it. She took full responsibility for that, and the actions that had followed.

What she hadn't been intelligent enough to realize was that she couldn't change it. She couldn't bring him into the world and make it all go away. Her love was not enough to make him a better man in the eyes of society. They would never see him as she did. They would never love him or respect him, not when he behaved like a man ashamed of himself.

And feckless woman that she was, she'd allowed society's opinion of her husband to color her own judgment and make her regret marrying him. She owed him an apology and she couldn't bring herself to deliver it because her pride had yet to let go of the insistence that he owed her an apology as well. He owed her . . . something.

But even deeper than all of this was the realization that after days of avoiding him, she missed him. And she was afraid to approach him because of it. Afraid that he might reject her, as was his right.

So she hid. And as her wounds festered, she began to entertain the notion that she was beginning to understand why Grey hid as he did.

And if one managed to avoid unpleasantness long enough, avoidance soon became determination.

"Your Grace!"

Rose turned to face the direction of the call, the puppy jerking to alertness at the movement. Already fiercely loyal to his mistress, he let out a sharp bark at the footman hurrying toward her.

"Yes?" Rose shushed the dog. "What is it?" Had something happened to Grey?

The handsome young man paused to bow. "Begging your pardon, Your Grace, but you have a visitor waiting upon you in the rose parlor. A Lady Devane. She was told you were not at home, but she pushed her way in." The man's eyes were bright with anxiety. "Given the circumstances, it was thought best if I came directly to fetch you."

Given the circumstances indeed. Good Lord, what was Lady Devane thinking in coming to Grey's home? All of society—even Grey himself—believed her responsible for the attack on him.

If Grey found her there . . .

Rose thrust Heathcliff into the young man's arms. "Take him back to the stables, please. I will attend to Lady Devane. You were right to find me."

The footman smiled, obviously soothed by her taking charge of the situation. He bowed again and turned in the direction of the stables, Heathcliff high on his shoulder.

It was unladylike—though this was hardly the time for decorum—Rose hitched her butter yellow skirts and ran toward the house. She was gasping for breath by the time she reached the terrace doors, and she paused but a moment to catch her breath before pulling them open and rushing through the house to the rose parlor.

The housekeeper paced just outside the door, wringing her hands. She looked up at the sound of Rose's heels clicking on the floor. Relief washed over her face. "Your Grace, I'm so sorry. The lady refused to leave."

"It's all right." And it was. Rose braced a hand against the wall and took a few deep breaths to slow her heart and the frenzy of her lungs. "Have tea and biscuits brought in."

The older woman's eyes widened. "You intend to entertain her, then?"

Rose nodded, fixing a grim smile on her lips. "She braved coming here for a reason. The least I can do is hear her out. Advise the servants to keep discussion to a minimum, please. I'd rather the duke hear about this from me rather than his valet."

Round cheeks flushed red, but she didn't deny the servants' tendency to gossip. "Of course, Your Grace. Right away."

When the housekeeper scurried off, Rose took a moment to smooth her hair and skirts before entering the parlor. Lady Devane stood near one of the windows, and turned gracefully as the door closed.

"Good morning, Duchess."

"Lady Devane." Rose inclined her head. "This is unexpected."

Then slightly—and only slightly, Rose realized—the woman chuckled. "I should imagine. I appreciate you receiving me, madam. I thought perhaps you'd set the dogs on me."

Rose smiled at the absurd notion. "And deny my curiosity the satisfaction of discovering what could have possibly brought you here? I think not." She gestured to one of the comfortable sofas rather than the little stiff-backed chairs. "Will you sit?"

"Thank you." The elegant blonde sank down onto the edge of the cushion and removed her gloves. She wore a dark blue morning gown and matching hat that brought out the brightness of her eyes and the creaminess of her complexion. She looked cool, composed, and flawless. Not at all like Rose felt.

"I've sent for tea," Rose commented, unable to think of anything else to say as she also sat—across from the countess.

Lady Devane arched a fine, golden brow. "I must confess I did not expect such hospitality."

"I might not be certain of what to think of you, madam, but I should like to think I'd never be so rude as to forget my manners."

Green eyes sought hers and held for what felt like an eternity. Did she suspect Rose of lying?

"Forgive my bluntness, but I would think that your husband's wishes would trump manners any day."

"My husband has never told me who I can and cannot receive in my own home. Of course, that might change once he learns of your visit."

Lady Devane smiled slightly. "Indeed. I will be brief, then, and spare you as much discomfort as I can."

"His reaction will be what it will be despite how long you stay, Lady Devane. You may as well take your time. It's been some time since I've had a caller." She hadn't meant to admit that, but there it was, hanging in the air between them.

The countess nodded. "Then I am truly glad I chose today to make my call, and will do my best to make it worthy of your reception."

The tea arrived before they could take their conversation further, which was just as well. Rose had the feeling that once Lady Devane began talking, an interruption would not be so welcome.

The housekeeper set the tray on the table between them, her anxious gaze flittered back and forth between Rose and her visitor. Rose thanked her and dismissed her, though it was painfully obvious the woman was loath to leave.

"Your staff is very protective," Lady Devane remarked once they were alone once more. "How very fortunate you are."

Rose inclined her head as she poured a cup of tea for each of them. "That depends on the situation, I suspect." She smiled a little as she added the cream and sugar, pausing to inquire as to how Lady Devane preferred her refreshment. "Now that you have set my household aflutter, perhaps you'd care to enlighten me as to the nature of your call?"

Taking a sip from the delicate china, Lady Devane made a slight "Mmm" of acquiescence. "Pardon my impertinence, but I notice you've been out of society as of late."

"That's hardly an impertinence, Lady Devane. It is truth."

"Still, it occurs to me that the reason for your absence may be a subject you do not wish to discuss."

Rose met her curious gaze with a direct one of her own. Why should she not be direct and answer honestly when this woman played such a huge part in her current situation?

"I've been absent because I find I have no wish nor the patience to be talked about so blatantly. Neither do I have the desire to be questioned about my husband or listen to the wild speculation circulating about him, our marriage, or myself for that matter." Her tone had grown louder and the fire in her cheeks hotter with every word. "Surely, you can understand why I feel that way, Lady Devane?" And now that she said it, she suddenly felt as though she had a better understanding of Grey, but would that understanding benefit either of them?

The older woman's smile was sympathetic, even rueful, but not the gloating triumph Rose somewhat expected. "I am sorry for that. But do you not think that hiding here like some kind of guilty criminal only serves to worsen matters?"

That struck a nerve. In fact, it struck several. "A guilty criminal, madam? I'm sure you know nothing about guilt or criminal behavior, do you?"

This time her companion did not smile. She flushed—and rightfully so. "I know what it is to be treated as such. That is why I feel I have some justification in speaking plainly to you."

And she hadn't been speaking plainly prior to this? "By all means, then, speak as plainly as you wish."

Lady Devane set her cup on her saucer and leaned forward, resting her forearms on her knees. Her expression was resolute, her gaze unwavering. "I know avoiding society seems the best—and most comfortable—course right now, but I strongly advise you not to hide here for long, Your Grace. We both know what that has done for your husband."

Hiding. Yes, she was hiding. Just like Grey. Yet Rose wanted to defend him, if not herself. "And we both know who is responsible for that, Lady Devane."

Smooth ivory cheeks reddened, but the lady did not look away. "I will assume as much responsibility as I should own, madam. The rest must fall on the duke, where it belongs."

"He never would have become a recluse were it not for the vicious attack you launched upon him." Why not just get it all out into the open and have done with it?

"He was the worst sort of man and I found that foolishly attractive, I admit. I will also admit to wishing that someone would ruin that pretty face of his and show him what it was like to be treated so poorly. But I would never dream of doing such damage myself, and I would certainly never dream of asking another to carry out revenge that is rightfully mine."

"Rightfully?" Temper spiked her pitch. "Is maiming a man for life the kind of revenge you think rightfully yours, madam? Because I find that disgusting."

The other woman leaned away from the vehemence in Rose's words. "Your husband ruined me, Your Grace. I will be plain—he took my virginity, and refused to marry me when the situation came to light."

Rose might have made some sound were her throat not so tight. She had no idea what to say and seemingly no ability to speak at all. She had known that Grey was different then, but to think that he had been so totally without honor was shocking.

Lady Devane continued, her tone considerably cooler than it had been. "Were it not for Lord Devane's kindness I do not know what might have become of me. So you see, I meant it when I said you must be an extraordinary woman to inspire His

Grace to marry." Then, as though remembering herself, she shook her head. "Forgive me. He is obviously a changed man, and I am not here to relive the petty tragedies of my past."

"He ruined you, so you ruined him." It made sense in a macabre sort of way. Still, Rose found it difficult to justify Lady Devane's actions. She couldn't justify Grey's either.

"I did nothing," her companion replied with a bitter twist of her lips. "I married the first man who would have me and I was happy for it. But one night, in the company of someone I hold very dear, and who thinks the world of me, I remarked on how I would like to see Ryeton pay for what he had done to me. My friend took my wish to heart." She paused to allow Rose to fill in the rest of the tale herself.

"You mean that someone else had Grey attacked because of the damage to your honor? Who?"

Lady Devane shook her head. "I will not reveal his identity. Not to you, nor to your husband, Duchess."

Rose regarded her closely, her head swimming with all that she had just learned. "You love this person."

"Very much."

"Enough to take responsibility for a crime that is not yours. Enough to endure years of gossip and accusations."

The blonde nodded. "I would endure that and more to protect him. But despite that, I refused to hide away and let the gossips deem me guilty. At first I wanted to do just that, but Lord Devane brought me back into the world and taught me that the only way I would ever regain my self-respect was to face those who would sneer at me. Let them think me guilty. I know the truth. And now so do you."

Rose shook her head—a desperate attempt to sort everything out so it made sense rather than seem like some kind of dream. "I appreciate your candor, Lady Devane, but I'm not completely certain I understand why you've decided to share this with me now."

The older woman's smile turned kind, and patient. "Yes you do. Because it is important that you do not hide from them. You must show them that they have no power over you, that you will not be dictated to by their pettiness. If you do not do this now, they will have won, and it will become more and more difficult for you to regain your place in society." There was a pleading light in her eyes. "For Ryeton's sake, you must be strong enough for both of you. If you do not stand up to them, he will never be the man you want him to be."

"I do not want him to be anything other than the man he is." And God willing, never, ever return to the man he used to be.

That had better not be pity in Lady Devane's pretty eyes. "The man you know him to be is different from the man he's become, is he not? Both of you deserve better than that."

"Why would you defend a man who ruined you?"

"Because I realized that he didn't ruin *me*. I let him ruin my reputation because I was young and impetuous. And perhaps I feel responsible for him, and see you as a way to redeem myself of my past sins. I know all too well what it is like to feel like an outcast from society."

Bemused, Rose smiled because she did not know what else to do. "I'm not sure what I think of being used as a doorway to redemption."

Lady Devane smiled as well. "Think of it as kindly advice, then, from a woman who has seen her share of scandal and weathered it as well. Gossips are like vultures, going after the wounded and the dying. Thrive, and they cannot harm you."

Rose's smile grew. "That is sage advice indeed."

The other woman rose to her feet. "I have taken up enough of your time, but I hope you will reflect upon our conversation positively. I also hope to see you out in society again soon."

Rose stood also, offering Lady Devane her hand. "I believe you shall. Thank you for calling."

"Thank you for receiving me," Lady Devane murmured as she closed her fingers around Rose's. She shook hands like a man, something Rose respected. "By the way, you have my permission to share this conversation with your husband, not that I expected you would do otherwise."

"I appreciate that. Good day, Lady Devane."

"Good day, Duchess."

She hadn't made it two feet when the door to the parlor flew open, revealing Grey, chest heaving in fury, eyes bright as flame. His terrible gaze fell upon Lady Devane. "What the hell are you doing here?"

If only the meeting with his secretary had ended sooner Grey might have prevented Rose seeing him so dangerously close to losing control. He might have prevented her seeing Lady Devane at all.

To her credit, Margaret—Maggie he used to call her—didn't flinch at the sight of him, even though he huffed and puffed like an ogre and purposefully hadn't worn his mask. He wasn't going to hide the sight and shame of it from her. She looked at him serenely, with a touch of pity in her big eyes.

He had the ungentlemanly urge to punch her in the face. How dare she, of all people come to his home and poison Rose's mind with God only knew what kind of venom against him. Of course, whatever she said about it, it was undoubtedly true and he would deserve every insult. But Rose . . .

He didn't want Rose to know what he had done to this woman.

But Margaret merely sank into a deep curtsey before him, held his gaze and said, "I was just on my way out, Your Grace. My apologies."

He might have grunted, he wasn't sure. Then she rose gracefully and swept past him like the Queen of goddamned Sheba. The door clicked quietly shut behind her, and Grey turned his gaze toward his wife.

She wasn't looking at him with hatred in her eyes, which was good. Still, that didn't calm the fury—betrayal?—churning in his gut. "Why would you entertain that woman in my home? Do you despise me that much?"

Rose blinked. "I don't despise you at all, you lumbering oaf. You make it sound like I invited her, which I didn't. Although I refuse to apologize for seeing her. She was very enlightening."

"I wager she was," he growled.

His wife arched a brow. "She didn't do it, you know."

He scowled. "Do what?" Make Rose disgusted by him?

"Have you attacked. She wasn't responsible. Someone acted out of a perverted sense of biblical justice on her behalf, but it wasn't her."

He snorted. "Of course she would tell you that." That Rose believed this didn't hurt as much as it made him angry that she was so easily duped. But what was Margaret's motive? To further her revenge by making Rose believe her innocent?

The gaze that locked with his told him he was every kind of idiot. "If that woman had decided to have revenge on you, Grey, it wouldn't have been your face she sliced. If you think about it, you'll realize that as well. Someone she cares for very much had you attacked—someone she would rather take the blame for than give up as the actual culprit."

It was on the tip of his tongue to argue, call her naïve and gullible, but then he took her advice and thought about it. And then he wanted to smack his head against the wall for not having the clarity to see it before. But of course, he'd been wounded and bitter and had his tail tucked between his legs. He'd been too blind to see it before. It was only with Rose that the truth seemed to sink in.

Margaret had a brother, Michael. She always talked fondly of him, though the man rarely ventured out into public. He was a recluse, just like Grey had become. There'd been rumors of an illness, but perhaps the sickness had been of the mind rather than the body as Grey had first thought. Maggie used to say how protective she was toward him, and he toward her. They would do anything for one another.

As sudden as his fury had appeared when he learned of Lady Devane's presence in his home, it banked and disappeared. Oh, it would be easy to cling to his old anger and bitterness, but something inside him knew the truth from the lie he'd allowed himself to believe all these years. It was easier to think of someone retaliating against him because he'd wronged her. Easier to think of himself as the sole injured party even though he knew he was so much more—or perhaps less.

And now he saw it all so clearly, and he realized that the person who had truly suffered during all of this was Margaret. She'd lost her reputation because of him, and the illusion of her honor because of her brother. And yet, she'd never once backed down or hid her face.

To think he'd resented her for prancing about society as though she had nothing to feel ashamed of, and now he knew it to be true.

"You know who it is, don't you?" Rose whispered, coming to stand directly in front of him. He could smell the springlike dew of her perfume, feel the delicate heat of her body through his clothes. It was like a balm for his soul having her so close, and yet she tormented him like the most skilled captor.

"Yes," he replied softly. "I think I do."

"What are you going to do?"

He thought for a second, but the answer was clear. "Nothing. I'm not going to do a thing. It's better in the past." What could he do that wouldn't cause more ruination? If he hadn't behaved so despicably toward Margaret she never would have come to hate him, and the attack wouldn't have happened. But if he retaliated now, he would only be hurting a woman he'd already hurt enough. She obviously loved her brother enough to take responsibility for his actions—and that was a love Grey understood. He'd do anything for his brothers and his sister as well.

Soft fingers touched his face. "You don't want revenge?"

He glanced down at her and saw something in her eyes that took his breath away. "No," he replied hoarsely. "I don't. But I would like my wife back."

She smiled, and the shattered fragments of his heart glued themselves back together. "I think that can be arranged, if you are willing to forgive her for thinking only of herself."

"I can, if she can forgive me for being less than she deserves."

Tears blossomed in the wide curve of her bottom lashes. "Less? That's not true. Every day you prove yourself to be more than I could ever want."

Grey pulled her close, and pressed his mouth against hers, drawing her into a hungry kiss that consumed them both until he carried her to the sofa and made love to her on the delicate brocade. Though it had only been days since he'd felt her body wrapped around his, it seemed as though weeks had passed, she felt so good.

Afterward, as he held her in his arms, feeling a

peculiar and humbling tightness in his throat, he did something he hadn't done in a long time.

He thanked God for what He had given him, and promised, that if the Almighty gave him just a little bit longer with Rose that he would try to be a better person.

And this time, he meant it.

Chapter 22

"Do you plan to attend the charity ball at Saint's Row this Thursday evening?" Eve asked as she and Rose took a break from their shopping to enjoy low tea at a quaint little West End shop.

Rose selected a small sandwich from the plate between them on the lacy tablecloth. Her heart, shameful as it was, kicked up a fuss at the mention of the ball. "I do not know." She wanted to go. She wanted to go very badly, but she was anxious about attending, despite her conversation with Lady Devane the day before.

Eve kept her features perfectly schooled, but Rose saw the slight tightening of her friend's lips. "Staying home does you no good, Rose. Why should Ryeton ever leave the house if you are always there? The man needs incentive."

She wasn't certain that whether or not she went out mattered one whit to Grey, but Rose didn't say that. Oh, she knew that Grey wanted her to be happy, and of course he cared about her, but he wasn't about to change his mind about society just because she decided to put on a mask and attend a charity ball.

Of course, he might attend. After all, it had been at a masked ball that she managed to seduce him. Perhaps she could convince him to attend again. Even if he kept to the shadows, it would be better than going alone.

Wouldn't it?

"Very well," she capitulated. "You have convinced me. I will go to the ball."

Eve's face lit up. "Brilliant! Oh, it will be so much more fun with you there. Lately Gregory's insisted on introducing me to all of his political cronies. Do you have any idea how utterly boorish politics can be? Honestly, running an empire should be much more interesting."

Rose smiled. It was good to see her friend happy. For a little bit, she'd worried that Eve might pine for her absent mystery lover—and that she might make a bad marriage just because it was expected of her. Now, she had to admit, it seemed as though her friend truly cared for her fiancé, and he for her.

After a few moments silence, her friend leaned her head and shoulders over the table and whispered, "Is it true that Lady Devane called on you yesterday?"

The servants couldn't have gossiped about that, could they? They seemed so loyal to Grey it seemed unlikely, and yet that same loyalty might have caused some loose lips out of a sense of justice. More than likely, however, someone had seen the lady's carriage roll up the drive to Ryeton House.

Sighing, Rose nodded. She hadn't intended to tell Eve about the visit—not that she didn't trust her friend, but because she thought of her conversation with Lady Devane as something to keep in confidence. The truth wasn't hers to tell.

"It is true," she admitted. "She didn't stay very long, but she paid me a visit."

Eve's eyes widened. "What did she want? Did Ryeton see her?"

"She wanted to offer me advice, and, yes, Grey saw her."

"Advice on what?" Eve scowled as though personally injured. Obviously she thought no one but herself properly equipped to give Rose advice. "What happened when they saw each other?"

"You sound a little too gleeful," Rose admonished. "What do you think they did? Shag on the carpet?"

Her friend's pink lips fell into a perfect O. "What did you just say?"

Rose flushed. "Nothing worth repeating. Forgive me. Grey was angry at first, but they were civil toward each other."

"If I were him I would have kicked her posterior out of the house immediately. I can't believe you received her."

This was a conversation she did not want to have, but if it came down to this or what they discussed, Rose would rather the former. "It's never been proven that Lady Devane was behind the attack on Grey. Furthermore, it's never been proven that said attack was unwarranted."

Another shocked expression. Eve was beginning to look like a fish gasping for air. "I cannot believe you just said that."

Rose shrugged. "It's true. Grey himself doubted her involvement, and I know for a fact that now he doesn't hold Lady Devane responsible for his injuries at all. As for the other, it is well known what kind of gentleman my husband once was—and that's not much of one at all. He was a scoundrel of the worst kind."

"You don't seem the least upset by that knowledge."

"I'm not. He's no longer that same man. I know there are some who do not believe a man can change, but Grey has."

"Spoken like a woman in love."

Rose looked away. "Yes, well . . . a wife should be well aware of her husband's faults and virtues, should she not?"

Now it was Eve who looked uncomfortable. "I know very little about Mr. Gregory, despite our long acquaintance."

Reaching across the table, Rose settled her hand atop one of the smaller woman's. "You will come to know him. That is one of the great aspects of marriage."

"Has Ryeton improved upon closer association?"

"Yes." Then she grinned. "And no. His virtues are great, but so are his faults. Of course, I'm sure he feels the same about me."

"I doubt it," Eve remarked with a bit of a smirk. "He's no doubt grateful you wanted him—especially after knowing him as well as you do."

"Maybe." For some reason she was struck with

the memory of Lady Devane saying Grey would not marry her once he'd ruined her. He had married Rose as quickly as possible. Surely that said something, not only for how much he had indeed changed, but for how deep his regard for her ran.

Her friend regarded her over the rim of her teacup. "Have you told him you love him yet?"

Now it was Rose's turn to gape. "No! I mean, that is none of your concern."

Eve arched a brow. "Of course it is my concern, you are my best friend. Everything that happens in your life is my concern. When do you plan to let him know how you feel?"

"I don't know." She'd said it that one time, when he'd fallen asleep, and never found the courage to say it again, especially since he'd had plenty of time to say the same words to her and had yet to utter them.

"Perhaps hearing how you feel is exactly the kind of motivation he needs to accompany you to the ball."

Rose took a sip of tea rather than laugh outright. The only incentive she could think of that might possibly get Grey to that ball was a team of wild horses and half a dozen very strong men.

But that didn't stop a kernel of hope from budding in her breast. The idea of having Grey attend the ball with her thrilled her to no end. She didn't care that it would give the gossips fodder for a month, or that they would be stared at like side show attractions, it would be worth it to walk into Saint's Row on his arm.

"I'll ask him," she heard herself say. "I'll ask him to come with me."

Eve stilled, watching her with an expression Rose could only describe as surprise. "Really?"

She nodded. "I will. I'm tired of hiding, and I want to go to the ball. Most of all, I want my husband to come with me, but that won't happen if I don't at least try."

Her friend grinned. "That's the spirit. When are you going to ask him?"

"Tonight," Rose replied with a determined frown. "I'll ask him tonight." That way she couldn't turn coward and change her mind.

Or at least there was less chance of that happening.

"He wouldn't dare turn you down," Eve insisted. "Not if you ask him at the most opportune moment." She waggled her eyebrows lewdly.

Rose cursed herself for blushing. "An expert on the male sex, are you now?"

Eve shrugged, flashing a sly smile. "Enough of one."

That made Rose laugh, because the idea of any woman actually understanding how a man thought and acted was ridiculous to say the least. "You tell yourself that if it makes you happy."

Eve chuckled as well. "Ah, well I can always dream, can I not?" Then she nonchalantly plucked a cookie from the tray and leveled a suddenly serious gaze at Rose. "Now, tell me about this advice Lady Devane gave you."

Caught. Rose sighed. "It was about Grey."

Her friend nodded, obviously noting her pained expression. "You don't wish to betray her confidence or your husband. I understand."

Relief washed over her, sharp but welcome. "I appreciate your understanding."

"Still, it must have been odd to discuss Ryeton with a woman who once knew him intimately. Did that vex you at all?"

"A little, but not so much as I thought it would."

"Probably because he's yours now and not hers." Eve grinned. "I would think there's a certain satisfaction in that."

Rose smiled in return. "I'd be lying if I said otherwise. I'm sure there are those who would call me a fool to believe that he would ever remain faithful to his marriage vows, but I do believe it, Eve. He will not betray me. Never. I reckon I might very well be the only woman he's ever been involved with who could have said those words with confidence."

Eve's lips puckered at the corners—a parody of a smile. "Remind me why you think so highly of this reprobate."

Laughing, Rose shook her head. "Because he's never been anything but kind and generous to me. Because he makes me smile—he makes me laugh. He can also make me angrier than anyone else in the world, and because when I'm with him I feel as though I am where I am supposed to be."

Puckered lips blew a gusty sigh. "That must be lovely."

"It is," Rose admitted truthfully, picking up her cup. "It really is."

But it would be so much lovelier if she could know for certain that Grey felt the same way.

Grey was sweating by the time he and Archer finished their game of lawn tennis, though it was a cool day and the sun hid behind large fluffy clouds. Despite that his shirt stuck to his back and his hair to his head, he felt good. Exercise did wonderful things to clear the mind.

He mopped his face with a small towel as he and Archer walked up the steps to the terrace where a frosty pitcher of lemonade waited for them. Grey poured them each a glass as they sat, each propping his feet on the table.

"Good game," Grey commented after taking a refreshing drink. "Thank you."

His brother, who was dressed casually in white and beige the same as Grey, smiled. Archer was looking a little wilted as well, a fact that pleased Grey. It was good to know he could still keep his younger sibling on his toes. "Thank you. I don't think I've ever run so much in my life. Least not in my adult years."

"Nor I. We used to run all the time as boys, remember?"

Archer's grin grew. "I remember Tryst trying to keep up. Poor little bastard."

Grey's brows quirked. "He's not little anymore." He took another deep drink. "By the way, have you heard from him lately?"

"Mm." Archer swallowed and set his empty glass on the table. He reached for the pitcher. "Got a letter just the other day. Says he hopes to be home by the end of the season. Something about a business venture."

Grey shook his head. "Boy never stops working."

"He's not a boy anymore either. He must be what? Damn near thirty."

"Twenty-eight," Grey replied, holding his glass out to be refilled as well. "He'll be home for his birthday." It was a nice thought, knowing that Tryst was coming home. He missed his youngest brother. And he wanted him to meet Rose. Probably—undoubtedly—he'd met her in the past, but not as his sister-in-law.

Hopefully Rose would still think well of him by then.

What the hell was wrong with him? Moping and whining over a woman? He'd never done this in the past. He'd never cared if they liked him for longer than a night. Hell, he hadn't cared if the affection had lasted that long. Now, here he was crossing his fingers that his wife would still like him by the end of the summer. It was pathetic.

If her opinion mattered so much, why didn't he endeavor to do more to earn it? All he had to do was go out into public. With her.

The very thought made him grind his teeth. He could just imagine the sneers, the whispers. Being stared at like some kind of circus attraction.

At least he no longer had to worry about anyone trying to kill him again—or harming Rose for that matter. Maggie's brother wouldn't do anything without thinking his sister wanted it. And Grey was pretty sure the dowager Lady Devane was done with him.

At one time his male pride would have demanded

he pursue her just to prove that no woman could resist him. What shite. Now he was simply happy for it. It was good for a man to realize that he wasn't the Almighty's gift to womankind.

He lifted his gaze to find Archer watching him strangely. "What?"

"Are you certain you are fine with me giving Bronte away?"

No, he wasn't fine at all, damn it. And every time he thought of it, it was like a knife in the ribs, but it was his own fault, so the only person he could be angry at for it was himself. "It's good."

"I don't believe you."

"It really doesn't matter does it?"

"Of course it does. Tell her you want to do it."

"And ruin her wedding day? I don't think so. Better that I watch from an alcove, or better yet, don't attend at all." His earlier fire of indignation had burned out and he resigned himself to the fact that he would do whatever his sister asked, even if that meant not attending her wedding. He'd dumped a lot of shame upon his family. He refused to add more.

"Don't be an arse."

"She doesn't want me there, Arch." And that was the end of the conversation.

"Who doesn't want you?" A sweet and familiar feminine voice asked from behind him.

Grey smiled over his shoulder at Rose as he removed his feet from the table. "No one. We're just discussing details of Bronte's wedding."

Rose's lips curved as she walked toward him. "Gentlemen discussing wedding details? I think the world must be ending." Picking up his glass, she took a drink of lemonade. It was an innocent, innocuous gesture—and one of the most arousing things he'd ever seen.

Archer chuckled, seemingly obviously to Grey's dumb state. "Lucifer is putting on his ice skates as we speak. And on that note, I'm afraid it is time for me to take my leave. I promised Mama I would escort both she and Bronte to the ball tonight, and I have yet to find a suitable mask."

"I look forward to trying to ascertain your identity this evening," Rose remarked with a smile that seemed only slightly strained. Regardless, the sight filled Grey with unease.

"As do I." Archer bowed over her hand before leaning down to whisper, "Arse," in Grey's ear and punched him in the arm. Hard.

Sometimes, Grey hated his brother.

Rose wasted no time. As soon as Archer had left them, she turned to Grey with a determined glint in her dark eyes. "May I speak to you?"

"Of course. You don't have to ask permission, Rose. You are my wife." This was making him slightly squeamish. He knew something unpleasant was coming.

His suspicions were confirmed when she chose to remain standing rather than join him at the table. "I want you to come with me to the ball at Saint's Row tonight. I know I should have asked before this, but I thought . . . I thought it would be better to wait until the last moment."

Because she thought it would be harder for him to refuse? Pressure wrapped around his heart, squeezing painfully. It was a simple request, one any wife might make of her husband, and one most husbands would accept. And the significance of the ball was not lost on him. Their first tryst had happened at a masked ball at Saint's Row—and it was once again a Thursday evening. Providence couldn't have chosen better.

"You'd have a better time without me." It wasn't a direct refusal.

She folded her arms beneath the swell of her lovely bosom. "No, I won't. And I don't understand how you can expect me to face the gossips on my own."

"I don't expect you to do anything. You seem to be the one with the expectations." Oh, yes, this was good. Getting defensive was so manly of him.

"Is it wrong of me to expect you to act like a husband?"

"Plenty of husbands do not attend balls with their wives."

"Yes, but those wives generally find someone to keep them company later."

Heat rushed to Grey's cheeks as the meaning of her words struck him. "Are you planning to take a lover, Rose?"

"Of course not." She regarded him as though he were a bothersome child. "I just want you to come with me. You are a duke, for heaven's sake. You can tell them all to go to hell and get away with it. You have nothing to be afraid of."

She couldn't seem to get further than that. She thought he was afraid. That he was a coward. That stung. No, that pissed him off. But how could he make her understand?

"I'm not afraid of them, Rose." Not really. "I just don't want to be around those people. I don't like them."

"You can't dislike *all* of them." All her disdain was missing was a good eye-rolling.

Grey rose to his feet, uncomfortable with having her look down upon him. He already felt her revulsion, he wouldn't add to it by making himself low. "When I was . . . injured, do you remember anyone coming to visit me? Other than family members."

She frowned, her gaze unfocused as she looked inward. "I seem to remember one or two gentlemen at first."

He was surprised she hadn't recognized them when she met them with Archer. "Westhaver Blackbourne, the Earl of Autley, and my cousin, Aiden Kane. Two of my fellows in debauchery. Yes, they came for a bit, and then they stopped coming as well. No one cared, Rose."

"So, you lock yourself away because you feel sorry for yourself?"

An exasperated sigh escaped his lips as he raked a hand through his hair. "What I'm saying is that no one cares if I show my face or not. I have no friends, other than you. Why in the name of God would I want to go where I'm not wanted?"

"I'm not enough incentive?"

"Christ, I never said that!" Lord she was good at making this all about her. As though he didn't want to go just to injure her.

"You don't have to." Her lower lip jutted ever so slightly.

"What is this Rose? Some sort of 'if you loved me you'd go to the party' ploy?"

She paled save for two bright spots of color on her cheeks. "That's low, even for you. No, it's not a ploy, Grey. It's a simple truth. If I meant anything to you, you wouldn't make me face the gossips alone."

"It's not about the gossips, Rose. And this sure as hell is not about you."

"What is it about, then?"

"It's about me. Those people pretended to be my friends. They kowtowed and kissed my arse like I was the king. I wasn't worth the attention then, and I don't want their attention now."

"So this is about your pride, then?"

"I'm ashamed!" he shouted, patience gone. Christ, had he really admitted to it? Yes, he had, and it felt good, like a huge weight lifting from his back. "I'm ashamed of the fact that I wasn't a good enough person to keep the two friends I had besides your father. I'm ashamed of who I was and I'm ashamed that you've learned even a fraction of it. I'm ashamed of how I've hidden and justified it all and I'm ashamed that I've tainted you with my rotten reputation—a well deserved one at that. And I'm ashamed that I had my head too far up my own arse to see how desperate your father had become. I could have helped him. I should have helped him."

She stared at him, eyes wide, mouth slightly parted. Her lips moved but nothing came out. She was speechless—something he would have paused and congratulated himself for if he could stop his own tongue.

Grey continued, "I hurt people, Rose. Not just women. I cuckolded men who considered me a friend and never once thought of how betrayed they must have felt. I used women for my own pleasure, and considered them worth a second go if I could remember their name the next day. I deserve this scar. I deserve much worse, and I've never understood how God could have seen fit to let me off so easily. And I'm afraid. Does that make you happy to hear me admit it? I'm afraid that if I waltz back into that world, that those vultures will welcome me with open arms and I'll become that man again."

He'd rather die than be that bastard again.

Rose came to him, her soft hands cupping his face. "You don't deserve that scar, Grey. I don't care what you've done. And you don't deserve to carry this guilt around anymore. You're not that man anymore. I know that even if you don't."

He eyed her warily. "How do you know?"

"Because that man wouldn't have taken in the wife and child of a deceased friend. Papa knew he could trust you to look after us, Grey. Doesn't that tell you anything? If you were still that man you never would have married me, and you certainly wouldn't waste all this breath trying to convince me how awful you are."

He scowled. "Your father told me to keep my hands off of you."

She smiled sweetly. "And he told me to stay away from you. We both must take the blame for our marriage, though I refuse to see it as a bad thing. Do you?"

"No. But I think you will."

"And I think you are an idiot." She kissed him lightly on the lips and stepped back. "I will never regret marrying you, Greyden Kane, but neither will I live in the world you created for yourself. I'm going out into society and I'm going to let them talk. I know who my friends are, and that's all that is important. But I am not going to let wounded pride and embarrassment keep me from enjoying myself. Neither should you. It's time to let go of the past, Grey. There's nothing for you there."

He watched her in stunned silence as she moved toward the door. Hand on the knob, she turned once more to flash a soft and hopeful smile at him. "If you change your mind, I will be at Saint's Row tonight attending Lady Devane's masked charity ball. It would be the perfect opportunity to assuage her of the responsibility for the attack on you, don't you think? And the perfect time for you to start living again."

Would it? It sounded like the perfect opportunity for him to throw himself at the mercy of wolves.

"I'm not threatening you, Grey. I love you, I do with all my heart, but I'll only wait so long. I can only take your rejection of the things that are important to me for so long. I don't ever want to lose you, but I'm not sure you're going to give me a choice."

And with that hanging over him like a knife waiting to plunge into his chest, she opened the door and walked out. He was left alone, the way he had always preferred it until Rose came along.

How could she love him when she didn't really know him? Hell, he didn't know himself.

Chapter 23

Eve and Lady Rothchild would be coming by to collect her at exactly nine o'clock, so Rose made certain she was dressed and ready by eight thirty just to be safe. Unfortunately, that gave her plenty of time to pace the length of the rose parlor as she waited.

She wore a beautiful Worth gown of dark blue silk patterned with Japanese blossoms in shades of plum, gold, and white. The neckline was cut low and square, trimmed with delicate gold piping that also trimmed the short cap sleeves. The snug bodice fastened up the back with a row of tiny hidden buttons that ran almost all the way down to the bustle. The skirt was drawn up slightly, to reveal a pleated gold underskirt that resembled the sheaves of a fan.

Heather had braided her hair beginning at the nape of her neck, and then brought the thick rope up, pinning and tucking and arranging until Rose was left with a stylish but dramatically different hairstyle, ornamented with an Oriental comb. She completed the look with a pair of dainty gold dangles for her ears and a set of matching gold bangles on either arm. The gold shone warmly against the rich blue of her gloves—dyed, of course, to match her gown, as were her slippers.

"If you don't mind me sayin', madam, you look right beautiful," Heather had gushed with a strong measure of pride.

Rose smiled at the maid. She was so glad Heather had decided to stay with her rather than return to the country with her mother. Some days, the other woman's presence was vastly comforting. "If I am at all pleasant to look at, it is all due to your skills, Heather. Thank you."

And now, pacing the parlor, she had to admit that she did feel lovely, but what did it matter when the one man she wanted to admire her wouldn't be there? She strongly suspected that he wasn't about to show his face to her at all before she left. No doubt he was brooding upstairs in their bedroom, or perhaps in his study, wishing to God that he'd had the sense to stay the hell away from her as her father asked of him.

God knew there had been a few moments as of late when she'd thought the very same.

And then she realized that she would rather be miserable with Grey than content with any other man. How pathetic and deranged was that?

A knock at the door sent her heart tripping erratically. So much so that she had to press her hand over her chest in a feeble attempt to still the foolish organ. Was it Grey?

"Come in."

It was Westford. Rose wilted in disappointment.

"Beg your pardon, Your Grace, but Lady Rothchild's carriage just pulled up."

Rose's gaze flew to the clock on the mantel. It was one minute to nine. Where had the time gone?

"Thank you, Westford. Will you get my wrap, please?"

He bowed and backed out of the doorway as Rose gathered up her reticule and her mask—a silly little thing made of starched silk and painted to resemble the geishas she'd once read about. She had thought to wear one of the masks she'd worn when she met Grey those two nights at Saint's Row, but she couldn't bring herself to touch them.

She'd meant what she said to him, she told herself as she left the parlor, spine rigid. He could only expect her to wait so long. But then what would she do? Take a lover? She couldn't imagine ever wanting another man. But perhaps the love she felt for Grey would fade someday, enough that she would find someone to share a part of her life with while Grey sat and watched his drift by.

Her stomach rolled. It couldn't be something she'd eaten as she hadn't had so much as a biscuit for hours. Her nerves wouldn't allow it.

She might think she was pregnant had she not learned from *Voluptuous* how to delay such happy occasions since her last menses.

No, she had to be honest, the idea of giving up on Grey—of never having the life she dreamed of with him—made her physically ill. She would not give up. But neither would she lock herself away in the house. She refused to stop living, just because her husband had forgotten how.

Of course, as luck would have it, she ran into Grey just as she entered the great hall on her way to the foyer. It was almost as though he was waiting for her, and for a moment her heart leapt, thinking that he might want to come with her. But alas, he wasn't dressed in evening clothes, nor did he wear one of his many masks. He wore those less and less around the house, now it seemed, but she didn't dare give herself credit for the change.

His gaze softened and warmed at the sight of her, the lines around his mouth and eyes easing. "You take my breath," he told her in a honey-rough voice that sent a tiny tremor down her spine.

Rose smiled, unable to hide her pleasure, even though she was disappointed. "Thank you."

"I wanted to give you this." He held out an envelope to her.

She took it. "What is it?"

"A bank draft for Lady Devane's cause." He cleared his throat. "I thought you might like to make a donation."

As tempting as it was, she didn't open it to peer at the amount. She'd do that later. How could he drive her to the very edge of distraction and be so amazingly wonderful? "That is very generous of you."

He shrugged. "It's only money. Someone else can make better use of it than I." Then he stood aside. "Your friends are waiting so I won't keep you any longer."

As she tucked the envelope in her reticule, Rose was reluctant to let him go just yet, but she knew she had no other choice. "I won't be late."

Grey smiled at her, but there was an edge of sadness to it. "Stay as long as you like. I'll be here whenever you come home." He leaned down to kiss her cheek. It felt so impersonal, so . . . final.

And because Eve and her mother were waiting, Rose couldn't ask him to ease her mind. She couldn't take the time to tell him how she felt and wrap her arms around him. All she could do was walk away.

"Good night, Grey."

Another sad smile. "Good night, Rosie."

Funny, but it sounded more like good-bye.

He was lonely.

The house without Rose in it seemed empty and cavernous, a pretty prison in which he was both prisoner and jailor.

It was still early in the evening, but he had no doubt that at that very moment Rose was dancing and laughing gaily at some witty remark her partner made expressly for her pleasure. Perhaps the man had his hand a little too low on Rose's back, held her a little too close. People would whisper, wondering how long it would take the dashing rogue to seduce Ruined Ryeton's neglected bride.

Just as they used to whisper when he set his sights on such a vulnerable woman.

His fists clenched as he stared out the window of his study, gaze focused on the stars that managed to twinkle through the clouds. He'd kill any man who dared impugn Rose's reputation.

Does that include you? A voice in his head whispered. He could have ignored it if a part of his mind hadn't paused for consideration. Of course his absence from these events harmed Rose. People would talk, it was their nature. What did they say about her? Did they pity her? Take wagers on how long it would take her to become a jade? Someone's mistress?

Before his marriage, his actions didn't reflect upon anyone but himself, but now there was Rose to consider. Rose, who had lost so much already, who had known the harsh breath of scandal more than she ever should. This was the girl who had taken such sweet care of him when he hadn't deserved it. Who had nursed him without complaint though he'd been an arse and worse to her at times. She never asked him for anything in the long years he'd known her.

Except that he attend one stupid ball with her.

She never asked for his heart though she freely offered hers. Love had always been a weakness in his eyes, but Rose made it a strength. A gift. Now that he thought upon it, Rose had loved him for years. No one would give as much of herself to someone she didn't care about—and she had given him so very much.

And how did he repay her? By allowing her to face the gossips alone, weather the ridicule and speculation. He offered her up as prey to men whose scruples were so low they were practically nonexistent. Men like the one he used to be. Years ago, if he'd stumbled upon a lady as socially vulnerable as Rose he would have stalked her and run her to ground as quickly as possible.

What the hell kind of husband was he? Was his pride—his petulant need to make some kind of foolish social statement—worth so much that he would throw the only person outside of his family who had ever truly loved him to the wolves? The *ton* didn't care if he ever attended a party or the theater. His absence didn't hurt anyone but himself—and now Rose.

It was laughable—in fact a harsh bark of laughter escaped his lips as he turned away from the window and raked a hand through his already mussed hair. He had promised her father he'd protect her. He had promised to stay away from her as well. If the latter could not be kept, then the former should.

But it wasn't just honor that ignited his blood, made the first sensations of life flow through his veins once more. He didn't want to be alone anymore. He didn't want to be without Rose. His place was with her, and hers with him. She was right, he was a coward. He'd been a terrible person and he'd suffered the consequences, but he hadn't been the only one to suffer. Maggie—Lady Devane also suffered, but instead of withdrawing from society, she made it look her in the eye. It wasn't about society facing him, it was about *him* facing society.

A better man would face up to all he had done and the people he had done it to. A better man would take his rightful place and accept every uncomfortable moment of it. If he truly was a changed man, as Rose believed him to be—as he *wanted* to be—then now was the time to do something about it, because hiding his face only made him more of the scum he always was.

Anticipation and irritation warred for dominance within him as Grey strode from the room, his boot heels hitting the floor with sharp thumps. As he climbed the stairs to his room, faces flashed through his mind—his mother, Archer, Trystan, Bronte, and Rose. These were the people he held most dear, the people who meant so much more to him than the people he'd hurt in the past, and yet they were the ones he injured now. How could he have been so blind? So stupid? No wonder Bronte didn't want him to give her away. She probably assumed he wouldn't want to anyway, that he wouldn't dare come out of his isolation for her. And no doubt he was a huge embarrassment to her, a young girl living under the shadow of her scandalous and reclusive older brother.

He reckoned Lady Devane held a similar opinion of her brother, Michael, but she'd protected him regardless.

Grey came to a sudden halt on the stairs, almost tripping as his feet froze. Was that what Bronte thought she was doing? By rejecting him, she was protecting him—giving him the perfect excuse to stay hidden away? As soon as he entertained the notion, he knew it to be true.

"Foolish little girl," he murmured. His heart didn't know whether to rejoice with understanding or weep with it. So many lives affected by his wounded pride and lack of common sense. The only life not affected was his own, because he'd stopped living long ago. Christ, he didn't know if he'd ever truly lived. Certainly he had gone through the motions.

That morning in Hyde Park had felt like living. Making love to Rose was life itself. She'd brought him back from the dead with her touch—her insistence that he was more than he ever thought he could be.

He didn't deserve her love or her high opinion, but he would rather die on this very staircase than lose it. In fact, he would do whatever necessary to keep it.

It would mean swallowing his pride—a task that left a bitter taste in the back of his mouth. It would mean facing his past and trying to make amends for all of the awful things he'd done. Some of those things could never be repaired. There would be people who despised him forever, and he didn't anticipate that any of his so-called friends would come to his aid, having abandoned him years ago.

But he had Rose, and God willing, she'd stand with him.

He hesitated at the top of the stairs, gripping the banister as a sudden, awful thought occurred to him. What if he did what she wanted and he lost her regardless? She told him she couldn't—wouldn't—wait forever for him, but what if society shunned him, and her by association? Rose was such a social creature, she'd wither without the glitter and gaiety.

Mouth set grimly, Grey made his way down the corridor to the bedroom he shared with Rose.

He knew what he had to do.

So this was why Grey liked masks, Rose thought as she drifted through the crowded ballroom at Saint's Row. Few people even spared a glance at her let alone acknowledged her. It was wonderful. Of course, Grey's disguise only worked when he was in a room with other masked people.

Would anyone there recognize him if he walked

through the door? Or perhaps if he drifted out of the shadows and asked her to dance? Perhaps, or perhaps not. They would never know because there wasn't even the remotest chance of Grey showing his face—partially hidden or not—there tonight at all.

Lady Devane had reacted deeply to the donation Grey sent. She'd looked at the amount and gasped before pressing her fingers to her mouth. "Why would he be so generous?" Her voice was ragged and faint.

Rose pressed her hand with her own. "I think it is meant to be a peace offering. A gesture of good-will."

Judging from the expression on the blonde woman's face, it was more like absolution. "I will be certain to include His Grace in my thank-you notes."

"I'm sure he'd appreciate that." Rose didn't add that Grey rarely received mail of his own that wasn't business or family related. No one ever tried to visit him either. He truly was all alone.

It was his own fault, she tried to remind herself as pity stirred within her breast. Surely there was someone here who would think of him kindly—as a friend?

As she glanced around, Rose couldn't help but wonder how many of these women had shared Grey's bed. She didn't want to know, truly. None of that mattered, and yet she couldn't help the thoughts swirling uninvited through her head. Maybe it was just as well that he avoided society.

"Your Grace?"

She turned at the familiar voice, thankful for the diversion. "Mr. Maxwell."

His face was partially obscured by a soft black mask with a lion's face painted on it, but Rose would know Kellan anywhere, especially when he spoke. "I hope I'm not interrupting?"

She smiled coolly. She hadn't forgotten the things he'd said at their last meeting, though they seemed so unimportant now. "My thoughts will wait. It is good to see you."

He stepped closer—not so much that it was improper, but enough to give them a little privacy of conversation. "I want to apologize to you for the things I said when we last met. It was very rude and boorish of me."

"But your intentions were good, so I find it impossible to despise you for it." She offered her hand, proving that she was sincere. "Let us be friends and not speak of it again."

"You're very good," he commented, wrapping his gloved fingers around hers.

"No, Mr. Maxwell, I am not. But I need all the friends I can get." Her tone wasn't as light as she would have liked, and the quip came out decidedly sharp.

"You will always have a friend in me," he assured her. "And in Lady Devane as well, I believe. She sang your praises very highly earlier."

"It's the money," Rose replied quickly. "It's obviously impaired her judgment."

Laughing, Kellan set a bright and sparkling dark gaze upon her. "I do not believe the lady ever allows her judgment to be impaired. She would not stand for it."

That was interesting. There was a taste of annoyance in Kellan's tone, mixed with a healthy dose of curiosity and respect. Could it be that her former suitor had a personal interest in Grey's former lover?

It was enough to make her head spin. "You are quite right," she agreed. "Lady Devane is nothing if not formidable. I find myself quite in awe of her. I wish I had half her courage."

"You have enough." It was clear that he respected her for it, just as it was clear that as much as he thought her brave for being there that night, he thought Grey all the more cowardly for not being there with her. And yet, since he hadn't said anything to that effect, Rose could not argue.

"Have you ever thought about going into politics, Mr. Maxwell?" she asked archly as she snapped open her fan. She cooled herself in a manner that had no secret meaning that she knew of. Whoever invented the "language" of the fan should have been slapped. What if a lady simply wanted to cool herself and not send a message? "I fancy you'd be quite good at it."

Kellan only smiled, taking no offense. Obviously he was too pleased with himself to regret the remark.

Torn between ire and amusement, Rose turned her head as she waved the fan in front of her face. It was so warm in the ballroom with all these bodies milling about that she was damp around the hairline. That would not do, as ladies were never supposed to be seen perspiring. A foolish notion, indeed as no one had the power to control the temperature of one's body, but who was she to dictate etiquette?

A gasp caught her attention, followed by a rush of whispers that filled the sudden silence that fell over the room. People stopped talking to turn and stare. People stopped dancing. Even the orchestra stopped playing.

Curious, Rose turned to see what everyone was staring at with such blatant shock.

Oh, dear God. Her eyes had to be deceiving her! But no, she knew who it was she saw standing just inside the ballroom doors, looking as though he owned the place, meeting every gaze with calm, ducal arrogance.

It was Grey.

And everyone else knew it was him as well, because unlike every other person in that ballroom, the Duke of Ryeton did not wear a mask.

Chapter 24

Hundreds of eyes watched him like vultures circling a wounded dog, but they didn't matter. Only one pair of eyes mattered to Grey at that moment.

It only made sense that he should be the only one in the room not wearing a mask. He had hidden himself for so long, that it felt somehow cleansing to put himself on such blatant display. He deserved this blatant attention. And on some level, he needed it.

Head high, he walked through the ballroom, the crowd parting for him. They didn't draw back so much that he couldn't hear their whispers.

"The nerve!"

"Did you see the scar?"

"Always did know how to make an entrance."

"He's so handsome!"

Grey stopped listening. It didn't matter what they said. All that mattered was finding Rose, and somehow he knew that she would be waiting at the end, letting him make this walk alone as he needed to do.

"Good evening, Your Grace," came a familiar

feminine voice. "How delightful to have you in attendance this evening."

Grey's gaze jerked to the woman at his right. Her face was mostly covered with a peacock feather mask, but he thought he recognized her jaw and the color of her hair. It was the stunned silence that fell over the crowd of onlookers that identified her for certain. She curtsied to him as though he was royalty. Amazing what a title could do even for the once lowest of men.

"Lady Devane," he replied with a bow. She was a brave woman indeed—and a good one. Not only did she welcome him to her ball, but she gave him opportunity to cut her if he wished, finally putting the blame of his attack on her shoulders. "Thank you for receiving me."

She rose with a smile and turned to address the gaping crowd. "His Grace, the Duke of Ryeton, has made the largest single donation this evening. Because of his generosity the children will have a new school next year." When she clapped her hands, others joined in as well.

And then the world stopped and there was nothing but Rose as she slipped from the crowd to stand before him. Grey forgot about Lady Devane. He forgot about everyone but her.

She wore a mask, but even if he hadn't recognized the hair and the dress he would have known it was her. He knew her scent, the shape of her mouth. He recognized her by the way his heart rejoiced at her nearness.

She stared at him, her mask doing nothing to conceal her wonder. "Why are you here?"

Grey smiled down at her. Did she notice that he'd pinned the rosette from the gown she'd worn their first night together to his lapel? "Because I hold you above my horse, my fortune, and my pride."

Her brow puckered. "I beg your pardon?"

"Those were the traits you said you required in a husband, were they not?"

Her face relaxed, and he thought he saw a glimmer of understanding in her dark eyes. "Yes. I believe they were. You came here just to tell me that?"

He laughed. Her face was so bright below the edge of her mask, her eyes damp and warm. It broke his heart—and buoyed it as well—to know he was responsible for all of that. "No. I came here to dance with my wife. And to do this." He took her face in his hands and kissed her in front of the entire ballroom. He didn't care about the gasps or that everyone could see. He didn't care what they said or whether or not his behavior was proper.

He was a duke, damn it. A scandalous one at that.

When he lifted his head, Rose's eyes fluttered open. Her breath came in short, gentle heaves. "I'm very glad you decided that could not wait until I got home."

Grey offered his arm. "Shall we?"

"There's no music." But she took his arm anyway.

The orchestra had stopped playing shortly a[illegible]r he walked in. Grey turned his gaze in their [illegible] tion, nodded at the leader and once again t[illegible] was filled with music.

"Well, damn my eyes, some things never change. You're just as arrogant as always!"

A dark haired, blue-eyed man stood before him, tall and rangy and grinning broadly from ear to ear. It took a second—longer than it should have—for Grey to place him. "Aiden?"

His cousin took his hand and clapped him soundly on the arm. "It's good to see you, Grey. Damn good." Then to Rose, "Please excuse my crude language, Your Grace. I'm just happy to see your husband."

And Grey was happy to see him, he realized. Perhaps his friends hadn't deserted him after all.

Damn if it didn't bring a lump to this throat.

"No apologies are necessary," Rose informed him brightly. "I'm always happy to meet family. Perhaps you might join us some night for dinner at Ryeton House?"

Aiden smiled at her. "I would be honored, thank you. I'll let the two of you get on with your dance. I'll talk to you later, Grey."

Grey watched his cousin walk away before continuing with Rose out onto the dance floor, where other couples now twirled and pranced. He couldn't find the words to express himself so he remained silent, but Rose seemed to understand and squeezed his arm to her side.

It had been a long time since Grey danced, but the steps came back to him readily enough. They joined the set with other couples and no one cut him or treated him like a leper. If anything, he was treated with polite—and sometimes exuberant—curiosity. Others who had known him better once upon a time watched with trepidation, as though they thought he might spout horns at any moment.

Regardless, no one was openly rude to his face—or to Rose's, and that was what mattered.

He ran into Westhaver Blackbourne as well, who was also happy to see him. "I thought we'd lost you," he said candidly as Rose conversed with her friend Eve. "When you had the servants tell Aiden and me to go away, I thought I should never see you again."

Grey frowned. "I don't remember telling the servants to say that, but I was so out of my wits on laudanum I probably said all manner of things I didn't mean. My apologies, old man."

His old friend shrugged. "None of it matters anymore. It's easy to see what brought you back to the land of the living." He nodded at Rose. "She's a beautiful woman."

"She is," Grey agreed without hesitation. "Inside and out."

West flashed a roguish grin. "They all are, my friend. It just takes the right one to make us realize that."

Grey would argue that not all women were beautiful inside or out, but thought better of it. West always did have a way of twisting words until you believed he knew exactly what he was talking about.

When his friend took his leave—after extorting a promise that Grey would join him at his club someday—Grey turned to Rose. He didn't think he'd be at the club anytime in the immediate future, but he would go. One more small step into life again.

Lady Eve excused herself and Rose took both of Grey's hands in her own. "Let's go home," she said.

He arched his brows. "Already? I thought you would want to stay for a while."

Dark eyes flashed. "No, I want to take you home where women can't stare at you like hyenas after a baby chick."

He laughed—loudly, which caught a fair bit of attention. "Surely I'm more threatening than a chick?"

She smiled, ruining her petulant expression. "A puppy perhaps."

Grey stepped closer so that their torsos touched. It was totally improper behavior, but the gossips already had so much to talk about, one more thing would hardly matter. "Is that all you want to take me home for? To protect me?"

Her gaze turned coy. "I received the newest edition of *Voluptuous* today. I thought I might read to you."

Was it just him or had the temperature in the room suddenly climbed ten degrees. "Let's go."

He grabbed her by the hand and started weaving their way toward the door. People stopped him to say hello, and he was forced to speak to them rather than be as rude as he wanted. A good fifteen minutes passed before he and Rose finally made it to the entrance of the ballroom, only to have Vienne La Rieux descend upon them.

"*Monsieur et Madame le Duc*!" she cried, clasping her hands together in front of her breast—abundantly displayed above a peacock-colored gown that must have cost a small fortune. "Finally, you leave my club together, *non*?"

Grey winked at her. "At last, madam. But we may want a room again someday."

The French woman grinned, delighting in Rose's obvious embarrassment. "*Mais oui!* An anniversary present, Your Grace. On the house."

He thanked her and bade her farewell.

"She knew?" Rose's tone was incredulous as they made their way closer to the exit. "How could she know?"

Grey shrugged. "The woman seems to know deuced near everything that happens here." They were almost to the foyer.

And then Archer showed up, with his mother and Bronte in tow.

"Oh, ho!" his brother cried, clasping him close in a fierce embrace. "Did you think you'd escape without saying hello?" Then, for Grey's ears alone, "I'm so frigging proud of you I could just piss."

"Please don't." Grey gently pushed him away, meeting the other man's bright gaze with a lump in his throat. "But thank you."

His mother hugged him as well, so overcome that she began to weep. Grey didn't know what to do with her, but Archer gave her a handkerchief and Rose discreetly took her aside so she could compose herself.

That left Grey with Bronte, who looked as though she was on the verge of tears as well, her blue eyes watery behind her mask.

"You," he said firmly. "Let you and I get one

thing straight right now. I don't care if you've already asked Archer. I don't care what your groom's family wants, or who you think you're trying to protect. I will give you away, or there will be no wedding. Is that understood?"

The cupid's bow of his sister's mouth trembled and for a moment he thought he had been wrong about her and now she hated him, but then she threw herself into his arms, laughing.

"I love you," she whispered against his ear before kissing his cheek.

She was gone before Grey could even hug her back, which was probably just as well given the burning in his eyes.

"We'll be all over the scandal rags tomorrow," Archer crowed with a bit too much enthusiasm.

"No doubt," Grey agreed. "I'm afraid I have provided enough entertainment for one evening. Dinner tomorrow?"

His family accepted the invitation with quiet aplomb and a great deal of unspoken pride, but it was obvious all the same. Then they left him and Rose to finally make their escape. He had just gotten situated in the carriage and told the driver to go on when she plopped herself down in his lap and wrapped her arms around his neck.

"Why did you come here tonight?" she asked. "Other than the fact that you've finally come to your senses and realize you love me."

Chuckling, Grey reached up and untied the ribbons that held her mask. The pretty silk fell away to reveal the beautiful face beneath. "I missed you," he replied honestly. "And you were right—about everything. I'm tired of drifting through life. I want to live again—with you."

A lone tear trickled down her cheek. "I think that might be the most romantic thing you've ever said to me."

He grinned. "I have more."

She pressed her fingers to his lips. "I'm tired of talking." She kissed him, teasing his lips with the ripe curves of hers, sliding her tongue inside to rub against his in a sensual rhythm that had him fisting his hands in her skirts.

By the time they reached Mayfair, Grey's hair was mussed, Rose's skirts crushed, and he was harder than an oratory competition for mutes.

"I can't believe you came," she told him as they entered the house, arms wrapped around each other. "I'm so proud of you."

"I wouldn't have done it without you."

She shook her head. "You did it for yourself not for me."

Perhaps that was true, and perhaps it wasn't. He had no interest in discussing it tonight. "It's just the beginning," he promised. "I'm going to go wherever you want to go from now on. Within reason."

She laughed. "Of course. We can't have you attending a musicale just to please me, can we?" She gazed up at him. "You know, I think I'm going to want to spend plenty of evenings at home as well. That time I spent out of society had some very soothing moments."

"Of course," he agreed, thinking about all the things they could do to one another at home. Alone. "There has to be moderation."

Upstairs in their bedroom, he undressed her, unbuttoning each tiny button one by one until she sighed in exasperation. "In a hurry?" he teased.

His wife got her revenge, when clad only in her chemise and stockings, she turned those nimble fingers of hers to his cravat, working the knot so slowly he thought he might go mad. She worsened the torment by slowly rubbing her hips against his thigh. His cock was so rigid he could hang clothes on it, and the need to bury himself inside her consumed him.

Still, a skilled lover knows when to have patience—and a man in love knows that his woman's pleasure comes far, far before his own. So, as ready as he was, Grey was in no hurry to let this night end, not when it might prove to be the best of his new-found life.

Wearing only his trousers, he took Rose's hand and led her to their bed. He climbed onto the mattress and pulled her down beside him, lying so that they were face-to-face.

Warm fingers came up to gently touch the scar that ran down his face. Odd, but he hadn't thought of it at all that evening. In fact, he'd almost forgot about it.

"I heard you that night," he admitted. "When you told me you loved me."

Her head tilted. "I thought you were asleep."

"No." He held her gaze as he raised his own hand to brush the softness of her cheek. "I should have said it then, but I love you too, Rose. So much."

Her smile was smug. "I know." She kissed him again. "Make love to me."

His entire body pulsed. "I intend to, but there's one thing I have to do first."

Rose frowned. "What's that?"

Grey pulled the brand-new copy of *Voluptuous* from beneath the pillow where he'd hidden it before going to the ball. "There's a story in here that I want to read to you."

At Avon Books, we know your passion for romance—once you finish one of our novels, you find yourself wanting more.

May we tempt you with . . .

- **Excerpts** from our upcoming releases.
- Entertaining **extras**, including authors' personal photo albums and book lists.
- Behind-the-scenes **scoop** on your favorite characters and series.
- **Sweepstakes** for the chance to win free books, romantic getaways, and other fun prizes.
- Writing **tips** from our authors and editors.
- **Blog** with our authors and find out why they love to write romance.
- **Exclusive content** that's not contained within the pages of our novels.

Join us at
www.avonbooks.com